Praise for Amy Lynn Green

"Green nails all four voices of her alternating narrators: women knocked down by disappointment who find hope and unlikely camaraderie through the pages of a book. This is an uplifting read for dark times, featuring strong and unique characters uniting toward a common goal. It also has crossover appeal for fans of historical fiction from Jennifer Ryan and Kate Quinn."

—*Library Journal* starred review of *The Blackout Book Club*

"The characters' trajectories from strangers to close friends will warm readers' hearts. Bookworms will take to this."

—*Publishers Weekly* on *The Blackout Book Club*

"Green proves to be a first-rate author in her remarkable first novel about humanity and patriotism. . . . Green brilliantly creates a limitless and captivating reading experience with the nuance and wisdom of a seasoned writer. The timeless dichotomy of forgiveness and justice rings with contemporary relevance, and Johanna will be a well-loved heroine for her gumption, humility, and wit."

—*Booklist* starred review of *Things We Didn't Say*

"*The Blackout Book Club* is a fabulous novel that will warm the hearts of readers everywhere. Amy Lynn Green gives us a poignant look at life on the home front during WWII and how comfort and camaraderie can be found in the shared love of books. This will be a wonderful book club read!"

—Madeline Martin, *New York Times* bestselling author of *The Last Bookshop in London*

"*The Blackout Book Club* is an ode to books and libraries, but it's also an ode to human connection. Amy Lynn Green's entire cast of characters comes vividly to life, each woman with a distinct voice that makes the reader feel as much like her friend as her fellow book club members are. I couldn't put this book down!"

—Addison Armstrong, author of *The Light of Luna Park* and *The War Librarian*

"*The Blackout Book Club* is an engaging story that illustrates the power of books to unite and encourage us in trying times. The wonderfully diverse cast of quirky characters brings to life the shared worries and hopes of people on the WWII home front. A wonderful read."

—Lynn Austin, author of *Long Way Home*

"A salute to the power of books and of friendship! Not only does the writing sparkle with Green's trademark wit, but the characters become your dear friends, slowly exposing the hurts and secrets that have shaped them. Come to *The Blackout Book Club* for the fun—stay for the depth."

—Sarah Sundin, bestselling and award-winning author of *Until Leaves Fall in Paris*

The FOXHOLE VICTORY TOUR

Books by Amy Lynn Green

Things We Didn't Say

The Lines Between Us

The Blackout Book Club

The Foxhole Victory Tour

The FOXHOLE VICTORY TOUR

AMY LYNN GREEN

a division of Baker Publishing Group
Minneapolis, Minnesota

Published by Bethany House Publishers
Minneapolis, Minnesota
www.bethanyhouse.com

Bethany House Publishers is a division of
Baker Publishing Group, Grand Rapids, Michigan

Printed in the United States of America

Library of Congress Cataloging-in-Publication Data
Names: Green, Amy Lynn, author.
Title: The Foxhole Victory Tour / Amy Lynn Green.
Description: Minneapolis, Minnesota : Bethany House Publishers, a division of Baker Publishing Group, 2024.
Identifiers: LCCN 2023031465 | ISBN 9780764239571 (paper) | ISBN 9780764242779 (casebound) | ISBN 9781493445189 (ebook)
Subjects: LCGFT: Christian fiction. | Novels.
Classification: LCC PS3607.R4299 F69 2024 | DDC 813/.6—dc23/eng/20230711
LC record available at https://lccn.loc.gov/2023031465

This is a work of historical reconstruction; the appearances of certain historical figures are therefore inevitable. All other characters, however, are products of the author's imagination, and any resemblance to actual persons, living or dead, is coincidental.

Baker Publishing Group publications use paper produced from sustainable forestry practices and post-consumer waste whenever possible.

24 25 26 27 28 29 30 7 6 5 4 3 2 1

"A small USO unit is aboard this troopship, girls and men who are going out to entertain troops wherever they may be sent. These are not the big names who go out with blasts of publicity and maintain their radio contracts. These are girls who can sing and dance and look pretty and men who can do magic and pantomimists and tellers of jokes. They have few properties and none of the tricks of light and color which dress up the theater. But there is something very gallant about them."

—John Steinbeck, *New York Herald Tribune*, June 1943

1

February 22, 1943
Minneapolis, Minnesota

Maggie McCleod had exactly twenty-four measures to get her heels back on. The trouble was, she had to keep wailing on her trumpet at the same time, which made the whole operation much more complicated.

As she riffed on the crescendo of "Rhapsody in Blue," she tried to work her bare left foot deeper into the high heel. The motion was hidden from the audience by the hem of her gown, but her grimace as her toes jammed partway in could be spotted by anyone with a keen eye. Swollen again. No surprise after the band members had been forced to run to catch the train to Minneapolis.

Come on, come on. A measure skipped by without her as she fumbled with the strap, trying to force it over her heel.

It was easy enough to wriggle the shoes off at the start of each concert, right after Maggie took her spot on the stage. Just a discreet motion shielded by her gown's long hemline while the audience listened to Catherine Duquette, first-chair violinist, give her polished introduction to the Swinging

Sweethearts. Replacing the heels before the final bows was trickier, but Maggie had never had this much trouble.

In front of her, conductor Martin Simmons tilted his head back theatrically with the final swell of the upbeat tune, his baton twitching wildly, as if trying to juice the last bit of energy out of "his girls." Beyond him, the audience filling the plush seats of Northrop Auditorium clapped enthusiastically.

"A good show," they'd say during intermission. *"Didn't those girls play like men?"*

At least, that's what they'd say if she didn't give them something more interesting to talk about by tripping to the microphone. It was tradition for the soloist of the previous piece to dismiss the audience for intermission, reciting the standard lines their promoter churned out. Tonight that was Maggie, shoes on or off.

On Simmons's cue, Maggie curtsied with the others, deeper than usual, letting her hook the heel's strap with her finger and give it a frantic tug.

No one else could hear the tiny snap, but Maggie froze. *Perfect. Just super.*

She silently cursed Simmons for choosing the ridiculous uniform, their promoter for showcasing it on publicity kits, and even women like Catherine who made walking in heels seem effortless.

Simmons, arms spread apart in his circus ringmaster stance, was staring at Maggie, punctuating her cue with his thick eyebrows. One of her fellow brass players elbowed her in case she'd forgotten.

There was nothing for it but to scoop up the broken heel, letting it dangle from her free hand, and limp to the microphone.

The gathered audience stared, and she gave them a smile. Might as well defuse the tension. "Never fear, everyone, I wasn't injured. Just a wardrobe issue." She held up the shoe, and the concern turned to chuckling. "Not the most practical of uniforms, but you all came for the glamour, and the Swinging Sweethearts deliver at any cost."

It wasn't how she was supposed to start the speech—the script called for her to mention the venue and thank everyone for being there—but it felt good to say it out loud, despite the slight discomfort on the faces of the first few rows past the stage lights. She'd always hated the posters with condescending slogans like "While our boys are off at war, the women have joined the band . . . and these sweeties sure can swing!"

She warmed to the speech, drawing closer to the microphone to make sure even the back row would hear. "I hope you've enjoyed our all-girls extravaganza, even if it was just our name that drew you in. Come to think of it, you don't see Tommy Dorsey or Glenn Miller changing their band names to 'The Bachelors of Rhythm' or 'The Dashing Dreamboats.' Maybe it would sell more tickets—or maybe that's just for us women."

More laughter, and this time she glanced across the stage at Simmons, who was frozen in place. Good thing he couldn't actually murder her with his baton in front of this many witnesses.

Anyway, this was his fault. He was the one who dressed them up like dolls, scolded anyone who seemed to be gaining weight, and told their promoter to feature posters with photographs that made them look more like pinup girls than serious musicians. "The crowds come to get an earful *and* an eyeful," she'd heard him say.

Well, he was getting an earful now, and it served him right.

Mr. Simmons was already gesturing frantically to the band to leave the stage, but the women's eyes were mostly on her, including a horrified Catherine Duquette, cupid-bow mouth in a perfect O.

Better finish this quickly.

"The program will continue after intermission. So listen to us—close your eyes if you need to—and see if you don't get the best music you've ever heard from this all-girl band." She gave a small bow. "Thank you."

The applause that followed was probably the same volume as usual, but it felt different. Special. It was for her specifically. Not just her as one instrument in dozens, another gown in a sea of sweethearts.

She refused to look over her shoulder at Simmons as she filed backstage with her fellow band members. As she did, Catherine turned, clutching her violin case. "Was that . . . planned?"

Catherine looked the very image of demure womanhood, her auburn hair pinned with a pearl hair comb, with only one curl falling out by her ear. Even that was probably intentional. She'd never gone onstage with a wrinkle in her gown, much less lost a shoe and embarrassed their conductor in front of an audience.

"Of course not. Help a girl out, would you?" Without waiting for an answer, Maggie grabbed the shorter woman's shoulder, steadying herself as she pulled off her other shoe without tearing her gown's hem. That done, she flared her toes against the scuffed boards of backstage, enjoying the freedom of being gloriously barefoot. "Thanks."

"Why did you . . . ?" Catherine began, then bit her lip and tried again. "That wasn't the speech we're meant to give."

Noticed that, did you? Maggie fought rolling her eyes and just shrugged. "It came to me, that's all. Didn't you like my improvisation?"

"I don't . . . it's just . . ." She seemed to give up on explaining the faux pas and settled for "Mr. Simmons will be upset."

"That's why I don't plan to let him find me." Maggie hiked her skirt up enough that she wouldn't trip over it and gave a little wave. "See ya onstage." With that, she made a beeline for an abandoned stack of scenery, an ideal place to hide until the end of intermission.

Maggie leaned against the wall, breathing out deeply. She'd actually gone and done it, said what she'd been thinking for ten long months now.

For once, she wished her father had been in the audience. He hadn't fully approved of her joining the Sweethearts, but he'd always raised her to speak her mind. But he was still back in Chicago and hadn't even been able to break free from his mission work to attend one of the shows they'd put on near her home in the Windy City.

As confident as Maggie had tried to sound to Catherine, she couldn't help worrying. This was her third job since she'd moved out on her own a year and a half ago. She hadn't cared when she was fired from the soda fountain for slapping a handsy customer or when she walked out from the munitions factory when she found out the male employees were paid more. Those had been ways to pay the bills, nothing more. But the Sweethearts, despite their ridiculous name, had been her dream, a chance to play music professionally. If she'd ruined it by running her mouth again . . .

"It'll blow over," she muttered, willing it to be true. She could talk her way out of nearly anything, after all.

At least, that's what she hoped.

2

February 22, 1943
Minneapolis, Minnesota

Catherine Duquette pretended to admire the Northrop Auditorium chandeliers as the audience streamed past her, hoping against hope that no one would talk to her.

It wasn't strictly required, but Mr. Simmons always liked his girls to mingle with the crowds during intermission to make connections for future bookings. That wouldn't be so bad, except it required her to speak coherently to strangers.

Still, there was no way around it. Better to make an appearance and be seen by Mr. Simmons, murmur a few thank-yous to compliments on the show, then hurry backstage with some excuse or another.

To pass the time, Catherine took covert glances at the gowns worn by the women of the audience, some draped in furs to keep the chill of the winter night away. The frigid season and the seriousness of wartime ensured that most of the colors and prints were subdued shades of blues and grays. But she caught a glimpse of a stunning cream dotted-swiss gown with a tiered skirt, and a gold number with a sweetheart neckline designed to show off a sapphire necklace.

The men she mostly ignored, except that, as usual, her heart raced slightly when she saw a glimpse of Brillantined black hair. A moment later, the turn of a head and the appearance of a rotund belly proved it wasn't Leo.

Of course it wasn't. He couldn't be here, lounging in a Minneapolis performance hall. He was somewhere across the ocean. At least, she prayed he was, and not in a field hospital or buried in foreign soil.

Don't think about that. Whenever her mind drifted to Leo during shows, her performance suffered.

A flash of color caught her eye, and Catherine squinted at the woman emerging from the auditorium's side door just to be sure. Yes, she knew that fur coat, a dark tuxedo-front mink with turned-back cuffs over a burgundy gown. That her mother was wearing an old coat proved she was at least attempting to cut back on new fashion for the war effort.

Catherine bit her lip. She'd worried about coming back to the Twin Cities, although she hadn't said a word about the Sweethearts' schedule to either parent.

The second Mother's eyes caught hers, they sparkled, bottle green like a traffic light and outlined with winged liner to make them seem larger. "Catherine!" she squealed, nearly trampling several audience members to clear a path to her, arms spread wide for a hug. Catherine breathed in the familiar scent of Evening in Paris, the one constant in her mother's life. "You were magnificent, as always."

"I didn't know you'd come," she said, forcing a smile.

Her mother had already changed her expression to an exaggerated pout. "Come now, be honest, *ma chérie*. Were you *ever* going to tell me about your show? Ah," she said, waving a manicured finger in the air before Catherine could speak. "I've guessed it. You were embarrassed of your *maman*."

"No, of course not. I—I thought you were living in New York until . . ." Catherine choked on the ending she couldn't bring herself to voice: until the divorce proceedings went to court.

"Ah, I see," Mother said, leaning in conspiratorially. "I am, of course, but those dratted lawyers are always making me pop back into town. Imagine how delighted I was to have this to look forward to." She took Catherine's arm to lead her out of the flow of traffic, pausing to greet an acquaintance Catherine pretended to remember and waving at a couple across the room before turning back to her daughter. "Honestly, it was divine, seeing all you ladies up there. I couldn't have been prouder."

"Thank you," Catherine murmured, all that was usually required of her in conversations like this.

"Do you remember how your father groused about starting lessons when you were so young. 'Vivienne, imagine the *expense*.'" Her imitation of Gerald Duquette, complete with gruff, smoke-grated voice, was quite good. "I told him that it would be worth it one day, and wasn't I right?"

"Yes, Mama." That was always the right answer . . . as long as Catherine's father wasn't around.

Whether it was that stray thought or a familiar lurching gait that caught her attention, Catherine found her gaze drifting toward the crowd—and the one man striding determinedly in their direction.

No. Not both of them. The sick feeling in her stomach intensified as he took measured steps across the gleaming terrazzo floor toward them, but she discarded a momentary thought of fleeing.

"Catherine," he said coolly, not even directing the slightest acknowledgment toward Mother.

"What are you doing here, Father?" It was terribly rude, but Catherine hadn't been able to help blurting it out. Father never read the entertainment notices in the newspaper. His order was strictly Business, News, and sometimes Editorials, but never something as trivial as music or theater.

"*I* certainly didn't invite him," Mother inserted, as if this were at all in question. Her face didn't wear the same stormy glower as her estranged husband, but she'd taken on a haughty, head-tilted posture that had the same effect.

"Arthur brought me a playbill with your photograph in it," Father said, disgust lacing his voice, as if she'd been plastered across town on a circus flyer clad in a lion-tamer's bikini instead of a perfectly respectable glamour shot with her violin.

Catherine felt a fleeting burst of anger at Father's favorite employee, but poor Arthur likely had no idea of the tension he'd caused. She turned up the brightness of her smile to a level that would break blackout regulations. "Yes, our promoter thinks people respond best to a local connection."

"I see." Catherine knew that tone well. It meant Father had weighed all the details and passed final judgment. "I just finished speaking to that director of yours—"

"Conductor," Mother corrected, forcing her way back into the conversation and angling her narrow shoulders to step between the two of them. "Honestly, Gerald, even an uncultured boor like you should know that. I suppose you think intermission is called the seventh inning stretch."

Father ignored her, a skill which, Catherine had recently realized, had allowed him to remain unhappily married to Mother for twenty-two years. "He told me he wasn't aware you were only touring for a year."

Catherine felt her ears burn and knew it would only be a matter of seconds before the flush crept up her neck and to her cheeks. "I—I meant to tell him. The timing just never seemed right."

That wasn't entirely true. Some part of Catherine had

hoped that she'd be able to negotiate with Father, or even that, with the divorce proceedings taking up so much of his time, he might forget.

A foolish hope, she now realized as she looked at her father's immovable face. He had more gray around his temples than she remembered.

"I see. Well, I took the liberty of breaking the news to him. He wasn't happy, of course—all the more reason you ought to have given him notice from the start—but he said he certainly wouldn't want to keep a young woman in his band without her parents' approval."

The words made Catherine flinch. Persuading her father to agree to one year of touring "to get this music business out of your system" had seemed like a dream come true. But here she was, eleven months in and barely started. When she took her place onstage, none of the difficulties of the tour came to mind. She could only think about the dear friends she'd made in her fellow musicians, the improvements in her skill, the sheer freedom of touring through glittering ballrooms and big cities across the country . . .

Mother brushed Father aside with the flat of her hand, a gesture that might look playful if you overlooked the spite in her tone. "Oh, stop being such a boor, Gerald. No amount of bluster can keep my Catherine away from music, can it, *ma chérie*?"

Catherine searched for a response, but Mother didn't seem to need one, her attention fixed on her estranged husband.

Father, on the other hand, hadn't taken his eyes off Catherine, his words clipped and businesslike. "It is, however, not up to you. Catherine and I had an agreement, and I'm sure she wouldn't be so foolish as to break her word, not with her future at stake."

The words were very proper. No promise of disinheritance, no reminder that most musicians at her level wouldn't be able to survive on their salary, no threats. Those wouldn't come out until she dared to cross him.

Just now, Catherine was feeling remarkably low on daring. She wasn't like Maggie, who could speak her mind and grit her teeth against the reaction. Her parents' slowly rising voices were already attracting stares, and she licked her dry lips in an attempt to speak. "Can we discuss this after the performance, please? I really ought to—"

"There's nothing more to discuss," Father interrupted. "One month, Catherine. That's final."

Mother sniffed. "Delightful. Then I'll be sure to tell the concertmaster of the New York Philharmonic to schedule Catherine's audition for mid-March."

"My audition?" Catherine asked, hating how helpless her question sounded. Surely her mother hadn't. . . . She wasn't ready, not for performances at that level. Her year with the Sweethearts was the first time she'd ever played with other musicians.

"I was just going to tell you before we were *interrupted*." She glared at Father, then turned back to Catherine. "It's a magnificent opportunity. I may have been forced to give up my career after getting married, but I still have my connections."

That was a slanted version of the real story. From what Catherine had heard, her mother, a Parisian-born opera singer, had been struggling financially and had married Father as a way out. But Catherine knew Mother had told her rendition of the story so often that she believed it was true.

"I must say, he was fascinated when he heard I had such a talented daughter. 'Where have you been hiding her away?' he asked." She gave her usual trill of a laugh. "Of course, the real question was, *Who* was hiding her away?"

Father's voice was little more than a growl at this point. "That's unfair, Vivienne. I've always wanted the best for

Catherine—which doesn't include the life you lived in Paris, half-starving in a tiny apartment with a ruined reputation."

Catherine cast desperately about for a way of escape and saw two of the Sweethearts' woodwind players whispering to each other and discreetly pointing in their direction. Were they close enough to hear?

If not, they soon would be. Vivienne Lavigne-Duquette and Gerald Duquette were known in society gossip rags for their tempestuous public rows. Catherine usually managed to play the peacemaker and remained invisible whenever possible.

Not this time. She struggled to breathe as more and more people turned and whispered, gesturing to her parents, who now stood directly facing each other, their voices continuing to rise.

"You mustn't pretend, Gerald. You want *your* best and always have. The rest of us might as well not even exist."

Father scoffed. "Really, Vivienne, you seem determined to make it impossible for *anyone* to forget about you, even if that means making a scene."

"I really must be getting back," Catherine finally said. Both pairs of eyes turned to her, sharp as daggers, cutting the courage out of her so she could only add, "Enjoy the rest of the program, Father, Mother."

Now. Now. She had to leave now. Before they shouted after her, before she was in the middle once again. Catherine nearly tripped over her hem in her hurry to escape, blinking back tears.

What was she going to do? If Mr. Simmons had already agreed to dismiss her from the Sweethearts—and she didn't doubt her father could bribe or coerce him to do so—then she had very few choices before her. She could return to the Duquette mansion on Summit Avenue and marry a suitable husband like her father wanted. Or she could run off to

New York and live with her mother and whatever man was currently in her life, riding her coattails into a prestigious audition she wasn't prepared for.

Her parents were dividing her and her future up like she was another bank account or vacation property for their attorneys to quarrel over.

A few deep breaths backstage were all she could spare before one of her fellow violinists tugged her to join the others for the second half of the performance. Catherine took her seat in the front row, smoothed her skirt, and ran a hand across her violin's lustrous finish to soothe her shattered nerves.

The bitter tightness returned to her throat, like a bowstring pulled until it snapped. How would she focus on concertos and key signatures now?

The way you always do, she reminded herself, settling into her place and smiling vaguely as Mr. Simmons stepped up to lead them in tuning their instruments. She breathed in deeply, tucked her violin close against her, and let her bow join the discordant cacophony necessary to produce beautiful music. For a few moments, she could play something ugly, venting her emotions into those loud, uncensored notes.

Then, when the curtain rose, Catherine would forget that her mother and father were in the audience, waiting to confront each other again after the final curtain. She would forget the impending deadline, the audition, everything but the music. And she would play the best she ever had.

3

February 22, 1943
Minneapolis, Minnesota

So much for hoping it would blow over, Maggie thought as Mr. Simmons charged toward her with the fury of a Midwestern blizzard.

Their conductor didn't even let her get backstage, pouncing the moment the curtains separated them from the audience. "Maggie McCleod, don't you dare sneak away!"

The small part of her that hoped Simmons had taken her speech as the joke it was meant to be disappeared instantly. She'd seen bar fight aggressors more composed than Martin Simmons, his wiry eyebrows knit down, reducing his eyes to slits.

This time there wasn't anywhere to hide, and Maggie had no intention of running away.

"You disgraced the entire band with that speech," he practically shouted, pushing past one of the oboe players, who let out a squeak and scattered backstage with the others, giving Maggie one last wide-eyed stare.

Some friends they were. Maggie could practically hear the whispers of backstage gossip now: *"Can you believe what Maggie did?" "She'll get what's coming to her this time." "Serves her right, if you ask me."*

Maggie made a show of smoothing out her skirt before raising her head to look at Simmons, his arms crossed and shoulders squared to give him an additional inch of height on her. "There's no need to yell. I can hear you just fine—and so can the audience members."

This prompted what she could only describe as a growl, though he did lower his voice somewhat. "Do you know who I spoke to over intermission?"

"A fan praising my comedic timing?"

As expected, no flicker of amusement broke the scowl on Mr. Simmons's face. "A member of Rockefeller Center's advisory board. Who was, up until your untimely blunder, considering inviting us to perform in our largest venue yet. He informed me he's no longer interested and said to 'tell your girls to stick to music.'"

At that, even Maggie had to wince. It was one thing to offend their manager and another to lose a performance opportunity.

"I take disrespect seriously, Miss McCleod," he continued. "Very seriously. A band is only as good—"

"As its reputation," she finished the often-quoted statement with a bland smile. "Well, if telling the truth into a microphone hurts our band, maybe we have bigger problems."

"That's exactly the attitude I'm talking about." He waggled an accusing finger at her like he was scolding a child. "You've been nothing but trouble since the day you joined us."

That wasn't strictly true. She'd waited to be trouble until the third or fourth day. That was when she'd snuck out of the hotel to attend a performance of one of their rival bands and got caught on the way back in. Somehow, Maggie knew pointing this out wouldn't help her case.

"Don't try to tell me that I couldn't find anyone to replace you. By tomorrow morning, I could have a dozen lady trumpeters lined up who would do anything to perform with a band of this caliber."

Maggie decided to take the offensive. "If I'm so replaceable, then replace me."

He blinked, and for one triumphant moment, she was sure she'd called his bluff. Then he smiled, oily as a pan of sausages. "All right. You're fired. And don't think I haven't wanted to say those words for a long time."

The hum of activity past the audience curtain seemed to fade as blood rushed to Maggie's face. *Now you've done it.*

With great effort, she kept her face even, unwilling to give Simmons the satisfaction of seeing the reaction he wanted. "Fine, if that's the way it has to be." The words came out with remarkable calm, given how her stomach had just bottomed out.

"And once I'm through," Simmons continued, straightening his tie, "everyone in the industry will have you on their blacklist."

Hearing those words stung, especially knowing that with his connections, they weren't empty threats. But there wasn't a chance Maggie would show it. "If it gets me away from you, it'll be worth it."

Walk away with your head high. That's what mattered most, since she still had to face the others backstage to snatch her trumpet case and broken heels from where she'd stashed them. Maggie did her best to look aloof, ignoring the whispers of the other women and hurrying away as quickly as she could in bare feet.

Her mind raced as she wove in and out of audience members in the crowded atrium. Simmons was right: the Sweethearts would be able to find another trumpet player. But what would she find to do next?

Their chaperone wouldn't let him actually throw her out

onto the street tonight, but she'd have to have a plan by morning when the Sweethearts moved to the next stop on their tour.

There was always the option to live with her father or her sister's family while she looked for a new job.

Maggie dismissed the idea almost as quickly as it had come. It wasn't that they wouldn't be happy to see her. But the thought of admitting to her family that she'd failed *again* rankled. There had to be something else. She'd figure it out on her own.

"Excuse me!" a voice called, stopping her short, "young lady?"

She turned to see two men in evening dress fighting the current of the crowd to get to her. They looked like a comedy duo, opposites in every way. One was short with a thick moustache dominating his tanned face, and every energetic step reminded Maggie of a tin wind-up soldier. Next to him, dressed in reserved gray, was a balding fellow with glasses who, though not fat, was broad-shouldered and stiff, like a living wardrobe.

"What can I do for you gentlemen?" she asked, fixing on a cheery smile. No need to let the whole world know she'd been canned.

"That was some speech you made before intermission," Tin Soldier enthused. "The way you got a laugh and made a point all at once was gold-medal stuff. You really laid it out, Miss . . ."

"McCleod. Maggie McCleod." She set her trumpet case down and stuck out her hand, bracing herself for the vigorous pumping that followed.

"Sterling Warner," he said, "and I'm delighted to meet a musician with such a hidden talent."

"It must be hidden pretty well. I sure haven't found it yet." The quip slipped out before she could stop it.

Mr. Warner chuckled, his shoulders shaking and a light

of genuine amusement in his eyes. "See? I told you." She frowned, not sure how to respond, before she realized that he was directing the comment to the tall, unsmiling man beside him. "She's a natural, Douglas. We've got to have her."

Maggie could only stare at the energetic man. "I'm sorry, what?"

"The girl has promise, I suppose," Douglas said in a grudging sort of way, ignoring her question. "But it's risky, taking an unknown without experience."

"That unit of yours is all unknowns," Mr. Warner countered, blithely unbothered. "She's clearly used to touring."

Maggie took a step forward, clearing her throat. "I'm also used to people talking *to* me, not *through* me."

"There it is again. That wit of hers. Just the ticket." Before Maggie had to resort to stomping her foot to get attention, Mr. Warner put a hand on her arm, the other splayed out in dramatic fashion. "Miss McCleod, any chance we could tempt you away from this gig for a job with the USO camp shows?"

A job? In the music business that had just supposedly slammed its door on her? She tried to sound cautious, even professional. "I'm listening."

And listen she did, since Mr. Sterling Warner—movie producer and member of the Hollywood Victory Committee—barely let her get another word in edgewise. Turns out, the United Service Organization had started a division to organize small groups of performers to entertain American troops at bases, in hospitals, and even overseas near the front lines. The bespectacled man with him, introduced as Floyd Douglas, was a USO talent manager.

"We are in a bind," Douglas admitted. "We scheduled a sibling acrobat act for one of our variety units, but they dropped out at the last minute. We're shipping out from New York in just over a week."

"I see," Maggie said slowly, trying to take it all in.

Douglas gave a succinct summary of the schedule—grueling, commitment—three months, March through May, and salary—eighty-five dollars monthly, plus lodging and transportation—all peppered with so much propaganda from Mr. Warner that Maggie half expected his suitcoat to turn star-spangled.

"So I'd be performing trumpet solos for the GIs?" she clarified.

Douglas nodded. "Up to three shows a day, depending on the number of troops in a given area."

"And we'd want you to toss in some of that funny business between songs," Mr. Warner added. "The boys'll just love a female comedienne, and you've got the chops for it."

Maggie stared at him doubtfully. Sure, she could drop a one-liner every now and then off the cuff, but performing comedy in front of an audience?

"You sure this isn't some racket?" she asked, out of habit more than anything else. She had enough street smarts to tell when someone was running a con, and this didn't have that feel.

"Of course not," Douglas said, looking baffled that she'd ask such a question. "You can look over the contract with a lawyer if that would be of service to you."

"So what do you say, Miss McCleod?" Mr. Warner asked. "Are you willing to consider our offer?"

It wasn't the warning of a difficult schedule that made her pause—she was used to hard work—nor the danger of the tour, which actually appealed to her. It was one simple, stray thought: *What will Dad think?*

Her father, a Salvation Army preacher, had certain . . . misgivings about the entertainment world.

I'll worry about that later.

"I can do you one better," she said. "I'll accept it here and now."

"That's the spirit!" Mr. Warner slapped her on the back, then, apparently realizing she wasn't "one of the boys," chuckled and shook her hand instead.

"I'll do my best," Maggie promised. It was flattering, really. A genuine Hollywood type thought she was talented and funny enough to be hired on the spot.

There were still some questions for Maggie—no, she didn't have an agent; no, she wasn't in a musicians' union; yes, she owned her own instrument—and Douglas was midway through worries about whether they could expedite a passport when a delicate cough interrupted. "Excuse me."

They all turned, and even though Maggie had recognized the voice, it was still a surprise to see Catherine, tilting her head so her diamond earrings glittered in the chandeliers' light. How long had she been standing there?

Douglas was all detached politeness. "How might we be of service, miss?"

"I couldn't help but overhear. . . . I don't suppose you're looking for two performers for your show?"

Maggie tried to swallow away the feeling of jealousy the innocent question raised in her. Why would Catherine want to leave a band where she was the first-chair soloist and adored by all?

Instead of being charmed by Catherine's wide-eyed hopefulness, Douglas shifted, raising a hand to adjust his bow tie. "Well, I—"

"Because if so, I'd like to volunteer." She gave a smile that drew out the dimples in her cheeks. "My name is Catherine Duquette."

"Ah yes, the violinist," Mr. Warner enthused. "Charmed, I'm sure." He gave Douglas a significant look, which he didn't seem to notice.

"Pleased to meet you, Miss Duquette," he said, "but I'm not sure you know what you'd be getting into."

"Oh, but I do. I read all about the USO tours in *Billboard* magazine." She went on to talk about how noble and patriotic it was, but Maggie stopped listening. She already knew what Douglas would say.

All of the Sweethearts had to meet a certain standard of pretty, and Maggie grudgingly dressed up and did her hair like the rest. But this was Catherine Duquette. She would make a field full of female-deprived GIs go crazy with the slightest flutter of her eyelashes, and she could play Vivaldi's "Four Seasons" with enough passion to make an audience weep. She was as good as hired, and for a moment, Maggie resented it. It wasn't fair, her elbowing into a deal Maggie had gotten fair and square.

So she was surprised when Douglas interrupted with a cool "Thank you for your interest, Miss Duquette, but we don't need another musician for this variety unit."

"Oh. I see." Even Catherine's smile couldn't stand up under his dismissal, and in the awkward silence that followed, she took a step back. "Are . . . are you quite sure?"

In spite of herself, Maggie felt a tug of compassion at the desperation in Catherine's voice. Maybe even Catherine, with her fancy jewelry and Parisian perfume, had as good a reason to get out of Dodge as Maggie did. After all, everyone had their secrets.

And an awful thought crossed her mind, just for a moment: What would Simmons do if he lost two performers, including his star violinist, in one night?

"Better not pass this chance up, fellows," she found herself saying. "Catherine's a real pro. The best we have, in fact."

The shocked look Catherine sent her was worth the gambit by itself.

But Douglas didn't relax his stiff posture. "A solo violin

isn't our usual act. Too quiet to hear when we're unable to use a microphone."

"She can dance too," Maggie added. Well, anyway, Maggie had seen her swirling around on the dance floor a time or two when they had a break between sets at a ballroom performance. "And didn't you say you needed to fill in for a duo?"

As Douglas wavered, his face still registering disapproval, she wondered why she was risking her own future by speaking up for Catherine's sake. After all, they hadn't signed any papers yet. Beside her, Catherine gripped Maggie's arm, threatening to cut off the circulation.

Mr. Warner put up his hand and glanced over at his friend. "A moment, ladies, if you don't mind."

Maggie nodded graciously, hauling Catherine several steps away and pretending like she wasn't straining to hear every word through the genteel chatter of the atrium.

Mr. Warner's voice was lower in tone but not volume. "What's the problem, Douglas? She's a cut above the usual all-American girls you trot out for shows like this."

"I've got instincts, Warnie, that's all. And I've learned to trust them."

"Trust me instead this time. You won't regret it, I'll tell you that. She's a real looker."

After a long pause, Douglas nodded, muttering something about Mr. Warner being better at horse races than he was.

Well. Maggie wasn't sure how to take the conversation. They hadn't said a thing about *her* looks.

Who cares? Sure, Maggie was taller than most women and had a too-big nose, and no one would ever describe her as slender or glamorous, but once the curtain rose, it was talent that mattered. Wasn't it?

She managed to straighten up and not look like she'd been eavesdropping as the two men returned. "All right," Douglas said, his face back to a standard disinterested expression. "If you're interested in rounding out our variety unit, we'd be pleased to offer you a contract, Miss Duquette."

"I accept," she said quickly, as if they might change their minds.

"Excellent, excellent!" Mr. Warner enthused, pumping her hand and Maggie's in turn. "You'll be heroes to those boys. Just you wait!"

"Not so loud, please," Catherine blurted, glancing about as if a mobster were lurking behind one of the pillars, ready to pounce. Or, more likely, she didn't want Mr. Simmons to hear that his star violinist had just jumped ship.

As if in confirmation, after taking Douglas's card and instructions to meet him in the lobby of the Hotel Nicollet the next day to sign the contract, Catherine bit her lip nervously. "We'll have to tell Mr. Simmons first thing tomorrow. The poor dear, losing two of us at once. What will he say?"

Maggie snorted. *Dear* was a word only Catherine and Simmons's mother used to describe him. "Good thing we won't be around to hear it." But that raised another practical detail. "Mr. Douglas said they wouldn't start paying for lodging until next week at the tour's start. What'll we do until then?" She had some wages saved up, but she didn't want to bleed them out on a rented room.

For a moment, Catherine frowned, too, then her China-blue eyes lit up. "I have just the thing!"

4

February 23, 1943
St. Paul, Minnesota

Despite the fact that Catherine had known Lorraine Maynard since they were children, she still felt like a door-to-door salesman standing on the stoop with her traveling trunk at her feet. After all, it had been a long time, and so much had changed.

However, when the door burst open in response to her knock, Lorraine beamed so widely that Catherine's nervousness faded away. "Catherine! It's a *delight* to see you."

"Hello, Lorraine dear." She hugged her friend, and only then did it become apparent that she was seven months pregnant. The high-waisted aqua dress she wore fell around her in soft pleats, obscuring her condition, though she'd written to Catherine to tell her the good news. "Thank you so much for taking us in."

"With all your touring, I was starting to think I'd have to buy a ticket in order to see you. Harrison insists that loud music would upset the baby, so I'd have had to sneak off to the concert hall under some pretense or other. Wouldn't that have been grand?" Lorraine opened the door wider, letting them pass with all the formality and grace of the lady of the house, never mind that she'd only been married a year. "Do come in."

Beside her, Maggie shifted, clutching her startlingly small suitcase, and Catherine stepped aside to indicate her. "Allow me to introduce my fellow musician, Miss Margaret McCleod."

"Any friend of Catherine's is a friend of mine," Lorraine said, tittering a laugh. Maggie looked less amused, likely unsure of what to do with the tiny blonde whirlwind who was already inspecting their luggage. "My, you've traveled so far! You must be exhausted." She tugged the handle to Catherine's trunk. "I'll have our chauffer bring up your things. Catherine, dear, what do you have in here? Bowling balls? Solid concrete? A dead body, perhaps?"

She chose not to encourage her by rising to that comment. "I was gone for quite a long time." Some days, you simply didn't feel like a tweed skirt and needed something loose and flowing, and then there were the shoes and accessories required to match.

The entryway of the Queen Anne–style house wasn't as foreboding as her parents' sprawling manor, though the hardwood floors gleamed and the antique gilt mirror looked like it hadn't seen a fingerprint smudge in a decade. An eyesore of a geometric painting took up the rest of the wall. "A present from Arthur's travels," Lorraine said, noticing her looking that way. "Cubism, he called it. It was all the rage in Paris before the war."

To Catherine's eye, it was the sort of style that might make people go to war. "Your brother certainly has . . . unique tastes in gifts."

"But enough about that," Lorraine said, catching her arm like they were back at boarding school, giggling about exams and boys and who would get the starring role in the school program. "The telegram you sent me last night was just too dramatic. An overseas venture? You must tell all."

Though Lorraine's voice was casual, her sunny features were sharply attentive. Did she suspect something was amiss?

"It's quite the long story. Perhaps we ought to see Maggie to her room first?"

Lorraine caught her hint as the plea for privacy that it was. "Of course. Do follow me."

Catherine waited downstairs while Lorraine ushered Maggie away, giving a tour as she went. Following the sound of a big band record, she wandered through an archway and into the morning room.

This, she could tell, was her friend's favorite room of the house. It seemed *warmer* than the rest. The furniture was arranged near tall windows that probably caught the light just so as it rose in the east. The lace tablecloth had a few light stains from tea, and the smell of roses lingered in the air.

She sat in one of the petite cushioned chairs. On the table next to her, a tiny dove-gray hat was a few knitted rows from completion. Catherine stroked the soft yarn.

"How are you, dear?" she began, once Lorraine joined her.

"The doctor says everything's coming along. Mainly, my back aches, my feet are swollen, and I'm bored to tears." Lorraine slumped on the divan and propped the aforementioned feet up. "Harrison's in New York for some dreary board meetings this week, and I've been driving the housekeeper just crazy hunting for something to do. It's a godsend that you came when you did." She paused, a sparkle of mischief in her eyes. "Now, tell me all about it."

Instead of drawing out the mystery further, Catherine spilled all the details of the USO job and her reasons for taking it. There was only one part she left out: the fact that she hadn't told her parents, nor was she planning to do so . . . not until it was too late for them to do anything about it.

Lorraine inserted appropriate exclamations, then frowned. "Isn't it dangerous, though?"

"Not at all." Catherine passed the half-truth off with what she hoped was a reassuring smile. "And it will mean the world to our boys in uniform."

"I'm sure, but, Catherine, a variety act?" Lorraine had taken up her knitting, and it seemed to Catherine that even the soft sound of the needles formed a tsk of disapproval. "It's not exactly a step toward a serious musical career."

That, at least, she could answer. "Oh, but dozens of Hollywood stars are joining USO tours. It's quite the prestigious thing to do."

Lorraine sighed, looking down at the tiny hat. "And I suppose it doesn't bother you that you'll miss the birth of your goddaughter or godson?"

Catherine counted the months. Of course. That would explain her friend's hesitance. "Aren't first babies usually late?"

"Not over a month late."

"I'm sorry, Lorraine." She gave her friend her best pleading look. "But you know how much this means to me."

"Yes, I suppose I do." The silence that fell between them wasn't entirely comfortable.

Catherine shifted in her seat. Should she ask? If she didn't, it would bother her for the next three months. With effort, she kept the tone of her voice casual. "Have there been . . . any letters for me? From Leo?"

"That pilot of yours?" Lorraine shook her head. "Nothing since October, like I told you. I'm sorry, Catherine."

It was the answer she was expecting, but it still fell like a blow. She took a breath and pressed on. "And they really did stop arriving? You didn't . . . Father didn't . . . interfere?"

Instead of being irritated at the implication, Lorraine was

all compassion. "You know I'd be the last person to come between you and a fellow who's clearly sent you head over heels. I promise I didn't tell your family or hide any letters or meddle in any way."

As much of a betrayal as it would have been, Catherine had been almost hoping for some other explanation, one that would mean Leo was alive and well, merely chased off by her interfering family. "I believe you," she whispered, feeling her shoulders droop.

Lorraine was at her side in an instant. "Oh, Catherine, I do hope nothing's happened to your beau. But, you know, I didn't think it was right, him courting you behind your family's back."

Of course Lorraine wouldn't understand. She'd married a respectable financier at age nineteen. "You know what Father would say if he knew about Leo. And only because he's a farmer's son, not for any real reason."

"Yes, I suppose so." Her friend's bright smile returned with a determined air. "Everything will work out, Catherine. I'm sure of it." Whether she meant that Leo was healthy and well, only unable to write for some reason, or that she would pick up the bits of a broken heart and move on, Catherine wasn't sure.

"Hallo in the house!" a familiar voice called, echoing loudly down the hall. "Anyone home?"

Catherine gripped the arm of her chair. Panic flared through her as she directed a cutting glance at her friend. "You didn't tell me Arthur was coming."

Lorraine fluttered her eyelashes as if her appointment with her brother had simply slipped her mind. "Oh, I didn't?"

Catherine didn't comment on Lorraine's terrible acting abilities, wondering instead if she could duck out the glass door leading to the patio.

"Well, if it isn't our Cathy!" Arthur DeVos stepped into

view through the doorway, arms akimbo in a loud mustard-colored suit like he was leading a parade, a look of genuine astonishment on his face.

"Isn't it delightful?" Lorraine said, rising on tiptoe to buss her brother on the cheek. "Catherine's staying with me for a while. And of course I knew you would want to say hello."

"Do I ever!" He marched over and caught Catherine up in a hug, burying her nose in his suit lapel until she could smell his particular brand of cigar. "It's been a good long while, Cathy. How the heck are you?"

Pushing away, she made sure her smile was on the tepid side while still being polite. "Very well, thank you."

This was a disaster. Arthur, in addition to being Lorraine's brother and the target of her matchmaking skills, was Catherine's father's head sales manager at Duquette Lens Company. And he couldn't keep a secret. If Lorraine even hinted about the USO job, he'd report her newest adventure directly to Catherine's father in ten minutes flat.

Catherine riffled through a mental catalog of small talk. Not the weather, that would be exhausted too easily. Not the Swinging Sweethearts, Lorraine would tell him she'd quit. Once they moved to the dining room, she would be safe, since praising his sister's cook was one of Arthur's favorite subjects.

She finally blurted what the bores who came to dinner were always asking her father. "How's business these days?"

If he thought it was a lame attempt at conversation, he didn't show it. "Never been better! I tell ya, the war's been good for us, if it's not too gauche to say."

From the settee, Lorraine shot Catherine a look of despair, clearly knowing just how interested Catherine really was in this quarter's profit margins. With the assistance of a few well-timed nods and halfhearted responses, Catherine had

Arthur going for ten minutes straight without any hint of the conversation veering into personal territory.

By the time lunch was ready, Catherine had almost congratulated herself on a successful evasion when Lorraine stood. "Yes, that's all fascinating, Arthur, thank you. Now, don't you want to ask Catherine what *she's* been up to?"

Catherine did her best to indicate with a jerk of her head that this was not a subject she wanted to pursue. A frown of confusion crossed Lorraine's face, but the damage was done.

"Sure, sure. Didn't mean to go on like that." Arthur led the way into the hall, pausing to admire the painting he'd given his sister. "Your father tells me you're coming home soon, Cathy. Great news! When will that be, and how was the touring life?"

Catherine seethed inwardly and hoped that was all her father had indicated to the man everyone knew he hoped to call a son-in-law someday. Thankfully, Arthur seemed to be blissfully ignorant of this plan, somehow missing the hints from both Father and Lorraine and treating Catherine more like a buddy from his country club than a prospective wife.

She dodged the first portion of the question and focused on the second. "It's been a dream. I feel I've grown as a musician with a chance to perform in a full band."

"Whaddya know about that? And here all of us thought you couldn't get any better."

As always, Arthur, though sincere, was so over-the-top that it made Catherine's teeth ache. She had grown up with Lorraine's older brother, and he wasn't a bad sort. He filled his free time with a myriad of sports and hobbies, and could—and did—sing along with every song on the radio, but unlike the radio, there was no way to turn down the volume on his constant chatter.

That, at least, provided dozens of openings for changing

the subject. "And how about you? Still perfecting your golf swing?"

"No, no. I've moved on from that. No time. A pal of mine is going in with me to start a jazz club downtown."

"Is that so?" Catherine was delighted to hear how interested she sounded in the latest in Arthur's long line of ventures. Hopefully it would provide enough discussion to last them through lunch.

Lorraine tugged her aside just outside the dining room as Arthur barged on ahead. "What's wrong? You were shooting daggers at me the whole time."

Could she really not have guessed? "The second your brother hears about the USO job, he'll go straight to my family and tell them, that's what."

"But aren't *you* going to tell them?"

"Of course. After I leave."

Lorraine's look was part shock, part censure. "Catherine!"

"Honestly, Lorraine," Catherine said, exasperated. "I'm quite capable of making my own decisions. And one of them is that Arthur is not to know about the USO tour."

Her friend wrinkled her slightly upturned nose. "All right. But I don't like it."

An uneasy feeling made Catherine wonder if Lorraine might be right. She had made the decision quickly, uncharacteristically so. Had it been too hasty?

She shook her head to dispel her nervous second-guessing. Of course not. She'd spent most of her life trying to do what other people wanted. This was her golden opportunity, and she was going to take it.

Alone at last in her guest room, Catherine massaged her temples to get rid of the brewing headache. Once they'd invited her downstairs, Maggie had been an incalculable asset.

The subject of baseball came up, and she'd gotten into a discussion with Arthur about whether a women's league could fill the gap for enlisting male players. That had taken them clear through the soup and salad. Catherine had escaped soon after, pleading the need to unpack.

She tugged her trunk toward the center of the room, which, despite the rose-colored wallpaper and a bed done up in cream, still managed a thrown-together look from the mismatch of woods—oak for the writing desk, mahogany for the wardrobe, and a dark cherry for the bedframe.

After hanging up her dresses, she sighed. Better start drafting the news to her family while she still had the resolve. She opened up her jewelry box, which doubled as a stationery kit, and withdrew a piece of writing paper. Her hand brushed the packet of letters underneath, hidden when she was sure no more would be coming.

Part of her wanted to untie the ribbon that bound them and read them again, even though she had many lines memorized. The letters started with the hesitant tone of near strangers who had met by chance, but slowly, they'd become warmer, more personal. Leo was witty and a clever storyteller, but also thoughtful, asking for her stories in turn. She'd begun to share some of her hopes and fears with Leo, ones she knew her parents would never understand.

Just when she'd dared to write that she missed him and cared for him, Leo stopped writing back, and her next letters were returned by the army post. She'd never learned what happened to him, despite a desperate attempt to find out.

Will I see him on tour?

It was a silly hope. Sergeant Leo Wallace was one man in a great war, and she had no idea where he was stationed—even in his last letter four months ago, vigilant censors had prevented anything more specific than vague across-the-Atlantic language.

But still, wherever her USO variety unit landed, they'd be moving constantly, performing in front of thousands of men for months. That had to increase her odds. Why shouldn't he be in one of their audiences?

Unless he had become one more casualty of war, the army unable to notify her because Leo had never told his family about her.

She'd let that worry keep her up late at night many times. There were other explanations too, none of them pleasant. Maybe he'd met a beautiful Red Cross nurse and forgotten about her. Maybe something she'd said in her last letter tipped him off about her controlling family. Maybe he'd been captured by Germans and was even now starving in a prisoner-of-war camp.

Stop, she told herself, as she always did. *Fretting won't help*. But until now, she hadn't been able to replace worrying with actually doing something. Taking the USO job was a way to avoid choosing between her parents' competing plans for her future, yes, but there was also the small hope she'd be reunited with the man who had captured her heart.

"I *will* find you again," she whispered to the stack of letters. "Someday."

Suddenly, the sparse room felt cold and empty. If she were still with the Sweethearts, there would be a constant flurry of activity and conversation. Here, Lorraine was likely still entertaining Arthur, so that ruled out a visit downstairs. Maybe if she knocked on Maggie's door . . .

It was an unlikely idea. They'd never been close, even with all the shared rooms and railroad cars of touring. If anything, Catherine would have described Maggie as aloof, always making quips at others' expense, but rarely joining the other Sweethearts during moments of relaxation. She was talented—once, she'd even demonstrated her ability to play any little ditty one of the girls hummed by ear with hardly a mistake—but she'd never quite fit in.

Yet for some reason, Maggie had defended her to the USO talent agents. Maybe it was her way of reaching out in friendship, and if so, Catherine should reciprocate.

After tucking the letters safely away, Catherine slipped into the hall and tapped on Maggie's door, across from her own. "All unpacked?" she asked when it opened.

Maggie shrugged. "Didn't take long." She stepped aside, showing a room similar to Catherine's but painted in mint, and opened the wardrobe to reveal three dresses hanging there. That, Catherine supposed, would explain the size of the suitcase. How could a woman get by with so few clothing choices?

She'd read through the memos from the USO Mr. Douglas had given them, including their luggage allowances and what they ought to pack. Cold cream, perfume, bobby pins, stockings, and sunglasses were all listed, as well as clothes for onstage that would make them look like "the soldiers' best girls back home on an important Saturday night date."

From what she could see, none of Maggie's dresses fit that description. "Don't you think these are a bit . . . casual for performances?"

"They're all I have," Maggie said simply.

"We can remedy that." As she spoke, Catherine felt sure it was a brilliant idea, just the thing to take her mind off her worries about Arthur, her parents, and Leo.

"What do you mean?" Maggie's tone was dubious, as if Catherine was going to attack her with a machine gun.

"We are going to go shopping!"

5

February 24, 1943
Minneapolis, Minnesota

Maggie had never felt more like a cow up for auction than when the two Dayton's Department Store salesclerks roped her with the tape measure, reading the numbers that put her waist, hips, and bust on full display. The figures were probably larger than they should be. She'd never eaten so good in her life as she had with the Sweethearts—on someone else's dime.

Here in the Dayton's fitting room, shivering in her slip and underwear, Maggie almost wished for the simple brown or gray dresses of her childhood. She'd known she hadn't belonged here the minute she'd stepped through the fancy glass doors. By the time they'd glided up the newly installed escalators past displays of suits and golf clubs to the women's department, it was too late to run away, so she'd let Catherine haul her into a fitting room.

"We simply must get you a girdle," Catherine said appraisingly before turning toward the archway that led out to the clothing displays with slender mannequins modeling the latest styles. "Don't worry, Maggie. The girls and I will bring you everything you need."

Maggie sincerely doubted "need" would factor into it. This shopping trip had somehow transformed shy, mild-mannered Catherine into a maven of advice and enthusiasm.

Maggie sidled up to the sleepy-looking salesgirl and spoke in a low tone. "Listen, I need your help. Three dresses, all right? Four at the most. That's all I want to try on. And make sure they're reasonably priced."

The only response she got from the clerk was a noncommittal hum.

"I'm afraid we won't have time for alterations, but I'm sure we'll find something lovely to buy off the rack." Catherine shot a rapturous glance back at Maggie. "This is such fun!"

Fun. Some women found this sort of thing *fun*.

Maggie plopped down on the ivory cushions of the dainty bench and sighed. "That settles it. I'm doomed."

By the time Catherine returned, they'd had to recruit an employee from the menswear department to join the entourage, all of them carrying stacks of fabric in a rainbow of colors to hang on a golden rack for her inspection.

"Cotton dresses," she reminded Catherine, poking warily at the folds of a brilliant blue dress that fanned out in frills like a peacock's tail. "That's what the USO instructions recommended. Good for all climates, no matter where in the world we end up."

"They also said to bring at least one evening gown to perform in, and no one makes *those* in cotton." She thrust a rose-patterned monstrosity Maggie's way. "Why don't you give this one a try?"

Maggie held it out, frowning at the loud pattern. "Someone made this out of their old curtains, I bet."

"Well, it worked for Scarlett O'Hara," Catherine replied.

"Who's she?"

Catherine's mouth curved into a perfect pink O. "When was the last time you saw a movie?"

Maggie didn't have the heart to tell her the answer was never—her father had thought most of Hollywood was thoroughly hell-bound. Whatever her own feelings on the eternal destiny of the film industry, she did agree a ticket was a waste of a perfectly good dime.

She pulled the privacy curtain over the alcove of her fitting room, dress draped over her arm. Underfoot, her shoes left small imprints on the green velvet carpet. The mahogany trim classed it up plenty, but Maggie still couldn't help feeling like she was walking on an enormous billiards table.

The curtain dress, it turned out, needed someone with the figure of a curtain rod, not broad shoulders and ample hips like Maggie's.

Also rejected was a "darling" floral day dress, an "enchanting" pink off-the-shoulder gown, and an "exquisite" silk number in a color Catherine called "taupe" and Maggie called "ugly."

Catherine looked despairingly between the clerks at that comment, receiving obligatory sympathy in return. "Maggie, you are entirely too picky."

"I accepted this one." Maggie held up the gray-blue gingham shirtwaist dress that she'd tried on somewhere in the middle of their spree. It was, she'd been told, on sale.

"That old thing? I don't know how it wandered into the stack. It's not elegant enough."

"It's got mother-of-pearl buttons," Maggie protested, quoting the salesclerk.

Catherine fanned herself in a mock swoon. "Oh! The extravagance."

That was the annoyance that had worked its way under Maggie's skin like a sliver of wood. Catherine meant well, sure, but she didn't understand: things she thought of as necessities really were extravagances to people like Maggie.

She'd almost put her foot down and said one new dress was more than enough, thank you, when she saw Catherine's next selection, a flowing evening gown in deep green.

Well. It couldn't hurt to try on one more.

This time, Maggie could step out from behind the curtain with ease instead of mincing her way over in a fitted skirt. Standing before the full-length mirror, she dared a glance.

This dress wasn't made for someone as slim as a cigarette holder. The emerald-green material didn't glitter with sequins, but the skirt fell like a waterfall down to her ankles, and its cap sleeves and squared neckline didn't squeeze out her curves, but they weren't hidden either.

She straightened her shoulders in the mirror, glancing toward the others, who, for once, weren't sharing opinions. "It's not *as* terrible," she admitted, waiting for Catherine to tell her it wasn't her color or bring up girdles again.

But Catherine's stare broke into a beaming smile. "What do you mean? You look stunning, Maggie. Doesn't she look stunning, Jeannie? Patty?"

The other two women nodded obligingly. When had Catherine learned the salesclerks' names?

When Maggie heard the price, she nearly collapsed, quickly figuring how many hours of good, solid work she'd be spending in an eyeblink.

Still, her new USO salary was decent. It's not like she had anyone back home to support, and the Foxhole Circuit packing list *had* said their performance clothes ought to be special.

Maggie ran her hand over the subtle beading along the neckline and sighed. "Fine. I'll take it."

Catherine wasted no time in gushing her approval, and Jeannie and Patty looked equally delighted.

As Catherine tried to wheedle them into bringing out silk stockings from the back room, since none were to be had on the sales floor, Maggie settled back. For the first time, when she thought of an audience full of applauding GIs, she could picture herself onstage in front of them.

"I'll knock 'em dead," she whispered to the ostentatious fitting room. "Just you wait and see."

6

March 1, 1943
Union Depot, St. Paul, Minnesota

Arthur drove his sporty Aston Martin like a tank, rarely slowing for yellow lights and plowing through the morning's traffic without regard for potential danger. From the front seat, Catherine tried not to show she was beginning to despair of arriving at Union Depot alive.

"Nice day for a train ride, eh?" Arthur mused, taking a hand off the steering wheel to fix his tie, a garish polka-dotted thing. "I'm surprised your band doesn't have a bus to get you ladies to the station."

"Yeah, you'd think they'd be better about details like that," Maggie said. A quick glance to the backseat showed her drilling a look into Catherine's skull that shouted, *"Tell him, already."*

Which Catherine steadfastly ignored. She felt bad about leaving Arthur in the dark—worse, even, than not telling Mother or Father—but he'd hear about it soon enough. She'd posted her letters this morning, giving her parents an overview of the USO camp shows and their mission.

"Never mind," Arthur said. "It's a good excuse to see you off." And there was no chance of their being late with the way Arthur drove. He pulled up to the sidewalk outside of the bustling station, stopping an inch away from another car's fender, and hauled their luggage out, whistling all the way.

While Maggie stood off to the side, Catherine let Arthur hug her. "I hope the jazz club works out," she said a bit lamely.

"Thanks," Arthur said, beaming. "All the best to you and your band, Cathy. Make us folks at home proud!"

"I'll try." She hesitated, ashamed by his enthusiasm. Maybe she could give him a bit of honesty this close to her escape. After all, he couldn't stop her now. The contract had been signed. "And Arthur . . ."

"What's that?" he prompted, already halfway into his Aston Martin. Maybe it was her tone, but he suddenly looked serious for once.

That, more than anything else, made her lose her nerve to tell him the truth. "Thanks for the ride."

The sober look in his brown eyes disappeared so quickly Catherine wondered if she'd imagined it, replaced by his usual affable smile. "Anytime, anytime at all, Cathy. And I mean that. So long!" With that, he tipped his hat, slammed the car door, and careened away like he had a life insurance policy he wanted to cash out.

Looking up at the steps to the depot, Catherine felt a surge of excitement, despite being sore from needle pokes and calloused from practicing solo violin arrangements.

The rest of their preparations for departure hadn't been nearly so fun as shopping at Dayton's. Floyd Douglas worked them through the paces with businesslike efficiency to prepare them to ship out. The checklist included a hurried physical, inoculations against malaria, cholera, and at least three other exotic-sounding diseases, and the just-in-time arrival of their passports and USO ID cards, with strict instructions to carry them at all times.

Careful not to trip in her white oxford pumps, Catherine marched up the steps to the depot with confidence, dressed in a burgundy serge travel suit. Maggie followed behind, wearing a practical raincoat. With the boy she'd flagged down left to handle their luggage, they were free to find Mr. Douglas and board the train for adventure.

Once they'd gone past the neoclassical pillars, Catherine stopped short. The main concourse was unexpectedly dark, and a quick glance up told her why. Unlike in her girlhood, the beautiful arched skylights were painted over with tar, enfolding the rows of benches below in shadow.

Maggie must've noticed her staring because she tilted her chin at the new décor. "I heard it's to protect the station from air raids so the Fort Snelling boys can sneak through."

"Of course," she said, suddenly subdued. It made one think, knowing that the Axis powers could bomb them anywhere in the country.

If it were up to her, she'd stop and admire the hustle and bustle of the station, but Maggie was bearing down on their platform with the assured pace of someone who had grown up in a city. Train stations weren't new to Catherine, of course. In the past, though, she had settled into Pullman lounges, with appointments like wide velvet divans, tile murals, and even a solarium with a bar service, not to mention the master lounge sleeping cars.

Coach class was something else altogether, but Catherine was glad they had secured tickets at all. With train travel essential for military personnel, she had heard stories of vacationers who stayed up all night to queue up for tickets home, only to be told they'd all sold out.

Once they stepped aboard, Douglas promptly let the rhythm of the rails lull him into a doze, while Maggie opened a blank notebook, working on the banter for her routine. That was all right with Catherine. She preferred peaceful journeys.

As the train rolled onward and the views of the city faded to countryside, Catherine gave another glance to Maggie, making sure she was absorbed in her thoughts. Then she opened her handbag to take out the letter she'd placed there this morning, written in Leo's slanted hand. He'd drawn a caricature of himself poking out of a miniature train engine in the margin, exaggerating his square jaw. He was quite the artist, and though she had no photograph of him, seeing his self-portrait always made her smile.

> *I rode on my first ever troop train today. I can't wait to get over there and show those Jerries not to pick a fight with us Yanks. We're all in a celebratory mood, though for me it's bittersweet. Catherine, maybe it's bold of me to say it, but I don't care: I wish more than anything that this train was bringing me closer to you instead of farther away.*

She creased the letter again and tucked it back in the inner pocket of her bag. Maybe this one was bringing them closer together. She could only hope.

When she closed her eyes, she could still see the Sweethearts' name on the marquee of the Surf Ballroom, hear their instruments tuning, smell the mixture of mud and rain and new grass that had been in the air the evening she met Leo Wallace.

May 1942
Clear Lake, Iowa

Catherine couldn't help but be impressed by the interior of the Surf Ballroom. A massive hardwood floor, new enough not to be scuffed by decades of dancers, shone under the light of globe chandeliers hanging from the midnight-blue ceiling. The elevated platform for the band was spacious and trimmed with red curtains, framed on either side with artificial palm trees to match the ballroom's name.

Though they were miles away from any real beach, Catherine understood the choice of décor. There was a particular romance to the ocean, one she had felt every summer when her family traveled to the shores of Virginia or California at whatever resort her mother thought would be a good escape from boredom that year. The salty breeze and warm sand, surrounded by strangers stretched out in the sun, made one feel that anything could happen.

The Sweethearts set up onstage, ready to perform a full set of swing tunes and popular big band hits, saving their classical pieces for more formal events. Soon eager dancers crowded through the doors, from bobby-socked youngsters to middle-aged couples, all ready to foxtrot the night and their troubles away. A few of the young men were dressed in uniform, on leave from one of the nearby forts. When Catherine caught glimpses of them as they danced past the stage, she thought they held their sweethearts a little closer and stole kisses more often than the other couples.

It must have been an hour in before Catherine noticed a young man with jet-black hair sitting alone at one of the booths along the side of the ballroom, lounging with an arm draped over its wooden back so he could face the stage. He wore a brown tweed suit, the fabric too heavy for the warm weather, indicating, perhaps, that it was the only suit he owned. Regardless, he wore it well, and no matter how many others jitterbugged past, Catherine couldn't spot a more handsome man in the crowd.

Song after song, he didn't stand to ask a girl to dance or meander over to the bar to order a drink. His eyes remained fixed on the platform and—unless Catherine was wrong—specifically on her.

Maybe he was shy and had been dragged there by a friend, though something about the way he interacted with others, smiling easily, made her doubt that. Well, perhaps he had some physical reason he couldn't dance. It was none of her business, anyway, she told herself as they finished "Stardust."

After the applause, Mr. Simmons indicated each of the sections in turn, and Catherine gave a deep curtsy with her other string players. As she rose, she saw the handsome wallflower putting two fingers in his mouth to let out a whistle more at home in a ballpark than a ballroom as he stepped away from the edge of the dance floor.

Was he . . . coming this way?

The owner of the ballroom took over the microphone to announce an upcoming dance benefiting war bonds. Their conductor had told the Sweethearts this was their cue to leave for their mid-set break, a chance to rest or "freshen up" in the powder room. Catherine's hands moved by rote to tuck her violin in its case, her eyes on the handsome wallflower who was indeed approaching the bandstand.

Go over to him, the daring side of her, the one that had gathered the courage to join the Sweethearts in the first place, insisted. If he wasn't waiting to speak with her, she could simply walk past.

"Ahem." Just as she'd hoped, the young man reached forward to touch her arm as she went by. Up close, she could see his eyes were an entrancing shade of dark blue, like the sky at twilight. Words escaped her, and she tried her very hardest not to stare, or at least not to look like she was staring.

Having captured her attention, the wallflower bowed elaborately. "Good evening, Miss Duquette. May I have a dance?"

She didn't ask how he knew her name. Much to her embarrassment, her face was featured on several of the playbills used to advertise the Sweethearts' performances. "I . . . but there isn't any music playing."

"Then I'll make some. I can whistle about half of the notes in 'Yankee Doodle.'" He sounded so hopeful that Catherine didn't think he was teasing her.

She laughed at the feigned desperation on his face. "Maybe instead you could buy me a soda, Mr. . . ."

His face broke into a smile worthy of a cinema poster. "Leo Wallace, soon-to-be pilot of an army fighter plane. And I'd be honored."

He looked the part with his confident bearing, debonair attitude, and dark hair that, even in the ballroom, seemed to be slightly mussed by the wind. He took her arm like they were old friends, completely comfortable with each other, instead of strangers who had just learned each other's names. "I had no idea coming here tonight that I'd be treated to such a beautiful performance."

She would not blush. She would not. "Thank you. Do you know much about music?"

He'd led her to the dining area. The ceiling had a green-and-cream pattern of an awning, and the walls were painted with beachside views of crashing waves, as if they'd stepped into a soda fountain on the Atlantic City boardwalk.

Leo shook his head. "I'm afraid I don't. Visual art is more my area. My old man's a farmer, but after the war is over, I'm hoping to make a living as an illustrator."

"Tell me, then, what does your artist's eye think of the murals?"

He turned to see the wall she indicated, pulling Catherine slightly closer in the process. "It's not the Sistine Chapel or anything, but they're not bad. Gives the place some atmosphere." His voice dropped in volume, like he was telling her a secret. "Though I'll admit to being more taken by one of its enchanting occupants."

After buying her a grape soda, they took a table off in the corner. Leo told her about his extensive flying experience, breathtaking stories of daring climbs and near misses, then asked her what it was like to travel with the Sweethearts. She found herself sharing about the thrill of curtains rising and the exhaustion of traveling without a space to oneself, the soda that offered the pretext for their conversation nearly untouched. How long had it been since someone had listened, really *listened*, to what she had to say?

"Catherine." The new voice startled Catherine into remembering that there were, in fact, other people in the world than just the two of them. Namely, Maggie McCleod, calling in a too-loud voice just outside the dining area. "Show's about to start."

Catherine supposed she should be grateful—Mr. Simmons didn't take kindly to missing musicians—but Maggie's interruption felt like an unwelcome reveille to a deep sleep. "I'm sorry," she said, standing, "but I have to go. If our band leader notices I'm late . . ."

"Sure. I understand." Leo joined her, moving with her as if reluctant to leave her side. "Guess now I know how Cinderella's prince must have felt. I don't suppose you'd leave a shoe behind for me?"

An idea occurred to her. "We'll be performing here again tomorrow night."

"Really?" When she nodded, he whirled her around like they were in the middle of a foxtrot. "Then I'll be here. Waiting. For any chance I have to see you again."

Catherine felt her heart beating faster as she hurried away. She took her place onstage and glanced at Mr. Simmons, taking over the stage with his impeccable tuxedo and commanding glare. The Sweethearts' conductor had warned them against going on dates or even talking to young men on their tour, knowing he could start to lose members of his band if a romance sparked.

Is that what this is? The start of a romance? Catherine found herself hoping it might be. The way Leo talked to her, listened to her, smiled at her . . . it was so different from the way her parents treated each other.

The next day, she found herself taking extra time on her makeup and hair, all the while wondering, worrying. What if Leo had changed his mind? What if he never came, or worse, came but danced with someone else?

But when she hurried through the doors of the Surf, violin case tucked under her arm, there he was, in the same suit but with a different tie.

Maggie McCleod, of all people, was talking to him. If it had been any other member of the Sweethearts, Catherine might suspect she was trying to steal Leo's attentions. That didn't seem to be a danger with Maggie. She faced Leo with arms crossed, her hair still pressed flat in the back where she'd slept on it. Even her voice didn't hold a trace of flirtation, sounding more like an interrogation than a friendly chat.

But Catherine forgot all about that the moment Leo looked up and saw her, a broad smile filling his face.

She'd almost made it to him when Mr. Simmons tapped his baton on his music stand and looked in her direction, halting her in place. She couldn't do anything to jeopardize her future with the Sweethearts.

Catherine changed directions, heading for the steps to the stage instead, sending Leo a look that begged him to understand.

She shouldn't have worried.

"Remember," he mouthed. *"One dance."*

Instead of joining her fellow brass players, Maggie paused by Catherine's chair, giving her a long look with something lingering underneath it that Catherine didn't like. She tried to ignore it, tuning her bowstrings with practiced ease.

Finally, Maggie spoke. "I thought you said he was from a small farming town near here."

Catherine's brief interlude with a handsome soldier the night before hadn't gone unnoticed by the other Sweethearts. They'd surrounded her to demand the details on the way back to the hotel. She'd pretended not to care for the attention, but the truth was, there was something giddy about being the lead in a romance that seemed to come straight off the Hollywood silver screen. But she hadn't realized Maggie had been listening too.

"He is." She'd been delighted by his humorous stories of the chickens his parents raised.

Maggie shook her head. "When I asked him, he said he was from Chicago like me."

"He was probably born there." *And couldn't wait to get away*, she chose not to add. Catherine had been to the city several times and found it dirty and ugly.

"Seems strange, that's all." Maggie's gaze drifted from her to across the room, where Leo was sitting in the corner booth—their booth. "Maybe you shouldn't be cozying up to someone you just met."

A prickle of resentment rose in Catherine's stomach, and her words came out with a bite to them. "He's just a local boy about to enlist, looking to have a nice evening out." And yet some foolish part of her felt there was something more. A connection, perhaps. Certainly an attraction. Leo had, after all, chosen her, out of all the women in the room.

If Maggie saw any of that in Catherine's face, she didn't comment on it, just gave a short nod. "Maybe. Just . . . be careful."

The comment wasn't entirely a surprise. Maggie was the renowned pessimist of the group, always telling them how to hold their purses so they couldn't get snatched or mocking the romantic comedies the other girls watched when they had free time. Whether it was her nature or upbringing, Catherine couldn't say, but it had never annoyed her like it did now.

Of course, a well-bred lady didn't let on, so she raised her violin to her chin and turned away. Some chips on people's shoulders couldn't be repaired.

There were no clocks on the walls of the Surf, probably to allow patrons to lose track of time, so Catherine simply watched Leo Wallace, standing alone at the back of the ballroom, waiting to dance with her. Never had an evening seemed to stretch so slowly.

When the appointed hour for their break finally arrived, a local barbershop quartet started a six-song set to keep the Saturday night crowd swirling on the dance floor.

With a glance over her shoulder at her friends from the band, Catherine slipped onto the hardwood floor and toward Leo's bench.

The way he smiled and took her hand as the quartet crooned "In the Good Old Summertime" gave her a glowing feeling she'd never had before.

The crowd packed on the dance floor had thinned, perhaps because the taut harmonies weren't as upbeat as the jazz music the Sweethearts had been playing. Leo didn't seem to mind. His hand against her waist felt like it belonged there, and their steps moved perfectly in time. Somehow, she doubted that Leo had benefited from private dance lessons like she had, but he was a natural.

As they slowly moved back and forth, Catherine tried to tell herself this was a simple favor to a departing soldier, that she could say good-bye and not feel a sense of longing for what might have been. But she knew in her heart it was a lie.

"What's wrong?" Leo had stopped, and she realized she had too, right in the middle of the dance floor.

She tried unsuccessfully to conceal the worry in her voice. "It's . . . it's going to be over so soon."

"Hey, now. A lady as pretty as you shouldn't worry about things like that." He gently guided her back into the steps of the dance. "Just enjoy the moment—and the music."

As they danced in time, the quartet's songs flew by in the background. In fact, she'd forgotten all about them until Leo began singing along with their warbling tones in a lovely tenor voice, holding her gaze like he'd held her hand just moments before, "'Let me call you sweetheart, I'm in love with you.'"

By the time Catherine hurried back onstage to finish their performance, Leo had secured her promise to write to him—and one sweet but lingering kiss, given as a seal of that promise when a handshake just wouldn't do. She hoped she hadn't shown it, but inside she felt like a bottle of shaken champagne, bubbling over in a joyous fizz.

That night, she began a letter giving Leo her friend Lorraine's address to reply to. Surely her friend would forward them along to the next stop on the tour. If only they hadn't had to say good-bye.

It all felt like a dream, not something that happened to real people, certainly not shy women like Catherine: to be noticed, listened to, even *kissed* by a handsome soldier. Maybe he would forget all about her as soon as basic training began.

But maybe, she allowed herself to hope, they'd found a spark of love that, against all odds, would last the war.

7

March 1, 1943
Union Station, Chicago, Illinois

At this time of day, the Union Station concourse was full of people hefting luggage, slouching on the benches, jostling children, and above all, checking their watches. Only the blacked-out barrel vaults of the skylight and the occasional men in uniform served as a reminder that there was a war on.

Maggie walked with purpose, ignoring the arched trusses and chandeliers to get to the entrance. The telegram she'd sent to her father specified the pillar underneath the golden Goddess of Night holding an owl, but the seating area near it was full, so Maggie searched for the closest bare patch of bench that would allow her to keep an eye on the archway. By the time she made her way to an empty area, it had been partially blocked by a tall young man in an impeccable dark suit holding a newspaper, half of which he'd scattered on the seat next to him.

She cleared her throat, but the sound was lost in the station's hubbub. "Excuse me."

He looked up, and Maggie almost forgot the question she

meant to ask. Not that he was handsome, exactly—neck too long, slightly receding hairline, nose jutting out at a sharp angle—but his eyes were a bold blue under dark brows, the type that made a person stop and think, *Gee, that fellow must be somebody.*

In the next moment, though, she'd gotten ahold of herself and gestured to the bench. "Are these seats taken? By more than the daily stock market reports, I mean?"

With a sigh, he collected the stray pages and nodded to the opening, as if she needed his permission to sit in a public space.

"Thanks," she said, smoothing her skirt underneath her as she sat. The new blue gingham, actually, but somehow, Catherine had still managed to outdress her with something she'd probably had in her closet for ages.

The rows of benches facing one another were cramped to allow more seating for travelers, but it was still a surprise to Maggie that she could actually smell the perfume of the woman across from them. She had hunched shoulders, a pompadour that doubled her forehead height, and a narrow-eyed glare that Maggie thought might be a nearsighted squint until she spoke. "What do you have to say for yourself, young man?"

The tone was strident and impossible to ignore, and, looking around and seeing no other young man in sight, Maggie realized she must be addressing Newspaper Man.

He must have come to the same conclusion because he lowered the newspaper a few inches. "I'm sorry, do I know you?"

"Look around you!" she said, gesturing broadly. "The only men your age are in uniform. So what's your excuse?"

So that was it. It was true that there was a scarcity of young fellows in civilian clothes, but it took some kind of nerve to accost a total stranger. Maggie couldn't help glancing over to Newspaper Man, feeling the kind of interest she'd show in an auto crash or a police arrest.

Another sigh, this one deeper and more annoyed than the one Maggie had elicited. "I don't care to offer excuses."

The lack of a reaction didn't deter the perfumed woman, who shook a gloved finger at him. "You ought to have joined up right after Pearl Harbor like both of my boys."

"I'm sure you're very proud." The words were delivered with middle C monotony, so even Maggie couldn't tell if there was sarcasm buried in them.

"You're not even a married man with a family."

He held up his left hand, splaying long pale fingers, all of them bare of rings. "So I'm not." He proceeded to continue a very deliberate perusal of the headline about Joe DiMaggio leaving baseball to join the army.

"What do you have to say for yourself, then?" When he didn't answer, she leaned farther forward so that she had to be tottering on the very edge of the bench. "Well?"

This time, the shielding newsprint rustled but didn't lower. "I doubt anything I say will satisfy you, so I was planning to say nothing."

"Well, I never! In all my days . . ." But finding her exclamation refused to prompt another response from Newspaper Man or even a shifting of the Sports section to look her way, the outraged woman turned to Maggie, giving her a look that begged for commiseration.

Instead, Maggie stood and sat next to the woman, pitching her voice in a low, confidential tone and trying not to gag on a greenhouse's worth of floral scent that polluted the atmosphere. "I wouldn't harass that gentleman if I were you."

Disapproval marked her features. "You know him?"

She inclined her head in a slight nod. "And let's just say that certain government agents are assigned war work they aren't allowed to talk about."

She hadn't given the story much thought, but Maggie couldn't help wanting to make the woman feel foolish. Sure enough, her quick lie made the woman's eyes go as wide as dinner plates. "Is he really?"

She nodded solemnly—until Newspaper Man interrupted with a firm "I most certainly am not."

She winced. Good hearing, that one, even with the bustle of people around them. Apparently he hadn't been as aloof as he was trying to appear.

"And even if I were," he said, lowering the paper again, this time to deliver a glare to her of all people, "it would be a breach of national security to say so."

Maggie found herself going red all over, and she gritted her teeth to stop it. Fine. She'd been caught. Rude of the fellow not to play along. She almost said so as the woman blustered out further "I nevers!" before taking her leave, shooting both of them a disgusted backward glance.

Maggie steadily returned Newspaper Man's glare. What was he waiting for? An apology? "I was only trying to help. The way I see it, if you're a pacifist or 4-F or doing essential war work, what business of it is hers?"

He raised a brow, dark and thick. "True. Though it isn't any business of yours either."

Some thanks that was. "I don't see why . . ."

But when Newspaper Man stood and took up his small leather suitcase, a slight limp to his steps, she found herself trailing off without an audience.

As she searched the masses of moving people for his dark suit, another familiar figure caught her eye, dressed in a brown tweed skirt, practical as always. Maggie stood and waved to get her attention. She'd stopped under the wrong statue, the one holding a rooster and representing Day.

That, Maggie decided, weaving through the crowd, was

a better fit for Paulette anyway, with her honey-golden hair and sunny smile.

"Margaret!" Her older sister bustled over and kissed her on the cheek, something Maggie couldn't duck out of without offending her. The fact that she also offered a heavenly smelling paper bag made up for it. "I was so hoping I hadn't missed you!"

"I've got another ten minutes yet." Despite herself, she couldn't help looking over Paulette's shoulder. "Where's Dad?"

"He . . . couldn't make it." Paulette shrugged, fiddling with a few strands of long hair, always in a neat braid, not cut to her shoulders in the latest fashion. "A last-minute need at the corps."

Paulette probably wasn't lying. The population Dad cared for at the corps, the Salvation Army's name for their churches, often had unforeseen emergencies, but from the way her sister avoided Maggie's gaze, there was probably more to the story.

Their barrel-chested father had frowned in a mix of disapproval and confusion when Maggie explained that she was leaving home to join an all-girls band. "I know you've never liked jazz, or even classical, really—"

"Nonsense. I've tapped my toes to a Gershwin record on a Saturday night every now and again."

There was no need to dance around it. "Then why are you looking at me like I'm about to become the prodigal daughter?"

He'd tried to act surprised, said it wasn't so, but finally admitted, "It's not the sort of work I pictured for you, that's all. I had hoped . . ."

"That I'd be just like Paulette and Johnnie? Use my music in the church?"

He didn't look down in response to her challenging stare. "Is that such a terrible thing?"

It wasn't, but Maggie had never felt any kind of "calling," as the Salvationists put it, not to play the organ for a pastor-husband like Paulette, not to sing hymns in a mission church in China like John. All she'd felt was a rhythm in her bones and the undeniable joy of a trumpet solo.

Her father had sat in their worn-out armchair and looked at her with his serious, hooded eyes. "Do you remember why William Booth insisted the Salvation Army put together bands?"

Maggie suppressed a groan. "Yes, Dad. He said, 'Why should the devil have all the best tunes?'" As often as it was quoted in their house, she'd thought as a young girl that it was actually Scripture, buried somewhere in Second Chronicles. "But I'm not playing the devil's music."

"I'm sure not. But show me one person whose life has been changed by Bing Crosby." Of course, she couldn't, and he'd put a hand on her shoulder, his tone softening. "I don't mean to be harsh, Maggie. But remember, we're only on this earth for a short time. Why not do something that matters?"

"This does matter," she insisted stubbornly, and while he didn't argue further, she could tell by his tired sigh that he didn't believe her.

Or maybe he was just worried that his youngest daughter, out of his reach, traveling from city to city, might end up like some of the wayward folks he ministered to day in and day out.

That fear wasn't entirely without basis. Maggie had never been much for rules, as evidenced by the quick succession of jobs she'd lost by offending those in authority. But while she'd enjoyed the freedom and adventure the Sweethearts had offered, their chaperone had kept them all in line, and anyway, she'd heard enough sad stories from those on the streets to avoid any steps down that path.

"Are you all right, Maggie?" Her sister's voice, always full of care and concern, drew her attention back to where Paulette was waiting for a response. "I'm sure he wanted to come."

"Just disappointed. I was hoping to . . . say good-bye to him." Less complicated than saying she'd hoped they could part on better terms.

The way Paulette drooped made Maggie regret saying anything at all. "But you won't be gone long, will you?"

"Only a few months. Then I'll be back with plenty of stories."

If the smile Maggie gave was forced, Paulette clearly wanted to believe it was genuine badly enough not to mention it. Her sister chattered on about her two young children, asked about the tour, and reminded her not to trust anyone who offered to carry her luggage. Soon Maggie made her excuses and hurried back to her platform, clutching the bag Paulette had given her. A quick sniff through the brown paper, and Maggie's best guess was roast beef, probably on homemade rye bread, and one of Paulette's famous apple fritters, still warm. Her mouth watered.

God bless Paulette.

And God would, she figured. After all, Paulette didn't disappoint him.

The scent of cinnamon followed her into the crowded train car, where the coach-class passengers were rearranging themselves in a scramble of elbows and handbags and "excuse mes" as the conductor shouted a litany of the next stops.

They'd be passing through nearly all of them, settling in for another long stretch of rail travel into the night. No overnight stops in a hotel for them, no sir. Douglas had a schedule to keep, one that ended in their official audition and a steamer out of New York's harbor.

When Maggie stopped beside her seat, she was surprised to find it was already occupied by a woman with long lashes and dramatically arched eyebrows that made her look perpetually disapproving. She wore a suit that Catherine would call olive colored, the neckline plunging to a lacy suggestion of a blouse.

Maggie glanced over at Catherine, who gave her an apologetic shrug. The new seatmate continued to inspect her long nails, which were redder than a sunburnt lobster.

Since it didn't seem like Catherine was planning to make an introduction, Maggie cleared her throat to get the woman's attention. "You're our singer, I take it?"

The woman turned, displaying heavy gold earrings that should have made her lopsided, and nodded in acknowledgment. "Judith Blair, mezzo-soprano. You can call me Judith but never Judy."

"Nice to meet you." With a parting wave to Catherine, Maggie glanced around for another empty seat. With a carpetbag at her feet, a tiny embroidered pillow behind her neck, and a stack of magazines in her lap, it looked like Judith-never-Judy had practically moved in. Besides, Maggie had her notebook and her supper with her, and that would keep her busy for the rest of the journey.

If she could think of any jokes to write. Distracted by that thought, she didn't notice the hand outstretched into the aisle until the man it belonged to, a wiry middle-aged fellow in a striped suit so loud she wondered if he and Catherine's friend Arthur had the same tailor, cleared his throat. The skin around his eyes crinkled as she shook his hand. "As I live and breathe. Floyd, you were right when you said you snapped up the prettiest girls for this unit."

Ignoring that bit of flattery, Mr. Douglas indicated the shorter man. "May I introduce one of the other members of our humble troupe?"

"Humble?" the man said, chuckling, "I think you hired the wrong fellow. Howard Jones, at your service. Also known in my vaudeville days as"—he gestured grandly as if framing his name on a marquee—"Lightfoot Howie. Ventriloquist, harmonica player, tap dancer, and one-man show."

"Don't worry, I've made him promise he'll save a corner of the stage for the rest of you," Mr. Douglas said dryly. Did the man ever smile?

It was a relief to meet them. Maggie hadn't met many performers in her day, but these two didn't seem all that bad. A little eccentric maybe, but she had quirks of her own.

She spotted an empty aisle seat just behind them, one of the only spots remaining in the crowded car, and ducked into it. She set her paper sack on her lap before glancing over to her traveling companion, who was studying the station as the train lurched away.

"Ah yes," Mr. Douglas supplied from in front of them, "this is Mr. Gabriel Kaminski, our magician."

The man in the window seat turned, a bored expression on his face . . . that froze when he saw Maggie.

Oh, this is too perfect.

"Charmed to meet you, I'm sure," she said, with a devilish grin to Newspaper Man.

After another long day of travel and a night of getting what sleep they could, Maggie and the others had been shuttled to a small local theater. The backstage was sparse, a few stepladders and unused footlights gathering dust against the brick wall on one side and the ropes of the pulley system used to heave lights and scenery around onstage on the other. None of which they'd be able to use. They'd been warned that their tour performances might have only a bare-bones stage, if any.

Maggie glanced at the curtain. Just beyond it, a committee from the USO home office would soon gather, waiting for their official audition in a half hour, pens poised to write down everything she was doing wrong.

Were any of her jokes even funny? She hadn't had the guts to test them out on the others on the train, afraid she'd have to start over. Now she was starting to wonder if that had been a good idea.

"I should be the opening act," Judith demanded, her strident voice breaking into Maggie's worries. Even in their small circle, she'd already taken center stage. "As our only singer, it seems fitting."

"Nah, we need someone like me who can warm up a crowd," Howie argued.

"Couldn't we all go onstage together to be introduced at the start?" Catherine volunteered, only to duck back into her shyness like a soldier into a foxhole when the idea was roundly shot down.

Maggie was starting to realize the daunting nature of the task they'd been handed. Back with the Sweethearts, Mr. Simmons chose the songs they would perform, set the practice schedule, and picked the soloists. Maggie had never had to make a single decision the whole tour except how close to breakfast to roll out of bed. Now, they had nothing except the command to "put together a show that'll hold the troops' interest" and thirty minutes to do it in.

"Of course, we'll need a master of ceremonies," Howie said, giving what he probably thought was a masterful and ceremonial bow. "That way no one will miss a cue."

"Why not just turn the spotlight onto the next act?" Gabriel asked.

"Because we won't have a spotlight," Maggie pointed out.

It was the first time they'd really spoken since the train ride. Gabriel had made no reference to their earlier meeting at the station, as if he were hoping to pretend it hadn't happened. Maggie let it be. More fun to watch him squirm.

As their time ticked away, Howie thought they should alternate five-minute bits of their acts to keep everyone's attention, but Gabriel insisted they perform their whole set at once. Catherine didn't want to follow a comedian, thinking the switch to classical music would be too drastic. Judith wanted Gabriel to make her appear out of his magic cabinet, which he couldn't bring because of restrictions on the weight of his props.

Just when Maggie was ready to flee to the greenroom to tune her trumpet—any excuse to get away—the stage door creaked open, letting in sunlight and a burst of cold air. Maggie half-hoped it was Douglas to rescue her from this chaos. Instead, a short, dark-haired man in a corduroy suit hurried in with a package under his arm, stopping short as Howie flagged him down. "Say, mister, do you happen to know if they've got any cymbal sets around here?"

"Sorry. That I can't help you with." He hefted the package. "Just here to make a delivery." He seemed about to dash away again but gave the whole crew a shrewd sizing-up. "Are you lot the USO's latest show biz recruits?"

"We sure are," Maggie said. She hoped he hadn't overheard enough of their argument to pass anything along to the higher-ups along with the mail. "About to get shipped off to who-knows-where."

"Just make sure they put a return address on you so you can get back." He winked before ducking away into the theater. "Best of luck."

Swell. The delivery man was better at telling jokes than she was.

"I still say we ladies should get more time onstage," Judith insisted, raising her voice like saying it louder would make it more persuasive. "The troops are sick and tired of looking at other men."

Before Howie or Gabriel could protest, Maggie squared her shoulders and stepped into the middle of the circle. This was going nowhere. Someone was going to have to take charge.

"Listen, all of you. We only have—" she paused, remembering she wasn't wearing a wristwatch, so she yanked on Gabriel's arm to look at his. "Fifteen minutes to get our act together. Or that troopship will leave without us."

Howie gave a snort. "Douglas is all bluster. They're not going to turn us away the day before we ship out. Mark my words, this is just a formality."

He had a point, but Maggie couldn't help asking, "But what if it's not?"

The simple question brought a hush like the dimming of houselights before a performance, and she could almost see them worrying for the first time. What if one or several of them were given a thumbs-down from the USO brass and told to go home?

Maggie might know next to nothing about these three newcomers, but looking at the doubt on their faces, she could tell that they all wanted this badly.

In the sudden quiet, Maggie tried to imitate what her father called his major general voice. "Let's hear what everyone's got to perform and how long it runs. We can make changes after the audition, but we have to perform *something*, and fast."

"She's right," Gabriel said, and it would have been gratifying if he didn't sound pained to admit it. "Let's get this in as much order as we can."

By the time they'd talked through their acts, Howie realized his final tap dance could lead into one of Maggie's songs. Judith was finally convinced, with a masterful bit of flattery on Howie's part, that going last was more prestigious than being the opening act. And Catherine felt comfortable performing after Gabriel, who agreed to cut out one of his tricks to keep the run time shorter.

Douglas entered, clipboard in hand, just after they'd worked out what stage names Howie would use to introduce them. "Ready to step onstage, I hope?"

"Not really," Maggie wanted to reply, if only to buy a few more minutes to look over the jokes in her tattered notebook. But she forced herself to meet their new manager's eyes and smile confidently. "You bet."

She should probably listen to the others' acts to get a sense of what their show would be like as she waited backstage, but Maggie couldn't seem to tear herself away from her script, her mouth silently moving over the words. She was startled when she heard Howie call, "And now, armed with jokes and her trusty trumpet, our very own Miss Maggie McCleod!"

Imagine there's applause. Cheering even, Maggie told herself, stepping onstage, her heart pounding in her ears so loudly she might not have heard it anyway.

As she made for the center of the stage, she saw their judges for the first time. It was a small committee, just Douglas, two other men, and a woman, all in neutral colors that made them difficult to see in the dim lighting. Maggie had performed in all conditions, from a rainy Chicago street corner for a dozen toughs to audiences of hundreds with the Sweethearts. Yet somehow this handful of people felt more intimidating than all of them.

"Hello, everyone!" Maggie flinched as a zing of feedback echoed off the microphone and leaned back slightly. "It's good to be here. I'm coming to you all the way from . . ." She glanced offstage. "Sorry, just checking with the censors . . . apparently we're allowed to say where we've been, just not where we're going next, how we got there, who's there with us, or what the weather was like."

There. That wasn't so bad. She transitioned from the joke into her first music piece, an upbeat Gershwin number, and as the familiar notes poured out, Maggie started to relax, enough to make the next comedy bit a little more natural. By the end, she was firing off lines like she was a genuine radio regular.

Once backstage, Maggie leaned against the wall, taking in a deep breath as she tucked her trumpet in its case. Now, with the pressure off, she could listen to the rest of the acts. Gabriel . . . well, she couldn't judge his tricks from backstage, but from the sound of things, the appearances, disappearances, and transformations all went off as planned. Catherine, as always, made her instrument sing. And Judith crooned songs with her bluesy voice like the theater was packed with men who hadn't seen an American woman in months. All in all, Maggie felt that maybe this would work out after all.

When she finished her last song, they all came out to do their bows to the sparse applause of the committee members. Maggie felt her skin prickle with awkwardness the moment she rose to face them. What were they supposed to do now?

Thankfully, Douglas stood. "Thank you for your efforts. Please go backstage, and I'll meet you in the greenroom shortly after we deliberate."

As they filed out, Maggie caught a glimpse of another man joining the USO staff, clearly known by all of them if the smiles and handshakes were any indication.

Was that . . . the delivery man? The corduroy suit looked the same. What was he still doing here?

"Come along, now, m'dear," Howie whispered from behind her, giving her a tap with his cane that made her feel like a mule being prodded into a field. "They won't say anything while we're eavesdropping."

The atmosphere in the greenroom was far more relaxed than it had been backstage, or even on the train. Howie did a spontaneous two-step, spinning a startled Catherine around in a whirl. "We did it, ladies and gents! That's what I call a performance."

Gabriel took a seat at the scratched table shoved against the wall. "The acts did flow together reasonably well."

Meanwhile, Judith had sprawled over the entirety of the sagging couch in the corner, leaving no room for anyone to join her. "Don't sound so surprised, Mr. Mysterio. Just because none of us have made it big yet doesn't mean we don't have talent."

"Now what?" Maggie asked, taking the seat across from Gabriel.

"We wait," Howie said, shrugging.

That simple phrase seemed to end their celebrating, and Maggie found herself staring toward the door like a defendant waiting for the jury to return with a verdict.

After what felt like ages but was probably only a quarter of an hour, Douglas returned with a clipboard thick with paper. "Thank you for your patience. I have a few notes for you from the committee." He took a seat at the head of the table, the chair left open for him, and peered through his spectacles at Judith. "Miss Blair. Less sultry on 'Thanks for the Memories,' please. And practice a capella—the pitch was off on several pieces."

Though their singer nodded, Maggie was seated close enough to Judith to hear her mutter, "I'll show *him* something that's off."

He turned to Maggie just as she'd started to snicker, and she tried to recover. Thankfully, he glanced down at his clipboard with a frown. In the pause that followed, Maggie thought she might be sick, anticipating the criticism he'd level at her in front of everyone. Then he lifted his head. "Not a bad routine. If you give me your script, I'll mark the jokes that are inappropriate."

"Say what now?" Maggie blurted. This was the last thing she'd expected. There hadn't been anything that would even get the raise of an eyebrow out of her preacher-father.

"Army rules, you know. For example, the opening line mocking censorship policies will have to go. We wouldn't want anyone to think we were endangering our troops, now, would we?"

Maggie winced. She hadn't considered how that bit might come across. But Douglas hadn't said it was terrible, and she was sure she'd seen the committee chuckling here and there. That had to mean something.

Douglas moved on to his critique of Gabriel—the act was too long, and the Wondrous Wrist Guillotine wouldn't fit in the small footlocker he'd be allotted—and Howie—update the cultural references that were stuck in the 1920s. Maggie noticed with a twinge of resentment that the only negative comment Catherine received was that she'd have to play and speak louder, as many of their performances would be without microphones to amplify them.

"We're in, then?" Howie prompted when it looked like Douglas had finished.

"Your acts have all been approved," he confirmed, lowering his clipboard, the slightest twitch of a smile on his face. "Welcome to Variety Unit 14."

Maggie joined Howie in bursting into cheers, and even Catherine clapped at the good news. Although Gabriel and Judith tried to look aloof, she could tell they were pleased as well. "Oh," Douglas said, "and one more thing. A friend of the USO told me to pass on his congratulations to all of you for a job well done. Did you happen to meet a middle-aged fellow on your way in?"

Howie frowned. "Backstage before the audition, sure."

"Do you know who that was?" Somehow Maggie got the idea Douglas was barely suppressing a laugh at their expense.

"Not a delivery man?" Maggie offered, which despite not being a joke, prompted a loud guffaw from their manager.

When he'd gotten himself together, his voice was triumphant. "That, my friends, was comedian, movie star, and host of the top radio variety show in the country, Bob Hope himself."

8

March 3, 1943
New York City, New York

Catherine rolled the cuffs of her brand-new uniform sleeves. The muddy khaki of the barely tailored jacket and skirt wouldn't be featured in any department store window, but she didn't dare say so and risk coming off as prissy. At least the patriotically colored USO camp shows patch broke up the monotony, if only slightly.

Thank goodness she hadn't been wearing this in front of Bob Hope. For that matter, thank goodness she hadn't known Bob Hope was in the audience when she performed. She hadn't seen any of his movies—she preferred dramas to the comedies he clowned around in—but like nearly everyone in America, she'd listened to his radio show. The fact that he'd actually approved of their performance was thrilling.

Catherine filed back into the greenroom with the other performers, all swathed in khaki, and nearly laughed. Howie, who couldn't be more than a few inches over five feet, tripped over the cuffs of his pants, and Judith nearly burst out of her tailored blouse with her curvy figure, though she insisted she didn't need to move up to a larger size. Maggie's height made the skirt's hem creep up to her knees, and her red cable-knit socks couldn't be regulation. Of the group, only Gabriel looked like he actually belonged in uniform.

Catherine had noticed Gabriel had a pronounced limp, though she was careful to keep from staring at it. That, of course, would explain why a man who appeared to be in his thirties hadn't enlisted or been drafted.

How difficult it must be for him, with many of his friends likely in the service. She couldn't help wondering what his story might be but certainly didn't ask. There was something intimidating about the man, to the point that she'd had to work up the courage even to bid him good morning and only received a curt nod in response.

Howie, on the other hand, proved very easy to talk to. It was more difficult to get him to stop. She sat down beside him on chairs that were either designed to be uncomfortable or ended up that way by entropy. "I enjoyed your tap routine," she said, more to make conversation than anything else. "You're an excellent dancer."

"Well, I ought to be. My wife and I performed vaudeville together for almost two decades until . . ." He trailed off, twirling his wedding ring. "Well, it took longer than I expected to adjust after her passing."

Ah, a widower. Before she could offer her sympathies, Maggie interrupted, as usual unaware of the emotions of those around her. "Any guesses where we're going tomorrow?"

Howie straightened, the sad look disappearing from his eyes. "My money's on England. Our troops there are giving the Brits a devil of a time when on leave, I hear. They could use something worthwhile to do."

Catherine's breath caught, allowing herself to hope. "Oh!

Wouldn't that be wonderful? The Royal Opera House, St. Paul's Cathedral, the White Cliffs of Dover . . ."

"Don't get your hopes up. I'm told there will be no side excursions or sightseeing allowed," Gabriel said. Maggie rolled her eyes, but Catherine felt better knowing that someone else planned to follow the rules.

Still, to be so close to such amazing places and not be able to explore them was a blow. "I suppose not." Then she brightened again. "But just think, Jane Austen and William Shakespeare might have trod the very same ground."

Before they could speculate further, Mr. Douglas, dressed in a navy pinstripe suit just a little too nipped in at the shoulders to hang well on him, entered. "Very good. Now that you're in proper attire, a few further formalities." If he cared that most of their uniforms looked like secondhand costumes, he didn't mention it. Instead, he drew out a sheaf of papers from his portfolio, tapping them on the table to even them out, somewhat unnecessarily, since he proceeded to give one to each of them.

"This," he said with a dramatic flair that made Catherine wonder if he had missed his calling by going into talent management, "is an oath of secrecy that each of you will need to sign. I expect you to read it carefully and take it seriously. Any violation of these terms during the next three months will be treated as treason."

Catherine felt a sudden nervous tension in her stomach, though a glance around told her that no one else seemed affected by this announcement. No need to overreact.

"Sure, sure," Judith said, snapping her fingers for a pen, which Mr. Douglas gave her with an expression of distaste. "Uncle Sam won't have any troubles from me." She scrawled her name without even pretending to read the agreement.

"I'm not sure you understand the seriousness of this document."

Catherine certainly did. The document wasn't long, but the terse language prohibited releasing any information—verbally, in writing, or through photographs—about the tour unless specifically permitted by the army, including troop and ship movements or numbers.

Suddenly, the uniforms they wore seemed to come with more responsibility. They weren't playacting for a costume ball. This really was the US Army, and that meant the potential for danger.

Oh, her mother would just die if she knew where her only daughter was now. She was all for drama, deception, and danger, of course, but mostly of the social variety that wouldn't require getting her hands dirty, much less traveling to a war zone.

It doesn't matter what Mother would think. This is my decision. Catherine took the pen Judith offered and wrote her name on the agreement in the fine, even script she'd learned in boarding school, not one flourish shaking with nerves.

"I can't think we'd see anything worth spying on, anyway," Howie said. "Don't they send variety units like ours to hospitals and base camps?"

To Catherine's surprise, this obvious fish for information didn't go unrewarded. "Some will, yes. The USO is starting to organize their camp shows into different circuits, one to visit the sick and wounded at military hospitals, another to bases stateside. And, of course, there's the Foxhole Circuit, the one you will be joining, which performs for troops deployed overseas."

In her letter, Catherine had assured her parents that there would be no danger at all, and that she'd likely be playing to soldiers in training. "Is it safe?"

"I'm sure the army means to bring us all back in one piece," Maggie quipped.

"That is the goal. And I almost forgot." Mr. Douglas,

who Catherine suspected never forgot anything and merely waited to check it off his schedule, stood and pulled a crate away from the wall. "Fresh from the quartermaster corps." He lifted the lid and set a gas mask down on the table. Catherine couldn't help shuddering at the grotesque, featureless apparatus.

"Golly, what's wrong, Catherine?" Maggie muttered. "You'd think Douglas just plopped down a severed head."

"I've never seen one up close before, that's all." But given the comparison, she couldn't unsee it: the stiff black rubber forehead, the prominent snout, the blank eyes, staring into nothingness. Would they actually have to wear this?

Howie grunted, taking it up and holding it like Hamlet held a skull. "Thought I was done with you, old friend." In response to a questioning look from Catherine, he added, "I was a doughboy in the first war, you know."

"You'll need to keep it with you," Mr. Douglas instructed, "in addition to wearing your uniform whenever you're in public, except for performances. Let both remind you that you are under the command of the army for the duration of the tour. Above all, you will follow orders—no matter the circumstances."

Catherine frowned. The man emphasized at least half of his words, as if they were schoolchildren waiting for the opportunity to misbehave instead of professionals on tour.

"Yes, sir," Howie said with mock seriousness, firing off a perfect salute that hadn't gotten rusty since his days in the last war, though he likely hadn't gotten away with a lopsided grin then.

Mr. Douglas didn't seem offended by the sarcasm, probably because he didn't notice it in his hurry to pass out a stack of memoranda with the rules and regulations that would govern their lives for the next several months.

"Does he think we're actually going to read all these?"

Maggie muttered to her as Mr. Douglas went on about censoring their mail.

Guiltily, Catherine let the page drop from where she'd already been starting in. No need to look like a goody-two-shoes. "Well, we wouldn't want to get in any trouble."

She was frozen by a cold stare from Mr. Douglas. "Miss Duquette, I assure you that you'll have plenty of time to exchange gossip on our voyage. If you would please give me your attention until then?"

"Sorry," she managed, sitting up straighter and tilting herself away from Maggie.

"The USO serves the enlisted men only," he went on, the interruption duly dealt with. "Some of our more famous performers are occasionally allowed to accept invitations to appear or dine at officers' clubs, but even they never perform there. Is that understood?"

They all nodded.

"Our ladies in particular will do well to note the section on codes of conduct for interacting with the men. I need not say that any hint of impropriety on your part would be disastrous."

"I can guess what they say," Judith said, a hint of mockery in her voice. "We're supposed to dress to impress but not to seduce. Sing sultry love songs without ever acting on them. Be the replacement for pinup girls and prostitutes but also act like wholesome angels." She fluttered her eyelashes innocently in the face of Mr. Douglas's stern expression. "Is that right?"

"Exactly," he snapped, without a trace of irony.

Catherine felt Maggie stiffen beside her. "Say, that doesn't seem fair."

"It certainly isn't, Miss McCleod, but it's necessary. And if you wish to be considered for future opportunities"—he drew out that last phrase with a meaningful pause—"then you'll be careful to keep your reputation spotless."

"'Future opportunities.' That's certainly cryptic," Judith said, letting the implied question hang in the air like a woman used to men spilling their secrets to her.

Mr. Douglas continued, directing his words to all of them. "I just got off a call with Abe Lastfogel—he's the manager of some of the celebrity tours—and it seems that Bob Hope stopped by his office and mentioned seeing you today. Apparently he was more impressed than I realized. He told me that if I see a particularly promising member of my variety unit, he might have a slot open in *The Pepsodent Show* tour."

Howie's head rose sharply from his cigarette case at that. "*The Pepsodent Show,* you say?" Everyone recognized the name of Bob Hope's radio show, sponsored by the toothpaste brand.

"Bob Hope will be leading the tour, of course, and other headliners will be Carole Landis, Francis Langford, and Jerry Colonna. The contract is for a full year at least, perhaps the duration of the war. It could be career-making, being an opening act for such big names."

That got Catherine's attention in a way the names of the glamorous Hollywood stars hadn't. A year of certified patriotic duty far from her parents' expectations and quarrels.

"Of course, I expect excellence from all of you, with or without an extended contract in the balance. But I should hope this news inspires an additional level of professionalism."

Catherine glanced around the table. The others were trying to hide it, but all of them had perked up at the mention of the celebrity tour with Bob Hope and his entourage. She supposed the pay and the experience would be welcome, but surely no one else wanted this the way she did.

"Are you saying that one of us here will be offered a USO contract with *The Pepsodent Show*?" Gabriel asked, frowning like he was trying to inspect the fine print of an agreement no one had made yet.

Mr. Douglas shook his head. "I wouldn't go quite that far. It's more that I've been invited to give a . . . strong recommendation. You'd still have to audition, I imagine."

The words were meant to temper their expectations, but Catherine knew from her mother's constant reminders that most doors in Hollywood were shut and locked to up-and-comers without wealth and connections. To find an open door like this . . . even if it was only a chance, it was the kind of chance that every entertainer dreamed of.

"Well, if that's all, then, care to step out and share a cigar to celebrate our departure?" Howie offered, clearly speaking only to Mr. Douglas. "I ponied up for a few imported Havanas for the occasion."

He escorted Mr. Douglas out of the greenroom with a monologue about how he'd shaken Al Jolson's hand at a Broadway performance in the '20s.

Judith watched them go, then slapped her book of rules down on the table. "Disgusting."

Catherine nodded, trying to find some common ground with her fellow traveler. "I don't care for the smell of smoke either."

Judith looked at her incredulously. "Not *that*. I mean Lightning Howie making the first move so soon, getting Douglas alone like that, offering him an expensive cigar. He's playing dirty."

Catherine had the unsteady feeling that she was being trapped in a conversation without knowing what to say next. But she was used to it from interacting with her mother and had a list of stock phrases to offer up. "I'm sorry?"

Judith's mouth twisted into a sneer, though Catherine felt

she was only getting caught in the crossfire. "Oh, come on, you don't think he'll chat Floyd up, trying to get that contract? The little bantam rooster thinks he's so charming."

That was something Catherine hadn't considered. "You heard him, though. It will come down to our performance."

"Sure, that's what he *said*. Head start or no, don't fret. The job's as good as mine." She winked, but Catherine was quite sure it wasn't meant as a joke.

Oh dear. After the time they'd all shared on the train and the way they'd worked together to complete the audition, she'd hoped this tour might be as enjoyable as her time with the Sweethearts. Now, instead of fellow entertainers, she was surrounded by competitors.

Not that she planned to give up without a fight. Catherine didn't consider herself conceited, but she knew that years of private lessons—the best money could buy—had given her considerable ability, and there was her appearance to consider. Her mother had often told her that her looks would take her far in life, and while Catherine had hated hearing it at the time, maybe she was right after all.

Maggie drew back her chair with a scrape. "As far as I'm concerned, the rest of you can duke it out."

"You're not interested in the contract?" Catherine knew she sounded suspicious, but it would be just like Maggie to pretend she was above such petty concerns.

Maggie shook her head. "I took this job on a whim. It's a free trip around the world for a few months and a paycheck, nothing more."

"Sure, sure, you say that *now*," Judith scoffed.

Maggie bristled at the woman's unconvinced tone. "Listen, Judith, one thing you should know about me right off the bat: I always say what I mean. And I don't change my mind easily."

That, at least, Catherine knew to be true.

"Then I'm sure you'll tell Floyd that, won't you?" Judith said, with a casualness that seemed false to Catherine. "Just so he's aware."

"Sure," she said. "Happy to interrupt the smoke break." In the doorway, she paused. "Oh, and all of you might want to enjoy the chilly weather while you can."

"What do you mean by that?" Gabriel asked, looking up from the book of rules that he'd been studying the whole time.

Maggie seemed to enjoy being the center of attention, cocking her head slightly and letting the pause drag out a moment. "I happened to be standing right outside Douglas's office when Lastfogel called him. Couldn't help listening, you know?"

Catherine held her breath, leaning forward. "And?"

"Ladies and gents," she said, a smile tugging at the corners of her mouth, "we are headed to North Africa."

9

March 4, 1943
Atlantic Ocean

The *John Ericsson* must have hit a patch of rough water because Maggie found herself gripping her bunk's steel frame for balance. Her stomach lodged a protest, not so much seasick as plain old hungry. Normally there would be two meals a day on the troopship, eaten in shifts, but tonight, since they'd had an embarkment time to hit, there had been no dinner. She'd only eaten a sandwich handed to her on the docks, ham and Swiss on soggy bread with a scrap of tomato and the slightest hint of lettuce.

"What's army food like, do you think?" she asked her roommates. They'd crammed all three women of the troupe into one tiny compartment.

"Probably nothing good with so many thousands to feed from a ship's galley," Judith said tartly.

Even if her predictions were right, Maggie would survive. Before Paulette took over the cooking, their father, bless his widower heart, had prepared dinners that were often underdone, overdone, or a mess of something on sale at the butcher's.

"I don't think I can eat anything." Catherine's voice was not quite a moan, but she was curled up on her bunk, her eyes shut.

"You'll have to eat something during the two weeks we're at sea," Maggie said practically. "Might as well test it out early."

All three wore their uniforms, modeled after the Women's Auxiliary Army Corps. Maggie, for one, didn't mind being wrapped in khaki like everyone else on the ship. It made a girl feel like she belonged. That and the canvas musette bag with its mess kit tucked inside, footlockers for their instruments and props, and official ID cards, and she really was in the army now.

Just as Maggie had started to work out the double knots on her boots, the sudden piercing sound of a klaxon kicked her heart into a drumroll. This close to American waters, it had to be a drill, but the high-pitched siren had a way of hammering in your head like a demolition crew.

"Where the devil are we supposed to go?" Judith demanded, pressing her hands against her ears to dampen the sound.

"Deck 4A, wherever that is." Maggie hadn't been paying much attention to those details while they'd been ferried over to the troopship, instead taking in all six hundred feet of her from bow to stern.

"I asked a crew member to point it out as we boarded," Catherine said, and Maggie barely suppressed a snicker. Of course she had.

Catherine dragged herself up, wobbling unsteadily for a moment. "Follow me."

They had only a few flights of cramped stairs to climb before reaching the deck, where Catherine led them in a direct path to a cluster of passengers in khaki. Lifeboats were trussed up near the railing, waiting for the call to abandon ship that could sound at any time in waters where U-boats prowled for victims.

Here, the sound of the klaxon didn't reverberate shrilly against the walls, but the cold Atlantic breeze could knife them in the back. Spring on the ocean was no primrose-and-sunshine affair. Maggie suddenly envied the wool winter uniforms given to performers sent to England, shivering against a particularly chilly blast.

In the sea of army caps, Maggie spotted a head taller than the rest with a gleam of dark brown pomaded hair that was practically blinding in the bright sunlight, belonging to their resident magician. "There they are," she said to the others, squirming through the crowd to get to Douglas, Gabriel, and Howie, who'd been hustled off to the narrow hammocks with the enlisted men instead of the more private quarters granted to officers, the fifty nurses onboard, and the USO women. Being surrounded by bodies on all sides provided shelter from the wind, and Maggie's shivering slowed.

A crew member, broad-shouldered and pacing with authority beside the lifeboats, hurried the dozens assigned to this deck along with an impatient gesture. "Eight minutes," he bellowed, his voice carrying to the back of the group. "That's how long it takes to freeze in the Atlantic in March."

Well. Maybe Maggie could take notes from him on dramatic timing.

"This ship only has lifeboat capacity for a third of its occupants," the crew member continued, pacing by the railing and giving all of them a look of extreme seriousness, "so if the klaxon sounds for a genuine U-boat attack, arrive to this location as soon as possible. Everyone else will be relying on their floatation devices until rescue arrives."

It didn't seem like an exaggeration as Maggie glanced from

the few lifeboats to the large group huddled in the March wind, waiting for the drill to be over.

"That's awful," Catherine whispered, her eyes wide.

Howie shrugged. "Never fear, Miss Catherine, I'm sure they'd give preference to the ladies."

Catherine didn't seem reassured, her face pale and her body so wispy thin that she might need rigging to keep her in place if the wind picked up. Not for the first time, Maggie wondered if she should have advocated for Catherine in the first place. Maybe it would have been better for her to stay behind.

Satisfied that he'd sufficiently sobered the landlubbers, the crew member continued his shouted speech. "You will keep your canteen of water and emergency rations on you at all times, as well as your Mae West, in case of emergency."

"Mae West?" Maggie mouthed to Gabriel, who nodded, apparently knowing what the instruction meant.

"These." He patted the deflated life preserver they'd been given to wear around their necks and must have noticed her continued confusion because he added, "Named for the, er, generous chest proportions."

To his credit, Gabriel looked uncomfortable giving the explanation, but Maggie still huffed in annoyance. Reducing any woman, even one as famous as the Hollywood actress, to her bosom size felt demeaning.

The crewman went through a list of regulations: no one was to smoke or use a flashlight on deck; there would be absolutely no tossing trash into the ocean, as it would be a clear signal to U-boats of their path; and anyone who fell overboard would not be rescued.

"As if a floating body wouldn't be more of a signal to the Germans than a few cigarette butts," Maggie muttered.

Judith snorted a laugh, but Gabriel, never one to pick up on a joke, frowned. "It's probably something they say to scare the GIs out of doing something foolish."

That was a fair enough point, she figured. A bunch of fellows in their early twenties cooped up with nothing to do probably had to be warned away from careless pranks.

Maggie started to shiver again, envying the men for their sturdy trousers, while their uniforms cut off midcalf and let in an awful draft, even with stockings on. As she shifted from one leg to another, she noticed a blond soldier with chapped, red ears under his regulation-shorn haircut leering at them.

Noticing he'd attracted her attention, he pushed his way over. "Hey there, gals. If you come down to our bunks, we can help you pass the time." Now that he'd opened his mouth, she could see he gave new meaning to *buck private,* with a gap-toothed smile giving him a wholesome farm boy appearance he clearly didn't deserve.

Catherine was already flushing beet red, but Maggie turned away, deliberately not making eye contact. She'd long since learned not to give fellows like that the time of day. They always hated being ignored.

As if to prove her point, Buck Private picked up his pace and cut in front of them, blocking their way off the deck. "Say, I was talking to you gals."

A sharp burst of applause cut Maggie off before she could tell him to get lost. Gabriel, a stiff smile on his face. "Thank you, sir, for volunteering!" he said in his performance voice, resonant and upbeat, like a trumpet to his usual bassoon.

Buck Private stiffened, and his eyes went to Gabriel's uniform to confirm that he wasn't an officer slumming with the enlisted men for the drill. That settled, the sneer reappeared on his face. "Volunteering for what?"

"These *ladies*"—Gabriel emphasized the word—"and I are with the USO camp shows, responsible for your entertainment on this voyage. My magic act requires audience participation, so I'll mark you down for . . . being sawed in half, let's say."

Catherine made a sort of choking sound, and Buck Private actually growled, fists white-knuckled at his side.

"Unless you'd rather I report you to your commanding officer for harassment," Gabriel went on coolly.

"It's not worth it," Maggie said quietly, before Buck Private could do something stupid.

But he knew it, too, and with one parting curse aimed at Gabriel, fell in with the crowd streaming back to their quarters.

"You shouldn't have done that," Maggie blurted. "If you pick a fight with every GI who ogles us, you'll leave a trail of sawed-in-half bodies from here to Algiers and back again."

Sure enough, like she'd expected, Gabriel's eyebrows knit into a frown. "Pardon me for being a gentleman."

"He was only trying to help," Catherine said, looking as if she might die on the spot without a change of subject.

"Maybe, but we have to be respected for ourselves, not because a man swoops in to rescue us." She had been responding to Catherine, but she didn't look away from Gabriel, though trying to figure out what was going on under his stony expression was darn near impossible.

Gabriel only stepped back slightly. "I see. And if you do ever need help?"

"I'll be sure to let you know." Maggie tried to lighten the mood by giving him a slap on the back, but it felt false. "No need to worry about us. We'll be fine."

"I'm sure. If that's all, I should go below deck and prepare my props for our first performance." He walked away stiffly, and even though Maggie knew it was probably to conceal his limp, it sure did look furious.

"I can't believe you said that," Catherine whispered.

"Was anything I said not true?"

Her eyelashes fluttered at the unexpected question. "Well, no."

Maggie rolled her eyes. That was the trouble with girls like Catherine. All women knew certain fundamental truths, but hardly anyone was willing to speak them out loud so something could be done about them.

She'd learned how to hold her own against men like Buck Private. It was men like Gabriel that she didn't know how to respond to.

Anyway, she wasn't about to chase after their magician and explain her whole life story to prove she really could take care of herself. *"No need to worry about us. We'll be fine."*

She'd said that before, a long time ago. As she made her way belowdecks, the ship shifting beneath her, she couldn't help remembering their tiny apartment that smelled of drying socks and the angry voices that cut through the pinging of the radiator. . . .

OCTOBER 1931
CHICAGO, ILLINOIS

Maggie opened her eyes and rolled over on the bed she shared with Paulette. Immediately pain banged a snare drumbeat against her forehead.

Drumbeat. Her brother's drum. The band . . .

She lifted a hand to the bandage around her head—and remembered what had happened earlier that day.

She had been playing "What a Friend We Have in Jesus" on her trumpet with the Salvation Army band after Dad's street-corner sermon, Auntie Tabitha's strong soprano and John's drum helping them keep time. Some folks stopped to listen. Most ignored them, walking right past. But soon they'd gathered a group of rowdies who started hurling abuse, then rubbish from the ground.

If they'd been baseball pitches, nearly every throw would

have been called a ball. The troublemakers probably didn't mean to hit anyone, just cause a stir.

But an empty bottle had collided midair with a scrap of hubcap, raining down chunks of glass and shunting the metal away from its trajectory. That's what Maggie had been told, anyway. At the time, all she'd known was that something was coming toward her face too fast to duck. Then the shouts and the throbbing and the pavement under her knees and Dad's arms around her.

The doctor had visited their apartment to stitch up the gash and told her, real serious, to get some rest.

Maggie wasn't very good at resting.

"Golly," she whispered into the darkness, as close to a swear as she was allowed to get. Had she been stoned? Like the apostle Paul? That had to count for something with God. Or maybe she'd at least get an interesting-looking scar.

Outside her room, she could hear voices, and a crack of light spilled in through the doorway.

Was that what had woken her?

She could hear the words through the thin walls and the hiss of the radiator. "When I think about the cowardice it takes to attack a child. . . ."

It was Dad, and madder than she'd ever heard him.

Maggie stood. She could tell from her sister's quiet breathing that she was still asleep. Avoiding the worst of the creaking floorboards, Maggie edged nearer to the door.

". . . glad to hear that she's going to be all right, of course. But our point remains. This is a dangerous part of town, particularly for the girls."

It was Captain Eugene Rogers, Auntie Tabitha's husband. Maggie didn't call him uncle, mostly because he never talked to her or any of the other junior cadets from the corps. Too busy doing important adult things, she guessed. Like trying to worry her dad, saying Chicago was dangerous just because a piece of trash hit her.

"What are you trying to say, Eugene?"

"We thought—that is, Tabitha and I wanted to suggest—that you speak to the divisional commander about a new posting."

What? They couldn't! Dad wouldn't let them.

Maggie clapped her hand over her mouth to keep from yelling it. To her surprise, Dad didn't immediately blurt out the same thing, his voice weary. "So you're giving me my farewell orders, is that it?"

Farewell orders were what transferred officers to a new place. Maggie was good at sorting out the Salvation Army code by now. Her mother hadn't died two years ago, she was *promoted to Glory*. *Churches* were *corps*, *preachers* were *officers*, and the parsonage provided by the Salvation Army was their *quarters*. It was only when she went to school for the first time that Maggie had learned there were different civilian words for the things and people that filled her life.

"Not at all. But I'm concerned that this environment might not be best for someone with young children. After what happened to Maggie today . . ."

She expected Dad to say that it was a freak accident, that the injury looked worse than it was, that the doctor had told her she'd heal just fine. Instead, he sighed. "I should never have let her join the band."

Maggie's jaw dropped. She'd never loved anything the way she did playing that trumpet. He was just upset, that was all. There was no way she'd stay inside all day cooking and scrubbing floors for the maternity home like Paulette.

"I won't leave here. I have a calling."

Maggie nearly cheered. Good for Dad.

Until he went on, "But there may be another way. My wife's father has offered to pay tuition for the children at a school several hours away. It's a good school, but until now, I hadn't considered . . ."

"Perhaps that could be their mission," Auntie Tabitha said gently. Her voice startled Maggie. She had thought Captain Rogers was there alone. How could Auntie Tabitha agree with him?

"Maybe," Dad replied, and even though his tone wavered, it still felt like a betrayal.

It was almost torture to wait until the good-byes were said and the front door creaked shut, but as soon as it did, Maggie exploded from her room, not caring if she woke her siblings. "You're sending us away?"

She had the satisfaction of seeing a fleeting expression of surprise flicker over her father's face. James McCleod wouldn't be truly startled by anything short of the Second Coming of Jesus, and maybe he'd put even that on his agenda.

Sure enough, by the time he spoke, his voice was mild. "I am considering it. You would start in the spring term. There would be plenty of time to prepare."

A glance at her father's face told her he was serious.

At eleven, Maggie was the youngest of the McCleod clan—but also the most stubborn. If she agreed to go off to this school, Paulette and John probably would too.

"No," she said, folding her arms. "We're staying with you. This is our home." Leave Chicago? Leave Dad and the women at the maternity home and Auntie Tabitha and the band? Just to go to some dumb boarding school? Never.

"I know it's hard," Dad said, stooping down so she could see his serious brown eyes at her level. "But I can't—this isn't a safe place for you and your sister."

She wanted to argue, to ask what place was safe, really, what with bank robbers and car crashes and Charles Lindbergh's baby getting snatched right out of their fancy home. But that didn't seem like it would help.

Try something else. Think.

Their family had to stick together, especially now. Promotion or not, they'd already lost Mama. There was no way she'd say good-bye to Dad over a little cut on the forehead.

"If God called you here, and he gave us to you, then maybe he called us here too."

Maggie wasn't sure if she believed what she was saying—God probably didn't take much time to think about kids like her—but she said it all confident anyway.

And like Peter at Pentecost, she'd spoken just the right words. Maggie knew from the look on her father's face that she'd won.

He ran a hand lightly over her hair, stopping at the bandage wrapped around her forehead. "If anything happens to you or your sister . . ."

"Don't worry about us, Dad. We'll be fine. I promise I'll be careful." More than careful. She'd be tough, independent. She'd never complain again about being cold when the winter lasted half the year or tired when her feet were sore from marching around at Christmastime playing carols to anyone who would listen.

From now on, she determined, Dad wouldn't have to worry about her. She would take care of herself.

10

March 5, 1943
Atlantic Ocean

"I loathe boats," Catherine moaned, pressing herself against the wall of their cabin to steady herself. The route from New York to Casablanca, Morocco, would take two weeks, they'd been told, give or take a few days for weather conditions, and even after a full day at sea, she still couldn't get used to the sensation of the world tilting underfoot.

"Mmm, yes. It *is* impossible to apply mascara on these blasted things," Judith said, her smoky voice sounding bored. "Help a lady out, darling?"

Catherine shook her head. "My hands wouldn't be steady enough. Perhaps you could leave it off, just for today?"

Judith stared in horror, as if Catherine had suggested stepping out without her clothes on. "At my age? Never."

Catherine frowned. She'd placed Judith eight, maybe ten years older than her twenty-one. Then again, there were fine wrinkle lines on her face around her high cheekbones, visible only now before makeup and powder were applied.

"Stared long enough to guess?" Judith raised an eyebrow at

her in the mirror. "I'm nearly forty, that much you'd know if you snuck a look at my USO identification card." Something Catherine had never considered doing.

"I didn't mean . . . that is, you certainly don't look it." Always the correct response, she knew, when discussing a woman's age.

"Maybe. But I'm a singer and an actress, and in my world, there are only three types of female roles: Juliet, Lady Macbeth, and the crone from Julius Caesar. And if I don't catch a break soon, I'll find myself in the long gap between those last two." She applied powder with an expert touch, softening the lines on her face, then took out the rouge.

Catherine thought about picking up the pocket mirror and examining her own reflection but decided against it. "I can't imagine how dreadful I look. How I'm going to perform is beyond me." They hadn't given a show their first night at sea, letting everyone settle into routine, but the USO had worked out a schedule of on-deck shows for the rest of the voyage, rotating as many men as could fit into the audience.

"You'll manage." Judith took a bottle from her vanity pouch and swallowed a pill in a quick motion.

Since the cabin was small, Catherine was close enough to read the label. *Mothersill's Seasick Remedy*, it said, with a block print of waves running along the bottom. "Do you suppose I could . . . ?"

"Sorry, doll." Judith shook the bottle, clearly half-empty. "Not enough to share. It's every woman for herself out here."

Yes, she supposed that's the way it would be. No one was here to do her any favors. If anything, now that they were all trying for the same opportunity, Judith wanted her to fail. Maybe Maggie did, too, despite what she said about not wanting the Pepsodent contract.

They'll be disappointed, then. Catherine took up her violin case with a new resolve. Seasick or not, she would perform, and she would impress.

Soon, the bracing cold of the open air on the deck acted as a shock, distracting her from the nauseous feeling in her stomach, but Catherine still trembled with nerves as she stood before the gathered men, just in time for Howie to introduce her.

It took some getting used to, pulling the bow across the strings when the world was tilting around her, but Catherine set her feet apart for balance and pressed on.

The music enfolded her, drawing her back into the dance halls and hotel ballrooms and auditoriums around the country where she'd seen the same expression on the audiences' faces—the feeling of being transported far away. The music helped her forget, for a moment, about her nausea and fears and homesickness.

She'd worried that the program was weighted too heavily toward classical music. "Won't the boys get bored?" she'd asked Mr. Douglas on the train ride.

He shook his head. "You might be surprised. Of course, they love comedy and the latest hits, but they're not so lowbrow that they can't appreciate a little culture."

And so she leaned into the violin, swaying back and forth, letting the sounds of Vivaldi and springtime and hope carry through the salty air.

When the last note faded, she saw wide-eyed GIs who applauded the moment the spell of the music was broken, a few poking fingers in their mouths to whistle.

Even if Leo wasn't here, these were America's boys, willing to sacrifice everything for the cause. The least they could do was give them something to smile about along the way.

The mess hall was a din of chaos, a long, narrow room with a table down the center, like a trough in a barnyard. Men would slap their trays down and eat as they shuffled down its length, their dinnerware to be cleared by the time they reached the end. Despite the noise of hundreds of rowdy men and the short time frame, most managed to scarf down a full meal, and Catherine would do the same.

It was so radically different from her mother's table etiquette lessons that Catherine giggled. Imagine, telling these men to keep their elbows tucked in and never to use the salad fork for the salmon. The troupe had taken their first breakfast after embarkment in the officers' dining room, but after that, as Mr. Douglas had reminded them, "We're here for the enlisted men."

Catherine filed along, receiving a heaping helping of roast beef that appeared to have been boiled to death—along with stares from most of the men around her.

Despite the noise, the soldier next to her grinned and spoke-shout, "Well, miss, how do you like the army welcome? Only two meals a day and nowhere to sit down and eat 'em."

She smiled back, trying to think of what to say in this absurd situation. "It's not so bad. At least my stomach has settled enough to eat." Setting her tray down, she offered him a hand. "Catherine Duquette, one of the USO performers."

A silly start. He could certainly see the patch and armband identifying her as such, and outside of a unit of nurses headed for an evacuation hospital, they were the only women on the vessel.

Still, the freckled, fair-haired soldier didn't seem to mind. "Buddy Montrose, 703rd Railway Grand Division," he said, "which is a fancy way of saying I work on trains. They sent us straight out from Fort Snelling just a month ago. That's where I hail from."

Catherine blinked in disbelief, recognizing the army outpost only a few miles from her home. "Really? I'm from St. Paul too."

Buddy seemed to find this grand news. "Well, whaddya know. Whereabouts?"

She decided not to mention her family's Tudor Revival behemoth on Summit Avenue, afraid he'd immediately write her off as a snob. "Closer to the west side."

"Then I bet you've gotten pancakes at Mickey's Diner."

Again, she decided against informing him that Duquettes didn't eat at any establishment that ended with *diner*.

"Don't make me envious, or I won't feel like eating this," she teased, dodging the question. This launched Buddy into a description of the smell of bacon fried up in the diner car that had the men around him practically salivating.

"You don't happen to know if there are any army air force units aboard with us, do you?" she put in when Buddy found a gap in the conversation.

He tilted his head. "Don't think so. Most of them came over back in November with the initial invasion force."

"Oh. I see." That ruled out the possibility of Leo being somewhere on the ship. Worse, the November date triggered a dread deep in her stomach. Leo's last letter had been dated in October. She, like all Americans, had read the headlines about Operation Torch and the Americans' victory over the Nazi-supporting Vichy French governments of Morocco and Algeria. But she hadn't really considered that Leo might be part of it. His letters had been vague enough not to draw the heavy blackouts of censors, but she'd deduced that he was stationed somewhere in Europe. From there, his unit, the 2nd Bombardment Group, might have been called to Africa's coast to join the invasion. If so, the odds that he'd stopped writing because he'd been killed or captured increased substantially.

Don't think about it. It was possible that even if he was in North Africa, he'd simply been wounded or so overwhelmed with the carnage of battle that he'd stepped away from writing. Perhaps he'd attend one of their performances and see her onstage in her shimmering gown, the gold lamé with the draped asymmetrical neckline. *"Oh, Catherine,"* he'd say, searching her eyes with his deep-blue ones, *"I'm sorry I never explained myself. But now that you're here . . ."*

"Hey!" Catherine startled to see another soldier teasingly cuff Buddy on the shoulder. "Stop monopolizing the lady."

They all laughed, and the conversation turned to lighter things: card games, baseball teams, and how the army was a ticket to world travel. Whenever she contributed anything, the men seemed to hang on her every word. It was gratifying, though exhausting.

As they were pushed out of the mess hall to let the next batch of men inside, Catherine felt more settled. She could do this. All these boys really wanted was a sense that everything was normal. A conversation with a pretty girl who reminded them of home.

Still, the face she pictured when she closed her eyes in their tiny cabin that night wasn't any of the friendly fellows she'd spoken with that day or who had greeted her after their performance on deck. It was a handsome pilot in an ill-fitting brown suit, staring into her eyes and singing, "Let Me Call You Sweetheart."

I know we'll meet again, he'd written in his last letter, the one before she'd poured out her heart to him. "Not even a war can separate us." For a long time, Catherine had been too lost in grief and worry to believe it. But now, as she crossed the ocean that had kept them apart, she began to hope it might be possible.

11

MARCH 19, 1943
CASABLANCA, MOROCCO

"Well," Maggie said, eyeing the weathered boards and cross-hatched barricade that formed the makeshift stage, "it's no performance hall, but it'll do."

"Will it hold our weight?" Gabriel asked dubiously, testing it with one boot.

"Of course. The corps of engineers built it just yesterday in anticipation of our arrival." Douglas looked deeply offended on their behalf by any question of the stage's stability.

"From bombing-run ruins, probably," Judith joked in a mutter, but Maggie wasn't about to complain. It was better than pitching back and forth on the troop ship while soldiers craned and shoved to get closer to the front.

"Just take care that your heels don't get caught in the cracks, ladies," Douglas went on, waving over the soldiers who hauled in their crates of props. There had been many volunteers, for that duty and every other since they'd debarked from the gangplank. It really made a girl feel like a celebrity, the way they were cheered and met with enthusiasm wherever they went.

Maggie had been dying to take a look around the city, but to her disappointment, the minute they stepped onto the street flanking the busy Casablanca harbor, Douglas had corralled them into three jeeps, jostling them toward their first performance outside of the city, for the staff and patients of the 8th Evacuation Hospital.

At least the open tops of the rugged vehicles had allowed her a good view of Casablanca. The stucco buildings, whitewashed to protect against the summer sun, lined streets capped with graceful sculpted arches. Elegant palm trees lent an exotic air even to the modern French parts of town, but something about it still reminded her of Chicago. Buying and selling, cars and carts hurrying by, a mix of languages spoken everywhere you turned, expensive villas only streets away from falling-apart sections that people warned you to stay away from. Cities were like that, even thousands of miles away from home.

The whole time, Maggie had cursed the silly army regulation that prevented them from bringing cameras. What she wouldn't give for a snapshot of the sights to bring home. There was nothing to be done about it, of course. National security and all that. She'd just have to buy a few postcards.

The road out of the city took them through the suburbs, greener and less desert-like than she'd expected. From there, they'd arrived at the tent city that was one of the American outposts, teeming with soldiers far enough from the front lines to be bored, a prime audience for the USO.

By the time they'd changed from their uniforms into their performance duds, a crowd had formed: doctors, nurses, and troops set up on the nearby airstrip.

Maggie tried not to let preshow nerves take over as Howie clambered onstage to test out the boards with the beat of his shiny black tap shoes. It was hard to hear his ventriloquy and hammed-up jokes over the men's laughter.

I hope I get half that reaction.

On the troopship, since they'd performed in such tough conditions, she'd stuck to only a few trumpet pieces, no jokes needed. This was the first time she'd go through her whole routine, about twenty minutes of material. And this audience wasn't a bunch of seasick greenhorns. These men had been part of the invasion force. They'd seen their fellow soldiers mowed down by remorseless bullets, faced fire from German tanks, huddled in ditches while waiting for the planes overhead to pass by, and seen friends fall to enemy fire far from home.

And a small part of her wondered, *Why would they find your little jokes funny*?

She shook her head, clearing out the thought. No sense in giving in to nerves. Anyway, these boys were so starved for the sight of a woman—any woman—that she'd probably bring down the house just by stepping onstage, even wearing her cotton dress, much simpler than Judith and Catherine's glamorous gowns.

She hadn't had the courage to try the emerald silk yet. The other two women were supposed to be the sultry sirens, while she'd taken the part of the mouthy girl next door. The idea of putting on eveningwear felt uncomfortable, like an itchy wig that anyone could mark as unnatural from yards away. Until she got used to performing, she'd leave the gown at the bottom of her trunk wrapped in the brown paper the Dayton's clerk had swathed it in.

The other performers were clustered at stage right, where they could peer around the wooden frame and watch the soldiers, but Maggie worried that would only increase the nagging stage fright rumbling around inside her, so she inspected their stash of props instead. Most of them had stowed away their things in standard army footlockers, except Gabriel, whose blue leather trunk with polished gold fittings would actually be seen onstage. It probably had a hidden compartment or secret bottom. She took a step closer, sliding her fingers along the latch.

"I probably don't need to tell you that those props are extremely delicate and my livelihood depends on them." Maggie pulled back her hand and tried not to look guilty as Gabriel strode toward her, his face grim. "But I will anyway."

"I'm sorry, I . . . the goldfish." Really, what was it about Gabriel that made her start babbling nonsense? She tried again. "I watched the disappearing goldfish trick three times on the troopship and couldn't figure it out."

"You're not meant to." In his costume, a formal coat and tails ensemble, he looked ready to dash off to a ball, though the traces of dust on the cuffs of his pants betrayed his actual surroundings. He picked up the gold-tipped cane leaning against the trunk and inspected it closely, as if to make sure she hadn't tampered with it. "Now, if you'll excuse me, I'd rather unpack what I need for this performance in private."

She gave him a sardonic smile, her composure regained. "Ah yes, I forgot who I was talking to. Kaminski the Mysterious, master of illusions, creator of marvels, etc."

He gave her his usual blank stare before shaking his head. "Everything is a joke to you, isn't it, Miss McCleod?"

"My livelihood depends on them." When he didn't so much as crack a smile, she backed away. "Don't worry. I won't touch your precious props again. But I *am* going to figure out the deal with that goldfish."

"If you choose to spoil the illusion for yourself, that's your choice."

Maybe she'd only imagined a sense of humor on board the *John Ericsson*. Or maybe it was a temporary side effect of seasickness.

Then again, she hadn't exactly made it easy, teasing him and poking about in his things. She sighed. "Look, Mr. Kaminski—"

"You can call me Gabriel," he said.

That was a relief. The other performers had ditched formalities early on, using mostly first names, except for Mr. Douglas, who was so much a Mister he was probably called that in primary school.

"All right then, Gabriel. We've gotten off on the wrong foot, you and I. The way I see it, you think I'm an intolerable snoop"—he choked, but she continued calmly—"which I am. And I think you're an intolerable snob, which . . ." She trailed off, looking at him. "I guess you'll have to tell me if that's what you truly are."

"That depends, I suppose, on your definition."

She nodded sagely. "Exactly the sort of thing a snob would say." From the expression on his face, Gabriel hadn't picked up on the fact that she was only joking. Blast. Her sister always said that her sense of humor sometimes came off wrong. "What I mean is, I'm willing to give you a fresh start if you're willing to give me one."

Despite her fumbling, he seemed to consider this. "A truce, then? In the spirit of the Vichy French cooperating with the Allies?"

"I'm not sure the comparison's a good one for me, but I'll take it." The politics of this part of the world were so twisted up these days. Colonial rule and German collaboration and the Free French under de Gaulle, who were different from the Vichy French who America had been fighting until just a few months ago. It was hard to keep straight who was on whose side anymore.

Gabriel stuck out his hand, and she shook it, pleased that he was entering into the spirit of the thing. "I think you should go now."

She cocked her head. "What, tired of my company already? This isn't much of a truce."

"Not at all," Gabriel said conversationally, and was that a hint of mischief in his smile? "I only mean that Howie is introducing your act."

"Holy Joe!" She couldn't help startling, even though she knew it gave him extra satisfaction, because sure enough, Howie was halfway through billing her as the jazziest trumpeter ever to toot out a Duke Ellington tune. How had the time gone so fast? She snatched her trumpet from where it rested on one of the trunks and took a deep breath before stepping up the two grenade crates leading to the stage. A blinding light forced her to lower her lids to half-mast, the faces of the GIs disappearing in the sudden brilliance.

Shielding her eyes, she could see the trick: they'd turned on the antiaircraft spotlights for the performance. Oh, the ingenuity of the army.

She turned it into a comedic moment, staggering in an exaggerated way toward the microphone and raising her hands in the air. "I surrender!"

That got her first laugh of the evening, the sound echoing from the shifting shapes beyond the spotlight. Maybe not seeing their faces was a good thing. She hoped that would make it easier to remember the routine.

Deep breath. You can do this. All she had to do was get started, then she could focus on the music, letting the jazzy notes slip off her fingers and into the night.

"I'm glad to be here," she began, using the new introduction she'd workshopped after the USO committee had nixed her first one. "I'll admit, it took me a while to find the best way to do my part. I couldn't be a hostess at a canteen because of my two left feet, I flunked the WAAC typing test for army secretaries, and when the Red Cross found out I fainted at the sight of blood . . . well, I thought there was no hope for me."

Now that her eyes had begun to adjust, she saw a few men chuckling politely, all of them sitting on the ground and leaning forward, eagerly. As she swept her gaze first one way, then the other, she noticed Gabriel in the wings, standing by a wheeled tractor-looking generator they used to power the microphone.

Don't let him distract you.

"So I asked the local recruiter, 'What's left?'" Maggie lowered her voice to imitate a new character. "'Tell me about your skills,' he replied. 'Well, I enjoy mountain climbing, I've worked at a department store perfume counter, and I volunteer at a number of scrap drives.' 'So what you're telling me,' he said, 'is that you like to look down on people, you get paid to stink things up, and you've collected a lot of useless metals?'"

Maggie grinned, imitating the expression of the fictional recruiter. "'Lady, it's too bad you're a woman, because you'd make a perfect major general.'"

And just like she'd imagined it in all her daydreams, the men roared with laughter at the punchline. Officers, Howie had assured her, always made ideal butts of jokes, and she intended to get as much mileage out of that as possible.

Almost without thinking, she darted a quick glance offstage. It was difficult to tell with his top hat's brim casting half his face in shadow, but she could have sworn Gabriel was actually *smiling*.

Guess you can do this after all, Maggie old girl.

Report to the USO Home Office
Floyd Douglas, Foxhole Circuit, Variety Unit 14
March 21, 1943

I had planned for this to be a brief cover letter to the attached report of our progress thus far. However, I now find myself needing to clarify: we are all still alive and well and certainly not sunk to the bottom of the ocean by a U-boat. Soon after we arrived onshore in Casablanca, we learned that everyone in the United States thought otherwise.

It seems unconscionable to me that several reputable American newspapers actually printed this false information spread by the German propaganda radio. What is journalism coming to? I had to wait at the telegram office for hours to send word to my wife, along with a line of soldiers similarly reassuring worried relatives of their safety.

As for the voyage itself, our company delivered a tolerable set of performances on board the Ericsson. However, the vanishing quality of Mr. Kaminski's silk scarves was diminished somewhat by windblown sea spray, and Miss Duquette found heels were not conducive to violin sonatas performed on a tilting deck.

All members put forth an effort to mingle with the troops, which produced much goodwill, with one possible exception. Miss Blair, our singer, was once confronted for not wearing her "Mae West" life vest on deck. She responded that she was depending on her own (substantial) décolletage to keep her afloat. This nearly produced a riot among the troops.

So far, Casablanca has been a pleasant city. Given our relative freshness and the abundance of Allied troops in the vicinity, our schedule for the next several days is quite full (see the addendum to the report for details). As a result, I will conclude this letter with best wishes and a strong admonition to avoid subscribing to newspapers that print unverified rumors.

Sincerely,
Floyd Douglas

12

March 21, 1943
Casablanca, Morocco

Catherine took a deep breath. The spring breeze carried in the smells of the city: dust stirred up by the bustle in the street, mint tea being served on the balcony, and traditional Moroccan flatbread from the stand across from the hotel.

She'd chosen a gauzy headscarf and white dress with billowing sleeves specifically based on one of Ingrid Bergman's outfits in *Casablanca*, though she'd been disappointed to find out that, in addition to being filmed almost entirely on a California backlot, the movie's locations weren't even based on real places in the city. Judith had scoffed at her when she'd worked up the courage to ask the concierge at their hotel.

Still, from her perspective, Casablanca was every bit as charged with energy as it had seemed in the movie, home of spies and refugees, German agents and Allied sympathizers, French colonials in the *ville nouvelle,* Berber Muslims in the medina and Jews in the mellah, all crammed together in the ancient city. Catherine half expected Humphrey Bogart himself to appear in his ivory dinner jacket and black bow tie, squinting into the bright sunlight.

Catherine and some of the other girls in the Sweethearts had gone to see the film *Casablanca* just before Valentine's Day, leaving the theater sighing over Bogart and arguing about the ending. Most of them had been upset by the pathos of the parting scene, but Catherine loved it. There was something even more romantic about bittersweet endings than perfectly happy ones.

It was Sunday, and even the USO took the day off. While they weren't allowed to dawdle off for sightseeing, Catherine had decided there was surely no harm in dashing across the street to the pharmacy to purchase seasickness medicine for the trip home. It was also a good excuse to use her French, practiced for years at her mother's insistence.

She rounded the corner of the hotel, cutting through the courtyard garden. Thick clusters of bougainvillea in a shade of pink too daring for Catherine to wear bloomed over the archway, letting down a scent like honeysuckle as she passed beneath. As she did, she heard a familiar braying laugh and glanced at the hotel's veranda, overlooking the gardens. Mr. Douglas and Howie were seated at a table near the railing, facing away from her. Both held drinks that glinted in the sunlight, Howie gesturing wildly, clearly in the middle of one of his tales.

Catherine pursed her lips. For all his sternness about the prohibition of sightseeing, it appeared Mr. Douglas had no qualms about indulging in a little recreation of his own, with the performer who seemed to be his new sidekick ever since the announcement of the Pepsodent contract with Bob Hope.

The only way to the main street was to pass by the veranda, but since she clearly hadn't been invited to the tête-à-tête and would be mortified if they felt obligated to invite her to join, Catherine decided to wait until the two men were occupied with a menu to sneak past. Once they were, she kept several large potted palms between her and their table, and was about to make her escape, when she heard Mr. Douglas say her name.

She froze as he went on. "She's the one that worries me."

"What about her?" Howie asked. "She's a mite shy but very easy on the eyes. Back in my day, I'd have given my two stripes and a left leg for a glimpse of a girl like her out in the trenches."

Without breathing too heavily, she edged closer. Mr. Douglas was sloshing his drink around in its glass, staring glumly at it. "That's just it. I've seen her type before. All smiles and idealism about cheering up the troops, but when she gets to the reality of it . . ." He shrugged. "She might crack under pressure. If I have to send her back in a few days after all this trouble . . ."

"Now, now," Howie said indulgently, "give her a chance, Floyd. People will surprise you sometimes. Anyway, surely she can last for ten more weeks."

Catherine noted with irritation that he didn't even consider the possibility of her being awarded the extended contract. *And why should he? Your manager thinks you'll quit halfway.*

"Some of the bigger stars haven't," Mr. Douglas countered. "Abe Lastfogel is forever having to shorten tours for the latest starlet who packs up her old kit bag and wants to wake up at home under a down comforter. We usually make some excuse about health or family troubles, but it's an embarrassment."

"I suppose not everyone's cut out for life on the road." Howie leaned back, and Catherine thought he'd seen her, but he only linked his hands behind his balding head and stretched. "Now, *I* was born for it, myself."

The more Catherine listened, the more she wanted to step

out from her cover and give them both a haughty stare. But the other part of her, the well-bred lady, cringed at the thought. What could she possibly say that wouldn't make things worse?

"I had to make some big promises to get the five of you onto this circuit so close to combat in Tunisia. Everything has to go perfectly."

"Don't worry so much, Floyd. It'll turn you gray before your time."

Mr. Douglas made a scoffing sound. "Anyway, at least we can count on Miss McCleod. As soon as I saw her, I knew she'd do just fine. Plenty of moxie." He took a long draught of his drink, sighing. "Bring us the girls, headquarters tells us, never once realizing how hard a job that is."

"I see your point." Howie nodded, as Catherine was sure he would no matter what Mr. Douglas said. "Pretty girls aren't meant for ugly wars."

From there, the conversation drifted to the Soviets and how long they could hold off Hitler's troops, but Catherine didn't stay. She hurried back the way she came as quickly as she could without drawing attention to herself. After all she'd overheard, she was in no mood for admiring architecture or reading French movie posters or even visiting the pharmacy. Once she'd made it safely inside the hotel's elevator, she blinked at the tears stinging her eyes.

So that's why Mr. Douglas had been so hesitant to sign her on that night after the performance. He thought she wouldn't be able to hack it, that she didn't have the—what had he called it?—the moxie that Maggie did.

Gratefully, neither of the other two women were hanging about their shared hotel room, leaving Catherine free to curl up on the bed and be properly miserable.

She caught a glimpse of herself in the gilt mirror on the wall, grimacing at the pale, teary face reflected there.

"Pretty girls aren't meant for ugly wars."

She turned away from the wall and took out her violin, practicing her most difficult piece with a forcefulness she'd never put into the notes before. No one needed to know what she'd overheard—or how much it hurt.

Suddenly, the clamor of voices in the street below felt more ominous, every shouted word and strange sight reminding her how very far she was from the department stores and dinner parties and orchestra hall footlights of home.

Had this all been a terrible mistake?

13

MARCH 23, 1943
FEDALA, MOROCCO

Maggie crossed her arms and tried not to look too embarrassed to be the last one chosen. It had happened often enough back when her brother's pals hadn't realized the scrawny, gangly girl in front of them could throw straight and swing hard. Ten years later, it still stung.

She'd been excited to hear that today their contractual obligation to spend time with the enlisted men after the shows meant a pickup baseball game . . . until the two captains had sorted everyone but her into a team.

Howie and Gabriel jogged over to separate groups of soldiers, shaking hands and meeting their new teammates. No one even looked back at her. She stared at the field, mostly packed dirt with a few scrubs of hardy desert grass, nothing like the manicured stadiums back home. "Which team's stuck with me, then?"

Almost as one, all of the men turned to her. "You're playing too?" the beanpole-tall team captain blurted, eyebrows racing to his hairline. When she nodded, he grinned and burst out, "Hot dog! Fellows, the lady's joining our team!"

No harm done, then. Of course they'd think she was here to watch, like Catherine, who, she noticed, had collected a group of soldiers sitting on the sawhorse benches to the side, surrounding her like bees around the waxy blossoms of the orange grove that framed the outfield. Catherine had already received so many gifts from admirers after their shows that she'd abandoned most of them in her hotel room when they left Casablanca to travel eastward along the coast.

"PFC Lawrence Wilcox, friends call me Lonnie," their captain said, stepping aside so Maggie could join their huddle. "You're not a catcher, by any chance?"

She shook her head. "Shortstop's more my position."

Her new teammates shifted uncomfortably, one of them opening his mouth to object, then closing it. They clearly weren't sure about trusting the important position to a woman.

"Swell," Lonnie said, gesturing to the bases, made of stuffed burlap supply bags. "The infield's all yours."

"Thank you." Now she'd better back up her bragging.

"I'd better take catcher," Gabriel said, reaching out for the mitt. He used the stiff leather to tap his leg brace. "Can't do much running these days." Maggie noticed that whenever they were around the troops, his limp was more prominent than usual, as if he was exaggerating it to make his 4-F status obvious and avoid questions.

"Hey, Wilcox, how're you planning to win with a gimp on your team?" The sudden interruption broke through their huddle, laced with such scorn that Maggie blinked in surprise. When she turned around, it was clear who had made the comment—the other team's captain, a fellow who looked so wholesomely all-American he could have been on a recruiting poster, though the derisive smirk on his face spoiled that look.

"Presumably," Gabriel said calmly, leveling a stare right across the plate to the All-American, "by playing like men instead of boys with schoolyard taunts."

There you go. She'd been about to tell Gabriel to ignore the taunter, but secretly, she'd hoped he would fire something back.

Clearly, the All-American's magazine of wit was out of bullets, so he settled for name-calling. "Bold words from a draft dodger."

This time, Lonnie stepped up before Gabriel could fire another round. "Aw, roll up your flaps, Alvin. Let's play ball."

That broke the tension, though Gabriel still held the stiff-lipped stance of someone who had more to say.

Maggie stationed herself between second and third base. It had been over two years since she'd last played, but hopefully rust couldn't build up in that amount of time. Not that these boys expected much of her. It was easier to exceed low expectations.

As the other team chose their batting order, the third baseman whistled a tune she'd heard a few times before on the tour, probably a marching song. She listened carefully to the jaunty melody, fixing it in her memory and picturing her fingers moving across her trumpet's valves. Maybe she'd work it into the next performance.

That is, until he started singing. The lyrics were about a 4-F fellow named Charlie, and the limerick-like lines were crude enough to be embarrassing. Was he trying to insult Gabriel too? No, he was too far away for their catcher to even hear him. Maybe it had just come to mind after Alvin made his mean joke.

"Hey," Maggie said, wishing she knew his name. "How about a different—"

Crack! Before she could finish, the first man up to bat hit the ball right toward her. Maggie nearly collided with the third baseman's legs as she dove to make the catch, and the ball hit her glove with a satisfying thwack. Ignoring the sudden burst of shouting, Maggie scrambled to her feet, turned around, and fired the ball all the way across the infield back to the first baseman. He caught her throw, foot on the base, just as the batter skidded up short. Their first out.

Alvin shaded his eyes from the sun, whistling appreciatively. "The dame's good." Louder, he shouted toward the infield, "What fellow taught you to play?"

Maggie snapped the ball directly to the pitcher with a glare at the man at bat. "My older sister, actually." Her brother, John, had helped too, but the way his comrades hooted with laughter told her she'd used the right punchline.

Unfortunately, Alvin seemed to be fairly able himself, his line drive landing him an easy jog to first base.

"Don't you let that fellow get past you," she said to her third baseman.

He cocked his head and gave her an odd look. "Whaddya want me to do, lady, tackle him?"

Maggie almost told him to give it a try, despite knowing he'd be depending on a straight and timely throw from his teammates to get an out. It was the principle of the thing.

But the next batter foiled her plans by hitting the ball high and long, and Alvin got a free pass right by Maggie. It rankled, but there was nothing she could do about it. At least, not until after the third out, when her own team lined up behind home plate. The batters before her turned in one run and two outs, with a man on first and third. Maggie could feel the pressure as she stepped up to the plate, facing Alvin on the slight rise of dirt that formed the pitcher's mound.

Of course he was a pitcher. Not every pitcher she'd known had swaggered with ego but a good many had. Came of being the center of attention, she figured, always under pressure and getting blame or praise for each win and loss.

He lazily tossed the ball into the air. "Let's see what you've got, girlie."

"Don't go easy on me," she replied, digging into batting stance. "I can take it."

Still, she noticed that the left fielder had jogged in close, sure she wouldn't be able to hit hard enough to reach the outfield.

To her frustration, she was overeager, swinging at a pitch that came across the plate too high. A rookie mistake. "Strike one!"

"Don't let him get in your head, Maggie." She didn't have to turn to recognize Gabriel's voice from his place at the rear of the batting line.

Right. She could do this. She had to.

When Alvin wound up again, Maggie drew in a breath and held it as the ball flew toward the plate . . . then cracked that ball straight over the left fielder's head.

She didn't miss the stunned expression that crossed Alvin's face before he had the sense to cover it up. By the time the left fielder chased the ball down from where it had rolled to the edge of the orange grove, she'd made it to third base, her sides heaving from the effort.

Lonnie, next up at bat, didn't give her much time to rest. His solid hit gave her a clear pass to home. As she tapped the stuffed burlap bag that served as a base, Maggie waved to the pitcher, still fuming.

"A woman's place is at home," she said, as innocently as she could, and even after weeks of busting up crowds of GIs, the laughter from her teammates, including Gabriel, was the best sound she'd heard yet.

By the time they had to call the game in the eighth inning so the performers could get ready for their evening show, Maggie's team had eked out a win by two runs.

"Nice showing out there," Gabriel said as they walked

back to the tents they'd been given as dressing rooms. "I hear they're starting a professional women's league back in the States if you're interested."

Had he actually complimented her? Maggie found herself standing a little bit straighter, ignoring the burning in her sore calves to keep stride with the taller man. "I already missed tryouts, I think." Besides, she wasn't good enough for that level of competition. "All I wanted was to put that smug sergeant in his place. Rotten of him to go on about your leg like that."

Instead of an angry retort like she was expecting, Gabriel shrugged, like it had been a long day. "He's the exception. That's the first time I've gotten flak out here. Most of the boys are too busy fighting and dying, I guess, to worry about why I'm not."

Maggie was surprised at his sudden honesty, but he didn't meet her eyes. "You'd serve if you could."

He was quiet for a moment, mopping sweat off his forehead. "I like to think so, yes. Though I have to admit, it's a relief to be here, to feel like I'm doing my part. And I plan to stay away as long as I can. The rest of the war, if possible."

So. For Gabriel, the contract was about more than the money or the connections. It was a way out from judgment back in the States.

"Kind of like running away, isn't it, though?" she said, and immediately regretted it. Whatever purpose Gabriel had found in entertaining the troops was loads better than the self-pity she'd seen engulf other men with disabilities from the Great War, many of them living on the streets.

Gabriel didn't seem offended, but he did stiffen the slightest bit. "I've wondered that myself. I'll let you know when I decide on the answer."

"I look forward to it," Maggie said, then changed the subject back to the baseball game—safer territory. Inside, she knew there was no way Gabriel would come through on that promise. It was like he was a book—a thick encyclopedia—that had opened up just a crack to show her what was written on a few of its pages, then closed again when she'd opened up her big mouth. Probably for good.

"Here, miss, let me help." The soldier who offered Maggie his hand had a shock of corn-silk blond hair and an anxious expression, as if the step up to the truck bed might make her collapse in a heap.

Maggie shielded her eyes from the morning sun with her hand. "I'm all right, thanks. But if you want to heave my footlocker up, I'd be grateful." No harm in letting the boys feel useful.

The soldier seemed pleased and lifted her heavy trunk like it was no more than a matchbox while she climbed into the two-ton truck. The fellows here were guarding and managing supply lines, since Fedala was a hub of petroleum storage and transport, and that meant they did their fair share of grunt work.

"Careful now," she warned, in case he decided to demonstrate his strength by tossing the footlocker. "My trumpet's in there."

"Of course," the man said earnestly, sliding it gently in place at the center of the truck bed. Then he took a step back, hesitating, before continuing. "I just wanted to say . . . that was some fine playing you did yesterday. Best I've ever heard, even better than the radio or the records."

Chances were, his praise was inflated because it had been so long since he'd heard anything more melodic than a bunkmate's snoring, but Maggie accepted the compliment with a nod all the same, glancing at the stripes on his arm indicating his rank. "Thank you, Sergeant . . ."

"Bates. Ricky Bates. You haven't got any idea how much it meant to us all. To me in particular." He fumbled in his pocket and pulled out a photograph, worn around the edges, and handed it up to Maggie. "That song you played toward the end there, the *Swan Lake* one. It's my wife's favorite ballet."

The woman in the photograph resembled a swan herself, dressed in a white wedding dress with a lace train, her long neck strung with pearls. "I'm so glad I included it." Usually, she only chose one classical piece from her repertoire per show, letting Catherine take most of that while she played big band and jazz.

Sergeant Bates took the snapshot back, smiling proudly at his wife before tucking her image away. "Hearing it again made me feel like she was sitting right here beside me." His eyes turned misty, and he might've been a courting lover beneath his sweetheart's window instead of a soldier in uniform at the tip of the Sahara.

Maggie couldn't think of anything to say, so she settled for "I'm sure she misses you."

He bobbed out a nod. "I don't mind telling you that spirits have been low these days, mine included. We all know we won't be guarding supply lines forever. But I feel like I'm ready for anything now. That music put the fight back into me."

"I-I'm glad." Maggie cleared her throat against the lump that had suddenly formed there. "We're happy to be here."

"I'm glad to hear it. Good luck to you!" He saluted her like she was a commanding officer.

Maggie scooted down the bench to where Judith and Howie were already seated closer to the cab, the prime spot to avoid the worst of the bumps in the road.

"What was that about?" Judith asked, gesturing to the sergeant, standing watch as if he needed to personally make sure they made it out of Fedala unscathed.

"Break the heart of a potential suitor, lassie?" Howie teased.

Maggie snorted. "He's married, Howie."

"That doesn't stop all men," Judith interjected wryly.

Maggie frowned. Honestly, what had happened to the woman to make her so cynical? She almost asked, but then Gabriel and Douglas came over to load the rest of the gear, and the question was forgotten.

Once they jerked to a start, Sergeant Bates waved at them as they rattled down the desert road. Maggie hummed the theme from *Swan Lake* and waved back until she couldn't see him any longer.

Traveling in a truck was hard on the tailbone, and by the time they stopped a few hours later to refuel, Maggie felt like she'd aged half a century in one morning. While Howie led the others in a spirited calisthenics regime that he'd learned at boot camp, Maggie spotted Douglas stepping aside to refill his canteen. She followed, stiffly. It was rare to get a moment alone with her manager.

"Mr. Douglas?"

He looked up from mopping his face with a wet handkerchief, and Maggie noticed for the first time that he shared their tired appearance, though his uniform was impeccably turned out. "Yes, Miss McCleod?"

"Earlier I told you that I wasn't interested in the contract extension opportunity with Bob Hope and his entourage. Well . . ." How much should she explain? If she told him about Sergeant Bates, he'd think she'd been dazzled by a small taste of fame. That wasn't it at all.

Maggie took a deep breath. If she could explain it to Douglas, maybe she'd be able to explain it to Father too. "Now that we've gotten this far, I've realized . . . well, that what we're doing *matters*. And I don't think I'll want to stop after three months."

No, it wasn't preaching the Gospel or serving the poor or

even performing hymns. Somehow, though, when Maggie played Gershwin or Tchaikovsky, she felt closer to God than she did even in church. That had to mean something, didn't it? And to know that it was actually helping someone like that sergeant clinched it for her.

Douglas was waiting for her to finish, head tilted, hand poised to replace the lid on his canteen.

"I'd like you to consider me for the Pepsodent contract, that's all." There, that wasn't so hard.

She even managed to stand strong under Douglas's scrutinizing expression. "It's a substantial commitment. Are you *quite* sure?"

"Very."

The pause that followed seemed to last a lifetime before their manager nodded crisply. "Then congratulations, Miss McCleod. You may count yourself as under observation and in the running."

14

MARCH 26, 1943
RABAT, MOROCCO

Catherine smiled until her cheeks hurt, waiting for the army photographer to capture a shot of her holding her violin as she stood between two beaming soldiers.

"Brilliant," he said, lowering his camera to reveal a face flushed red from the sun. "Thank you so much, Miss Duquette."

"I was honored to be asked." It was, she knew, one of the happier moments he was able to capture, rather than gathering images and footage of battles and the carnage afterward.

Over the past few weeks, she'd gotten used to posing for photographs in her uniform or one of her glittering gowns, a captured memory of the morale boost the USO had sent the soldiers' way.

Each time, she couldn't help thinking of the photograph she'd sent to Leo when he'd asked for it early on in their correspondence. She'd tried on three different outfits before settling on a light day dress with pleats gathered into the front bodice and a flounce to the skirt. He'd written back to tell her he kept the snapshot in a treasured place in his footlocker so he'd think of her every morning and night.

"Catherine!" Howie waved her over to a grove of palm trees like he was trying to help land a Flying Fortress. "Mail call."

She said a polite good-bye to the soldiers and rejoined her company, seated on the ground, all of them more excited about the news than she was. This was only the second time they'd received mail, forwarded by the whims of the Central Postal Headquarters in Algiers based on their variety unit's number and the schedule that only the USO and Mr. Douglas had access to. Apparently Rabat was a big enough city to warrant an army mail delivery.

Mr. Douglas stood in the center, holding a stack of envelopes and one package. She'd escaped the last mail delivery unscathed, and for once, she hoped Mother was enacting one of the famous frozen silences she inflicted on anyone who displeased her.

The first letter went to Maggie, a note from a sister that she started reading on the spot, and then Mr. Douglas held out the package. "It looks like Howard is the lucky recipient."

"Esther, you're a dear," Howie said, glancing at the address and making quick work of the paper wrapping with his pocketknife. "Mother of my late wife," he said, by way of explanation. "I joked about taking a government job, and she was so excited that I had finally taken serious employment that I didn't have the heart to explain."

Mr. Douglas continued thumbing through the stack. "Five letters, Mr. Kaminski?"

"Three sisters," he said, as usual, keeping his answers as short as strictly necessary.

"Oh, come on now, Gabriel," Maggie said, elbowing him.

"You don't expect us to believe that at least one of them isn't from a sweetheart back home?"

Catherine found herself exchanging glances with Judith. Was their comedian hinting at anything? Catherine had noticed that Maggie and Gabriel always seemed to be thrown together on their travel days. Granted, they spent a good amount of the time arguing or poking fun at each other, but still, seeing anyone get a rise out of their taciturn magician was significant.

"Yes," he said, fanning out the letters so she could see the names of the senders, "in fact, I do." Maggie grumbled a response, but—was Catherine imagining it?—seemed secretly pleased by the news.

"Well, I'll be!" They all turned to where Howie had unpacked a pair of socks, a melted chocolate bar, a letter stained with brown blotches from the same, and a small carton that he hefted in the air like an Olympic gold medal. "Lucky Strikes. Esther loves me after all."

Mr. Douglas continued through the stack. "From a Mr. Kenneth Barrow . . ."

"That's mine," Judith said, snatching it eagerly but making no move to open it in front of them.

"What's this?" Howie said, falling back in mock surprise. "Is this Mr. Barrow destined to be your third-time's-a-charm husband?" They were all aware of the many faults and foibles of the two other men she'd married and divorced.

She laughed, smacking him with the envelope. "Not a chance. He is the only man in my life, though." The smile she gave them revealed a softer side Catherine wasn't used to seeing.

She imagined this Mr. Barrow was the person Judith sometimes spent late nights writing to, using her army flashlight while the others slipped off to sleep, always shielding the letters if Catherine or Maggie passed too close. Surprising, given her general cynicism about love, but maybe it was only marriage she was opposed to.

There was one letter left, and Catherine breathed out in relief. Mr. Douglas was married with two grown children, so surely that one was for him. She'd have to come up with some explanation in case anyone pitied her for never hearing from home, something about her father's business and mother's social calendar, and how she was sure they'd write when they could . . .

"Miss Duquette? A moment, if you please." Mr. Douglas's voice was as effortlessly blank as ever, but Catherine still felt like a child called into her father's study to be interrogated about some infraction that Mother had reported to him.

Still, there was nothing for it but to step outside of the welcome shade and into the glare of the morning sun, several paces away from the rest of the company. "Yes?"

"I have a letter for you from a Gerald Duquette."

Was that all? Catherine had expected he'd find some way to contact her to express his disappointment and disapproval, despite the fact that she conspicuously hadn't sent the USO unit number that could be used to forward letters to her.

But something in Mr. Douglas's expression told her that wasn't the only concern. "Your father?" he asked.

"Yes." She took the slim envelope from him. Unlike Mother, Father was usually short and to the point. "Why didn't you deliver it like you did the others?"

"Because it did not arrive through the usual channels. It was given to me in Rabat from a major general there."

So that was it. Likely one of Father's Harvard friends was an officer, or he'd played golf with a senator who had a son in command. She forced her hands not to shake as she opened it, pulling it out to read the first lines.

Dear Catherine,

Your latest escapade, and its demonstration of a lack of judgment, was disappointing to say the least. I'm sure your mother had something to do with this, but I cannot stress enough that . . .

Catherine pushed it back into the envelope. She'd read it away from the others.

Before she could go, Mr. Douglas went on, "The officer in Rabat received it via the American embassy in Algiers. It was marked as priority." Several unspoken questions lingered between his words and lurked in his lowered brows.

"I, uh, must have neglected to leave him instructions for how to contact me." She forced a smile that she hoped would pass as genuine. "It was quite a whirlwind of last-minute activity."

"It was at that. Though that doesn't explain how he persuaded an army officer to play mail carrier."

So her neat dodge hadn't been effective. "My family is wealthy and well-connected," she said, deciding on the simple truth. He would likely find out sooner or later. "If they want something, they're usually able to make it happen."

"I see." And in the raise of his eyebrows, Catherine felt herself being dismissed again, the way Mr. Douglas had when discussing her with Howie on the veranda.

"Will there be anything else, Mr. Douglas?" Her posture was as stiff as her voice, but she couldn't wait to be away from this whole tiresome interview.

"One more thing." She braced herself for a scolding or a warning that the USO didn't show favoritism to the wealthy elite, but instead Mr. Douglas made a thorough study of his bootlaces before clearing his throat, his voice subdued. "My family, that is, my wife and children, were not always enthusiastic about my choice of career, particularly the amount of travel it required. Looking back at the outcome, I wish I had compromised, or at least made an effort to address their concerns."

Did he know the depths of her mother and father's disapproval? The two very different paths they'd planned for her life, and the fact that she'd gone AWOL from both of them?

No, he was merely trying to be helpful, assuming by her manner that there was tension in her family. "I'm sorry to hear that. But I'm sure it will all turn out fine in the end."

That he looked decidedly less sure gave Catherine her first glimpse of Floyd Douglas, talent agent and tour manager, as an actual beating-heart person. "Thank you for saying so."

This was where the conversation should end. Meddlers were never welcome, especially by grown men used to making their own decisions, but Catherine couldn't help adding, "I know it's none of my business, but . . . you might try apologizing."

"I think it might be too late for that."

It broke her heart to hear it, and she wanted to insist that relationships could always be healed, but that was the rosy glow of optimism speaking, not reality. She settled for giving him a small smile. "Just think about it. It might be worth your while."

"I'll keep that under consideration."

That was something, at least. "And thank you for delivering this letter," she said. "I look forward to reading it." Which was, perhaps, the biggest lie she'd ever told.

When he turned away after a hesitant nod, she folded the letter and pressed it into her pocket, determined to burn it in the nearest cookstove. The lines she'd already read were enough that she could guess what it said anyway.

He wouldn't have been so angry if you hadn't practically run away, part of her scolded.

Fine. She'd write to both Mother and Father again tonight,

telling them she was safe . . . and maybe, if she was feeling brave, telling them about the Bob Hope tour that might extend her time with the USO indefinitely.

For a moment, she allowed herself to imagine herself mingling with Hollywood stars, performing in front of them, making small talk over meals. If she took that daring leap to make a living in show business, she'd need her own connections, rather than borrowing her parents', and this was the way to make them.

Whatever her family thought, she'd made her choice, and as long as she could win this contract, she'd finally be out of their reach.

Report to the USO Home Office
Floyd Douglas, Foxhole Circuit, Variety Unit 14
March 28, 1943

Now that our route has taken us beyond the larger, coastal cities, our accommodations are no longer inns and hotels. See, for reference, my terrible handwriting. I'm writing this letter while hunched over in a pup tent that was designed for someone a foot shorter. The canvas cots and buzzing flies are prominent features; however, the most unusual changes are the slit trenches within tumbling distance of each tent. Should we hear an alarm shouted in the night, we were told to dive into them for cover from enemy fire.

I mention this because it should be impressed on future Foxhole Circuit performers, particularly the Hollywood set more accustomed to soirees than sandstorms, that "doing their bit" in this way will require actual sacrifice and risk. This is a real war zone.

Finally, as my colleague Mr. Warner requested "more color" in response to my previous efficient report, I will point out that I am a businessman, not an entertainer. Nevertheless, I hope the following anecdotes provide amusement:

- *Miss Duquette thought the phrase "embedded with the troops" implied more intimate relationships than sleeping in similar accommodations as our soldiers and was much relieved at my clarification.*
- *Upon finding him missing as we were ready to depart a tank company's encampment, young Mr. Kaminski found our old friend Howie Jones fast asleep—in the latrine.*
- *Miss Blair was presented with a coveted gift by an admirer at the last stop: a full tin of de-lousing powder.*
- *Miss McCleod is something of a baseball player, it*

turns out. She's been asked to autograph at least a dozen balls and has hit three home runs over the course of several games. How she'll be able to keep up this pace is beyond me, but it does make for good entertainment. Some of these boys could stand to be beaten by a woman more often.

Sincerely,
Floyd Douglas

15

March 28, 1943
Northeast of Fez, Morocco

Maggie stretched slowly as she ducked out of the tent, every muscle in her body protesting. Almost a week on the rugged part of their circuit, with pit latrines and canvas cots, was taking its toll.

When her two bunkmates had woken, she couldn't say, but now Catherine and Judith were kneeling outside, doing the best they could to clean the remnants of gluey oatmeal from their mess kits. "Glad you decided to join us," Judith said, barely glancing up.

"You missed breakfast." The look Catherine gave her reminded Maggie of a gently reproving mother.

"Oh no," Maggie said, shaking her head. "You can't make me feel guilty for sleeping in on the one day Douglas isn't beating down our door."

"Speaking of which," Judith said, wiping her hands on her uniform, "I'm in the market for a bath." She made a show of sniffing the air. "And believe me, you should be too."

"We can't take water from the Lyster bags." Catherine

gestured to the row of canvas monstrosities hanging from wooden frames between the tents. Each one had six spigots near the bottom and held treated water, kept cool by the evaporation off the canvas surface despite hanging in the sun all day. "They barely gave us a cup of it for doing dishes."

"Sounds like a river bathing mission is in order," Judith said, waggling her eyebrows. "I'm sure no one will mind if we remove our clothes to wash them too."

The idea was laughable, but Maggie played along. "Shh! Keep your voice down, or the soldiers will follow us for an encore performance."

Catherine blushed furiously, her eyes wide, and Maggie fought to keep from laughing at her terrified expression. "Absolutely not. I don't care how sweaty I get."

Judith rolled her eyes. "We're only joking, little Miss Prim."

"We'd probably cause an international incident if the locals saw us bathing in the nude." Still, it was a problem they'd have to solve eventually. Maggie was no tidy little housewife, but even she was starting to feel too grimy to go on.

She recalled the conversation she'd had with their jeep driver the evening before. Why not give it a go? "Come on, ladies, and bring your helmets. I'll show you how the soldiers do it."

Once they'd gathered their things, it was a short walk from the camp to the stream they'd seen while rattling in on a jeep. Maggie was sure the Sebou River was impressive at its widest point, but this particular offshoot looked to be waist high at its deepest. But the groundcover greenery was thick here, and several trees provided shade, drawing from the rich silt soil. Only the knobby bare rock of the far bank reminded her that she wasn't in the Midwest countryside on the way to a performance with the Sweethearts.

Well, that and the camels grazing lazily in the shade. Their herders stared at the three uniformed women as they passed, and Maggie gave them a wave before wondering how that translated to a different culture. She'd noticed the women of Morocco rarely appeared in public and never greeted strange men.

They continued downstream, where the gentle curve of the river provided an easy path to the water's edge.

"This can't be sanitary," Catherine said, eyeing a trio of mules tromping down to the opposite bank, their muddy hooves stirring up the water as they dipped their snouts in for a drink.

Maggie kept rolling up the sleeves of her uniform jacket. "A little pack-animal spit never hurt anyone." As she unbuckled her helmet and scooped it full of water, the other two followed her lead. A generous person might call it lukewarm at best. That was springtime for you, not nearly as hot as she'd imagined North Africa to be, especially overnight when she woke up shivering in her tent, reaching for her blanket.

"Are you sure about this?" Catherine asked, twisting a lock of her perfect auburn hair around her finger as if preparing to bid it good-bye forever once it made contact with the dishwater-colored stream. "I'm sure if we ask, one of the commanding officers would give us permission to use the chlorinated water."

"And get a lecture about how finicky females don't belong in an army camp?" Judith scoffed. "Not on your life. We'll do it like the troops or not at all."

Catherine still hesitated, looking down at her helmet.

Besides the tutorial from their jeep driver, Maggie had had to wash in a bucket several times in her childhood when the furnace in their low-rent apartment had broken and the pipes froze. She unknotted the kerchief that kept her unruly curls away from her forehead and scooped up a handful of water, splashing it on the crown of her head and patting it in before it could all run off into the dirt beneath her feet. "Just enough to get it damp," she explained. "You'll use most of it for rinsing."

The other two followed her lead, Catherine wincing as rivulets of water soaked into her blouse.

Maggie palmed the bar of scentless army soap she'd brought with her.

"Ugh," Judith said, pulling a face. "I'm suspicious of anything where the wrapper says it can be used to wash you, your mess kit, or your underwear."

"Well, it's what we've got." No sense in complaining about it. Maggie took off the wax paper and lathered it up as best she could. It was a delicious feeling, working the soap down to the roots of her hair. She could almost pretend she was in a shower back at home, until she looked around to see the desert foliage and watering herds surrounding them.

"What now?" Catherine asked, a stray iceberg of suds sliding toward her eye. She looked to Maggie with the air of someone waiting for expert advice.

"It's easier if someone else pours the water from your helmet to rinse," Maggie suggested. "That way, you can lean over and won't get the rest of you wet."

The women exchanged glances, as if wondering if they would be able to trust one of the other two, soap dripping down their foreheads like they'd been interrupted in the middle of a shower.

Judith was the first to laugh, and Maggie was surprised by the deep, rich sound. She'd heard Judith laugh before, of course, but it had always come off as a practiced, social type of giggle. This laugh, which she and Catherine soon joined, felt like a one a child would make, full of amusement at the absurdity of the picture they must make to the men watering their camels downstream.

"Here," Maggie said, taking up her helmet. "Who wants to give it a go first?"

Surprisingly, Catherine volunteered, stretching her elegant neck out as far as it would go, her long, wet hair trailing downward.

Maggie poured the water out, first slowly, then, accidentally, all at once, making Catherine shudder as the soap washed off her head and into whirling eddies of the stream. "That's cold!"

"Me next," Judith said, looking somehow younger with her thick long hair down around her shoulders. Catherine helped her, much more gracefully than Maggie.

When it was Maggie's turn, she crossed over to stand next to Judith, bracing herself for the downpour. Judith emptied her helmet without stinting, and Maggie felt the water soak into her collar and run down her back.

"That's enough." As she turned to step out from under the deluge, her foot slipped. Flailing in a vain attempt to regain her balance, she stumbled over a rock at the stream's edge and toppled over, landing ungracefully on her knees in the water.

"Are you all right?" Catherine asked, concern on her face, though Judith kept laughing.

"Just fine." Maggie stood, letting her sopping uniform drip into the stream. "It's what I get for being the resident know-it-all." She hoped they wouldn't run into Douglas on the way back, or she'd have some explaining to do, probably followed by a lecture about how public bathing *"wasn't fitting for a USO woman's reputation."*

"Come on, ladies," Maggie said, picking up her helmet and leading the way back to the bivouac area. "I've got to get back and set this mop with pins before it dries, or no man's going to want to look at me at tomorrow's show."

"Oh, I think a certain Gabriel Kaminski wouldn't mind," Judith said, squeezing her long hair out like it was a sponge.

Maggie groaned inwardly. She'd known this would be coming eventually, the way Judith nosed into everyone's business. At least none of the men were within earshot. Small mercies. "Don't we have something less frustrating to talk about? Politics, religion, bunions . . . *anything* else?"

"You're the only one he talks to, that's all," Catherine said, a familiar sappy smile spreading across her face. "I think it's sweet."

It was probably the first time the word *sweet* had been connected to Maggie in her whole life. "Half of the time, we're fighting about something or other."

"Exactly my point," Judith said, "and you should be glad it's only half of the time. With my second husband, the split was more like ninety-ten. But, oh, that ten was glorious."

"He doesn't think of me that way," Maggie interrupted before Judith could give them any more details about her romantic life.

Even that didn't wipe the knowing smile off of Judith's face. "Say what you like. I can spot an interested man even if I'm not planning to tie the knot again myself."

"Oh no? What about Mr. Kenneth Barrow?" Catherine said, a teasing lilt to her voice, and Maggie praised the heavens for the shift of focus onto someone else. "He certainly writes to you often enough."

Judith gave a braying laugh. "Funny you should mention that. Kenneth—he hates it when I call him Kenny—is my fourteen-year-old son." She paused, a slight frown creasing her face. "No, fifteen. I missed his birthday last week."

A son, eh? Maggie wouldn't have guessed, probably because she hadn't seen Judith as the maternal type.

"It must be hard, being away from him for so long," Catherine said, so sugar sweet with sympathy that in someone else, Maggie might suspect it was disingenuous.

Judith shrugged. "Can't complain. It's a steady paycheck, and that's not always a guarantee in the music world."

"Is his father . . . ?" Whatever Catherine had meant to ask trailed off in a decorous cough, though Judith had hardly been shy about her bad luck with men.

"He's a pirate," Judith said casually, swinging her helmet from its straps as she walked. "Or he was in *Pirates of Penzance*, when we met. That's about as good a picture of who Stanley Barrow is as you're likely to get. Should've listened to my mother—she warned me about him. Kenneth lives with her most of the time."

"Do you miss him?" Maggie asked.

"Sure." Judith cleared her throat, probably to get rid of the dust they were raising as they walked. It couldn't be actual emotion, could it? "All these years, I've told him I'd make it big someday and we'd never have to worry about money again. But it hasn't happened . . . yet."

Was Judith trying to make them feel guilty for going after the Pepsodent contract? Maybe. It would explain why she was suddenly so open about her personal life. And Maggie had to admit, after learning Judith had a son to provide for, her own reasons for wanting to join the tour seemed silly: a stubborn competitive streak and a desire to impress her father.

Still, there was nothing wrong with working for that contract just because someone else wanted it too.

"I'm sure he's very proud of you," Catherine said.

Maggie nodded in agreement, but inside she was thinking that as nice as it was to share a laugh over soaping up in the Sahara, these two women weren't going to get in the way of the Bob Hope contract, not if she could help it. After all, wasn't she putting in the most effort? While Judith and Catherine fussed over their makeup and gowns, she was the one out loading up the luggage, talking to the troops, and joining in a baseball game.

What if it's not enough? What if Douglas is looking for someone prettier or more talented?

She tried to wave away the doubt like one of the pesky Moroccan mosquitoes that multiplied in the spring. No point in thinking that way. If she wanted to increase her odds, she'd just have to work harder. They were all about to see just how good of a trouper Maggie McCleod could be.

16

April 2, 1943
Fez, Morocco

The C-47 gleamed in the morning light, and Catherine felt a thrill of excitement looking at the sleek lines of the transport aircraft. They'd be boarding soon, about to cross half of Morocco from the sky.

Mr. Douglas had explained that there weren't many American troops stationed between Fez and the Morocco-Algeria border, and the Atlas Mountains made the terrain slow going, even for rugged army vehicles. The few-and-far-between train routes were occupied with cargo transport, not passengers. That meant, for the first time on their tour, they'd be flying to their next destination.

This, at least, Catherine was prepared for, perhaps more than the others. She'd traveled in an airplane three times on various vacations, including to Paris with Mother when she'd turned sixteen.

As the crew hauled their luggage onboard, Maggie joined her, squinting suspiciously at the plane as if it might fail her novice inspection. "They call it the Skytrain," Catherine told her, proud to show off the knowledge she'd gained from a pilot at the last stop. Learning facts like this made her feel a little closer to Leo. "Isn't that a lovely name?"

Maggie only grunted. "Looks a little worse for the wear." She waved her hand at a number of dents near the star insignia on the wing. "Are those patched bullet holes?"

Catherine decided she simply wouldn't ask. "They told us it's perfectly safe."

"Oh, sure," Maggie muttered, clutching the bag their pilot had given each of them with instructions to use it if they felt sick.

Once they were given clearance to board, Catherine walked up to the boarding ladder with confidence, taking Mr. Douglas's hand to help her into the main cabin once she mounted the aluminum stairs.

The performers had been told to crowd together on the row of troop seats closest to the cockpit to make room for the handful of actual soldiers who would be traveling with them. Normally, the cabin would hold twenty-eight fully armed men, but their props and other cargo had reduced the number of passengers to twenty.

The Skytrain was reporting for use by a crew in training near Oujda, before departing for a location that no one would talk about but Catherine knew was Tunisia. They'd need a steady supply of soldiers there soon enough to push Hitler's forces out of the last German occupied stronghold in North Africa.

Maggie looked paler than ever, hunching over in her seat like she was already bumping through turbulence before they'd even left the ground. "This isn't natural, I tell you."

"Don't tell me you're frightened of a little old plane ride," Judith teased, never one to sound out a person to tell whether they were in the mood for a joke.

"Think about it," Maggie snapped, barely raising her head. "We'll be hurtling through the air at an ungodly speed through a war zone in a glorified tin can. Some things I'm allowed to be scared of."

Gabriel chimed in with a pacifying "Fair enough," then showed Catherine and Maggie how to fasten the buckle of their safety straps.

Catherine pulled hers as tight as she possibly could. It felt reassuring to be banded to the solid frame of the metal seat, though she was already overheated from the tightly packed bodies.

"Don't forget, we have our parachutes," Mr. Douglas said, patting a canvas bundle. "Just in case."

They'd been given only the most rudimentary crash course on how to use them, and Catherine chose to interpret that as a good sign that the army didn't anticipate even a hint of trouble while they flew over surrendered territory in broad daylight.

Though she'd experienced it before, the sensation of pulling away from the ground was always breathtaking, and Catherine did her best to peer out of the small window to watch the landscape recede beneath them. She could see the cluster of large tents, erected by the nomadic Berber people, that fringed the outskirts of the army camp. From above, the goatskin coverings looked like small brown squares against the spring grasslands. To the south, the Atlas Mountains towered into the distance, capped with snow at the top.

As they climbed in altitude, Catherine began to feel some of that wintery chill herself. On the ground, the afternoon sun had turned the thin metal fuselage into an oven. Now it offered little protection against the cold of the rising altitude. Catherine blew out a breath in a puff of white, tucking her hands into the cuffs of her sleeves for warmth.

"Is this bringing you back to your own GI days, Howie?" she asked, turning to her left.

He shook his head. "Nah. We only had a handful of planes in

the last war, mostly fighters and reconnaissance biplanes. They hauled us over the Atlantic by boat." He rapped his knuckles on the Skytrain's side. "Probably for the best. There aren't any bad memories for me. In fact, I met my wife on a plane."

"Really?" Catherine couldn't imagine that being crammed together with other passengers like this could possibly provide the atmosphere for romance.

"Yessir. We'd both paid fifty cents to go up with a barnstormer at the county fair just for the thrill of it. Afterward, I asked Sue if she'd like to take a shot at the midway games with me." He stared off into the distance and even let out a little sigh. "She got rings over all six milk bottles in seven tosses. I was a goner."

Suppressing a chuckle, Catherine smiled. "What a charming story. It sounds like the two of you were very well matched."

"You can say that again. Sue was the best part about my act too. Could sing like a nightingale, so light on her feet that she could dance circles around me, if you can believe it."

Catherine wasn't sure how much of this description was colored with the rosy glow of love, but decided to accept it all with a nod.

Howie's shoulders drooped as he sighed. "She was devastated when the doctors put her on bedrest. Wasn't much for reading, so we'd spend most nights listening to the radio together. And do you know what her favorite program was?"

"What?" Catherine asked, although she was beginning to suspect the answer.

"*The Pepsodent Show*," Howie proclaimed, cheerful again, like a light switch turned on. "Always made Sue laugh, even when she took a turn for the worse. And to think I might get a chance to perform with Bob Hope himself . . . she'd be pleased as punch."

"I'm sure," Catherine agreed, feeling guilty. She, like the

others, had been slightly annoyed by Howie's blatant pandering to Mr. Douglas over the past few weeks, always finding some excuse to pal around or offer him a compliment. Knowing that he wanted the contract to celebrate the memory of his late wife . . . well, it just went to show that you should be slow to judge a person.

As they flew, Catherine played Beethoven's Fifth Symphony in her head, trying to hear each of the entrances that would come with a full orchestra, letting a faint smile play over her lips in case Mr. Douglas glanced over. Yes, this was just like the flight they took to Bermuda to celebrate her grandmother's birthday. If, of course, you removed the gun ports in the windows, pretended there were reclining berths with soft blankets, and replaced the radio operator with a stewardess providing chewing gum and magazines.

A sudden series of bumps rapped Catherine's head against the metal of the fuselage behind her, ending the song and thoughts of sunny beaches. Her eyes flicked to the parachutes on the wall. Waiting.

"What was that?" Maggie shouted over the engine, making no effort to hide her alarm.

"This is nothing," Howie bragged, his booming voice cutting easily through the noise of the flight. "When I rode with that barnstormer, we looped and barrel-rolled our way through an entire circus advertisement. That relocated my stomach on the other side of my spine for about a week, I'd say."

A colorful way to describe it, but Catherine identified.

Don't show it. That's what mattered. She would be calm, confident, and full of moxie, just like Mr. Douglas wanted.

But the plane didn't level out like Catherine expected. Instead, it gave another jolt, ramming her against Maggie.

Were they landing already? It was, they had been told, a relatively short flight.

Be calm.

"Something's wrong," Maggie said, grabbing Catherine's arm like a hawk swooping toward its prey. "Something has to be wrong."

Confident.

"I'm sure it's nothing," Catherine said, but the shouts from the radio operator's compartment made her voice catch slightly at the end.

Full of—

A voice—the pilot's?—cut through the noise, demanding quiet. "Due to mechanical difficulties, we're required to make a forced landing."

"We're being shot down!" Judith cried shrilly.

Despite the stab of panic, Catherine forced her own mouth shut as the plane took a noticeable tilt downward. Pilots were trained for this sort of thing. They were landing, not crashing. Landing, that was all.

Someone shouted for everyone to fasten their safety straps, and Catherine checked hers, though she'd never unbuckled for a moment.

A sudden motion jarred her, and she couldn't keep from crying out, her voice mixing with others. The plane was going down. It didn't feel like a sudden, freefalling spiral, but it was no controlled, featherlight descent either.

And was that the smell of smoke?

No further instructions came from the pilot, who must have more important things to do than tell them how to prepare for impact, if he even—

The violent lurch of the plane beneath her snapped Catherine against her restraints, cutting into her before the plane groaned in the opposite direction, the cabin floor rattling with impact. All movement stopped. They'd landed.

Safely? Everyone seemed to be alive. Catherine's heart beat

staccato in her ears, and she clenched her fists to keep from crying out. It would only add to the chaos.

"Everyone out," a soldier bellowed, though the engine noise had stilled. "Now! Women first."

That startled Catherine out of her stunned relief to be alive. She tried to hurry, but she fumbled with the buckle, forgetting how the release mechanism worked.

Howie stooped over to help her, and she could see Judith and Maggie being herded through the cabin. "Th-thank you," she managed.

Instinctively, Catherine took a deep breath before staggering toward the entrance hatch, where smoke was already clouding the air, then stopped short. The boarding ladder was nowhere to be seen, but Mr. Douglas was waiting below, arms outstretched. "Take my hand!" he called to her, and though it was only four feet down to the ground, she felt like a paratrooper teetering before his first jump.

She leaned forward, clutching Mr. Douglas's entire arm, and leapt away from the plane. It was a terrifying moment before her feet landed on solid ground.

Get away, get out of the way. Catherine stumbled away from the plane, all while taking in their surroundings.

They had landed in a fallow field, deep gouges torn through the dirt where the plane had scraped its way to a stop. It rested at a crooked angle, but as far as Catherine could tell, all of its major parts were still intact, from wings to bomb bays to dorsal-like tail. The smoke came from the forward half of the plane. Already, it wasn't the billowing cloud it had been when she'd climbed down.

An almond tree about thirty yards away raised white-flowered branches invitingly, and Catherine ran toward it, glancing behind her as she did so. The others from the troupe followed, forming a huddle of sorts around her while the army recruits battled the flames.

Mr. Douglas's eyes scanned the group, his mouth moving in a silent tally, then relaxed as he realized he hadn't lost any members. "Is everyone all right?"

"Far from it," Catherine wanted to say, but everyone else was nodding after assessing themselves for any bumps and bruises.

"That does it. I am never stepping foot on a plane again," Maggie announced, collapsing on the ground, and though her voice was firm, Catherine had noticed her legs were shaking uncontrollably.

As men continued to duck out of the burning plane, an officer barked orders at the remaining soldiers, who began unloading crates, saving valuable military supplies.

Or preventing explosive material from catching fire, Catherine thought, taking a few hurried steps backward, though she knew she was far enough away.

But no explosion added to the chaos. The fire-fighting detachment must have been successful because the cloud of smoke faded to wisps, then stopped altogether, leaving an acrid smell behind. A series of whoops rose up from the other side of the plane.

"Now *that's* a sound I remember," Howie said, a brief smile creasing his lined face. "Victory after battle. They've put things to rights."

"Was it really a mechanical error?" Maggie pressed. "Or was there a German plane on our tail and they just didn't want to worry us?" She scanned the sky for the culprit, looking almost hopeful that this might be the case.

Gabriel shook his head. "I'm no expert, but I'd think we'd have done evasive maneuvers if the Luftwaffe was after us."

"Yes, well, that's just like the army," Judith said, adjusting her uniform as if she hadn't been shrieking in panic only moments earlier. "Sending us in a patched-up job like that. I'm surprised it even took off."

But she was all smiles when the handsome copilot jogged over to them. "It's all right now," he said. "Just a little engine trouble."

Maggie snorted. "If a busted plane and a fire is a 'little' trouble, I don't want to be around when things really fall apart."

He flashed her a grin. "Better be glad we caught it early and had a nice open stretch to land. Though we're awful sorry about the bumps."

"That's the risk we take, joining the army," Howie said, slapping the younger man on the back. He didn't comment on the military's gift for understatement. "Besides, we all made it out in one piece, didn't we?"

"I say we take the train next time," Maggie quipped, prompting laughter from everyone gathered—except Catherine.

How could they all be so casual? Catherine didn't dare speak, or her voice would give away her shattered nerves, and Howie and Mr. Douglas would exchange glances, thinking that she was too pretty and fragile to deal with the realities of being in a war zone. She leaned against the almond tree, hoping she wouldn't have nightmares tonight of falling out of the sky.

Then again, these were real performers, not like her, whose only experience before the Sweethearts was the occasional drawing room recital. Maybe they were just as rattled but were keeping up the act for Mr. Douglas's sake.

If so, all of them were better performers than she could ever hope to be.

From Sterling Warner to Floyd Douglas

April 1, 1943

Floyd,

Just had to drop you a line to say: keep up the good work in your reports, especially that last roundup of stories. Much better than your usual data-and-timetables stuff.

Between you and me, it's been rough, even back here. Another starlet—can't tell you who, slander and whatnot—called it quits this week, sobbing about the emotional toll of performing at hospitals. Not to mention the PR nightmare of that plane wreck in the Atlantic. Killed several of our performers, whole tour had to be cancelled. Awful stuff, war.

Stay safe out there, you and your troupe. And keep those reports coming. These days we could use something to lighten the load.

Warnie

Report to the USO Home Office
Floyd Douglas, Foxhole Circuit, Variety Unit 14
April 4, 1943

Tonight, I write this report grateful to be alive. Our near-miss emergency airplane landing (detailed in the attached report) was enough to sober all of us. Except Miss McCleod, of course. Though she seemed shaken, ten minutes after the incident, she was jotting notes based on the experience for her routine. An obliging army truck carried us the rest of the way to our destination, though we had to share passage with a howitzer and arrived only an hour before our performance time. Such is life on the Foxhole Circuit.

In the absence of an official committee, I took the liberty of denying the following joke: "Scrap drives go on by the hundreds back home, and I was all for them. That is, until I got here. See, I took a good look at the plane that got us partway here and think the wings were patched together by a few aluminum pots and my old Ford bumper."

Inappropriate? Certainly. Derogatory to our military? Indeed. Accurate? At least somewhat. In any case, I'm not alone among the troupe in saying I hope to never take to the skies out here again.

On a separate note, as Mr. Lastfogel requested an update on our performers with an eye to who might be worthy of the Pepsodent contract, I will attempt to give my impressions of all of them thus far.

Howard is a decent and established vaudeville performer, but his style of show is going out of vogue quickly. Still, he's a smash hit off the stage, palling around with the boys like everyone's favorite uncle.

Miss Blair knows how to work a crowd but has a narrow vocal range and her pitch tilts increasingly flat as her set goes on. She'd be just fine in a chorus or perhaps as an actress with some bit singing, but I don't see a solo radio career in her future.

Miss Duquette continues to play like she's in Carnegie Hall even when we're performing from the bed of a two-ton truck. However, she's not a natural at mingling with the troops and seems unsuited for rugged conditions.

Miss McCleod, on the other hand, doesn't have the glamour we're looking for, but her trumpet playing is fair enough, and she can get a roar of laughter from the most exhausted platoon.

As for the junior Mr. Kaminski . . . well, I'm afraid his

act hasn't lived up to my—admittedly high—expectations. I disclosed to the committee that I was the talent agent for his father, Simon Kaminski, during the three decades he was astounding audiences across the country. Gabriel executes his tricks flawlessly but mechanically, like he's reading off a script. Then again, the troops don't mind, and perhaps he'll get better with practice. It really isn't fair of me to compare him to Simon, but, ah, that's the double-edged sword of nepotism. He wanted to come on this tour quite badly. I got the sense that it was a kind of personal redemption for him as he's unable to serve in the military for the reasons noted in his file.

As you can see, my observations are inconclusive. At the moment, my recommendation for the contract is still anyone's game. I will update you if I'm further impressed—or disappointed—by anyone.

We have, as you know, a performance of personal interest coming next week. Once again, I would like to thank the USO leadership for allowing me to be assigned to this particular tour.

Sincerely,
Floyd Douglas

17

April 5, 1943
Oujda, Morocco

Maggie watched bubbles rise to the surface of the water in the bottom of her mess kit's pan, held over the coals of an abandoned cookfire. "Just a minute more."

Like she'd instructed him, Gabriel was holding his silk scarf taut against a canvas cot he'd dragged out of a pup tent for this operation. The bold white polka dots on a jet-black background were easily visible onstage, even from a distance.

As the boil reached a frantic pace, Maggie pulled the pan away. "Incoming," she said, tossing the water into the dirt, steam rising off the pan's steel surface as she hovered over the scarf. "Stretch it out good, now."

Gabriel tightened his grip, and she set the flat of the pan against the silk. It hissed as it made contact with the wet cloth, and the deep wrinkles disappeared as she pressed the pan back and forth, slow and steady.

"It's working," Gabriel noted, sounding faintly surprised.

"Of course it is. Didn't you believe me?" She ran the pan over the length of the scarf again, though it was already cooling and not as effective on the second pass. "How'd it get wrinkled so badly anyway?"

"We were in such a hurry to leave after the last show that some madness possessed me to let Howie help pack my props."

"Say no more." Their tap-dancing veteran wasn't known for being neat and orderly. He was currently sitting on an ammo crate in an olive grove on the other side of the road with the rest of their troupe, awaiting their transportation to the next performance. "Does that pass inspection now?"

Gabriel held the scarf up, inspecting the smaller wrinkles near the edges. "Normally, I'd say yes, but Douglas was insistent that our costumes look immaculate for the next performance."

Maggie poured a thin layer of water into the pan and returned it to the heat. "You noticed that too, huh?" Their morning meeting had been longer than usual, with their manager as jittery as if he'd consumed a whole pot of army coffee.

Gabriel shrugged. "Maybe someone important will be in the audience."

"Who, Winston Churchill?"

As usual, Gabriel seemed to miss the fact that she was joking. "Churchill met with Roosevelt at Casablanca in January. I don't think he'll be coming back anytime soon."

It's not as if Maggie actually expected the leaders of the free world to attend one of their variety shows. Still, Douglas was acting fishy if you asked her.

It was their last of a few days in and around Oujda, the headquarters for the Fifth Army. Maybe Lieutenant General Mark Clark, the army's commander, was high profile enough to allow for an exception to the rule barring officers from attending USO shows. Or maybe one of the war correspondents embedded with the troops had been assigned to cover the Foxhole Circuit.

Now it was Maggie's turn to be nervous. What if a journalist interviewed her and Dad read the article? None of her jokes leaned toward the risqué, but it was still hard to tell whether her father would approve. She hadn't mentioned that she was now a comedian in addition to being a musician. That felt like one more step away from the serious and sacred.

Trying to put that out of her mind, Maggie focused on her makeshift iron, running the heated surface around the hem of the scarf this time. "This is as good as we're going to get."

Gabriel fluttered the scarf into the air, eyeing it critically from both sides before nodding his approval. "That's the best it's looked since we left New York. How did you learn that trick?"

She had to laugh. "Growing up poor. It's amazing how many gadgets you can replace with a little elbow grease and some creativity."

"Well, I'm grateful you shared it with me."

She felt warm inside at the compliment. They'd come a long way from their hostile start, she and Gabriel. It helped to know that he wasn't trying to act smarter than everyone else—most of the time. He just liked to take time alone to think and sometimes used big words.

Maggie pretended to repack her mess kit as Gabriel folded the scarf into careful fourths . . . and then she reached over to snatch the scarf away. "Ha!"

"What are you—?" Gabriel protested, but it had only taken a second for Maggie to give the scarf a few tugs in the right place to confirm her suspicions. Sure enough, if you pinched one of the corners of the scarf and shook hard, like Gabriel did in his act, the smooth material turned inside out to reveal a plain black side.

"So *that's* how it works," she crowed, waving the half-changed material in the sky as proof.

"Put that down," Gabriel ordered, reaching to grab it back

like she was flaunting his underthings instead of a prop. "One of the soldiers will see."

Maggie dodged away at first, but Gabriel had longer arms. He turned the scarf back, spotted side out, and folded it into perfect quarters. "So where do you keep the polka dots that 'fall off' the scarf?"

He sighed. "In my sleeve."

"And they're paper, right?"

Another nod. "Is this why you offered to help me?"

She made her voice sound affronted. "Of course not. I did that because I'm a helpful sort of gal. Figuring out the trick is just a nice bonus."

"Mm-hmm," he said, clearly unconvinced. He unlatched the trunk to tuck the scarf inside, and Maggie got a glimpse of the reorganized contents: a top hat, a thick red cloak, an oversized deck of cards, and a portable stand that folded down to the size of a briefcase. No sign of the fishbowl. It must be tucked away to keep it from breaking.

"I hope you're happy," Gabriel said, closing the trunk before she could snoop further. "You won't enjoy that trick nearly so much now."

Maggie hated to admit it, but he had a point. There wasn't much thrill in knowing the magical scarf that loses its polka dots was just a double-sided cloth and some palmed papers. "Why do you think people like a good magic trick so much, if it depends on them being fooled?"

"Not fooled exactly." Gabriel's voice had taken on a thoughtful tone, the kind that made him sound like a professor. "Just . . . mystified. We live in an age where textbooks and experts can explain what stars are made of, where wind comes from, how a caterpillar becomes a butterfly, and everything else that was once a mystery."

Maggie tilted her head, having to work hard to keep up. "Is that so bad?"

He seemed to consider that for a moment. "Not really. But I think a small part of us longs to wonder. To study something beautiful without reducing it to a mechanical explanation. To be genuinely amazed by something we don't understand."

"Isn't that what church services are for?"

This time, he broke into an outright smile, and Maggie tried to keep from staring. Gabriel was handsome when he smiled. Not like a movie star or anything, but still, there was something magnetic about him. "Actually, yes. God isn't a cheap trick, of course. But he also can't be diagrammed or stored in a test tube. We all ought to be more comfortable with mystery, onstage and off."

"I always thought God was more like an orchestra concerto," Maggie blurted, instantly regretting it. "There's something about music that just . . ." She'd never explained this, not even to her father, and now it sounded silly. Nothing like Gabriel's deep professor-thoughts.

"What?" Gabriel prompted, when she trailed off.

Confound it. Now, when it counted, Maggie couldn't think of a single thing to say. "I can't explain it. But maybe that's the point. You know?"

To her relief, Gabriel didn't laugh, just looked at her with his serious dark eyes like she was just as smart as he was. "I haven't the slightest doubt God can be found in both illusions and in music. After all, David described God as a shepherd in his psalm. Maybe we all understand God better through the pursuit we're most familiar with."

That was the best sermon Maggie had heard in a long time. It made God sound . . . closer than she'd expected. "You know, Gabriel, sometimes I think I ought to follow you around just to hear you think."

Had she actually said that out loud?

Gabriel, too, seemed taken aback, but then he laughed, like

it was another one of her jokes. "Good news. We're trapped in each other's proximity for another several weeks. You'll soon be wishing you could get away from my thoughts."

Before Maggie could decide if she had the courage to say that it hadn't been a joke, not really, a sharp whistle drew their attention to Howie, standing among the olive trees. "Hey, you two! Join the show."

Gabriel squinted. "Is he juggling?"

Sure enough, as they jogged across the road, leaving their luggage behind, it was clear that Howie was keeping five—no, six—small orange spheres aloft. As he moved them neatly from one hand to the other, they seemed to blur together. Judith chanted encouragement, and even Maggie joined in, stepping into the welcome shade of the neat row of olive trees.

"Ta-da!" Howie proclaimed in his boisterous stage voice, catching four of the balls and letting the odd ones fall to the ground. Now, Maggie could tell that they were tangerines, and as he bowed, he tossed one to Judith, Gabriel, Douglas, and Maggie before bending down to pick up one for himself. "My treat."

After a week of army chow from field mess halls, Maggie wasn't about to turn down food, no matter how ostentatiously it was offered. She noted the last tangerine waiting in the grass, untouched. "Where's Catherine?"

"Where else?" Judith said, contempt obvious in her voice. "Posing for another glamour shot. This time with some antiaircraft guns."

"As long as she doesn't miss our departure, it's a good publicity opportunity for the USO," Douglas said, eating a quarter of his fruit at once. He didn't comment on the fact that, of all the variety unit members, Catherine easily received double the requests to pose for photos or sign autographs.

No need to dwell on that. Maggie sliced into the tangerine's skin with her fingernail, releasing a spray that smelled heavenly. The slices of fruit underneath were even better, the juice pooling on her tongue in the perfect mixture of sweet and tart.

She closed her eyes, savoring the taste, and when she opened them again, Howie was watching with his usual lopsided grin. "What do you think?"

"A thousand times better than canned peaches." Chicago didn't have much by way of fresh tropical fruit, especially for a family living on a preacher's salary. "Where'd you get these?"

"Traded some Arab farmers earlier this morning. Probably got ripped off. Our driver said that in November you could get a basket of tangerines for three Lucky Strikes or a chocolate bar. Now that the locals have gotten wise, the going rate's half a pack for a dozen."

"They're delicious," Douglas said, exposing smile lines on his face that Maggie hadn't noticed before. "Worth the inflation, certainly." He and Howie walked down the road toward the stream that watered the grove, discussing the finer points of wartime economics. Maggie watched them go.

"Odd for Howie to give up some of his precious, and over here, rare, American cigarettes." Gabriel's musing beside her drew her attention, as if he were reading her mind.

She nodded. "Unless he's playing nice to get Douglas on his side for the contract."

Maybe Douglas would see through the scheme and maybe not. Either way, her last wedge of fruit had a sour edge to it that hadn't been there before.

"Sometimes I envy you, Maggie," Gabriel added. "The rest of us all seem to be scrambling, putting on a show even offstage for Douglas's benefit, whereas you're free to enjoy the view."

She should tell him that she was back in the running for the contract, but what would Gabriel say if he knew? And anyway, it was true that she wasn't being phony around Douglas like Howie or Judith.

Judith stepped into the space between them, fanning herself lazily with a woven straw fan she'd picked up from a market vendor. "At least Howie is only trying to sweeten our tour manager up rather than outright bribing him."

There it was again, that constant cynicism that Judith doled out, trying to make everyone as suspicious as she was of humanity in general. "No one would do that," Maggie said.

"No?" Judith gave her a significant glance. "I'd say there's a good chance Douglas hands little Miss Duquette *The Pepsodent Show* tour like she's gotten everything else in life: on a platter with a silver spoon."

"She's got the same chance as the rest of us," Gabriel said.

"I don't know about that," Judith said casually, but Maggie recognized that tone, the sly look to the side, words trailing off significantly. It was the one the women of the Sweethearts used before doling out juicy gossip. And even though she hated herself for it, she leaned forward, waiting to hear what Judith would say next.

She didn't disappoint, tilting her chin at a dramatic angle. "I distinctly heard Catherine talking with Mr. Douglas about how rich her family is, and how they always get what they want. Then they lowered their voices and I didn't hear anything else until she said, 'Think about it. It might be worth your while.'"

That did sound suspicious, Maggie had to admit. "How did Mr. Douglas respond?" Gabriel asked, trying to feign disinterest.

Judith shrugged her angular shoulders. "Just that he'd 'keep it under consideration.'"

Maggie let out a sigh of relief. "Well, that's that, then. Sounds like a diplomatic no to me." Good for Douglas. She'd known he was too tight-laced to be bought off.

"Everyone has their price, even our rules-and-regulations manager." The cynical smile on Judith's face irritated her, but Maggie had to admit that the other woman had been in entertainment circles for far longer than she had. And who knew how much Catherine had offered to pay him?

"But that's not fair."

"Fair? Show business isn't fair, darling. It'll chew you up and spit you out if you let it, with nothing but a handful of chorus girl sequins and bad newspaper reviews to show for it."

The bitterness in Judith's tone made Maggie flinch. "Is that what happened to you?"

Whatever difficult place Judith had gone to, whatever memories she was lost in, were snapped away in a flash of her dark brown eyes. "Not after I get this contract. And I will."

Whatever Maggie was expecting from the way Douglas had stressed the importance of their next performance, another standard ragtag tent camp wasn't it. There was nothing at all of note to see, not even a distant landmark, like the tower of the Grand Mosque visible in Oujda.

Instead, black flies swarmed around them in plague-like quantities with every step, seeming to multiply as Maggie swatted them away. They were the reason Maggie and the others had been warned never to drink the standing water. The army surgeon, no longer needing to treat combat wounds from November's invasion, was kept quite busy with men who had contracted dysentery. "If you see someone running to the latrine like Rommel's on his tail, he's got the trots. You'll want to get out of the way," he had sagely informed them.

This bit of advice had nearly caused Catherine to die of mortification, and even Maggie had gotten the point. She filled up her canteen from one of the Lyster bags, feeling conspicuous even in her simple cotton dress.

"What's that?" Catherine asked, tilting her head toward the south.

Only then did Maggie hear the sound of shouting, down a slope to the airfield, where a cluster of men in uniform had gathered.

"Let's find out. It has to be more interesting than fly-swatting."

Maggie didn't wait to see if Catherine would follow and jogged over to see several men, including Howie, whose costume was in shambles, his dress suspenders visible, huddled around in a circle, shouting like they were at a boxing match. Oddly, they were all staring down at the ground. No one seemed to notice the women's approach, completely caught up in the drama in front of them.

Maggie wasn't tall enough to see what was going on, so she stepped closer, angling her shoulder and trying to push through. It wasn't effective, but as the men shifted back and forth, she glimpsed the object in the center of the circle, an empty metal container, knee high, with the word *PETROL* printed in large letters.

One of the men had told her that the flimsies, as the British called them, served as makeshift stoves in a pinch, modified into "Benghazi Burners." But if these men were frying eggs, why all the shouting?

When she was close enough to see into the container, it became clear. This was no cooking demonstration. Inside the flimsy, two scorpions circled each other, striking in a blur of pincers and tails.

Catherine let out a horrified yelp, and even Maggie gasped as the wickedly pointed creatures hissed and skittered up the sides. A few of the men turned, their faces turning from jubilant to contrite upon seeing her and Catherine decked out in their showtime finery.

"Sorry, ladies," one of them stammered out. "You weren't meant to see this."

Howie still couldn't tear his attention away from the gasoline-can combat, pumping his fist and shouting, "Get him!" accompanied by a war whoop that seemed to be pulled from an exaggerated Western radio show.

"Ugly little beasties, aren't they?" Maggie's voice was casual, but she didn't try for a second look as the scorpions fought to the death.

"I think I'm going to be sick," Catherine whispered, her face pale. Two of the men drew themselves away from the fray to step between them and the fight, as if shielding something inappropriate.

"Is this . . . something you boys do regularly?" Maggie asked, trying to cover up her discomfort.

The apologetic soldier nodded. "It's not high-class entertainment, but there's not much to do around here."

"And we kill the winner straight after," the other assured her, as if that made things any better. That prompted a small moan from Catherine, who banded her arms around her gold gown.

Maggie grinned in a way she hoped was convincing. "I guess I should thank you for making the desert a little safer, then."

She'd heard there were scorpions out here, but she'd never seen one, so she assumed they were either rare or one of Judith's exaggerations to get a reaction out of Catherine. What if there were more back at the camp, crawling into the shoes she'd left out to dry after yesterday's rain? *Ugh. What a thought.*

Cheers resounded from half of the men as the match presumably ended. She noticed that Howie accepted a handout of a few coins, three cigarettes, and half a chocolate bar from the tall, burly private doling out the winnings. "Thank you, my boy, and better luck next time."

"Let's hope my odds are better when we finally lead the assault on Italy," the private said good-naturedly, dimples appearing in his cheeks with a wry smile. He looked oddly familiar, though Maggie wasn't sure why.

She couldn't help aiming a jab Howie's way. "Taking what you can get from our soldiers' paychecks, I see."

She'd thought he'd see it as a joke, but his usually jovial face darkened. "What's it to you?"

"Nothing much. Just doesn't seem like something you'd want Douglas knowing about."

He reacted like she'd outright threatened to blackmail him. "It's not like you caught me patronizing a French bordello. Which, by the way, many of your hardworking soldiers aren't above doing."

She didn't rise to that bait, though she knew it was true. There was a lot of activity in the seamier parts of towns that the army didn't encourage but tacitly allowed.

"Anyway," he continued, "games of chance aren't strictly prohibited, not by the army and not by the USO."

"The lady does have a point, though," the burly private who Howie had taken his winnings from interjected unexpectedly. "Just because it's not expressly forbidden doesn't mean my father will like it. He always did make rules around the rules."

Maggie nodded along with him until his words sunk in. "Did you say . . . ?"

But the private was looking past her, and when she turned, she saw Douglas standing a few yards off, staring at them, more in shock than disapproval.

The private gave a casual wave. "Hey there, Pops. I figured you'd track me down sooner or later."

18

April 5, 1943
Oujda, Morocco

Pops? Catherine met Maggie's eyes, also wide. So she hadn't been the only one who didn't know Mr. Douglas's son was an enlisted man.

"Teddy," Mr. Douglas blurted, "how have you been?"

"I don't answer to Teddy out here, or even Theo. It's Private Douglas." Instead of embracing or giving each other a hearty handshake, Theo stood apart from his father, arms folded across his uniform. "What are you doing here, Pops?"

The edge to his tone told Catherine that this would not be a heartwarming reunion. She remembered her conversation with Mr. Douglas outside of Rabat. *"Less than enthusiastic,"* he'd said of his children's relationship with him.

Mr. Douglas, it turned out, had quite a gift for understatement.

"We should go," Catherine whispered to Maggie and Howie, but they made no move to disperse with the soldiers who had ducked away with the flimsy as soon as they spotted Mr. Douglas, perhaps confusing him with an officer.

And despite herself, Catherine felt it would be awkward to make their excuses now. If there was a pause in the conversation . . .

"Didn't you get my letter?" Mr. Douglas asked his son.

The private gave the barest hint of a nod. "I thought you were joking. Guess I shouldn't have underestimated you. Willing to cross an ocean to make sure your son was behaving himself, eh?"

"That was not how I intended it to come across."

"Well, here you are, after all." Even though Theo was clapping his hands together, he might as well have been slapping Mr. Douglas's face, the way the man winced. "Congratulations. Very theatrical."

"It wasn't like that." He shifted nervously and held out the parcel he'd held tucked under his arm. "I've brought you some sundry items from home, razors, chocolates, cigarettes. Difficult to get over here, I'm told."

Theo didn't step forward to claim the package. "One grand gesture can't make up for years of being away."

"I know that. I just—I just wanted to see you again."

"Well, now you've seen me." He turned stiffly, marching away like his commanding officer had barked an order to fall in. "Good-bye, Pops."

"Good-bye, Teddy."

Whether Mr. Douglas had repeated the nickname out of habit or to goad his son into turning around to correct him, the young man continued steadily on, his long shadow giving shade to the parched ground.

Catherine's family had never been particularly religious, but on the rare occasions they'd attended church for social reasons, she'd been drawn to a stained-glass window depicting the return of the prodigal son.

She was vague on the details, but there was something about the story of forgiveness and a welcome home that felt deeply true, the way a concerto arranged itself in beautiful, resonant harmonies.

This, it seemed, was not going to be that story.

Catherine knew she should leave to spare Mr. Douglas further embarrassment, but the forlorn look on the poor man's face compelled her to stay. "I'm sorry. We didn't mean to intrude."

"What?" He blinked, turning to her, as if just then realizing they were still there. "Oh. No, no. Don't worry about that. You were bound to discover my failings sooner or later."

She winced at the bluntness in his voice. "It can't be as bad as all that."

"Teddy and I never got along particularly well, but we had an especially sharp argument before he left to enlist." The story seemed to pour out of him unprompted as he stared off in the direction his son had walked away. "I told him he was throwing his life away by joining up, that I could pull some strings to get him into a protected job. He told me to . . ." Mr. Douglas coughed. "Well, he . . . refused."

Maggie toed the grass, seeming to want to look anywhere but at Mr. Douglas. "He'll get over it eventually, I bet." While she was probably trying to be helpful, Mr. Douglas seemed to deflate even more at the empty condolence.

"Yes, well, we'll see." He tore open a flap of the brown paper. "It's silly. But I'd hoped . . . I brought him this." He reached into the parcel and took out a baseball, crisply white with nary a grass stain in sight. "When Teddy was young, we'd go to the empty lot near the house and throw around a baseball every night, no matter how tired I was from work. But then I switched from insurance to agenting."

Howie grunted. "You had to look after your family."

"Yes, that's exactly what I said at the time." He palmed the ball, tossing and catching it with ease, without seeming to realize he was doing it. "And I worked hard, formed connections, made a name for myself—and lost my son."

"You haven't lost him. Not yet." Catherine spoke the words with more force than she'd meant to. There was just something about the sadness in Mr. Douglas's eyes. . . . It reminded her of the lost, lonely feeling that swirled inside her when she heard her parents shouting in another of their quarrels.

"Sorry about this, old boy," Howie said, slapping Mr. Douglas on the back. "I didn't know he was your son, or I wouldn't have joined in their game."

Catherine had a long career of offering smiles when she least felt like doing so, and she could spot the false smile Mr. Douglas offered them with the speed of a counterfeiter pointing out a false bill. "I am the one who should be sorry. I shouldn't have put all this on you. You'll be doing me a service if you forget all about it."

He handed Catherine his peace-offering parcel, one side still torn open, *Teddy* written on the brown paper as the only address. "Here. Find some GI who will want this. I'll be checking in with the Engineering Corps to test our microphones."

It was a reminder that soon, they'd perform for Theo's unit while he moped about in his tent, close enough to hear the applause, perhaps, but far enough away to send his father a message.

"Boy, that makes me spitting mad," Maggie said, shielding her face from the sun and looking after Mr. Douglas, trudging toward their stage with shoulders slumped. Howie took a few steps after him, but he seemed to think better of it, shaking his head sadly.

"Poor old Douglas comes all this way just to see his son, and he treats him like dirt," Maggie continued. "I'd have a few choice words for Theodore, I tell you what."

"I don't think your choice words would help," Catherine

said. Theo seemed far too guarded for that. He and Maggie would likely get into a shouting match that would echo through the barracks.

It really isn't any of your business, a reprimanding instinct lectured her, honed by years of Father's insistence on privacy and minding one's own affairs, unlike her meddling mother. It would be much easier to drift over to the stage and greet audience members before the show.

And yet . . . maybe it wouldn't do any harm to speak to Theo, listen to him, perhaps ask a few questions. After all, Mr. Douglas had come all this way. If there was anything at all Catherine could do to help, she ought to try.

She decided to try the makeshift canteen first, a plywood arrangement with a hand-painted sign, a few amenities, and a canvas awning shielding some tattered checkerboards. Sure enough, a group of soldiers stopped gawking long enough to ask if they could help her with anything.

Catherine turned on her most winning smile, bright as a spotlight, before she could think about what she was doing. "Actually, yes. I wonder if you could help me locate an old friend of mine."

She'd guessed correctly that Theo Douglas had leave that day, which would explain how he had time to go capture scorpions instead of jumping off the practice paratrooper towers that loomed in the distance. They'd eventually tracked him down kneeling by a water trough scrubbing his spare uniform.

He'd looked puzzled when she greeted him like an old friend, thanking her guides for their help to dismiss them. Then, slowly, awareness turned his expression sour. "Ah. You're one of Father's girls."

She didn't have to fake the outrage in her voice, drawing herself up straight. "*Excuse* me. What are you implying?"

At least Theo had the good manners to look embarrassed. "Sorry, I didn't mean that the way it sounded. Father was never one of those Hollywood philanderers. I only meant you're the latest in his endless quest for some big star."

"My *name* is Catherine Duquette."

He wiped his wet hands on his trousers and shook hers. She could smell the bland laundry soap on his skin. "Sounds like you already know who I am. Go on, then. Why are you here, Miss Duquette?"

This was it. Her last chance to avoid conflict by saying something trite like wanting to meet him since his father had talked so much about him.

"I just wanted to say that—I think you're being too harsh on your father. He's a good man, Theo."

In an instant, Theo crossed his arms across his chest, the wary look in his eyes turning stony cold. "If strangers have to tell me how good my own father is, maybe you're the one without the whole story."

Catherine stood mute. How could she argue with that? It was likely the same response she'd give if anyone tried to assure her of her parents' good intentions. "That's possible. But people do change, and I genuinely believe he's trying." A derisive snort from Theo was the only response she got. "Just give him a chance. And for goodness' sake, come to the USO show this afternoon."

"Why should I?"

Maybe she should have flirted, winked, and said that she'd hate to have him miss it. Dressed in her shining lamé gown, she probably made quite a picture. But it wouldn't have been sincere, so instead, she decided on the truth. "Because your father would be overjoyed to see you there. I rather think it's the entire reason he took this assignment."

Theo scoffed, turning back to give his jacket a particularly abrasive scrub. "Not likely. Like I said, it's just one more try to grab a rising star that'll never come. He can keep his show."

"Suit yourself." She certainly wasn't going to force him to attend the USO performance. Besides, a small part of her knew she was being hypocritical. Wouldn't she be wary if her family claimed to have changed? Once broken, trust was difficult to repair.

She knew Mr. Douglas as a manager and a man with the best of intentions, but she hadn't been there during the years of what Theo saw as neglect.

"One more thing." She set the parcel down next to the trough, far enough away that it wouldn't get wet, and tossed him the ball. It dropped too far to the left, forcing Theo to dive to catch it. Catherine had none of Maggie's skill at baseball. "He was trying to give this to you, along with an apology, but clearly the timing wasn't right."

The expression on Theo's face as he palmed the ball, tossing it into the air, was difficult to read. But he lifted his head and gave her a nod. "Thanks."

"You're welcome." Though Catherine wasn't sure she deserved any thanks. For all she knew, she'd only made things worse. But at least Theo's unit would have a brand-new baseball to use during their time off.

She walked away without looking back, trying, without much luck, not to feel guilty about the letter from her father, crumpled in a waste bin back in Rabat. Hadn't she done the same thing, not letting him have a chance to speak?

That's different. Father was almost certainly planning to guilt or manipulate her into returning home, and Mother was likely equally furious she'd missed the audition with the New York Philharmonic. They had nothing of Mr. Douglas's earnestness.

Still, for the first time since she'd gotten on the train in St. Paul, she wondered if she'd done the right thing in leaving the way she had.

There's no going back now. As the saying went, the show must go on, with or without the son of the prodigal father.

Catherine felt a tickle at her ear and adjusted the pin that held the artificial red rose in place, the one she tossed to the audience at the end of her act. While it made Maggie gag—really, the girl had no sense of romance—she loved the idea of leaving a trail of roses across the African battlefields.

Onstage, Mr. Douglas was giving his usual introduction to their show. "The USO is with you boys one hundred percent. We hope our program brings good memories from home, lifts your spirits, and . . ." His words faltered, his mouth going slack.

To her knowledge, Catherine had never seen Mr. Douglas at a loss for words, especially in his carefully memorized script, not even when one of his speeches was broken up by military police shouting at the front row to back away from the stage. Today, though, he couldn't seem to find his place again, just stared at the audience. Catherine followed his gaze.

There, lounging on the ground about three rows back, was Theo. Not beaming up at his father with a proud smile, but he was there and, from the looks of things, ready to enjoy the show.

Her heart fluttered in the way it did when a clashing chord resolved into harmony, and Catherine gave him a little wave from the wings of the stage.

"You're an insufferable bootlicker, you know that?"

Judith's voice in her ear made her startle, and when she whirled around, the woman was wearing a daring ensemble, maroon with a plunging neckline and fringed sleeves, and the same old scowl as ever.

"What do you mean?" Catherine replied, while onstage Mr. Douglas had recovered and was turning the stage over to Howie.

"I heard you went after Mr. Douglas's kid today." Her mouth took on a sardonic tilt. "What, did you promise him a kiss if he showed up?"

On cue, her face burned hot. "Certainly not! Why would I do that?"

"Because you know Mr. Douglas would reward you with the contract and a cash prize and half his kingdom."

"I don't intend to tell him." She had decided no such thing until that very moment, and it was clear from her expression that Judith didn't believe it, but it didn't seem right to take credit for Theo's change of heart.

"You've got the biggest bargaining chip in the game, and you're really going to toss it aside?"

She took a deep breath and forced herself to meet Judith's eyes. "People aren't bargaining chips, Judith."

For a moment, Judith's dramatic eyebrows rose in surprise, but she'd mastered her expression only a second later. "Everyone has their price, darling. You of all people should know that."

Catherine gritted her teeth against a nasty retort as Judith flounced away. She wouldn't let the diva's sour grapes ruin this moment for her. It certainly wouldn't have any effect on Mr. Douglas, who was watching his son like he was Roosevelt or Churchill, anxious to see if he laughed at Howie's antics.

Still, at the end of her act, she tossed her rose in the opposite direction from where Theo was sitting. No sense in looking like she was trying to curry favor with Mr. Douglas. If she was recommended for the contract, she wanted everyone to know that it was on her own merits, fair and square.

19

April 11, 1943
Oran, Algeria

The thing about breaking the rules, Maggie had learned, was that you needed the right timing.

The week before, they'd left the region around Oujda and crossed the border from Morocco into Algeria, then celebrated their entrance to a new country by taking to the stage for three shows in quick succession. From there, they'd worked their way eastward at an exhausting pace before arriving in the coastal city of Oran, a hub for American troops.

Now it was Sunday, their day off. Although Maggie had to share her room at the Hotel Continental with Judith, the other woman was occupied with her extensive makeup regimen to prepare for an evening date with an army officer. That left Maggie alone with a free afternoon just a short walk away from the Mediterranean in a city that was home to the chapel of Santa Cruz, an Ottoman citadel, and a rugged coast that had seen ancient conquerors and seaside battles. How was a girl supposed to stay inside with all that nearby?

Maggie gave the hotel lobby a surreptitious glance, making sure no one from the troupe had a similar idea, and saw no familiar faces among the guests flagging down uniformed bellhops or asking questions in French at the front desk.

She had changed into civilian clothes, her lightest white blouse and blue skirt. A man in uniform would blend in as just another soldier on leave, but women in army duds were much more conspicuous.

She'd just tied her hair back with a bandanna to keep it off her neck when a voice to her left startled her.

"If you're planning on seeing a bullfight, I'm told they converted the ring into a military hospital. Although sightseeing is against the rules, if you recall."

Gabriel, dressed in his perfectly pressed uniform, crossed from behind one of the courtyard's pillars to stand beside her.

It was like a magician, she supposed, to appear out of nowhere at the most unexpected times. It was also deeply annoying. "Keep your voice down, would you?" Maggie flinched at the sound of footsteps behind them, but when she turned, she only saw a porter conveying a load of luggage to the elevator.

Now that he'd caught her, she might as well make her pitch or risk him running back to Douglas and getting her a demerit next to her name on his almighty clipboard. "It's a beautiful afternoon for a walk by the ocean. Nothing dangerous, and I'll be back by dinner. All I'm asking is that you go back to your room and pretend you never saw me."

He didn't so much as uncross his arms, much less step out of the way. "It might not be safe for a woman to travel alone."

She'd thought of that, had even sized up the neighborhood of their hotel, but it was midafternoon, with plenty of daylight to return before dark. "I can hold my own. Anyway, nothing you say can stop me."

Gabriel sighed wearily. "I was fairly sure of that." She was just about to compliment him on his quick learning, when he added, "That's why I'm coming with you."

She hesitated, on the one hand, annoyed by the smugness in his tone, and on the other . . . it would be an easy way to get him to stop arguing with her in the hotel lobby where Douglas could see them at any moment. "All right. I could use the company."

They could get along for an afternoon, surely. And this way, she thought, smiling to herself at her cleverness, if he changed his mind and decided to report her to Douglas, he'd have to turn himself in too.

They stepped from under the hotel's awning into a swirl of unfamiliar sounds and smells. The streets, dotted with swaying shade from the occasional palm or cypress tree, were wide and well-maintained, and they dodged several buses taking travelers to and from the city's train station.

Only a few streets away, the bazaars their unit had driven past filled the air with color and sound. The produce stands, butcher stalls, and vendors sold goods and souvenirs of all kinds. A display of heaped spices and woven mats sat next to one of ceramic figurines of the Virgin Mary and across from a seller with a hutch of live rabbits. Some, spotting American visitors, shouted out pitches for their wares, but Maggie kept walking. Unlike Catherine, she couldn't speak a word to the locals in either French or Arabic.

The men and women who crowded the street were a mix of French, Arab, and even some Spaniards, with a few American soldiers on leave standing out in khaki drab. Older bearded men, protected from the sun by long robes and fezzes, sat in groups on sidewalk cafés drinking tea or playing dominoes, while a younger set walked about in American-style fashions, with pomaded hair and narrow neckties. Shoe shiners with boxes of brushes called out next to empty armchairs, eager to buff the dust from the street off the feet of the wealthy, and children dodged between legs, laughing and playing. The coverings and long skirts worn by the few Berber and Arab women she saw, no matter the heat, made Maggie vow never to complain again about having to wear heels to perform.

She closed her eyes and tried to get the feel of the city, letting the busyness of it surround her.

Gabriel's voice entered the sounds she'd immersed herself in. "Are you all right?" His face was creased in concern, and she realized how it must look to stop in the middle of the street like she'd gotten sunstroke.

"I'm fine. Just listening to the music."

He frowned, looking around the market as if expecting to see street performers.

She didn't bother explaining, since it would make her seem even crazier. To her, most places had a song, the rhythm and harmonies coming from all the everyday sounds. Oran's was a steady, ancient melody with a jaunty harmony fluting over it. As different from Chicago as ocean and desert, but still somehow similar.

Once they were past the sand-colored city walls, Maggie heard a different music, one she didn't have anything to compare to: the song of the sea.

Breakwaters jutted out into the busy harbor, and the fort on the jagged cliffs kept careful watch, the slope of the Atlas Mountains visible in the distance, as if someone had found a flat area near the sea and tossed a city into it. The water was clear and impossibly blue, like a second sky.

Maggie climbed as close as she dared, staying out of the way of the salty spray, her shoes sinking into the wet sand. She'd have to clean them off back at the hotel's shared bathroom to get rid of the evidence, but it was a small price to pay for being this close to the sea.

Gabriel sat down on one of the larger rocks, and Maggie

hoped the walk hadn't been too much for his braced leg. "I've never seen anything like this back home."

She thought about saying something poetic about the beauty of nature or whatnot, but that just wasn't her. "I'll say. I feel like I'm taking a vacation in someone else's life. Only I can't get too attached because it's all going to end soon."

"Some people might say it would be better to enjoy the moment."

"Some people are full of hot air," she joked, but Gabriel's face fell, so she added quickly, "Sorry, I didn't mean that. Anyway, it'll be something to tell my family about. None of them have been out of the country, except my brother, John, who does missionary work."

"Really? What country?"

Maggie found herself sketching out her colorful, religious family and the various adventures of growing up on Chicago's street corners, playing hymns and preaching to the outcasts of society. "It was a strange mix, you know? Dad was against drinking, dancing, and gambling and read to us from the family Bible after dinner every night. But I also celebrated my eighth birthday at the Salvation Army soup kitchen and sat in church next to prostitutes."

"That's why you weren't afraid to go out alone today," Gabriel said, more a statement than question.

She nodded anyway. "Big cities always feel like home to me. There are dangerous people out there, sure, but most are decent folks like any of us."

She turned away from the hypnotic waves to look at him and felt a different sort of pull. What did she really know about the man she'd been traveling with for weeks now? He didn't often speak up during travel or dinners, letting Judith and Howie carry most of the conversation. "How about you? Where did you grow up?"

Gradually, she drew Gabriel out to share stories of his

young life traveling the country with his father, also a magician. Then he described the varied personalities of his sisters—"all of whom talk so much there was rarely room for me to get a word in."

"What about that brace?" Maggie asked, a question that she'd been wondering for a while. "Have you always had to wear it?"

"No."

Maggie waited for him to go on, but Gabriel seemed to find that answer enough. Maybe she should have expected it to be a sensitive subject, but he'd been so open about everything else that she found herself surprised.

After a few moments of listening to the water break over the shore, Maggie cleared her throat. "The fish isn't real, right?"

His voice held genuine confusion. "Pardon?"

"I've figured that much out, anyway. The movement you see is just a silk tail swirling around."

He groaned, running a hand through his dark hair, which, Maggie had noticed when he sat down on a rock, had a bald patch starting near the back. She'd placed him somewhere in his thirties, so maybe it was inherited from his father. "This again?"

"If you're going to be all closed off about yourself, we have to talk about *something*. We can't just stand next to each other staring into the ocean in cold silence."

"Why not?"

Maggie studied his face until she was sure it wasn't a joke. The man genuinely thought that sounded like an ideal afternoon. "You are hopeless."

"Thank you," he replied gravely, and she thought she saw the twitch of a smile. "And to answer your question, yes, the goldfish in my act is artificial. It would be too difficult to keep a goldfish alive on a trek across Africa for a simple illusion."

She huffed. "Simple, he says. You're taunting me."

Gabriel let sand fall from his fingers for a moment, not denying the accusation. "If I gave you a hint, you'd have the trick figured out in a moment. That's why it's not wise for a magician to let anyone get too close. They might see things you'd rather keep hidden."

Well, well. The way Gabriel stared pointedly at her, she could guess he was talking about more than just his magic trick. Fine. If he didn't want to talk about his limp, that was fine with her. She could be cordial and businesslike, too, if she put her mind to it.

It felt like only an hour that they walked up and down the beach and climbed the rocky breakwater on the quay's eastern edge, but soon the sun threw down long palm shadows over the sand, and the sky turned the color of a melted cone of sherbet, pinks and oranges blurring together.

"We should probably be getting back," Maggie said reluctantly, dusting sand off her legs. "Early morning tomorrow and all that."

"What?" Gabriel feigned shock. "Was that a hint of responsibility I hear?"

"You bet it was. Just don't count on it happening again."

They joined several other travelers on the well-worn road into the city, including a group of GIs on leave who kept up a friendly chatter until they parted ways at the city gate.

"Companionable silence," Gabriel said unexpectedly.

Now it was Maggie's turn to quirk an eyebrow at him in confusion. "What's that?"

"You said earlier that we could stare out at the ocean in cold silence. I'd call it companionable silence. The sort you can share with a friend and not feel the need to fill the space."

She studied him, shifting uncomfortably. How long had it taken him to work up the courage to say that? "Why, Gabriel

Kaminski, I think the sea air's been good for you. That's the nicest thing you've ever said to me."

He took her arm as a car careened too close to the sidewalk and chuckled. "Just don't get any ideas about blackmailing me into breaking USO rules every Sunday."

She gave him a solid thwack on his arm. "You volunteered for this, buddy."

"Because I didn't want to have to search Oran's back alleys for you in the morning."

"Don't be so dramatic."

Teasing aside, she found she was grateful for Gabriel's company, for his thoughtful conversation and the reassuring strength of leaning against his arm, and not because the dimming light made the city feel threatening.

Back home, she'd always been one of the boys, palling around with her brother's friends. As the easy ask to go to the movies or dinner, she'd never suffered for a date, but her stern preacher-father had scared away anyone interested in going steady. Anyway, most of them would just as soon have her on their baseball team as their dance partner.

Gabriel felt different somehow.

It was the sun, maybe, or the ocean, tricking her into feeling like she was off on a grand adventure in one of those romance movies Catherine and the other Sweethearts had always been talking about back in America. All signs said Gabriel wasn't interested in her in that way. After all, he'd just described her as a friend, nothing more.

Still, what was the harm in pretending? As long as she felt like she was living someone else's life, why not enjoy strolling arm in arm with a young man?

They took in the evening sights of Oran in that same companionable silence, smelling tantalizing roast meat from restaurants, holding their breath when the foul coal-powered buses rumbled past, and watching swallows dip in the sunset, coming in to roost for the night.

As they turned a corner, Maggie stopped. Something seemed . . . out of place, like a discordant note in the usual bustle of the city.

Her eyes moved to the stately building dominating the block, a tricolored French flag flapping in the wind from its gate. The wall was marred with words scrawled in Arabic, the black paint still dripping. A crowd had gathered around it, mostly men, some clearly French, others Algerian. The two groups seemed to be divided, both staring at each other warily.

"We should go," Gabriel said, watching the crowd, his grip on her arm tightening.

"Just a minute. I want to find out what's happening." What was he worried about? Whatever the painted words said, no one here seemed violent. Most were simply muttering to one another in low tones. If the slogan was meant to spark discussion, it certainly had.

She thought back to the debris that had crashed into her head as a child on a Chicago street corner. Then again, it didn't take long for even peaceful scenes to turn ugly.

A young Algerian man wearing a fedora pointed at Gabriel's uniform, his voice full of excitement. "American!"

A string of French punctuated with a few English words followed, and the man's group of friends tightened around them. They didn't seem hostile—one even held out a hand for Gabriel to shake—but there were too many of them too close for Maggie's comfort. Besides that, she couldn't make out enough to understand what they wanted.

A shrill whistle added to the confusion, and she turned to see three men in dark uniforms marching in their direction. *Police,* shouted by the uniformed men and repeated by the bystanders hurrying to get out of the way, was one word that she recognized, but it didn't seem reassuring.

"Step back, please," Gabriel said, his voice rising with the heat of the people around them and the pitch of their voices. No one was listening to him, of course, worried that they'd be arrested. If he wasted time giving orders in a language no one here spoke, they'd be trampled for sure.

Maggie yanked on Gabriel's arm, pulling them both into the arch of a doorway just as a policeman grabbed the man who stood closest to the graffiti, hauling him away despite his protests.

That seemed to scare everyone else into clearing out, though Maggie noticed that the French residents were ignored entirely, left to look affronted and stare at the graffiti.

"What was that?" Gabriel asked, his voice shaking slightly.

"I don't know," Maggie said, "but we shouldn't have been in the middle of it." The safety of the hotel suddenly seemed far more inviting than stifling, and she let Gabriel take her arm again as they hurried down the street.

One of the policemen jogged over to them, perhaps noticing Gabriel's uniform. "Very sorry," he said, in heavily accented English filtered through a thick moustache. "Only some local—" He waved in the air like he was paging through an invisible dictionary for the right word.

"Protesters?" Maggie offered, and he shrugged, probably looking for something stronger. She decided not to tell the man that they'd been perfectly fine before he and his officers had made everyone panic.

"They protest, yes. Here, Morocco, everywhere. Now that you Americans are here, they think we French should leave." He chuckled to himself, as if the notion of an independent nation was a foolish one.

"Is that what the graffiti said?" Gabriel asked, pointing back toward the wall.

The policeman bobbed his head in a nod. "'Long Live America. Down with France. Algeria for Algerians.'" His words were laced with a disgust he didn't try to hide. "Please . . . go back to your hotel. And stay there. It is dangerous here."

But Maggie had to wonder, even as they obeyed the order, dangerous for whom?

"I'm sorry about all that," Gabriel said for the third time as they slipped into the lobby from the patio. "I should have insisted we stay here. We could have avoided that whole scene."

"You didn't have a choice, remember? I practically dragged you out sightseeing. Anyway, we're fine," Maggie reassured him, checking her skirt for any trace of their outing. "Just got a little up-close-and-personal experience with local politics, that's all."

Should she admit it?

Why not?

Still, Maggie didn't risk glancing over at Gabriel, unwilling to be caught blushing like a silly schoolgirl. "Although I have to say, I'm glad you were with me."

Gabriel laughed. "I could say the same about you. If it had been up to me, we would have been flattened when . . ."

The slight smile on his face dropped into dread, and Maggie turned to see Douglas storming toward them, his face red with anger. Maggie pulled her hand away from Gabriel's arm.

Oh no. This was like the day she'd been dismissed from the Sweethearts all over again. Would she lose this job too?

"There you are," Douglas said, his brows creased. "I see you've returned from your date."

"It wasn't a date," Maggie said hurriedly.

"Oh? Then Miss Blair was wrong in telling me that the two of you have been out together since we arrived at the hotel?"

How Judith had gotten this information, Maggie couldn't say, but she couldn't help being irritated at the insufferable tattletale. "Whatever she told you, I'm sure it was exaggerated."

Their tour manager cut an intimidating figure, dressed in his uniform, arms crossed and barring their way. "Would you care to explain yourself, then? I hope you won't deny that the two of you were out sightseeing against regulations."

"Well . . . yes," Gabriel said, but Maggie interrupted before he could go on. Better to let her take the brunt of this one. She gave Douglas the short version, taking care to emphasize that Gabriel had only tagged along because he'd felt obligated to escort her and leaving out the bit with the protesters. No need to make things worse than they already were.

Douglas's eyebrows remained sternly at half-mast. "The USO's rules are put in place for a reason. Do you realize that if we'd needed to make a last-minute change in schedule, I wouldn't have had the slightest idea where to find you?"

"Judith's been out to officers' clubs three evenings at least," Maggie protested. Though she knew it was a flimsy defense, it didn't seem fair not to bring it up.

"Which she clears with me in advance," Douglas said sternly, "*and* which is permitted under USO rules."

Well, that knocked out that line of reasoning. Maggie found herself surprised that Judith bothered about all of that with her devil-may-care attitude, but apparently, she'd figured out how to avoid lectures like this.

"If the two of you wish to have the slightest chance at the Pepsodent contract," Douglas continued, "you'll refrain from any further *excursions*."

That little barb stung, mostly because Gabriel visibly stiffened. She hadn't meant to do anything to hurt his chances in the competition.

"Yes, sir," they both chorused, like children forced to sit with dunce caps in the corner.

As soon as he was gone, Maggie turned to Gabriel. "Well, that wasn't the way I meant for this evening to end." How to apologize? It wasn't her fault, exactly, that he'd offered to come, but without her, Gabriel wouldn't be on Douglas's blacklist.

"I thought you weren't interested in the contract." His voice was as level as ever, but there was something vaguely accusatory in his gaze.

That's right. She hadn't told him, or any of her fellow performers, though they'd certainly find out now. "I-I wasn't, but . . ." She straightened. Why should she have to explain herself? It was really none of his business, and the betrayed look he was giving her was completely uncalled for. "Isn't a girl allowed to change her mind?"

"Of course." His words were gracious, but his voice was as cold as the ocean. He nodded. "Goodnight, Maggie."

Whatever magic spell she'd imagined the Mediterranean had cast over them was clearly over.

Maggie might have put a little too much force into the false snore she gave when she heard Judith open the door to their shared room. "You're not fooling anyone, darling. I know you're awake."

The springs on the other bed creaked as Judith threw herself on it, more like a child than a fully grown woman. "I heard Floyd cut your date with Mr. Kaminski short."

"It wasn't a date," Maggie insisted again, propping herself up on one elbow. Why did everyone insist on putting the two of them together as a couple?

Judith smirked, leaving a smudge of lipstick just above her upper lip. "Fine, an illicit rendezvous then. Have it your way.

Silly of you to try to sneak out of the room like that. As if I wouldn't notice and follow you to see what you were up to."

Maggie felt herself going red from anger. "You have no right to criticize. Didn't you just come from dining out with an officer?"

"Well, of course, dear. You certainly can't refuse one of our best and brightest, not during wartime when they haven't got much by way of female companionship."

Any attempt to make Judith feel guilty would be wasted time and effort. Instead, Maggie tried to beat some life into the pancake-flat pillows of the hotel's bed. "Anyway, you didn't have to rat us out."

Another shrug. "Break the rules, face the consequences." At least she didn't pretend she had only been worried about their safety or some nonsense. Judith might be a schemer, but she was straightforward about it.

"I didn't even want Gabriel to come along. He was only worried I couldn't look after myself."

Judith leaned back, and Maggie was slapped with a musky perfume. "Isn't that just like a man? Heaven knows how any women make their way in the world without them."

"Gabriel's not like that," Maggie found herself saying. "He means well."

"Hmm." This one syllable was delivered as Judith lifted hairpins from the dozens of places she had secreted them, until her dark brown hair dangled past her shoulders. "Better watch yourself, doll."

"Don't call me that." The reply was so instinctive that it took Maggie a moment to process what she had said. "What do you mean?"

Judith shrugged, the extravagant crepe bow on her shoulder rustling with the movement. "Just that our Gabriel is an ambitious young man. And he wants that contract at least as much as you do." She put a finger in the air, as if to interrupt a protest Maggie hadn't planned to make. "And don't try that nonsense about how you don't care about fame and fortune."

It was irritating to realize that by putting her name back into the running, she'd done just as Judith had predicted, but Maggie skipped over that. "Do you think he'll try to sabotage me like you did by turning us in to Douglas?"

Judith didn't even bother to defend herself, brushing her thick hair with even strokes. "Nah. Not his style. But if Douglas chooses you to audition for the Bob Hope tour, I wouldn't be surprised if Gabriel asks you to give it up so he can have it. Lays it on thick about how he needs it *so* much more than you. Maybe he's not as genuine as you think."

She shook her head, smirking at Judith. "You just don't trust men."

"True. But I also don't trust that one in particular. He's far too clever. Reminds me of my first husband: ambitious and charming with lots of practice creating illusions." She tapped her temple with a long red nail. "Keep a wary eye out, darling, that's all I'm saying."

It was only Judith trying to stir things up. Maggie had learned the woman was like a lit stick of dynamite. For her, blowing things apart wasn't malicious; it was her nature.

Still, as Maggie tried to sleep, the conversation raised a few doubts that hadn't been there before. Gabriel had spoken several times about what the contract would mean to him, and then there was his frustration when he'd learned Maggie was trying for it too. Was he trying to make her feel guilty about advancing her career?

Well, in any case, it wouldn't work. Maggie had always been one to go after what she wanted, and no man was going to stop her, not even one who called her a friend and looked spiffy in a tuxedo. If that was Gabriel's strategy, he'd soon find that he'd greatly underestimated Maggie McCleod.

Report to the USO Home Office
Floyd Douglas, Foxhole Circuit, Variety Unit 14
April 11, 1943

Very little time to write today (off to Algiers shortly with an intense schedule before us). We've added more performances, and the pace of touring is starting to wear on the troupe, myself included, but we all know we must maximize our time while we are here.

It should be noted for future groups that the no-sightseeing rule must be strictly enforced for the safety of the group. Today, two of my troupe members deliberately broke this rule. I had been seriously considering recommending Maggie McCleod to the committee for the Pepsodent contract as a comedienne who could, with the right script team, equal greats like Bob Hope or Abbot and Costello. The fact that she seems to be unable to follow the simplest of regulations is making me reconsider.

In the future, I would discourage coeducational variety units that include single women and single men, 4-F or not. Tour managers are not meant to double as prom chaperones.

Must get to bed. We're all exhausted, so I am hoping for a good night's sleep.

Sincerely,
Floyd Douglas

From Sterling Warner to Floyd Douglas

April 8, 1943

Floyd,

Had to drop you a line, since I searched your last report

a dozen times and didn't see a thing about Teddy. Did you find his unit? Get a chance to talk to him?

Spill the beans, Floyd. I want the details.

Your friend,
Warnie

From Floyd Douglas to Sterling Warner

April 11, 1943

Dear Warnie,

I know you think my reports ought to resemble some kind of diary, but I really don't think the USO is interested in my relationship with my son, which is why I left it out.

However, since you're an old friend . . .

Teddy attended the performance and told me afterward it was "a good show." And, best of all, after I've written unanswered letters to him for a full year, just yesterday, he sent me a postcard. With three sentences, none of them angry.

It's not much. But it's something. More than we had before, as you know. I can thank the USO for making it possible, as well as one of my performers. I have a hunch that Miss Catherine Duquette may have had something to do with my son's change of heart. There's more to our sheltered socialite than meets the eye, it seems.

That's all the time I have to spare for you—I'm sure you can use your Hollywood imagination and spin out the whole touching reunion. If you write it into a screenplay, be sure I get a cut of the profits.

Floyd

20

April 13, 1943
Algiers, Algeria

Catherine had stayed in hotels with marble ballrooms, champagne-and-caviar menus, and even a pool inlaid with tile mosaics designed to look like a Roman bath, but she'd never before slept in one with mosquito netting draped over the bed.

Still, the Hotel Aletti seemed like paradise after a long day of travel, not the least because her room was private. Maggie and Judith were in their own rooms several doors down, unable to argue or wake her up with snoring or make fun of her makeup routine.

With a contented sigh, she sprawled on the bed, staring at the tottering electric ceiling fan trying to make up for the heat of the stuffy third-floor room.

The windows were half-covered in a hasty swath of cardboard, presumably for blackout regulations, though a wide border of glass let the last of the evening's light into the gloomy room. Catherine pulled open the creaky French doors to explore the balcony. She stood still for a few moments, letting the sea air settle into her lungs and watching the stars wink from the night's horizon toward the Mediterranean bay that carved a blue-gray crescent into the steep hillside.

Alger la Blanche, the French called it. "A city clothed in white," she murmured, staring out at the lime-whitewashed buildings below, their outlines faintly visible even in the twilight. "Like a bride."

Her room had no private bath—"you have to have a uniform with at least four stripes for that," Mr. Douglas had told her when she asked—but there was a decent writing desk beside the bed. Back inside the room, Catherine took her dual jewelry box and stationery kit, and drew out her favorite fountain pen, an envelope, and a sheet of paper from underneath the packet of Leo's letters.

As she replaced it, she paused. The top one was folded outward, and Catherine could read some of the lines in the handwriting that had become so familiar to her in a few short months.

You know, Catherine, you're the most fascinating woman I've ever met. Promise me you'll write back soon.

The sight filled her with a pang of regret. If only she could write to him—and know her letter would reach him.

But that wasn't worth dwelling on. Fate had brought Leo to her in the first place. She had to believe they would find each other again.

Instead, she wrote a familiar St. Paul address on the envelope.

Dear Lorraine,

I must say, I've had more opportunities to practice my French in a month here than all our years at school, though

I've had to learn some additional military vocabulary. It truly is lovely here. I know you'd do anything to stand beside me now.

She paused the pen long enough that a blot gathered in the margin. Was that really true? As girls, she and her friend had dreamed together of travel and adventure, but maybe, married and expecting a child, Lorraine was beyond all that now. Catherine knew Father would have been perfectly happy if she had married well after completing her studies, like her friend. Though Mother would have been appalled, encouraging her daughter to dazzle the social scene while enjoying her youth and freedom.

Instead, she'd managed to choose a route that neither of them fully approved of.

Enough of that. This was Lorraine she was writing to, not her parents. No matter how hard she tried to put them out of her mind, they were still there whenever her thoughts drifted.

Catherine jotted a few cheerful and censor-approved highlights, leaving the letter on the blotter to be delivered to Mr. Douglas in the morning.

Just as she was getting out her nightdress to collapse for the evening, the high whine of sirens cut through the quiet.

Catherine gasped, and a moment later, the electric lights went out, leaving everything in blackness. An air raid. The hotel, it seemed, didn't trust their guests to turn off their lights, not when the stakes were approaching Nazi bombers.

What to do? She'd participated in drills back in America, with volunteer wardens handing out citations for those who forgot to pull the drapes, but never something like this.

While she debated, noises of confusion were already rising in the hallway. Fumbling with arms outstretched so as not to bruise herself on the furniture, she made her way to the door, where other guests were rushing about, ghostly shadows in the gloom.

Flashlights and even a few flickering candles cut swaths of light into the hallway's darkness, along with words bellowed in a commanding tone. "*Restez calmes, s'il vous plaît.*"

Mother would have been dismayed that the shock of the moment caused her to stare uncomprehendingly until the same voice spoke in English. "This is an air raid. Please be calm and proceed to the lower level."

Even if Catherine hadn't understood the instructions, the stampede of worried guests, stronger than any current, would have carried her down the stairs, past the main level, and down to the wine cellar. It was large enough to have space for all of the guests. Exposed brick walls peeked through an impressive stock of barrels and bottles. The blackout conditions, apparently, only applied aboveground, because dim electric lighting gave everything a bluish cast and left long shadows on the floor.

The hotel staff continued to shout commands, fighting to be heard over guests shouting the names of friends or protesting being shoved about.

"What are they saying?" a mustachioed man in shirtsleeves demanded of anyone within range.

"Stay calm and move farther in," Catherine translated. Sound advice. Mr. Douglas had told them that the hotel was nearly packed full, so their emergency shelter would soon be as well.

Catherine obeyed the command, pulling away from the press of people and searching for a familiar face.

There. Judith, wrapped in a long tweed overcoat, sat against the far wall, her musette bag at her feet, with a look that made others keep a ring of distance from her despite the instructions to move in closer. Catherine ducked around a rack of bottles, corks pointing outward, and sidled up next to her.

"I see you had time to dress." Judith undid a button on her coat to reveal the silk sheen of her negligee underneath. "A sweet colonel lent me this to keep us all decent down here. Though he took a good long look first."

Catherine blushed on Judith's behalf, shifting to shield her from anyone watching. "I hadn't changed for the night."

"Good luck for you." Judith reached into her musette bag and pulled out a fruit. "Orange?"

"No, thank you." How could anyone eat at a time like this?

Catherine shivered, watching Judith tear into the orange's peel, a mist of juice falling to the scuffed tile floor as the sirens continued to blare. "Did you bring all your belongings?"

"Near enough. With the lights gone out, the maids or the prostitutes who swarm the officers' quarters are probably rifling through all our valuables by now, taking anything that looks expensive." She regarded the rack of bottles next to them. "Should've brought a corkscrew. We could have made a party of this."

But Catherine wasn't listening, caught on Judith's first cynical observation. "Do you really think our rooms might be robbed?"

Judith shrugged. "Sure. Looted, I'd call it, given the circumstances. It happens all the time. But anything really worth taking will be in the hotel safe, which should be all right unless a Nazi misses the harbor and lays an egg right on top of us." As she threw out the army slang, she gave another appraising glance around her. "Maybe we could break a bottle open and claim it was tremors from the bombing."

Catherine could picture her wallet with her USO ID, her violin case, and worst of all, her jewelry box, abandoned on the writing desk. Anyone looking to profit from the extinguished lights and unlocked rooms would surely find it easy pickings. Inside were her pearl necklace, diamond earrings, a golden brooch from Grand-mère . . . and Leo's letters.

"How long until the planes are overhead?" she pressed, as a group of officers jostled in next to them.

Judith shrugged. "Depends on how much warning they get here. Quite a bit, probably, with the coastal defenses and all. I'd say fifteen, maybe twenty minutes?"

Plenty of time to slip back up to her third-floor room, grab her valuables, and get out.

If Judith was right. Who could say if she was an expert on air raids? But Catherine had to take the chance.

"I'll be back," she said, slipping through the flow of people shuffling into the available space, like a drowning woman flailing against the current.

Would she do it? Did she dare?

Don't think. Just act.

Uniformed members of the hotel staff hurried through the narrow walkways partitioned among the throngs, answering questions and offering assurances in French and broken English. Some dispensed blankets to those either ill-prepared for the chill of the cellar or embarrassed about being caught out in their nightclothes.

Catherine had almost reached the stairs when one of them blocked her way, his face somber. "*Arrêtez.* You cannot come this way."

"I must go back. My child is still—" she began in English before remembering and changing languages, pleading in French, "My daughter is missing. I must find her." The lie was the first thing to come to mind, the only reason they might let her out of the relative safety of the cellar.

Maybe he was a father, or perhaps her pleading eyes were more effective than her hasty falsehood, but the man stepped aside, glancing swiftly about as if to make sure the hotel manager wasn't watching, before handing her his candle. "*Dépêchez-vous.*"

Certainly, she would hurry. She banished the flicker of guilt for lying to the poor man, but it had to be done. Her violin was her livelihood, and the jewelry alone was worth her entire year's salary with the Sweethearts. But most irreplaceable of all were Leo's letters. She wasn't about to lose them, not after they had survived a cross-country journey, U-boat-threatened ocean, and trek through the desert.

She shielded the flame from any draft that might extinguish it, her heart pounding. No one she passed on the stairwell stopped her, all of them shouting names or questions over the sirens, heedless of the young woman going the wrong way, back into danger.

The third floor was eerily empty, and Catherine held the candle with a trembling hand, eyes scanning the room numbers to find her own. She'd pushed open the door to 308 when a sudden hush fell over the hall.

Having sounded the warning, the sirens left Algiers in the hands of God or Fate or whatever one believed in, and the only sound now would be the planes and their deadly cargo, dropped carelessly on the city.

Or the navy ships. The ones she had seen bobbing in the harbor from her balcony only an hour ago. She snatched her violin case from the foot of the bed and stumbled across the carpet to the writing desk.

A distant roar broke the silence, and Catherine held her breath, hand clutching the jewelry box. Could that be the drone of bomber engines? It had none of the menacing qualities that played behind the newsreels or in the war movies at the cinema, just an ordinary mechanical roar growing steadily louder.

The metal clamp of the ceiling fan began to clatter, the floor trembling beneath her. The planes were passing by now, surely not close enough to—

Some part of her recognized that the sound rocking through the room must be an explosion, though her mind only registered a concussive sound and violent jolt that nearly knocked her off her feet to the plush carpet below, followed by a sharp shattering.

Catherine cried out, tried to dodge away, but she felt pain against her face. Refusing to drop the violin case or jewelry box, she felt a warm trickle on her cheek. Blood.

She clenched her teeth against the woozy feeling that upended her stomach and made her ankles buckle, but the room still pitched around her. From the bombs or was she . . . ?

Vaguely, as her knees hit the hotel carpet and her eyes closed, she could hear that the sirens had started again, but soon, she couldn't hear them—or anything—anymore.

21

April 13, 1943
Algiers, Algeria

Leaning against the brick wall, Maggie had a new appreciation for their British allies and what they endured during the Blitz. Being underground should make her feel safer, but even here, the sirens worked their way into her head, setting her every nerve on edge.

A glance around made it easy to tell the military personnel from the civilians, even though most were in nightwear. The army and navy men were the ones who stood or sat stoically, some even chatting casually with fellow officers. Either they refused to show fear in front of their comrades, or they had simply gotten so used to bombings and death that hiding in the wine cellar of a fancy hotel during an air raid was a nonevent.

Maggie had practically been shoved against Gabriel and Howie in the press of fleeing hotel guests in the hallway, and they'd managed to signal Douglas to join them. "At least if we have to be trapped here, it's with friends and not strangers," Gabriel surprised her by saying.

Maggie agreed that, in a way, they were all friends by now. Oh, sure, Howie was a character, Catherine was Miss Prim, Judith bossed everyone around, Douglas had his rulebook and routines, and Gabriel was, well . . . Gabriel. But after so many weeks of being in one another's company almost all the time, Maggie was beginning to like them in spite of herself.

Once the sirens cut off, Howie kept up a near-constant mutter of swearing under his breath at the hotel staff for packing them in like sardines or not having the decency to let people smoke or whatever their latest infraction was.

"Won't he ever pipe down?" Maggie complained in a low tone to Gabriel, pinching the bridge of her nose to still an oncoming headache. "It's not like any of us are comfortable, but the hotel is doing the best they can."

"Go easy on him," Gabriel said, his voice lower still. "This is harder for him than he lets on."

Of course. Howie had served in the Great War. How many times had he heard sounds like these as he went over the top of the trenches and charged into no-man's-land? Only now did Maggie notice the way Howie's shoulders tensed every time there was a sudden noise, the deep breaths as he tried to calm himself, the hands jammed in his bathrobe pockets so no one could see them shake.

The ground underneath her trembled with an impact, and several gasps filled the quiet. Somewhere, a child began to cry.

"Not a direct hit to us." Howie's voice was raspy and far from his usual bluster. "They're probably aiming for the harbor."

Sure, sure. They wouldn't take aim on civilian targets, would they? Still, Maggie had noticed her share of boarded-up windows, crumbled garden walls, and even whole roofless buildings that testified to the fact that collateral damage was part of life here along the Algerian coast.

Next to them, a few officers playing cards by candlelight grumbled a complaint as Judith strode through their draw pile, wedging her way between Maggie and Howie. "There you are. Did you miss me?"

"What would we ever do without you, Judith?" Maggie asked dryly.

"Die of boredom, most likely," Judith said, examining her fingernails, as if the scuffle might have damaged one. She was wearing an oversized coat that revealed legs bare from the knee down, something that caught a glance from the men around them.

"Where's Miss Duquette?" Douglas asked, dutifully taking a roll call of his charges.

It was just what Maggie had been wondering as she searched the refugees in the dim light. Her auburn hair ought to stand out, but the scene was a mass of people and activity.

"I'm sure she'll find us," Maggie offered. Of all of them, Catherine would be the most likely to be the first downstairs, and therefore the deepest into the maze of bottles and barrels.

"Oh, she was already here," Judith said, "but she went back up to her room. To gather some valuables, I think."

They all stared at her, their voices overlapping. "Upstairs? The staff wouldn't let her do such a foolish thing."

"In the middle of an air raid? No valuable is worth that!"

"Why didn't you stop her?"

Judith chose to respond only to the last of them, a question voiced by Gabriel. "I learned a long time ago that if a woman is determined to do something stupid . . ."

Maggie hated the casual way Judith shrugged, like this was all some petty annoyance and not the middle of a war.

"Catherine's a practical girl," Howie said gruffly. "She wouldn't go through with it. And anyway, the hotel staff would have stopped her on the way up."

The same staff were currently stepping over seated guests, trying to pass along water, provide blankets, and answer questions shouted at them from all directions. Maggie had a feeling that one young woman, especially one as small and silent as Catherine, could easily slip past.

Maggie made up her mind. "I'm going to go get her."

"You certainly are not," Douglas snapped, grabbing her arm. Maggie pulled away, furious at being manhandled, but he did not relax his grip, using his large build to keep her from even moving toward the wine cellar steps. "Just because one member of our party flagrantly disobeyed regulations does not mean all of us will."

He was right, of course. After all, if Catherine had left at the start of the air raid, Maggie following her now would do no good, and if she'd been detained, then she wasn't in danger and would rejoin them soon.

As they waited, the sirens gave off a different pattern, apparently the all-clear signal, because Maggie could see many of her fellow basement refugees relax their posture as the employees declared something in French. The officers next to her swept up their cards midgame, good-naturedly challenging each other to a rematch in the morning. Just like that, the panic was over, and everyone went back to life as usual.

"How do we know it's safe to go up?" Douglas asked a passing bellhop.

He had Douglas repeat the question, then said, "Do not worry, *monsieur*. They are gone. The planes, they are easy to see coming across the Mediterranean. We always have the warning."

Maggie barely waited to hear the response before elbowing her way through the crowd, another skill she'd learned from her brother to navigate Chicago sidewalks, making her one of the first up the stairs and down the hall.

308. That was Catherine's number, several doors down from her own room.

Light flooded the hallways as the hotel's electricity was restored, and Maggie reached out to knock, but the door was ajar. She shoved it open, ready to give her fellow performer the what-for about wandering off during an air raid.

At first, she thought the room was empty, the movement of the crooked ceiling fan the only sound. Then the broken window drew her eye, and beneath it, Catherine slumped on the floor, surrounded by glass.

Maggie rushed to her side, turning her over. Still breathing, thank God, and the only blood seemed to be a two-inch cut on her chin and another on her lower arm, a few drops seeping through her sleeve onto the carpet. Hopefully, she had only fainted, maybe from shock at the explosion or the sight of her own blood. Her violin case lay discarded at her side, and a jewelry box had spilled its contents on the floor, its latch flung open.

"Hey!" Maggie said, wishing she knew more about what to do in times like this. "Catherine! Can you hear me?"

To her relief, Catherine's face twitched. That was good, wasn't it?

She tugged out a handkerchief—bless Paulette for insisting she always carry one—and dabbed at the cut on Catherine's chin. It was already partially crusted over, the excess blotting on the cloth, and the motion startled Catherine's blue eyes awake. Fear and then pain chased each other in her expression. "Where—what happened?"

"You were an idiot and could have gotten yourself killed, that's what."

It wasn't the most gracious way to summarize the accident, but wasn't it true? Sure, Catherine's family probably bought her a top-of-the-line violin, but no one went out in an air raid, no matter what valuables they'd left behind. It was just common sense.

Maggie rolled up Catherine's sleeve to get a better look at the second cut. This one was even shallower than the first, the uniform's thick cloth offering protection.

Catherine pinched her lips together, eyes full of fear. "Is it my face? Will it be scarred?"

"*That's* what you care about?" Maggie had started to think maybe Catherine was more than just a shallow debutante, but this was too much. "It's barely more than a scrape. You'll be fine."

From Catherine's hurt expression, she'd probably been a little too curt, but it would do her good to get her priorities sorted out. "What did you come back for, anyway?"

She hesitated for a full second. "I—Judith said that our belongings might be stolen in the confusion, so I came back to retrieve them."

"Whatever you've got in here, it wasn't worth it." Though Maggie had to admit as she crawled around to help Catherine gather the scattered pieces that these were heirloom-quality jewelry, not bits and bobs made of glass or paste.

The tip of a silver fountain pen poked out from where it had rolled under the bed, and when Maggie reached for it, her hand brushed paper. She pulled out a stack of papers.

They seemed to be letters, and she caught a glance of a name in bold script at the bottom of one before Catherine snatched them away: *Sergeant Leonard Wallace.*

She knew that name. Who . . . ?

Of course. A face came back to her memory from one of their ballroom performances back in the States, a good-looking man with a smile far too smooth to be sincere.

"Are you telling me you risked your life for a bunch of letters from that flyboy who dumped you?"

She knew about Catherine's beau. All of the Sweethearts

did, teasing Catherine every time a new letter came in, even though she tried to keep the relationship private. Most of the dreamier types thought it was "hopelessly romantic" that their own Cinderella had caught the heart of an army pilot after just one dance.

Until the letters stopped coming, and Catherine became more likely to cry than smile when someone brought up her soldier. Maggie had never pressed for details, letting the others whisper and gossip. Still, this was a bridge too far.

"Don't you dare say that," Catherine snapped, pulling the letters to her chest like Maggie might try to steal them. "Leo might be in a prisoner-of-war camp or even . . . even killed."

Maggie took a step back, startled. Had she ever seen Catherine annoyed, much less angry? "I'm sorry. I just assumed . . ."

With effort and a deep breath, Catherine regained her composure and spoke with icy calm. "Perhaps you shouldn't have opinions on situations you know nothing about."

It was a stupid thing to argue about since Maggie had spoken to him for all of five minutes and he was out of the picture now, but Maggie couldn't let it drop. Catherine was one of those love-at-first-sight types, which was the dumbest thing Maggie had ever heard. A fellow could hide a lot in letters, show you only the parts of himself he wanted you to see.

"Listen, it's none of my business. I just . . . didn't like the look of him."

Catherine shuffled toward her bed, raising one hand to her makeshift bandage. "I don't want to talk about it."

Maggie knew she should say something conciliatory like *"Sorry I got upset. I was worried about you, that's all. We all were."* But that felt like admitting that she'd done something wrong, and she hadn't. "Fine. Suit yourself."

Douglas and Gabriel arrived shortly thereafter, and deciding that Catherine didn't need to be rushed to the hospital so much as she needed a simple bandage, they turned in for the night, shaken but safe.

Looks like we got closer to the war than we'd planned, Maggie thought. The ground fighting had long since passed in Algeria since the surrender of the Vichy French government, but the Germans still seemed determined to do what damage they could from the sky and the seas.

Under the covers once more, Maggie tried to breathe deeply and think of peaceful things to help her drift off to sleep. Brahms lullaby. A sticky handful of Cracker Jack at a baseball game. The last few rays of summer sunsets. Anything but the wail of sirens and concussive booms of antiaircraft fire. Air raid or not, they'd be back to performing in the morning, and there was no room in their troupe for a tired, weak member.

22

April 14, 1943
Algiers, Algeria

To Catherine, the convent school where their driver dropped them off looked like it had been transported directly from Paris, with whitewashed walls, a manicured garden, and nuns giving a "*bonjour*" and a nod to the new Americans taking up residency.

The Aletti Hotel had turned them out. Several rooms had been damaged by the nearby bombing, and their troupe's rooms had been requisitioned for officers, sending the men to a Signal Corps barracks for their remaining days in Algiers and the women to bunk with the Women's Auxiliary Army Corps at the school, all to Mr. Douglas's chagrin, as the new distances required adjusting the travel schedule.

The sister led them to a long room that, judging by the piano backed against the far wall, had once been a music room before the army had rented out the space to house the WAACs.

Beds with thin mattresses and metal frames were lined in rows with an aisle down the middle, each neatly made, a blanket folded into a perfect square at the foot. Like all buildings in Algiers, the windows were hung with severe blackout fabric, but someone had taken the time to tie the curtains open with grosgrain ribbon. A Chinese checkers board occupying a battered end table and a shelf of well-worn books were the only signs that the ladies housed here had time for recreation.

"Where are our roommates?" Maggie asked, shoving her musette bag under an empty cot without bothering to hang up her performance dress.

"At dinner," Catherine said, passing on the reply the sister had given her in French to the same question. The WAACs enjoyed simple meals with the students rather than the usual army fare after being transported back to the convent from their work in the heart of Algiers at the post office and army headquarters. "They'll be up soon." It was a relief, in a way, to share lodging with so many. It gave her a good reason not to make forced conversation with Maggie, who still hadn't apologized for her rudeness the night before.

Judith kicked off her boots and stretched like a cat in the sunshine. "Better enjoy the peace now. As soon as the skirted soldiers get here, things'll get ugly."

Catherine frowned. "I don't know why you would think that."

"Trust me, doll. You'll see."

True to the sister's promise, Catherine had barely had time to lay out her slip to air it out for the next day's performance when she heard loud footsteps on the stairs, accompanied by a chatter of female voices and laughter.

"Brace yourself, gals," Judith said, though she didn't rise from where she was lounging on the cot.

It was silly, but Catherine couldn't help glancing down at her uniform to make sure it was tucked in and neat just as the WAACs burst into the room.

"Oh!" A doe-eyed brunette leading the charge drew up short and stared.

Catherine suddenly felt sympathy for the preserved gazelle head they'd all gaped at in the market on the way here. The women in uniform weren't hostile, but there was a marked stiffness in many of them as they filed into the room, their banter halted. It was likely just the army training, or maybe no one had told the WAACs they had three new bunkmates.

That theory was soon discarded when a woman with her uniform coat draped casually over her arm and a mischievous glint in her eyes approached them. "So you're the performers. We didn't know you'd be here so early."

"There's no evening show tonight," Maggie offered as an explanation, "and thanks for letting us bunk with you, ladies."

A new woman stepped through the bottleneck that had formed at the door. Unlike many of the others, who had ties undone and hats askew, her uniform was mannequin-crisp, and her short hair so blond it was almost white, not a hair of it out of place. "No need to thank us for following orders." The words were polite, but Catherine heard the unspoken subtext: *"We didn't have a choice."* Or maybe it was only Judith's open hostility coloring her imagination.

Maggie didn't seem to be deterred and offered the woman her hand. "I'm Maggie McCleod. And you are?"

"Senior Leader May Franklin."

"Senior Leader," Judith repeated, giving her usual wry half-smile. "What is this, the Girl Scouts?"

If possible, since her posture already put Catherine's former etiquette instructor to shame, Senior Leader Franklin stiffened even more, directing cutting blue eyes Judith's way. "That will be equivalent to the rank of master sergeant once the WAACs are assimilated into the army proper this summer."

"I see. Very nice." Judith's voice was thick with patronization, and Catherine felt she could die of embarrassment.

"I've been told you'll breakfast with us at six hundred hours," Senior Leader Franklin continued.

Maggie groaned softly, and Catherine was close enough to elbow her. Yes, it was early, but it wouldn't do to offend their hosts.

"We'll look forward to it," Catherine said, smiling winsomely. It was like trying to melt an iceberg with a cigarette lighter.

After delivering a few more regulations—keep their belongings neat and tidy, obey curfew regulations, no loitering about during the day when the night-shift switchboard girls were trying to sleep—Senior Leader Franklin waited, as if for them to sign a contract or swear an oath of obedience.

Judith barely raised her head where she lounged on her cot. "Guess we really are in the army now, girls," she said, sarcasm in her voice. "Complete with lumpy pillows and bossy sergeants."

Catherine wasn't the only one who gasped at that. Every woman in the room was now watching them, waiting for the senior leader's reaction. A muscle in her cheek tightened as she glared. "If you were under my charge, comments like that would get you written up for insubordination."

"Well, it's a good thing I didn't enlist, then."

The senior leader took a step closer. "We wouldn't have taken you if you had."

Rather than being offended, Judith tossed back her head and laughed. That, apparently, made Senior Leader Franklin think she'd won the round, because with one last dark glare, she swept from the room.

Subdued, Catherine sat on the edge of her cot, her fingers tucking tiny metal curlers into her hair like a gunner loading artillery. "I don't suppose they'll be coming to our show tomorrow night?" she whispered to Maggie.

Maggie paused, rummaging in her bag long enough to snort. "With her in charge? Not a chance. Anyway, since the WAACs work at the post office and headquarters and bunk all the way out here, it'd be a transportation nightmare to get all of them to the show near the men's camp and back again."

Everything she said made sense. Except . . . "It just feels like such a missed opportunity. These women work so hard. They deserve some entertainment just as much as the men, maybe more."

"Maybe. But there's nothing we can do about it."

Catherine looked over at their bunkmates, some whispering, one looking longingly at the silk gown spilling out of her footlocker. "Are you sure about that?"

Maggie waited, but Catherine's mind was still working, thinking through details, wondering. It was probably a silly idea. They'd never get permission. But maybe, just maybe, if they could . . .

What could it hurt to try?

The Army Central Postal Directory was a wonder of organization, with waist-high canvas bins of mail arranged in a maze that only the WAACs seemed to know the secret of navigating. A dozen of them were hunched over a long wooden trencher of a table filled with unsorted mail, their fingers and eyes flying across envelopes marked with names and regiment numbers. On the other side of the room were bins heaped even more precariously with packages wrapped up in brown paper.

The sight of all that productivity made Catherine hesitate. Maybe this had been a terrible idea after all.

As Maggie had predicted, the WAACs had not come to

their show the day before, and their second night had been full of more awkward exchanges. A few of the women snuck over to ooh and ahh over Catherine's costumes, while others had made arch remarks about how they'd had to earn the right to wear their uniform.

Well, they weren't wearing their uniforms today, at any rate.

Catherine glanced toward the door. There was still time to leave, to pretend they'd simply wanted to tour the facilities before their drivers arrived to transport them to the next stop. . . .

"Ladies!" Maggie announced, louder than the confined space required, and instantly, their arrival went from incognito to a full dress parade with a brass band.

So much for that idea. All eyes were on them now, the processing of mail halted as the WAAC women saw the three of them in full costume and stage makeup.

"We've gotten permission from the higher-ups to thank you for the hard work you've put in these past few months," Maggie went on, mercifully sticking to the script Catherine had given her when she'd agreed to be the spokesperson. "Since you couldn't take a day off to come hear the USO, the USO has come to you."

By now, the WAACs had realized what was happening. A few applauded as if the curtain were rising at a proper theater, while others glanced warily at a stately, middle-aged woman standing near the packages and watching Catherine and Maggie with interest. Her uniform sported gold adornments on her shoulder straps and lapels, indicating she was of a higher rank than Senior Leader Franklin, who was, as yet, nowhere to be seen.

Her introduction complete, Maggie raised her trumpet and blasted the opening notes of "The Boogie Woogie Bugle Boy." As Judith chimed in, Maggie pulled back on the volume. Together, Judith's rich, bluesy voice and Maggie's free-spirited playing—which bordered on improvisation, though Catherine knew how many hours she practiced—blended together beautifully, transforming the Central Postal Directory of Algiers into a Chicago jazz club.

Catherine moved to stand beside the woman in charge, who she soon learned was First Officer Martha Rogers, and attempted to explain over the music that they had indeed approved this with army authorities.

To their surprise, Mr. Douglas had accepted the idea with prompt approval, which for him bordered on enthusiasm. He'd made the necessary calls, telling them about other USO troupes who had given performances for a lone tank crew or roomful of injured men who hadn't been able to attend the main show. Judith had actually been the hardest one to convince, but Catherine had thrown in a pair of her silk stockings as a bribe to seal the deal.

Now it appeared Judith had no reservations at all. She had found her way onto a sorting bin and balanced on the wooden frame while belting out the song as if she was trying to be all three Andrews Sisters simultaneously. Many of the WAACs continued to sort mail, though admittedly at a slower pace, while others ceased their work entirely. One young woman even stepped away from her station at the parcels to join the second verse with a strong soprano, and Judith shifted into harmonies.

As the last note faded away, Senior Leader Franklin pushed a mail cart into the room, staring at the hubbub of applause. Catherine winced. Clearly, they'd had the good luck to arrive when she was out with a delivery truck, but it seemed that luck had run out.

Her mouth formed a perfect O before demanding, "*What* are you *doing* here?"

"We're only performing three songs," Catherine said,

fighting the urge to sink into the floorboards, because if she didn't say something, Maggie or Judith would. "Then we'll be on our way."

Senior Leader Franklin's hand gripped the cart even more tightly, and for a moment, Catherine was afraid she was going to ram it into them. "I think one is quite enough."

"Thank you, Senior Leader Franklin, for your concern," First Officer Rogers said gently, putting a hand on the younger woman's shoulder, "but this performance is approved. I believe it will be good for morale."

Ignoring the reproof, Franklin snatched up a handful of letters, carefully postmarked with names and regiment numbers, and waved them in Catherine's face. "What's good for morale is making sure soldiers about to go into battle receive their letters from home. How many will be left waiting while we waste time?"

Catherine's heart was beating faster now. She knew that tone, the rising tension in it. When used by either her mother or father, it had always been her cue to murmur her excuses and leave the dinner table or sitting room and hide until the argument passed by. Here, there was nowhere to go. Nothing to do except stay quiet and endure.

"Music isn't a waste of time," Maggie contested, her own tone warming slightly. "Honestly, it's nothing to get worked up about."

"Oh? When we first arrived, the men thought we were here to be pretty faces behind typewriters. I've spent three months proving we're more than that." She took another step toward Catherine, and she felt her breath catch. "I can't lose that. I won't."

"We're not here to bruise your ego, Scout Leader," Judith said, tossing her hair as she jumped down from the sorting bin, "just sing a few songs."

This time, Catherine was sure that things would end in

fisticuffs, the way Senior Leader Franklin lunged forward, ignoring First Officer Rogers's attempt to step between them. "How dare you—"

"Ladies!" The word burst out of Catherine before she could think better of it, and now everyone was staring at her instead of the impending fight. Why hadn't she just kept quiet?

She had no idea what to say next. Maggie or Howie would have a joke to lighten the mood, Gabriel some tactful logic, Mr. Douglas a no-nonsense explanation, but all she had was a fear of conflict and, maybe even stronger, a long weariness.

Hadn't it been just this way back in the Sweethearts? Women fighting for first chair and the higher pay that came with it, comparing their headshots on advertising posters, playing nice to one another's faces, then passing on petty insults and gossip behind closed doors? Catherine had always hated it, and to find it here in the middle of a war zone was too much.

She looked to Maggie for rescue, but she just tilted her head, as if to say, *"You got yourself into this. Better get out."*

Fine. She would. Catherine took a deep breath and looked Senior Leader Franklin in the eye. "We have something in common. We both know what it's like to be looked down on, to fight for respect and wonder when we'll be treated as equals."

When Senior Leader Franklin didn't protest, Catherine went on, her gaze now falling on the enlisted women sorting mail. "I'll admit, I haven't sacrificed what all of you have, but the way I see it, we women need to stick together."

Catherine closed her mouth tightly, hearing her heart pounding loudly in ears that were surely fire red. Had she . . . had she just said all that?

Then First Officer Rogers nodded. "Very aptly spoken," she said, a faint smile softening her stern features. "I believe, as the saying goes, the show should go on." Not even Senior Leader Franklin protested, seemingly out of arguments.

As she took up her bow, Catherine's opening notes faltered, her nerves taut from the confrontation and her unexpected speech, but soon she was lost in the music once again, letting Vivaldi's "Springtime" thread through the room and cover over the ugliness of war, like the ink of a postmark.

Next, Judith opened the floor to requests and took everyone on a journey to Oz with "Somewhere over the Rainbow," before Maggie capped things off with a few of the jokes from her routine.

"Speaking of mail," she said, gesturing to the full bins, "I hear some of you ladies are working as censors too. Let me tell you, my last letter to the States came back looking like Swiss cheese, so I've got a new strategy."

Maggie mimicked holding an invisible pencil, jotting down words as she spoke, "Dear Dad, Greetings from a place! After some time passes, I'll be at a different place, which I'm sure will be equally nice. The weather here is just like it always is at this time of year. I'm enjoying the local food, which is edible, and seeing the sights, which are visible. We are and will continue to be doing military sorts of things. Miss you all! Yours, Maggie."

The women burst into laughter and cheers at the joke, one they experienced firsthand every day. "Brilliant, isn't it?" Maggie said, folding her invisible envelope and giving the glue of the flap an exaggerated lick. "Use it yourself if you like, free of charge."

Catherine wondered how Maggie could improvise so well. It seemed like she'd just lifted the joke like a hat off a rack and tried it on for size, finding it a perfect fit. A tiny prickle of jealousy threatened to rise . . . until Catherine remembered the speech she'd just made. *"We women need to stick together."* Maybe that included the women of the variety unit too.

As they waved their good-byes over demands for an encore, First Officer Rogers gave her a hearty handshake. "Thank you so much for coming. It'll be all the ladies will talk about for weeks."

Senior Leader Franklin escorted them to the door. She had kept a steady pace of work through the performance, but Catherine had noticed her smiling at several of the jokes. When Catherine passed through the door, she stopped her. "You're not so bad after all, glamour girl."

"Thank you," Catherine said hesitantly, hating the fact that her response sounded more like a question. Still, she had spoken up, said what she really felt. It was a new feeling . . . but a nice one.

"If you ever decide you'd rather not fiddle through the entire war, you're welcome to enlist in the Women's Army Corps."

Catherine was quite sure she didn't have enough useful skills for the WAC—she wasn't proficient at typing, couldn't drive a car, and hadn't attended even a week of college—but Franklin's tone was more teasing than mocking, so Catherine smiled in return. "I'll keep that in mind."

They might not be leaving as friends, but they could at least be allies.

It was only a few blocks to the location of their second performance, the Allied Force Headquarters, a commandeered hotel where a fleet of WAAC secretaries filed papers, took dictation, and administrated nearly every aspect of the war.

The day was bright and clear, with few signs that they were strolling through a city in the crosshairs of Nazi bombers every night, beyond the dark curtains blocking most of the windows and a web of scaffolding against a crumbled wall.

Catherine let Maggie lead the way, glancing warily about her for pickpockets, who she'd been warned saw Americans as easy targets. As she did, Judith fell into step beside her. "Those were some pretty good lines you spouted off back there."

Don't let her get to you. "They weren't lines. Some of us actually say things because we believe them."

She scoffed lightly. "Sorry, but I don't buy it. I've been in enough women's dressing rooms to know that more backstabbing happens there than in the worst slums in the country."

There was some truth in what she said, Catherine knew, but she'd also seen the camaraderie that could thrive among women as well. "You can be as cynical as you like, but I stand by what I said. We're stronger together."

This time it was Maggie who made a face like she'd gotten a whiff of an Algerian tannery. Her steps quickened, causing Catherine to stumble in her attempt to keep up. "Yeah, well, if we're supposed to stick together, why throw your money at Douglas like you did?"

"My . . . what?" Catherine blinked, taken aback by the accusatory scowl on Maggie's face. "Do you . . . do you think I only got this job because I paid the USO to be here?" Some of the pettier members of the Sweethearts had suggested as much about her first-chair position in the band, but Maggie had been there when Mr. Douglas hired her. Yes, he'd needed to be talked into it, but not with a promise of her family's money.

But Maggie brushed off Catherine's outrage with a wave. "Not that. I'm talking about how you tried to bribe your way into getting the Pepsodent contract."

This was even more puzzling. "I never did anything of the kind."

"See? Didn't I tell you she'd deny it?" Judith said triumphantly.

"Deny what?" But even as she asked the question, the only possible answer came to her. It had to be some sort of sabotage, Judith spreading lies about her to ruin her reputation. Catherine felt heat rise to her face even without a single thing to be guilty for.

"Sorry, doll, but there's no ducking out of this one." Judith faced her head-on as they waited to cross a busy boulevard. "I heard you making your offer to Mr. Douglas when he gave you that letter back in Morocco."

The mention of the mail from her father triggered a memory. "What, exactly, do you think you heard me say?"

"That your rich family always got what they wanted, and that something might be worth Mr. Douglas's while."

Judith said it like it was a full confession, but when she didn't add anything more specific, Catherine asked, "Is that all?"

"Well . . . yes," Maggie admitted.

There didn't seem any way out of this except correcting the misinformation. Catherine kept walking straight ahead, trying to speak the ugly truth with dignity. "Since my personal life is apparently open for discussion, we were speaking about my somewhat contentious relationship with my family, as well as Mr. Douglas's rift with his son. I advised him that an apology might be worth his while. And that is all."

"Oh." Maggie looked properly chagrined, but Catherine noticed that Judith kept a skeptical smirk pasted on her face. Either she was keeping up an act, or she really couldn't force an innocent explanation to fit into her cynicism.

For a moment, Catherine thought they'd continue in silence toward the Hotel St. George, marked as the Allied Headquarters with conspicuous British, French, and

American flags flying from the balconies, but then Maggie added, "Well, it did sound suspicious, you have to admit."

She had to do nothing of the kind. "The worst part is that both of you believed the worst of me with only a few scraps of conversation as evidence."

"Oh, don't be such a snob," Judith said, rolling her eyes. "You'd have thought the same thing if you were in our place. If you ask me, you shouldn't be competing for the contract at all. Don't you have enough money already? No one's depending on you to make it big."

Should she tell Judith she was living off her own salary, not her father's allowance? Somehow, she was sure it would do very little good.

They'd reached the administrative building, and Maggie held the door open for them. "All right, Judith, enough of that. We all have our reasons for wanting the contract. All I'm asking for is a fair shot."

Catherine gave her a grateful look. "Which you always had. I hope you're convinced of that now."

They crossed the lovely shaded terrace and showed their identification to the guards at the front entrance of the former luxury resort. Then they were led into the command-and-communication center for the entire war. It was an odd juxtaposition with men in uniform stubbing out cigarettes on marble railings between Roman pillars and a secretary bustling past carrying a box marked *CLASSIFIED* with the efficiency of a maid delivering room service. Through one of the archways, Catherine could see a billiard table draped with maps and documents, chairs set up at each of the pockets.

While Judith flagged down someone to announce their arrival and set them up for the impromptu concert, Catherine took it all in. She'd just wondered if Eisenhower himself might hear some of their music when Maggie leaned against the wall next to her.

"So your family isn't too keen on you being out here?"

Maggie wasn't supposed to know that. No one was. In any case, Catherine didn't owe Maggie the details of her dysfunctional family. "No, they aren't."

"Huh." Maggie took out her trumpet, polishing a smudge off the bell with her handkerchief. "There was a time I'd have said we didn't have a thing in common. If you told me we're both the black sheep of our families, I'd have laughed."

That couldn't possibly be true. Not the way Catherine was in her family, anyway. "I don't find it particularly funny."

Maggie's face got a thoughtful cast to it. "You know, neither do I." As Judith called them over, arm in arm with an officer, she added, "And, hey . . . I'm sorry. For thinking that about you all these weeks."

Well. That was something, at least. Catherine found herself relaxing ever so slightly. Maybe they could finally begin to work together instead of against each other.

Report to the USO Home Office
Floyd Douglas, Foxhole Circuit, Variety Unit 14
April 18, 1943

I'm told bragging in this industry is overdone, so I'll only point out that few other USO units have been given a commendation by General Eisenhower. Our additional performances in Algiers for the WAACs on his staff recorded in the attached report did not delay our progress and were an excellent goodwill-building opportunity.

Despite a few setbacks, I've been impressed with the performers in my unit. None of them are aware that I gave up the Andrews Sisters base tour to take on a group of unknowns just for a chance to see my son. At the time, it felt like a demotion, maybe even a damaging move for my career. But I'm starting to wonder if this humble unit might be hiding a future star—or even more than one.

Even more importantly, perhaps, I find I'm genuinely coming to enjoy their company. Particularly since they're easy to beat at chess. (A much-needed relief from the monotony of travel in the convoy truck. A sergeant taught us to use palm sap on the bottom of the pieces to keep them in place as we ride.)

No further incidents of rule breaking—that I'm aware of, at least. Although Miss Judith Blair was very nearly arrested for dining with a naval officer at a local café. A military policeman interrupted their dinner, thinking Blair was a WAAC, who are not permitted to date officers. She produced her identification card and gave that poor MP a round dressing down. From the abbreviated (likely edited) version I received, his ears are probably still ringing.

Sincerely,
Floyd Douglas

P.S. This is Maggie McCleod. I offered to post this for Mr. Douglas after reading it over his shoulder, just so I could add this bit: I'd like to inform the USO Home Office that he has not, in fact, beaten everyone at chess. His record against me is 0–4, and he refuses to play me anymore. For someone so set on accuracy, you'd think he'd remember to record that bit of information.

From Sterling Warner to Floyd Douglas

April 15, 1943

Floyd,

I tell ya, I cheered when I got your last note. Good for you, and good for Teddy. Gosh, I'm glad to hear something good's come out of this sorry war.

Here's the Latest from Lastfogel (sounds like a newspaper column, doesn't it?): The Pepsodent Show is looking for more regulars for their radio program. Whoever you recommend may end up with a supporting-cast radio contract after the tour is up. Tell 'em that if you think it'll motivate them . . . or keep mum if it'll only make things tense. Any thoughts on the top contender?

I have a good feeling about this, Douglas. One of your unknowns is going to find that the path to stardom sometimes goes right through the Sahara.

Warnie

From Floyd Douglas to Sterling Warner

April 19, 1943

Dear Warnie,

You just have to be the first one to know, don't you,

you old snoop? Well, I'll play along. If I had to tell you today who I would recommend, it would be one of my last-minute additions that I discovered in St. Paul . . . but I couldn't say which one just yet.

It's maddening. Each has a piece of what we're looking for. Miss McCleod is confident and a natural entertainer—who has no professionalism or regard for rules. And Miss Duquette has virtuoso-level talent and natural grace, but she doesn't respond well to conflict or hardship. Is it too much to ask for a graduate of both an academy of the arts and the school of hard knocks?

Normally, I would say that we cannot expect change or growth in only a few weeks. However, life on the road is different. It accelerates everything: emotion, exhaustion, and—one can only hope—maturity. One of these young women may yet become the performer we need.

Here's hoping,
Floyd

23

April 20, 1943
South of Boghari, Algeria

"Looks like we finally found the Sahara." Maggie shielded her eyes to peer out of the jeep at the foothills of the Atlas Mountains, closer here than even in Fez. The rest of her view was a rolling landscape of yellow-green grass, palms, and sand in every direction.

"This is just the edge, I think," Howie said, replacing his uniform jacket, which he'd taken off at noon to keep from roasting in the open-topped vehicle.

They'd skirted the Sahara when they were heading south from Algiers to perform for small groups of soldiers guarding ammo dumps and completing desert training, but now Maggie could finally understand what gave North Africa its reputation for brutal weather. Away from the coastal breezes, even springtime temperatures became uncomfortable in the afternoon, and Douglas reminded them to fill their canteens at each stop. Out here, towns were smaller and covered in layers of dust, and only the stubborn, sturdy plants managed to break up the browns and tans with fringes of green.

The semi-arid wilderness south of the village of Boghari was, Douglas had informed them, as far toward the desert as they were going to venture. Even so, a glance at a map of the sprawling county was enough to show that they hadn't even traveled down a tenth of its length. Farther south, past the crosshatched Saharan Atlas range, roads were fewer and American military outposts more spread out, then non-existent. All attention was focused on the narrow corridor of ports, seaside roads, and railways for the transport of supplies and troops to Tunisia.

"Good thing, too," Maggie observed, trying to use the collar of her gas mask to fan herself. "If we got a flat tire out here, we'd have to haul the truck's carcass for a week to find a decent mechanic."

Their two jeeps were soon swarmed with a mob of a couple dozen soldiers as they approached the outpost. "Watch it!" Their driver hollered with the same intonation Maggie had heard a hundred times before by Chicago taxi drivers. "I'll run you all over. I swear it." Despite the warning, he decreased his pace to a crawl as they passed a tattered American flag, parking the jeep beside what must be the mess kitchen, a few outdoor ovens made of bricks and empty oil drums.

Judith was eyeing it too. "I suppose we can count out lamb and couscous like we had in Algiers."

"Don't remind me," Maggie groaned, her stomach reminding her it had been hours since they stopped for a lunch of canned field rations. It would probably be back to meat hash and stew, standard meals when far from the vibrant city markets of the coast.

They all hopped out, stretching stiff legs. The soldiers who ran over to them were among the most excited, and suntanned, that Maggie had yet met.

"We thought everyone had forgotten about us out here,"

one of them said, waving the men back to let the performers through.

"You're real!" another exclaimed, after reaching out to shake Maggie's hand. "I thought it was a joke when they said the USO was coming out here."

That was all it took to make Maggie feel guilty for whining about the food and the heat. These men had been out here in isolation for weeks or months with nary a movie palace or Moorish coffeeshop in sight.

The commanding officer of the post made his way through the crowd to give them a more official welcome. "I'll show you to your dressing rooms," he said, giving a chortle. "They're no Hollywood affair, let me tell you, but they'll double as your accommodations for the night."

Which, of course, meant they'd emptied out two tents for the purpose, one for the men, one for the women. Maggie, the tallest of the three, had become an expert at changing into a dress without being able to fully stand up.

The troupe followed him, their steps weary after a long day of travel, but something caught Maggie's eye, and she paused, squinting in the setting sun. The outpost was situated near the main road, on top of a hill that fell sharply away a few dozen yards past the barracks. Down the slope, a barbed-wire fence stood tall and stark against the dead grass. Deeper in, she could see several rude outbuildings clustered together.

"What's that? Another outpost?" She directed her question at the nearby soldier who'd noticed her staring. He had an earnest, round face, his hair in need of a trim to live up to regulation length.

"No, it's a labor camp for political prisoners. They're building a railroad."

"Oh." That made more sense, given the fence. "The only thing I'd ever want to do with this desert is get across it."

"Tell that to the poor devils pouring out sweat and blood to build it."

His tone, and the thought of conditions out here during the summer, sobered her. "What's your name, soldier?"

"Ira Levy, but my friends call me Monty."

She introduced herself in turn. "It doesn't seem right, an American army outpost near a labor camp."

Monty shrugged. "You're telling me. All we've heard from the brass is that they're doing their best, keeping the pressure on. They got the British POWs out of the camps right away, but everyone else . . . looks like they have to wait."

Maggie frowned. "Wait for what? The end of the war?"

"Maybe. We wouldn't want to anger the Vichy French, now that they're on our side. They're the ones that took away Algerian Jews' citizenship and rights. Without any orders from Germany either."

"So the people in the labor camp are Jewish?" If she squinted, she could see movement down by the buildings, likely the prisoners returning from a day's work.

"Not all of them. Some are refugees from Europe whose visas expired, others are communists or Spanish War soldiers or dissidents. All of them are worked nearly to death."

Maggie had read about Hitler's policies toward Jews, of course. Even before the war started, she'd seen the newsreels and thought things like *"That's a shame."* But she'd never been so close before. If she grabbed a canteen so she wouldn't get heatstroke on the way, she could climb down that hill and cross the stretch of sand to reach it in less than thirty minutes. "What's it like down there?"

"See for yourself." He handed her his binoculars, and she gripped the canvas strap, pausing for a moment, uncertain whether she wanted to know what the high-powered lenses would reveal.

Her father had taught her to always look the people they

served in the eye. *"Everyone deserves the simple human dignity of being seen."*

There was nothing else to do but raise the binoculars to her eyes and focus on the camp down the hill.

It wasn't their unkempt beards, sun-darkened skin, or tattered clothing that was most noticeable. It was the way they walked: grown men slumped over and trudging toward flimsy shelters for the night, weak and weary.

One of them looked up toward the hill, and she wondered how much of the American army outpost they could see and if they'd hoped these new occupiers would free them. How many months had gone by before they'd given up on that hope too?

"Awful, isn't it?"

When she moved the binoculars away and the scene faded, she blinked, focusing on Monty and the tent city behind him, filling with the smell of roast meat from the chow line. What had felt like suffering right next to her was suddenly distant as she stood under the American flag with a mile of desert and barbed wire and guard towers between them.

She handed the binoculars back. "And there's nothing we can do?"

Monty shook his head. "I think Roosevelt's trying, and journalists are campaigning for more direct action. Over in Morocco, there's a lawyer named Hélène Benetar who's petitioning the government, lining up jobs and housing for refugees, that sort of thing."

Maggie studied him for a long moment. "You sure know a lot about this."

"What else do I have to do, stuck out in the desert like this?" He said it casually, but Maggie didn't buy it. This meant more to him than just a topic to pass the time.

"Hey, Monty!" They both turned to see another soldier waving from the outdoor ovens Maggie had seen on the way in. "Get your sorry self over here. I'm not gonna take on KP duty alone."

"I have to go." Monty slung the binoculars around his neck and started to jog off, then paused. "Thank you."

She nodded. No need to ask him what he meant. It was a thanks for looking, for listening, for sharing some of the burden this fellow clearly carried for the prisoners down the hill: the guilt of knowing about an injustice but feeling helpless to stop it.

"Everything all right?"

Maggie forced her gaze off her corned beef and cabbage—not as bad as expected, giving cooking conditions—and looked up at Gabriel. "Sure. Why do you ask?"

He tapped her mess kit with his fork. "Usually you're finishing Catherine's plate if she doesn't want it all. But tonight you've barely touched yours."

Maggie glanced around. It was officially the end of mess, judging from the fact that Monty and the other soldier on KP duty were washing up, using a kettle suspended over a fire to boil hot water. Only the USO members were still sitting on the benches, watching the sun set behind the mountains.

"I stashed away a tangerine and ate it in the jeep," Maggie said, which was true, but that had been nearly eight hours before.

Gabriel raised an eyebrow. "You also said barely a dozen words to the soldiers you ate with."

"Better to let them talk, I figured." Douglas was always telling the performers that.

"*And* you haven't insulted me all evening."

That one was harder to counter. "They're not insults. Just spirited banter."

Gabriel was not one to be diverted, leaning forward like

Sherlock Holmes explaining his conclusion to a case. "Call it what you like. All I'm saying is that you're not yourself tonight." When she still didn't answer, he added, "Do you want to talk about it?"

"Maybe." Out of all the performers, Gabriel was the one who might understand, and she was touched that he cared, but . . .

She glanced at the others, who were listening to Howie spin some yarn about a vandalized ventriloquy dummy. "But I need to talk to Douglas first."

She'd told herself it wouldn't work, and Douglas wouldn't allow it anyway, but why not at least ask? She could hear Gabriel's braced leg dragging on the rough ground to follow her as she approached their manager, using the last light of day to look over their itinerary.

She sat down on the bench next to him and put on her best salesperson voice. "Mr. Douglas, I've got a pitch for you."

He looked up, the glare of the sunset off his spectacles making it difficult to judge his mood. "Go on."

"I think we ought to give a performance tonight, instead of in the morning. It's cooler now than it will be when the sun's up."

It was a flimsy argument, and Douglas clearly knew it. "Be that as it may, I doubt this outpost is equipped with any sort of stage illumination. That's why we scheduled our show for the morning in the first place."

Maggie sighed. It would be easier to build a railroad through the Sahara than get Douglas to change a schedule.

"Why this sudden interest in extracurricular shows?" Howie scooted closer, his story complete, and Judith and Catherine turned toward them as well. "First Catherine with those WAACs, now you. Not working hard enough already?"

"No," Maggie said quickly. If anything, though she'd never admit it, she was starting to feel worn down from the pace. "It's just I'd hoped . . ."

There was really no way to explain it other than the truth. Her words came out in a rush. "Maybe if we played now, the men in the labor camp could hear some of it from their barracks. By the time we perform tomorrow, they'll be marched back to the work site."

Douglas nodded. "Ah, I see." It seemed he and the others had heard about their imprisoned neighbors as well. "I do appreciate the sentiment, however, most of them don't speak English. Even if they did, we're far enough away that I doubt they'd hear us at all."

She'd already thought about that. "They'll hear me. My trumpet, I mean." That's why the Salvation Army loved brass instruments. They could cut through the din of cars and shouts and machinery the way nothing else could, even in a city like Chicago.

"Perhaps," Douglas said slowly.

"I say we at least try," Gabriel said, and Maggie shot him a grateful glance. "It's because of the Jews that we took Algiers without a fight. The day before Operation Torch, the Resistance took over all the strategic locations. Most of them were Jewish."

"I remember reading about that in the papers." But of course, the emphasis had been on American operatives' connections with local resistance groups. Maggie hadn't thought much about the Algerians involved or why they'd been determined to undermine their government.

"I think it's a lovely thought, whatever comes of it," Catherine ventured, and Howie nodded. Even Judith tossed out a casual "Why not?"

Douglas looked at his watch, then at the setting sun, his brow furrowed. Then he tugged his sleeve back over his watch and nodded. "We'll do it. I'll alert the commanding officer, though heaven knows how I'll explain it."

"Bill it as a campfire preview of tomorrow's show," Maggie

said helpfully to his retreating figure. She stood, retrieving her mess kit and packing it up without bothering to scrape it clean. That could come later. They had costumes to change into, instruments to tune, a program order to set . . .

"I wish I knew a song for them," she said, almost to herself. "A special one, something hopeful."

"How about 'The Star-Spangled Banner'?" Judith suggested.

Gabriel shook his head. "No good. These are Jewish refugees and Spanish War veterans. I doubt they've ever heard our national anthem."

"I suppose 'La Marseillaise' is out too, then," Catherine said.

"Definitely not."

Howie straightened, his dark eyes suddenly alert. "'Hatikvah.' It's a Jewish song, popular with the Zionists. Translated, it means 'The Hope.'"

While the suggestion seemed perfect, Maggie couldn't help feeling surprised that Howie, their resident clown, had made it. Her thoughts must have shown on her face because he ducked his head and fiddled with his helmet. "Howie Jones is my stage name. Catchier, you know. I was born Howard Lieberman. Not a practicing Jew, not anymore. But songs have a way of sticking with you."

Maggie understood. She had a whole hymnal in her mind from her growing up years. Which led her to ask, "Can you sing it?"

Howie shrugged. "Maybe. But we've still got the same problem. No microphone."

"No, I mean right now."

"Maggie learns music by ear," Catherine explained. "She can hear a song once and play it nearly perfectly."

Even Gabriel looked impressed at that, and Maggie wished Howie would just start singing already and take the attention away from her. She always hated the fuss people made about her ability, like it was some sort of magical power instead of a simple party trick. "Go on, then. Let's hear it."

"You can't make fun of me, now," he said, wagging a finger in Judith's direction. "I'm no Fred Astaire, singing and dancing at the same time."

"We won't," Maggie promised, and Judith nodded in agreement.

Howie closed his eyes like he was traveling far away, maybe back to family prayers around a table a long time ago, and sang in a thin tenor words that Maggie didn't recognize but could still feel somehow. They throbbed with longing and told a story that transcended language, the way you knew which of the planets went with which Holst movement just by the sound.

Maggie focused on the notes, her fingers moving through air as they would on valves, letting the melody write itself on her mind.

"Again," she said, when Howie had finished. Despite what Catherine claimed, she needed several repetitions to pull off her trick. Howie obliged, singing "Hatikvah" three times. By the last repetition, Gabriel had brought Maggie's trumpet, and she played along, faltering here and there, but accurately recreating most of the melody that had etched itself in her memory.

"I can do it," she finally said. "Howie, will you sing along while I play during the performance?"

He looked startled. "I don't—well, I'm no singer. Anyway, we just said they wouldn't be able to hear one voice."

"No, but it'll keep me on track if I forget the rhythm."

For a moment, Howie looked like he was going to turn her down flat, but then his gaze went to the rough bunkhouses past the barbed wire. "Well . . . all right. If you're sure it'll help."

"They're ready for you," Douglas said, indicating a clearing in the center of camp, where the thirty men of the outpost were struggling to find a comfortable place to sit on the rocky ground. Someone had made a campfire, and several lamps flickered on the ground. As Maggie got closer, she could see that they were made from C-ration cans, the grease inside smelling like leavings from the beef they'd just eaten. It gave the clearing a warm cast in the twilight.

They decided there was no need for costumes; their uniforms would do. Gabriel and Howie needed full daylight for their acts, but Judith agreed to start them off with a song that she belted out with surprising volume. Catherine turned toward the south and played so hard Maggie thought she'd snap her bowstrings. Still, Maggie doubted that more than a stray note carried down to the camp. This entire experiment was a desperate attempt, a prayer for a miracle.

The applause from the gathered company told Maggie that she was on. With no stage to take over, she simply stepped toward the campfire, raising her trumpet. They'd agreed on three songs, with "Hatikvah" last of all.

Near the end of her second solo, she felt the wind change and saw a shift in the curling smoke from the nearby fire. The labor camp was now downwind.

That was as close to a miracle as they were likely to get. Maggie took in a breath, letting it fill her all the way down, then nodded at Howie and let loose the first few notes of "Hatikvah."

The stark blast of her brass instrument wasn't the right sound for the haunting melody—a string quartet or a mournful piano solo would have been better—but it was loud. If the wind kept up, if the barracks inside the fence were as flimsy as they looked, maybe, maybe, some of them would hear.

As she played and Howie sang, something remarkable happened. One of the soldiers, clutching his dog tags like they were a talisman for prayer, stood and began singing along in Hebrew. Monty.

Maggie's eyes met his. She'd had a hunch about his heritage, sure, but it was good to see the fellow brave enough to take a stand. She'd heard that a lot of Jewish American soldiers even scratched out their religion on their dog tags, afraid of what would happen if the Germans captured them.

Monty repeated the simple verse with Howie as Maggie poured the notes out loud and clear, hoping they carried down the hill and into the labor camp.

Let them hear. Please. Let them hear.

Their show the next morning went back to their usual lighthearted fare, though Maggie couldn't help glancing down the hill, where workers had clambered into trucks to be carted away at dawn. Their small gesture hardly felt like enough, but it was all they had to offer.

The soldiers roared with laughter and demanded two encores before Mr. Douglas good-naturedly told them the troupe needed to move on. There were no jeeps to spare this time to transport them closer to the Tunisian border, only a rattling "deuce-and-a-half" cargo truck.

Howie and Judith had talked themselves into the cab of the truck with their driver, pleading age and a need to get some shut-eye. Catherine was leaning against the truck's tailgate, staring at the pockmarked road as it disappeared behind them, her face wistful, and Douglas seemed to be occupied taking notes to send back to the USO home office.

That left Maggie and Gabriel to sit on the fold-down troop seats that lined the side of the truck, propping their feet up on the luggage secured down the center.

This time, he didn't suggest bringing out the chess board as they had on previous treks. "It was a good show last night."

Maggie shifted to look back in the direction of the outpost and the labor camp. "In its own way, I guess."

"There was one thing I wondered, though." He shifted forward, and Maggie was again taken aback by how intense his eyes could be. It felt like he could see straight through you. "You knew that song by heart, rhythm included. You didn't need Howie to sing with you, did you?"

It sounded like he already knew the answer, but she shrugged anyway. "Not really."

"So why did you ask him to?"

Maggie thought back to another one of her father's old sayings before they went to the Salvation Army corps' Sunday meeting. *"Do you know why we sing hymns?"* he would ask, stooping down to adjust her misbuttoned sweater or brush her mussed hair. *"We sing to God, of course, but we also sing to each other. When we've almost forgotten what we believe, the words of the songs remind us."*

He'd sung those old reminders when Maggie had woken up with a nightmare, on days when the pews were nearly empty, during Mother's sickness, and even after her death. And when he couldn't sing, when his throat was choked with tears and memories, Maggie had watched him listen to others around him repeat words of hope.

She let the memories linger for a moment, then looked back at Gabriel, waiting in companionable silence for her answer. "I asked him to sing because he needed to."

Gabriel didn't react, his face impassive. Then he shook his head. "Just when I think I have you figured out, you continue to surprise me, Maggie McCleod."

Maggie smiled impishly at him. "Well, if you're going to be so flattering, why don't you just ask me out on a date and get it over with?"

Did I really say that out loud? Judith and Catherine's teasing must be getting to her.

Surprise flickered over Gabriel's face, and she laughed, though she felt a nervous flutter in her stomach as she waited for his response. That was the safest way to do things. Make everything into a joke. That way, your real feelings were safe.

So she was surprised when instead of brushing the comment aside, Gabriel looked intently at her. "If I were a sort of man looking to go on a date, I certainly might."

That sort of response fairly demanded a question, and Maggie couldn't resist. "What's that supposed to mean?"

For a moment, he looked like he might not answer. "There's no way to escape me," she said, gesturing to their surroundings, "and we've got a long drive ahead of us."

He acknowledged that fact with a nod. "There's not much to tell. I decided several years ago I wouldn't be settling down and raising a family."

"Really?" She couldn't hide her surprise. "I'm not angling for a free ticket to the movies, but you seem like the most settling-down sort of fellow I've ever met. Responsible, hardworking." She stopped herself just short of saying *good-looking*. That felt far too personal. "Stubborn, too, but most women wouldn't hold that against you."

This was quickly moving out of teasing territory, but Maggie wasn't sure how to get it back.

"Marriage," he went on, glancing over at Catherine and Douglas, still occupied in their tasks, "is not part of my plan."

"Ah." Maybe it was as simple as that. Gabriel did seem like the sort to have a highly annotated life plan, probably drawn up at age ten, with diagrams and checklists.

"There's no chance of you changing that plan?" Maggie knew it sounded desperate, but she had to know, and this might be the only time she and Gabriel were able to talk alone.

"No," he said simply, and if she hadn't been watching him

closely, she might have missed his hand drifting down to the brace on his leg.

Was it something about his injury that kept him from wanting a family? Did he think he was somehow less worthy because he wasn't able to walk perfectly or serve in the military like others?

For a moment, she wanted to reassure him, but then she looked at the closed-off expression on his face. Maybe it wasn't any of her business. Gabriel could mind his own affairs. If he ever decided to trust her, he knew where to find her.

Still, during the rest of the ride, the space between them never closed, even when they hit a stretch of road full of potholes and it would have been easy for Gabriel to slide closer, and the small gap of bench between them felt a little bit lonely.

24

April 23, 1943
Navarin Airfield, Sétif Province, Algeria

"Maggie!" When Maggie rolled over with a sleepy moan, Catherine tugged on her arm, her irritation rising. "You have to wake up. Our driver is here."

"Mmmph" was Maggie's articulate reply, swatting Catherine away like she was a fly.

"Oh, don't be ridiculous." Really, Catherine enjoyed a good lazy morning as much as anyone but not when they had a show to get to.

As Catherine tugged Maggie's blanket away, Judith took the less gracious route of splashing water from a nearby washbasin in Maggie's face, following it up with a curt "Now get up, or we'll leave you behind."

That combination seemed to spark some life into her, though she still stumbled sluggishly to gather her things.

Catherine felt a twinge of guilt. *Poor dear*. They'd had long days of travel that week across the rural roads, and Maggie seemed to have worn herself out, playing baseball and staying up late talking with soldiers after each show.

They were all tired by this point in the tour, but Catherine hoped that the combination of powder and sunglasses covered up the bags under her eyes and that the greasiness of her hair after too long without a bath was hidden by a chignon tucked under her helmet. At least last night, they'd bunked with a group of Red Cross nurses with an actual roof over their heads, a welcome change.

Outside of the utilitarian barracks, the driver who greeted them stood at sharp attention, his hair cut so close to his head that it was barely visible. "Sergeant Clyde Stark, at your service." He made a show of opening the doors of the jeep for them, and Catherine murmured her thanks. *Betty Sue*, the white letters under the windshield proclaimed.

"Y'all just pile in, now," Sergeant Stark said after securing their luggage. "You can see the sights on the way. We've got to get a move on if you want to set up for the show."

Their lodging was located outside a small village, where camels likely outnumbered the population, so the roads here weren't anything like the paved boulevards leading from the larger cities. This one was pocked with holes and debris, and Sergeant Stark seemed to be steering Betty Sue toward each and every one of them.

"He's taking the 'off-road' bit of 'off-road vehicle' too literally," Maggie muttered, closing her eyes.

Thankfully, Sergeant Stark didn't seem to hear over the noise of his enthusiastic explanation of how to tell Roman ruins from Phoenician ones.

"There's no need to make up time," Catherine assured him, interrupting as yet another bump jarred her spine. "We're quite fine with a, uh, slower pace."

"Not to worry. They put me on this job because of my driving record." The brag was timed with a straight shot through an especially deep pothole that had Catherine grasping for something to hold on to.

She tried to keep her eyes on the road, and her stomach settled. "What unit are you with, Sergeant Stark?"

"Me? I'm a proud tail gunner with the Second Bombardment Group."

She'd asked the routine question dozens of times, always listening for that very answer, so now she wasn't sure she'd really heard it. "Did you say . . . the *Second* Bombardment Group?"

"Sure did."

It was the same direction she'd written on every letter sent to Leo after his deployment. Could it be?

Sergeant Stark glanced over at her, and Catherine knew she had to say something to cover up her shock. "And I assume you first came to North Africa in November?" The date of the American invasion . . . and the time when Leo had stopped writing.

"No, ma'am. We were patrolling the Eastern Seaboard back in the States for U-boats and then did some training in Montana. We've been in Africa for less than a week."

A frown briefly flitted across her face before she could stop it. That wasn't right. Leo had specifically written to her about training across the ocean. Then again, Catherine had never quite been able to sort out the jumble that was military unit organization. Perhaps the 2nd Bombardment Group had been divided into two or more companies.

Which means Leo might not be here after all.

Catherine couldn't bring herself to ask Sergeant Stark if he knew Leo, not with Maggie seated beside her, knowing the torrent of mockery it would unleash, particularly after the incident with the letters during the air raid. If Leo really was here in this small town in the Algerian desert, Maggie wouldn't spoil their reunion.

Her heart began beating faster at just the thought. They were discouraged from stepping out with admirers and "stage door Johnnies," as Mr. Douglas called them, after their shows, and instead instructed to mingle with groups of soldiers. Surely, though, she could arrange some sort of private meeting, however brief.

That was, if Leo was stationed here, if he wasn't on duty and was able to see the show, if she could find him, speak to him, hold him again.

As they drove the five miles to the airfield where they were set to perform, Sergeant Stark narrated the drive, pointing out olive groves and barley fields swaying in the breeze, the green welcome after their brief time in a more arid region of Algeria. Catherine did her best to focus and not think about Leo. Better not to let her hopes rise too high.

Still, she found herself taking off her sunglasses as their vehicle approached the canvas neighborhood of pup tents, searching for a familiar debonair smile.

"Here we are," Sergeant Stark said, parking the jeep next to the type of rough wooden stage they'd become accustomed to on their tour.

Any hope they'd had of clean costumes faded as a swirl of dust hit them, pummeled by the winds that swept across the flat terrain—a sirocco, the locals called it. Catherine could feel a few of her curls wrenching loose with the force of it.

Sergeant Stark hopped out quickly to open the doors for them once again. "Better hold on to your hats because . . ." He broke off, his mouth gaping as he stared at Catherine.

She'd gotten a similar reaction before, with women scarcer than ice cream sundaes out here, and often just as drooled over. "I can't imagine I look all that glamorous after this wind," Catherine said, smiling to relieve any embarrassment he might feel.

"Sorry. I—I'm sorry." He shook his head like he was trying to dislodge something stuck there. "It's just . . . you look like someone, I mean . . . I thought for a moment I recognized you."

"I must have one of those faces." Catherine smiled modestly, the way she always did when someone mistook her for someone more famous—Rita Hayworth came up the most often. "But I can assure you, I've never gotten anywhere near Hollywood."

Their once-vigilant driver seemed to have completely lost his train of thought. "Uh, ladies, before I forget, we'd be obliged if you'd stay away from the planes."

"We're not especially interested in aircraft," Maggie said with a laugh. "But can I ask why?" Her voice was casual, but Catherine could see the familiar light of curiosity in her eyes. Telling Maggie not to do something was a sure way to guarantee her interest in it.

"Oh, security and all that," he said vaguely. "The pilots are touchy about it."

Catherine tilted her head. "Is that so?" They'd performed several times for army and navy air groups before, even sometimes for RAF fighters when the British army was nearby, and they'd never once received such a warning. One tail gunner had even given them a tour of a Flying Fortress, bragging about its features like he'd welded them himself.

But Sergeant Stark didn't seem keen to discuss the subject further, touching his hand to his helmet like he was tipping his hat. "See you at the show, ladies. Break a leg." He rushed off as if the future of the North Africa campaign rested on a message he needed to deliver.

"Funny thing to say, isn't it?" Maggie asked, mirroring Catherine's thoughts.

"Maybe these troops are training with a new, secret aircraft," Catherine offered. If that was the case, they certainly didn't have anything to worry about from her. There was only one thing on her mind: this was Leo Wallace's unit, and if luck was on her side, finally, after months of silence and waiting and wondering, he'd be in the audience this afternoon.

Catherine adjusted the petticoats that gave fullness to her gown's skirt, her palms slick with sweat. *You look fine,* she tried to reassure herself, listening to Gabriel's act stretch out interminably onstage while she waited.

Now that she was this close to possibly being reunited with the man she had dreamed of for months, everything felt uncertain. Leo had met her when she was a demure musician in a black evening gown back in Iowa and fallen for her through carefully written letters. Today, she was exhausted, dusty, and far from home.

Then again, he would be changed too. Combat did that to a fellow, or so some of the men had said. Maybe that's why he stopped writing: he felt he wasn't the same man she had met at the Surf Ballroom.

Well, if he gave her the chance, she meant to prove him wrong.

At the last minute, she'd decided to risk questioning from Mr. Douglas by playing "Let Me Call You Sweetheart" as her final number, which was not in the USO-approved routine.

"You're on, doll." Judith nudged her as Howie announced her act onstage.

With one last pat at her hair to make sure the red flower was tucked neatly in place, Catherine rounded the rough backstage, climbing onto the platform that looked out on the airfield's runway.

She opened her eyes, looking over the crowd, searching for Leo's handsome face. He had to be here, he just had to.

The applause, as always, was thunderous, but this time, Catherine heard something usually reserved for Maggie and Howie's acts: laughter. Some of the men were pointing, turning to one another, not with whispers but with shouts and cheers.

Almost instantly, Catherine could feel her face burning. This felt like more than the usual stares and enthusiasm. Did she have a lipstick smear on her cheek, perhaps? Or maybe her slip was poking out from her hem.

The din continued even as she lifted her violin in a vain attempt to begin the program. What were they saying? Amid all the noise, it was hard to tell. One thing was sure: either Leo was not present among the men, or he was hidden from her view.

As the clapping died down, she could hear isolated voices from among the seated soldiers.

"Where's the swimsuit, Red?"

"You can take that dress off anytime."

"This'll be a show for sure!"

What in the world? Catherine stepped up to the microphone at the center of the stage, staring at the mob—she'd never thought of the audience that way before, but this one certainly was—trying to think of what to say. "Today, I-I'll be playing several selections for all of you. . . ."

But her words were drowned out as the scattered cries coalesced into one shout, repeated over and over: "Red Bombshell." A few of the men near the front tried to jump onto the stage, held back by military police stationed on the fringes.

Shaken, Catherine decided the only thing to do was begin playing. That restored some bit of order, but between songs, the cheer of "Red Bombshell" continued.

She gave the abbreviated program of two songs, hoping Howie would recognize the closing number and take it as a cue to announce the next act. "Let Me Call You Sweetheart" would have to wait. She was in no state to debut a new song now.

The moment the last strain eased off her bow, she gave

a perfunctory curtsy and made a direct line offstage to the renewed cheers of "Red Bombshell," along with any number of offers to meet her after the show. She didn't pluck the flower out of her hair and toss it. The way this crowd was going, it might have caused a stampede.

A chorus of wolf whistles followed her, and Judith, waiting by the steps, barked over her shoulder in a strident voice, "Leave her alone, you vultures!"

In spite of herself, Catherine's legs shook as she ducked backstage, away from the spotlight and the chanting. Onstage, Howie was trying to restore order, or at least change the subject, by reciting one of his humor bits.

I didn't see him. Given how the performance had gone, she wasn't sure whether to be disappointed or relieved that Leo wasn't in the audience.

"You all right, darling?" Judith asked. Her gaze wasn't set to its usual world-weary amusement. In fact, she actually looked concerned.

"Fine." Though Catherine couldn't deny that her ears were still burning from embarrassment. "It's just . . . I'm confused. Did they advertise our show as a burlesque?" But she hadn't noticed any unusual reception when Maggie had stepped onstage.

"Men are beasts, that's all." Judith waved her hand as if dismissing half of the world's population in one go. "I should know, I married two of them before I got wise and gave up."

"That nickname they shouted . . . have you heard it before?"

Catherine had been afraid it was some awful innuendo, but Judith shook her head. "Can't say that I have." She gave Catherine one last pat on the shoulder. "You'll be all right. Must dash—it's my turn onstage."

Before Catherine could take a deep breath to attempt to

regain her composure, Mr. Douglas strode over, clipboard in hand, his face more flushed than usual. "What the dickens was all that about?"

"I-I wish I knew," Catherine said, doing her best to keep a waver out of her voice. It certainly wasn't anything she'd said or done on the way here, and the gown she wore wasn't a slinky scarlet number, just her usual gold gown and pearl necklace. Elegant, yes, and she'd attracted more than a few whistles at past performances, but this display was something different entirely.

Maggie drifted over, slapping Catherine on the back like they were teammates at the end of a baseball tournament. "Good thing we'll be moving on tomorrow, eh? This lot isn't worth our time."

"I just don't understand," Catherine repeated. From what she could hear, Judith's singing wasn't prompting a particularly raucous reaction.

"Don't let it bother you. I'm sure it's an isolated thing."

Something in the other woman's tone made Catherine turn to study her. She'd long ago noticed that Maggie's emotions might as well be written on her face in newspaper-headline type, and now she looked very much like someone who knew more than she was telling.

"All right," Catherine said, narrowing her eyes, "what is going on, Maggie? And don't bother lying."

Whatever mental argument Maggie had been having with herself settled, and she looked up, determined. "There's something you need to see."

Neither bothered to ask Mr. Douglas for permission, and Catherine followed her to the very area Sergeant Stark had warned them away from and which, apparently, Maggie had already visited before the performance.

Several B-17s were lined up in an orderly row, despite the rugged state of the airfield, and Maggie stopped before the second of them. Catherine craned her neck up at it and frowned.

The plane was painted with one of the more salacious examples of nose art she'd seen: an auburn-haired woman with stiletto heels posing in a red bikini that just barely qualified her heaving bosom for decency, leaning provocatively against an artillery shell. The words *Red Bombshell* were scrawled next to it.

How crude. It didn't say much about the army's respect for women, did it? She started to turn away, but a second glance at the painting's face caused her to stop short. Even after blinking, the facts were undeniable. Take away the flirtatious expression, and the face of the woman on the plane's nose art was a dead ringer for *her*. Same hair, same cheekbones, same eyes, even the same small beauty mark under her left eye.

"How . . . ? Who . . . ?" But the answer came to her before she could even fully form the question, and her chest tightened with panic.

As far as she knew, there was only one person in this part of the world with access to her photograph and the artistic talent to get the likeness so exact: Leo.

Catherine changed into her uniform, buttoned all the way to her chin, and replaced her sunglasses and scarf before seeking out Sergeant Stark, who sobered the minute he heard her demand.

His prominent Adam's apple bobbed above his uniform collar as he swallowed hard. "Listen, ma'am, I don't know what's going on, but . . ."

"Bring me to him," Catherine repeated, never flinching.

"Roger." He bobbed his head in a nod, like she was suddenly a major general giving orders. "Right away."

He led her to one of the tents situated on the edge of the airfield with a beautiful view of the mountains.

Once there, he paused, standing in the worn grass, as if wondering how a person could knock on a tent, then cleared his throat. "Someone to see you, Wallace." He glanced helplessly back at Catherine.

"You may go," she said, accidentally slipping into the tone Mother used to dismiss the housekeeper, but Sergeant Stark didn't seem to mind and hightailed it to safety.

As well he should. There was about to be a sustained strategic bombing the likes of which this airfield had never seen.

The tent flap trembled, and Catherine realized Leo had been hiding from her. Maybe he'd seen her from a distance, or maybe they had a bulletin board and had received one of the USO flyers that listed her name.

Leo Wallace emerged from the tent, shuffling his boots and straightening to look up, no trace of surprise on his face. At least, she thought with satisfaction, he, too, was far from the striking figure she'd danced with at the Surf. Thinner, the fair skin of his face chapped with sunburn, though his eyes were the same shade that she now recognized as the blue of the Mediterranean Sea.

Stop looking at his eyes. She was supposed to be angry, wasn't she?

Still, a small part of her desperately wanted to hear he'd meant the painting as a misguided compliment, that there was a reasonable answer to why he'd stopped writing, that everything would be all right between them if they could simply start over.

"Catherine," he said, after a slight hesitation.

"Leo." She tried to make the one word as cool as possible, letting the silence stretch, making him the first to speak.

"So you know," he said, having the decency to look ashamed.

"Only that you've humiliated me," she said, as if that wasn't enough. "I came to get an explanation."

He nodded miserably. "It's like this." The deep breath he drew in reminded Catherine of the uneasy figures she'd seen in line for confessional on the occasions her father wanted them to be seen at church. "Whenever we stopped at a USO dance or a Red Cross club, I'd flirt with a gal who seemed interesting and get her address, tell her to write to me. That way, I'd get a letter nearly every mail call to show off to my buddies."

The words, delivered so quickly that some of them blurred together, hit her like stinging grains of sand in the wind, eroding her hope that this might end in apology and reconciliation.

"Every . . ." she stammered in disbelief. "How many women were you writing to?"

He shrugged. "Most of them trailed off after a letter or two. Those hostesses meet hundreds of soldiers a day, you know? Only a few, like you, kept writing."

"How many?"

He winced like he'd cut himself shaving, then admitted, "Seven."

Her Leo, her star-crossed lover, the first man to see her for who she really was, was nothing more than a glorified con artist. Worse, he had used her, and other women, playing with their hearts for his own entertainment.

It wouldn't have worked, a voice inside her insisted, *if you hadn't been so desperate for someone to love you that you'd jump at the first man who took notice of you.*

Deep down, she knew it was true, but she couldn't think about that, not now.

"I see." She kept her tone even, unwilling to let him hear how he'd hurt her. "And when did you paint your plane with my picture? Which, I should add, is a generous term for such a crude drawing."

"Back in September, when we started maneuvers in the Atlantic."

"Which you also lied to me about." Perhaps she was twisting the knife, but he was the one who had stabbed himself with it.

Leo bobbed out a nod. "I thought it would be more exciting if I was a pilot off in England going on bombing runs, not a flight mechanic stranded stateside."

So Leo wasn't even a pilot. All his stories about his flying experiences were likely lies as well. Had she ever known one true thing about this man?

"I stopped writing to all of them, honest. It just . . . didn't feel right anymore."

It never had been right, but Catherine had too many questions she needed answers for to waste time with something so self-evident. "But you didn't tell me—or any of the other women—the truth about why."

"What was I supposed to say?" he asked imploringly, as if he actually expected her to give him an answer. "It started out as something to pass the time. A joke. Nothing serious. I didn't mean for anyone to actually start caring about me like you did."

She wanted to snap back that she'd never felt anything for him, but the words she had written were proof enough that she had, and she hated that he could tell.

"It was a terrible thing to do," she managed instead.

"I know. But look, no one from home writes to me, not even my mother. I was lonely, all right? Lonely and bored and . . . well, I never dreamed you'd come here." He trailed off, looking away from her. "But I guess you're not interested in my excuses."

He was right about that. She'd been about to say "I hope you're ashamed of yourself," but she knew at a glance he was. It wasn't enough, of course, to outweigh the humiliation he'd caused her. In fact, his misery made her angrier. By being sorry, he'd even robbed her of a decent tirade. What was she supposed to say now? *"Oh, I forgive you Leo, let's be friends, maybe I'll send you a postcard every now and then"*?

No. Never.

She had to make him understand, to really feel what he had done to her. "I was sick with worry for months, half-convinced you were dead and that no one knew how to contact me. One of the reasons I came on this tour was to find you."

"Oh." If possible, he looked even more crestfallen. "I never thought—"

"No," she interrupted, "you didn't." When Catherine thought of Leo reading her letters, her poetry, out loud for laughs to the men of his unit, she could just die on the spot. Echoes of the "Red Bombshell" cheer seemed to resound even here. Would they ever leave her?

She had to get away from here, from him.

The last time they'd parted, she'd given Leo a kiss. Now she didn't even give him a final wave or farewell as she walked away into the desert alone, tears she'd managed to hide from him stinging at her eyes.

She had been wrong when she left the movie theater after *Casablanca* as a starry-eyed innocent. She did not like unhappy endings.

25

April 24, 1943
Navarin Airfield, Sétif Province, Algeria

Of all the people who could have met Maggie by their truck at the edge of the airfield the next morning, only Adolf Hitler himself would have been less welcome than Sergeant Leo Wallace.

"*You*," Maggie said, not bothering to hide the disgust in her tone. Sergeant Wallace, the scum, stood at attention for a brief second before realizing it was only a USO performer, not a commanding officer, who addressed him. "What are you doing here? Don't you have training to get to?"

He nodded, shifting uncomfortably. "I'm missing mess to be here. She . . . she told you?"

What did he think, that Maggie growled at every GI trying to be friendly? "More or less."

For all his faults, Sergeant Wallace didn't wilt under her glare like a coward. It had that effect on some men when she fired it like a fastball to their face. "I just thought I'd see you all off."

"Haven't you done enough damage already?" Judith demanded, coming up behind Maggie. "Now scram."

Thankfully, the two of them were the only ones from the troupe at the meeting place, because Maggie had a feeling she was going to say a few things she wouldn't want Floyd Douglas to jot down on his clipboard. She was tired, sore from a night of poor sleep in an army tent, and coming down with a headache and a cough, and Wallace had just offered himself up as the perfect target for her bad mood.

"Do you think she'll let me apologize?" he said, his voice hesitant. "I did a rotten job of it yesterday."

Wallace was a looker, she'd give Catherine that. Not even the sleazy type who ogled women up and down like they were no more than living pinup girls. He had a boyish mischievousness to him that he unleashed on them now.

Grudgingly, Maggie wondered if they were being too hard on him. After all, everyone did something stupid every now and then. She only wished he hadn't dragged Catherine into it. When she'd told the story of Wallace's villainy, she'd tried to hide her hurt, but it was obvious that this young man—or at least the man she'd thought he was—had meant more to her than she'd admitted.

"Listen, I was raised to believe that everyone gets a second chance." Wallace looked almost hopeful, until Maggie added, "From God. So I'd recommend you say your apologies in your prayers and leave Catherine be."

"And I wasn't even raised to believe that," Judith put in, "so don't push your luck. Although, I gotta say, I like your plane's makeover." She indicated the B-17s poking their noses onto the airfield.

Sure enough, even from a dozen yards away, Maggie could see the change. The painting of the Red Bombshell—Maggie refused to think of it as Catherine—was now cloaked from collarbone to the ankles in a formal black gown. Only her face, arms, and the heels remained, poking out just under the dress's crude hem.

Not Wallace's work. If the slapdash brushstrokes without any attempt at detail or shading weren't enough to indicate that, the shock on his face was. Not even the carefree flyboy could be that much of an actor.

"Well, what do you know about that?" Maggie fought the urge to laugh, unsuccessfully. Even snorted once.

"A much better look," Judith declared like a critic at the Art Institute of Chicago. "And don't you go giving it a thigh-high slit or plunging bust once we're gone, you hear?"

"I won't," he said fervently.

"Go on," Maggie said. "That's as much peace of mind as you're going to get from us."

Wallace looked like he was going to protest again, then must've reconsidered, because he nodded and jogged off to finish the war in his own way. Whatever regrets he had, he'd have to figure out how to battle through them.

Just in time. Catherine's swollen eyes and the way she looked fearfully in all directions before hurrying out from the tent barracks to join them told Maggie they'd been right to drive Wallace off. She reached out a hand to help the slight girl up into the truck. Catherine murmured her thanks and slid down the bench as far down as she could go.

"Did you . . . ?" Maggie mouthed at Judith, indicating the plane.

Judith snorted, not attempting to lower her voice. "You kidding? Think I keep a tin of black paint with my stage makeup?"

It was a fair point, and besides, Judith's snoring had woken Maggie twice during the night. The close quarters of a shared pup tent weren't made for secrecy.

Maggie took a seat on the now-familiar benches, stifling a yawn. Today's route would be a longer one over rocky terrain.

Once the men joined them, they were off to Constantine, ever closer to the Tunisian border, for several days of performances. Lots of American units had clustered there, newly arrived and ready to get sent over to the real fighting. Maggie had felt tired just hearing Douglas give them the rundown. Of course, she hadn't let on. He had to be close to making his decision about the Pepsodent contract, and any display of weariness would be as good as giving up.

That's why, when they finally loaded up and rattled away, she took out a postcard she'd bought back in Algiers and started scribbling a few lines instead of taking a nap, her pencil jerking with each bump in the road.

"Writing a letter home?" Gabriel asked, raising a brow in surprise. Once again, he'd chosen to sit next to her, something the others now expected, saving the seat for him, and Maggie couldn't deny that it gave her a secret pleasure to have someone actually seek out her company. Oddly, he wore his helmet, though the performers usually abandoned them for travel, except on sunny days when it offered a bit of shade.

Maggie nodded. Unlike Judith, who liked to scrawl her letters late at night, Maggie chose to use every available nighttime moment for sleeping. "My dad's used to my handwriting being terrible." She stifled a cough in the elbow of her uniform. Wouldn't do to have Douglas hear and think she was getting sick. "Though this is a new low, even for me."

"There's not much space anyway," he pointed out.

That had been the idea behind the postcard. Trying to fill a whole page of writing paper with news for her father felt daunting. Though Maggie told herself it was because she was being careful for the censors, she knew that wasn't quite it.

"How do you tell someone who doesn't know what it's like?" she found herself asking. "Being out here, traveling around, performing."

Gabriel looked out at the coastal road. "I'm not sure I can

say. My father was the real performer, before he retired a few years ago. He understood from experience. I learned everything I know from him, even borrowed his props."

Now that he mentioned it, some of the props did seem more worn than she would have expected.

He lowered his voice. "Even Mr. Douglas is a friend of my father's. Before auditioning for this tour, I was working as a legal assistant in a suburb of Chicago."

"No!" she said, acting as scandalized as if he'd said he was a bookie or a mobster. And the truth was, though a desk job did seem to fit Gabriel, the news still surprised her, considering how comfortable he was onstage. "Well, you must have inherited some natural talent. Lucky you. I don't have much of a pool to draw from."

"Preachers aren't performers, is that it?"

Was Gabriel actually asking a personal question? She almost teased him about it, given how notoriously closed off he'd been about his own life, but stopped, feeling that it might ruin the trust that had started to build between them.

"Not exactly. If I were going around the world with a Salvation Army band, dear old Dad wouldn't blink an eye, but he sees shows like this as a waste of time." She looked down at the postcard, picturing it sitting on the worn kitchen table next to Dad's thick falling-apart Bible. "But I'd hoped . . ."

Gabriel's voice was quiet, not attracting attention from the performers on the other side of the troop seats. "You hoped what?"

"That he'd change his mind once I told him about the soldiers and what our songs mean to them. But I can never figure out how to say it."

Maggie hadn't voiced it before, and putting it into words made it seem more . . . fragile, like the intricate ceramic tiles for sale at the market, displayed on velvet and safely out of reach of passing mules or grasping children.

"It sounds to me like you're hoping to change your own mind."

Her first instinct was to protest, which probably meant he was right. "Maybe I do need a little more persuading."

His gaze, as always, felt intense, like she was in the focus of a crack sniper. "What would it take, do you think? For you or your father?"

It felt silly, but Maggie forced herself to be honest. "If I got to tour with Bob Hope, I'd feel like I'd really made it, like I was doing something that mattered, you know?"

"I see." He turned, closed off like he always was whenever someone mentioned the Pepsodent contract.

It was a rotten thing to be in a competition with each other, Maggie decided. It would have been better if Douglas had never told them about it, just sprung it on them at the end.

"Well, I'm sure your father's very proud of you," he said.

"At least one of us is." Her father was like how she imagined God probably was. You knew he loved you but also that he had expectations, spoken or unspoken, and most of the time, Maggie felt like she was falling just short of measuring up.

Not out here, though. Every day was a reminder of her purpose, the difference she was making. If only she could put it into words.

She signed her name at the bottom of the postcard in surrender. It would have to do. She'd give Dad the full story when she went back home again . . . or at least, she'd try.

A couple of bone-rattling hours later, they stopped to refuel, and Maggie stood up slowly, feeling an ache that seemed to go deeper than the usual soreness. She'd better go to sleep as soon as they made it to their hotel in Constantine.

Howie gave her a hand down from the truck in his usual courtly way, and as she took it, something caught her eye.

"Taking up a side career in painting, Howie?" she asked, turning his hand over to show the small flecks of black paint there.

"Not sure what you're implying, Miss McCleod." He whistled a jaunty, innocent tune and ambled toward the shade of a nearby fig tree.

If he wanted to be coy about it, fine, but she wasn't obligated to play along. She hurried to catch up with him. "Where'd you find the paint?"

This time, Howie didn't pretend ignorance. "The Signal Corps had several gallons of blackout paint left over from their last post near the coast. We decided to give it a higher purpose."

She couldn't help jibing him. "It wasn't exactly fine art."

He reared back in exaggerated effrontery. "I'd like to see Norman Rockwell himself do better while sneaking around a military encampment at midnight with nothing but a pocket flashlight for illumination. Besides, I had to balance on Gabriel's shoulders to get to the top parts."

The image of the older man swaying and cursing in the dark while flailing a paintbrush was enough to make her laugh out loud. She glanced over at Gabriel, suddenly understanding the helmet jammed down low over his forehead, likely covering up a number of stubborn paint drippings impossible to get out without proper shower facilities. Laughing, she gave Howie a peck on the cheek. "You're both wonderful."

"Anything for our gals," Howie said, with a wink. "Although I have a feeling Gabriel would welcome that gesture of appreciation too."

Maggie willed herself not to blush. First Judith and Catherine, and now Howie? "I don't think he's interested in me like that."

"If you say so." Howie mimed a shushing motion. "Now,

don't say another word about the incident with the plane. If I know Douglas, he'll feel honor bound to court-martial us for defacement of military property."

They shared a laugh, and it made Maggie remember times back at the Salvation Army corps when she'd heard Great War veterans reminiscing about their war buddies, the fellows who had their backs, literally and figuratively. Something in her had always wished she could experience that kind of loyalty and dedication.

Well, they hadn't been in a pitched firefight, but Maggie was starting to feel like their little variety unit might just be her war buddies.

"More tea," Maggie said. Or, more accurately, tried to say. The words came out barely over a croak, and Gabriel raised an eyebrow for clarification. She gestured at the engraved silver teapot, and he passed it her way.

They'd made it to Constantine later than planned, and Maggie had fallen into a deep sleep immediately after their performance, barely rousing when Judith pounded on her door to wake her the next morning. The fact that it was Easter Sunday, a celebration of resurrection, made it all the more insulting that she felt like death warmed up.

"Everything all right today, Maggie?" Gabriel asked, studying her far too carefully for her comfort. Maybe he'd noticed her flushed cheeks or the slight shiver that traced through her when she wasn't careful to control it.

"She's just sane enough not to be a morning person like the rest of you fools," Howie grumbled, sipping his second black coffee. They all learned early on that Howie was used to the late-night performances of the vaudeville circuit, and he considered anything earlier than ten o'clock—or, as Howie preferred, ten hundred hours—practically indecent.

To avoid answering Gabriel's question, Maggie took a gulp of tea, scalding the inside of her mouth. Just what she needed on top of everything else. But if Douglas knew how sore her throat was, he might not let her perform tomorrow.

All she needed was another night of good sleep, and she wouldn't wake up feeling like she had spent the night in the desert with no canteen, her forehead burning up.

Pharmacie. Catherine had told her that was French for *drugstore*, and Maggie figured she could sneak away for some lozenges. It would have been easier to take Catherine with her, but she hadn't even come down to the hotel's courtyard for breakfast, pleading the need for more rest, an excuse both Judith and Maggie pretended to believe.

So far, Maggie hadn't needled her with a single "I told you so" about Sergeant Wallace. She hoped Catherine would snap out of her heartbreak soon, though. It was awfully awkward, tiptoeing around her.

Maggie curled her hand around the cup of tea, the strong spearmint scent rising to her nose. "Just a little tired. It'll pass."

Gabriel took a swig of his own tea, seeming content not to push the matter.

Not Judith. "Oh? Then how do you explain the coughing fit that made everyone in the elevator turn away from us?"

Was it her headache, or was Judith's voice exceptionally loud? Douglas looked up from his coffee, a frown on his face, as if he meant to enter the conversation.

"It was nothing. Say, this is a nice restaurant, isn't it?" Maggie said, after a quick glare in Judith's direction. It was a lousy attempt at a distraction, but all she could think of at the moment.

The courtyard was a study in symmetry, framed by two marble fountains, with crimson-draped tables set up in a diamond shape, graceful potted palms situated halfway between each to form a screen of greenery. Their server seemed to disapprove greatly when they'd requested an extra chair to accommodate five of them. He now wove toward them, two trays of breakfast food expertly balanced.

"Sure," Judith said, her eyes narrowed, clearly seeing through the dodge.

Maggie wasted no time digging into her shakshuka as soon as it was placed in front of her, partly because it smelled like heaven, and partly so she wouldn't be asked to talk with her mouth full. A slice of her knife bled yoke from the poached egg into the peppers and tomatoes, and the first bite was warm with bursts of garlic.

"Delicious," she said, even though it hurt to swallow. This, at least, felt right. Dad always insisted their Easter breakfast be celebratory, which usually meant a doughnut from the bakery down the block. Maggie took another mouthful in his honor.

"Are you quite sure you're all right, Miss McCleod?" Douglas asked, turning on the assessing glance of a talent agent whose performers paid his bills.

This had to end here. She didn't bother to adopt a respectful tone, looking their manager straight in the eye. "Don't worry about me, Mr. Douglas. I'll be onstage, ready—"

She meant to say "ready to play," but her cough chose that moment to reappear, and she pressed her napkin to her mouth to muffle the sound, pretending she'd choked on a bit of tomato. "Anyway, I'll be sure to take it easy today." At least after she went to the pharmacy and got in her hour of practice and her morning stretches.

Douglas reluctantly nodded. "Very good. But please let me know if your condition worsens. I'm sure your act is demanding on your vocal cords."

She acknowledged Douglas's request with a nod, though she knew she'd do no such thing.

If these last several performances had had decent microphones, that would have helped, but very few camps had the right equipment. She'd had to shout her jokes out for the last week, once even into a megaphone for a crowd of several hundred.

Thankfully, Howie rescued her with his usual banter, and Maggie managed to force down half of her dish. She made a show of declining Gabriel's invitation for anyone in the troupe to join him for an Easter service at a nearby church. Dad would be horrified, but she was in no condition to listen to a sermon in French, much less try to croak out hymns. "I think I'll go up to my room instead," she said, for Douglas's benefit. "Maybe take a nap."

"One moment, Maggie," Gabriel blurted, scraping out his chair so suddenly it nearly toppled over. "Could I have a word with you?"

Behind him, Judith gave her a waggle of her arched eyebrows, which Maggie steadfastly ignored. *Friends. We're just friends, that's all.* No need to make things uncomfortable with teasing.

She obligingly followed Gabriel over to one of the fountains, surrounded by a hexagon of black and white tiles. The water that trickled out of the stone pedestal in the center formed a soothing background noise, but peaceful atmosphere or not, if he was going to suggest a visit to the doctor, she'd slug him.

Instead, he said, "I wondered if you'd be interested in being my assistant tomorrow. That is, for my act." He rubbed the back of his neck, looking profoundly uncomfortable.

The question was so unexpected that Maggie took a few beats to process, the fountain trickling merrily in the background. "Catherine looks better in a gown," she blurted, a tinge of jealousy coloring her voice. Where had that come from?

He frowned. "I'm not asking Catherine. I'm asking you." When she didn't respond, he forged ahead, not quite looking her in the eye. "I only thought, since you're feeling poorly today, that it might be better to give your voice a rest, but still have a way to participate. Just for a few performances."

"It'll pass. I'm sure of it." But was she sure? From the look on his face, Gabriel certainly wasn't convinced, and for a moment, Maggie allowed herself to consider the idea. It would only be temporary, until her voice came back. "Besides, I don't know how to be a magician's assistant."

He seemed to seize on this as an opening. "It's not difficult. You'd fetch my props, display them to the audience, and distract their attention to aid my sleight of hand."

Maggie winced. So she'd be a set piece to look at, just like when she'd been a part of the Swinging Sweethearts. "I don't know, Gabriel. It doesn't sound like it's for me."

"I had a feeling you might say that. But if you'd consider . . ." Gabriel trailed off as he made a thorough study of the mosaic pattern. "I also thought if we worked together, that is, if the act belonged to both of us, then maybe if Mr. Douglas awarded me the Pepsodent contract . . ." This time, when he looked up again, he seemed almost hopeful. "We could stay together. If you wanted to."

So there it was, out in the open. Gabriel had no intention of giving up his fight for the Pepsodent contract, not even after hearing what it meant to her to win it, just like Judith had warned her. "I could ride your coattails, you mean."

"That's not it at all," he protested.

He probably hadn't meant to be offensive, but the fact was, if she joined his act, she'd be admitting defeat. "And what if I want to get the contract without you? On my own merits?"

"I see." Any trace of vulnerability was gone, faded back into the professional mask of a master of illusions. "If that's how you feel, then I withdraw the offer and apologize for offending you." With that and a nod good-bye, Gabriel was gone, leaving Maggie's head swirling like she was back under the blinding stage lights.

She could have handled that better. Someone like Catherine would have known how to be more gracious in turning him down. Still, she hadn't come all the way across the ocean and through the desert just to end up as a pretty face standing silently beside the real talent. No, she would perform her act at every show they had left, no matter how she felt. Even if she didn't get the Pepsodent contract, at least she'd be able to leave with dignity.

And, a traitorous part of her admitted, at least she wouldn't need to find out if Judith was right after all, and Gabriel's interest in her was nothing but smoke and mirrors.

Report to the USO Home Office
Floyd Douglas, Foxhole Circuit, Variety Unit 14
April 25, 1943

We've traveled over a thousand miles in North Africa and are nearly to the border of Tunisia.

I've tried to be upbeat around the performers, but reports from the front reveal that our estimates that the active combat in Tunisia would be over by the time we arrived were overly optimistic. I have no intentions of turning back—after all, what is the point of a schedule if it's not maintained?—but we may be closer to enemy fire than originally planned. Since at least two other variety show units have performed in a combat zone, I know the USO will give us its blessing to proceed. Perhaps you might also give us your prayers.

As for the state of our troupe, there seems to have been some interpersonal tension among the ladies. Something to do with a soldier, I believe, although I'll admit the details are vague. I try not to listen when the subject of romance comes up. A balding man of forty-four is never welcome in those sorts of conversations. That said, it doesn't seem to be anything that will impact the success of the tour.

Finally, and most importantly, I have enclosed a petition signed by my performers—and, it should be noted, myself—regarding the labor camps still allowed to operate in North Africa. I believe there have been journalists making a similar protest, and I can stand by the accuracy of the description enclosed. It's a blight on our nation's reputation to have an American flag flying within view of barbed wire and slave labor. I'm sure our few voices matter little, but I promised them that I would put our protest on record.

Sincerely,
Floyd Douglas

From Abe Lastfogel to Floyd Douglas

April 20, 1943

Floyd,

I'm pleased to pass on some good news. See the enclosed article about your merry little band, with a focus on Miss Duquette. It sounds like they skimped on the details, hard knocks, etc., but that's the newspaper business for you.

I must say, I'm not sure how you worked a feature out from all the way in Algeria, but it's been publicity gold. The AP picked it up, and it's been seen all around the country. We've already gotten more inquiries than we know what to do with from people wanting to audition or donate.

Good work, Douglas. I knew it wasn't a waste, putting you with that little variety unit.

And by the way, better get me the name of your recommended performer soon. We've got PR materials to print, you know. I saw Bob Hope at a bond drive performance last week, and he remembered your group and asked after you. Don't let us down!

Abe Lastfogel

26

April 25, 1943
Constantine, Algeria

Catherine splashed a handful of water on her face, not bothering to wait for it to warm. She needed the cold to shock her swollen eyes into some semblance of normalcy and distract her from the thoughts of *him*.

No matter how often she told herself he wasn't worth it, Leo's rejection still stung. She felt like a violin with a snapped bowstring, everything she attempted slightly off. For a while, she'd been able to claim exhaustion to avoid speaking to the others on the road, then she threw herself into the performance once they arrived in Constantine. Now, though, it was Sunday, and she was left alone with her thoughts and memories of a relationship that could have been and never really was.

Get dressed, go for a walk, do something, anything. It was sound advice, but all Catherine wanted to do was stay in her room and be properly miserable.

She'd only just changed into her uniform when a knock sounded at the door. It was a polite tap, so probably not

Judith or Maggie, who either banged on the door or threw it open without knocking at all.

"Coming," she called, catching a glance of herself in the mirror, face wan and eyes red. How dreadful she looked. "*Un moment, s'il vous plaît.*"

Once she'd made an effort, futile though it seemed, to powder away the worst of the damage, she opened the door to reveal Mr. Douglas standing at a respectful distance, his hands clasped behind his back. "I'm sorry to bother you," he began, and his tentative tone made her realize her eyes were likely still red, though there was nothing she could do about it now.

"Is everything all right?" she asked. Maybe there had been some last-minute change in the schedule and they were calling the tour short before entering Tunisia. At the moment, that might be more a relief than a disappointment.

"Oh, of course." Mr. Douglas produced a newspaper from behind his back. "To the contrary, actually. The USO home office sent this to me, and I thought you might like to see it."

Beneath the masthead of the *Minneapolis Star-Journal* was a picture of Catherine, wearing her uniform and arm in arm with two soldiers looking adoringly at her. She recognized it as the army photograph taken in Rabat, with a fittingly exotic backdrop of palm trees and the fender of a parked Jeep.

Her eyes scanned the first few lines of the article.

While the citizens stateside send best wishes to our boys in uniform, the USO's variety units are delivering it to them. Catherine Duquette, daughter of socialite darling Vivienne Lavinge-Duquette, is a member of one such unit.

The following description—mostly saccharine praise of her violin music "filling the Sahara" and mentioning how hungry the soldiers were for the sight of a woman in eveningwear—barely qualified as news.

Clearly, the reporter who had tacked a byline onto the article hadn't been present at one of their shows, or he'd know they hadn't traveled by train through Africa, nor did they actually reach the Sahara proper.

Catherine paused halfway, noticing Mr. Douglas was waiting for her reaction. "It's . . . very nice. Though there seem to be a few factual errors."

"Yes, I noticed that too, but it's to be expected, these days," he said, his tone condemning the entire field of journalism as little more than novelists writing short form. "In any case, the USO office says they saw a spike in interest and donations after its publication, more even than when a celebrity tour is announced."

"I'm surprised to hear that."

Mr. Douglas shook his head. "You learn, working in show business, that people can become cynical where celebrities are concerned. They assume the stars and starlets are just coming out here for the publicity. It's ordinary people like you who they admire. And deservedly so."

"I . . . I'm glad it was helpful," she said, keeping her real thoughts hidden. "Do you mind if I keep the article?"

"Please do. I had hoped it might . . ." He hemmed and hawed his way to a complete sentence. "In any case, I'm glad your efforts have been acknowledged."

He was trying to cheer her up, Catherine realized. From the way he'd avoided her since they'd left Leo's airfield, she felt sure someone, likely Judith, had given him the gossip. This attempt to make her feel better was sweet, and, at the same time, an utter failure. "Thank you," she said, putting her entire stage presence into making it convincing. "I appreciate it."

The moment he said his polite good-byes and she'd shut

the door, Catherine sat on the edge of the bed to read the rest of the article, her suspicions growing with each line.

> *"Most girls will never get this kind of chance," Miss Duquette said. "I'm proud to be launching my career by serving our boys. Remember my name. You'll see it in lights someday."*

"I never said that," Catherine whispered to the crumpled page, as if the reporter who took the information from her mother might hear it and print a retraction. "Would never say it."

But she knew who would. In fact, she'd actually heard her mother express similar sentiments before.

Sure enough, the article that had begun with a mention of her mother's name ended with a quote attributed to Vivienne:

> *"I'm so proud of my daughter for her sacrifice and service. Young ladies of America, take note—if you have the talent and the moxie, there's more than one way to serve your country."*

Well. Catherine tossed the newspaper to the floor, not sure, despite Mr. Douglas's kind intentions, that she could keep the thing a moment longer.

Don't overreact, she chided herself.

After all, besides the fact that there was no mention of the other members of her variety unit—probably because Mother didn't know their names or bother to take the time to find out—there were no glaring omissions in the article, no facts that were blatantly untrue. But still, to have someone put words in her mouth, to use her for attention like this . . . it was nothing short of infuriating.

But Catherine knew just how Mother would respond. She'd open her dark-lined eyes just slightly, drawing out her words. "Now, *chérie,* don't be so dramatic. This kind of publicity is just what you need—I was doing you a favor. Trust me."

The trouble was that Catherine didn't. She never really had. And now she was sure that, even half a world away with an ocean between them, she still hadn't managed to escape her mother.

Flushed from the afternoon sun, Catherine tottered into the cool of the hotel's lobby on sore feet, regretting letting Maggie talk her into an outing.

The three women had visited a recreational club for enlisted men, something Catherine had thought would keep her mind off Leo. Maggie, despite an awful cough, had spent the whole morning and early afternoon beating everyone at chess, pool, table tennis, and every other game available. Meanwhile, Judith had drawn a circle of admirers swigging coffee around a lunch table. That left Catherine alone trying to hold up her end of an interminable conversation with a group of flyers about the latest Western they'd seen on leave.

She'd made her excuses early, claiming the need to take an afternoon nap, which she fully intended to do. Whether it was all the noise or the heat, her head ached.

Her steps were slow as she made her way through the lobby, though even in her dour mood, she couldn't help but be impressed once again by its elegance. While other buildings in the city tried to evoke a Parisian feel, the Grand Hotel Cirta flaunted its Moorish architecture, from the intricate scrolled arches of the bleach-white exterior to the colorful tiling and dangling brass lamps in the lobby. The vaulted dining room with its massive wooden tables and wallpaper with a gold netlike *sebka* motif, large enough for a feast of hundreds, was a sight to behold.

"Boy, it really makes you feel like you're *someplace*, you know?"

Although the inane comment from the person next to her was spoken in English, Catherine nodded absently without turning her head . . . until she realized she recognized the voice. *But it can't be . . .*

She turned slowly, and Arthur DeVos himself, dressed for the heat in a white suit with a fairway-green tie and pocket square, stood next to her in the hotel on the border of Algeria and Tunisia. "Hullo, Cathy," he said cheerfully. "I tried to send a message to your room earlier, but you were out. Glad we finally caught up."

She made no effort to stop staring. "Arthur, what are you doing here?"

Never one to be bothered by abrupt questions, Arthur flashed his easy smile. "Officially? Here on business. You know, Duquette Lens looking to expand internationally and all that."

"And unofficially?" But Catherine was fairly sure she knew the answer. While Duquette Lens had factories in London, Bern, and Copenhagen, she was confident expansion to Algeria was not in her father's plans.

To his credit, Arthur didn't try to hide it. "Your family thought you might need someone to check in on you," he admitted. "Seems your last letter had your father worried. He figured if he sent me instead of just a telegram, you'd have someone you knew to escort you on the voyage home. Soon, if it all works out."

Home. Of course, Father would have heard her news that she might join *The Pepsodent Show* tour if she was chosen as a threat. But she hadn't counted on the length that he would go to keep his daughter within his grasp.

"Great place to visit, this. I've got a tour all booked up of the old Roman ruins later today," Arthur was saying. "Constantine's named after a Roman emperor, you know. They've got heaps of old citadels and temples out here—and most of them in heaps too." He chuckled at his own joke, not noticing Catherine's sudden silence.

No, that isn't it, Catherine decided as Arthur's brown eyes turned back to watch her steadily. *He notices, but is trying to cover up the awkwardness.*

She should be angry, furious. First Mother's newspaper article making the tour seem like it was all her idea, then Father sending Arthur to pressure her into leaving. It was a new low for both of them.

And yet, try as she might to work out the appropriate amount of outrage, Catherine found she was as empty as the tank of a jeep a few miles out from a supply station. Her legs suddenly felt weak, the weariness from long days and sleepless nights finally taking their toll, and she rocked forward slightly before catching herself.

"Say, you don't look so good, Cathy," Arthur said, his eyebrows bunching in concern as he took her arm. "Have you eaten lunch?"

"A little," she managed, and before she could add that she didn't care to, he was herding her toward the hotel's entrance.

"Come along, then. I'll give you the whole story over tea and pastries. Do they have afternoon tea here, or is that only the Brits?"

She didn't protest, mostly because crossing the road and being seated at a table near a tall, lace-curtained window gave her time to think.

"What looks good? My treat, of course." His voice, including the badly pronounced "*Merci*" he offered their waiter, seemed to boom off the small walls, drawing stares.

Catherine studied the menu. It was deeply unfair that Arthur's news had left her without any appetite because the café had quite a selection of delicious French pastries. "I'm not sure which to choose," she said, speaking quietly and hoping he'd mirror her.

"Go whole hog, then—order 'em all." He cracked his knuckles and settled back into his chair. "You don't mind doing the talking, do you? I studied a French phrase book on the way over, but my accent's so bad I'd probably challenge someone to a fight while trying to get a cup of Darjeeling."

Catherine decided not to argue with him and ordered four pastries, plus two cups of mint tea. When they arrived, Arthur sawed the *pain au chocolat* in half like it was a log of firewood, pieces of delicate pastry flaking onto the clean white tablecloth. "This way we can both try 'em all."

Catherine would have been happy with one unmangled croissant, but she took the offered half and watched in horror as Arthur dipped his into his tea.

"So," she began, "my father sent you to bully me into coming home."

His hand paused on the way to his mouth, tea dripping off the soggy end of the pastry onto his saucer, and the hurt expression that momentarily crossed his face made her regret her choice of words. This wasn't his fault, after all. "It's because he cares about you, Cathy. Honest. Or I wouldn't have come. You know that."

"Do I?" She asked the question automatically, because neither of her parents had been the sort to dote over their daughter. Her mother had been too busy with her dress appointments and social calendar to bother with Catherine until she came of age, and her father made no secret of the fact that he wished she'd been a boy, able to take over the family business directly instead of finding a son-in-law for the role.

"He wants to make sure you're safe. This close to the war zone is no place for a lady."

Hadn't she heard that every step of the way from the very beginning? *"Pretty girls aren't meant for ugly wars."* She had been so determined to prove them wrong, and where had that gotten her? Painted nearly in the nude on the nose of a plane, hoarse and exhausted on the way into a battlefield, homesick and lonely and so very tired of being stared at and whistled at and ogled.

This wasn't the career she dreamed of or the adventure she'd hoped it would be. She'd thought it was her chance to escape from her parents and maybe even find herself and find her true love, but all she had found was heartbreak.

"Besides," Arthur went on, a grin tugging at his face, "my sister would want me to remind you that your godchild will be born any day now. We might make it home in time for the big event."

"Of course. I . . ." Catherine trailed off, unwilling to admit to the soon-to-be uncle that she had all but forgotten the approaching due date. Despite her dread of facing Father, at least Lorraine would be delighted to see her.

"I'm sure it's been real rewarding, the work you've done out here," Arthur said around a mouthful, a flake of pastry landing, unheeded, on his round chin. "But you've done more than your fair share. Time to come home, don't you think?"

That was her cue to speak, but Catherine couldn't yet find the words, letting the silence linger in the chatter of French mingling around them.

So her father thought staying was a foolish idea. Well, maybe it was. If she was honest, with all claims of noble motives aside, she knew her leaving had been an intentional slap in her family's face, a cry for independence, or maybe even attention. How could she be surprised when they responded?

"I'm sorry for the position my father put you in, Arthur,"

she found herself saying, "but he shouldn't have worried. My contract is up at the end of May, so I'll soon be boarding a steamer back to the United States. If I'm offered an extension to another tour, I will be declining it."

Saying the words out loud gave her a sense of relief. No more decisions to make, no more living from a trunk and straggling into a bed—or cot—in a new city each night. Back to regular meals and laundry service and warm baths drawn up whenever one felt the urge. Yes, back to her family's demands and the pressure to find a suitable husband, but at least whoever she found wouldn't hurt her the way Leo had.

"That's just it." Arthur took a big bite of the *chausson aux pommes*, forgetting, apparently, that he had planned to sample only half of each. "I've had a talk with your boss, that Douglas fellow."

Arthur had talked to Mr. Douglas? Catherine wondered how that conversation had gone. She couldn't picture them getting along.

"He agreed to let you off early. Two days from now, just after the rest of your performances here in Constantine. Said conditions would be rougher in Tunisia, maybe even dangerous, and it wouldn't be right to keep you if your family was worried." He wiped filling-stained fingers on his napkin and leaned back in his chair enough to infringe on the space of the person behind him.

Of course Mr. Douglas would allow her to leave early. He was likely surprised she'd made it this far.

Two days. So soon. And yet that would mean only a couple more performances until she could be free. Not have to face Maggie's pitying buck-up hints. Not have to put on a smile again and again while under a spotlight. Not have to banter small talk with soldiers who reminded her of Leo.

"All right," she said. "It seems to be for the best."

Arthur gave a relieved nod as he cut into a fruit tart. "Just so, just so. I'll send your father a telegram tonight to let him know."

"Thank you," Catherine said, genuinely grateful to be saved the task, though the bite of croissant she took to oblige Arthur had lost all of its buttery warmth, now bitter as the swallow of tea that followed it.

If even her own manager was willing to let her go so easily, Catherine was sure she had done all she could. It was time to go home and face the music.

27

April 26, 1943
Constantine, Algeria

Maggie sucked in her stomach as Judith fastened the clasps on the back of her gown. She tried not to think about the rack of girdles at Dayton's that she'd refused to go near.

"There you are," Judith said, tugging the last clasp closed, the fabric pulled tightly around her middle. "Why have you been wearing those old cotton things when you've got this stashed away? You're a stunner."

"I was waiting for the right occasion," Maggie said, brushing the compliment off with a laugh.

If only she felt as good as she looked. She hadn't *exactly* kept her promise to Douglas to rest the day before, and the fever she'd pushed back with some medicine from the pharmacy was now threatening to go another round against her. But she could keep the coughing in with effort, at least long enough for a twenty-minute set onstage.

Maggie twirled in the mirror, letting the green silk fall against her legs.

Let Gabriel see her now. He could keep his glamorous magician's assistant position. She would do just fine on her own.

It was petty, Maggie knew, making a statement like this about her solo act. But the way she looked at it, there was no harm in getting a little extra dressed up every now and again, if only to show Douglas that she really was serious about entertaining the soldiers. If they wanted to see a dolled-up glamour girl . . . well, she'd give it to them.

"Go on, pucker up," Judith said, holding up a tube of red lipstick. "You can't go out with a bare face after putting a dress like that on."

Maggie had to laugh at that. "Can you imagine what the valve of my trumpet would look like at the end of the performance if I did?" No, the dress was enough, though she did compromise by letting Judith dust rouge on her face.

"Borrowed from Her Majesty," Judith said, putting a finger over her lips. "Don't tell. My shade would be far too dark for you."

Not that Catherine was likely to notice. She'd been distant all day, all weekend, really, still distracted over her pilot. When did hurt turn into self-pity? Maggie wondered. No friend would let Catherine sulk around forever.

"You're still looking pale," Judith observed, tsking.

"I'm feeling fine now," Maggie said, which was a lie, but if she told Judith the truth, she'd spread the news to Douglas that Maggie was practically two feet in the grave. With a little bit of makeup, her symptoms were well hidden. At least, she hoped so. She'd down another pill on her way out the door, just to be safe.

You can do this, she commanded herself. A McCleod could get through anything, no quitting, no excuses. As children, she and her siblings had risen every Sunday to the strains of "I'm in the Lord's Army" belted out by Dad, and no matter how early it was, no matter how cold it was outside or how bitter the wind might be, they'd marched down to the corps meeting place without complaining.

She ran a hand over the silk. She'd muster up that same determination now, regardless of how she felt—and look good doing it.

When Maggie stepped out onstage, letting the emerald silk swish around her ankles, the men erupted in whistles and shouts, and she couldn't help grinning. Oh, she'd gotten applause before, of course, but never a reaction like this. She mimed looking around in all directions. "What's all the noise about? Did the Germans surrender?" This time laughter mixed with the whoops and cheers.

Halfway through her first song, she started to wonder if it had been a mistake to borrow Judith's heels, her knees locking in an attempt to keep her balance. Formal footwear, always her nemesis, no matter what side of the ocean she was on.

Just a little dizzy, that's all. She tried to take deep breaths in between the notes, but she choked a few times on a cough, missing a few beats. She made a joke about it at the end of her song, blaming breathing in the desert sand.

Today's audience was a group of paratroopers, fresh from training, sent in to support the ground troops. Most of them looked barely old enough to shave, much less plummet through the air into a war zone. They didn't seem to mind that this wasn't her best performance, cheering like she was an A-list star straight from Broadway.

By the time she launched into "A String of Pearls," her most demanding piece, it was getting harder to ignore the headache, spots of dizziness distracting her from even the familiar melody. *Just a little more.* Then she could perform her closing bit and drag herself offstage and rest. But the song required long stretches of connected notes, and Maggie found her lungs couldn't sustain them.

She eked out the last few notes and instead of her usual bow she gave a wide curtsy, displaying a little leg, feeling both ladylike and dizzy. Time for the last joke.

"All the Boy Scouts back home have their trusty plane-spotter guides, and they could tell a B-17 from an A-29 on a foggy day while blindfolded. Seems to me they'll have to make some changes to the Superman radio show, now that their audience is getting so sophisticated. Soon, you'll hear, 'It's a bird, it's a P-39 Airacobra, it's Superman!'"

Thankfully, that got a round of laughs, because imitating a deep radio announcer voice triggered the rasp in her throat. She stifled the cough as best she could, knowing the men were waiting for the next line. *Got to push on.*

She forced her girl-next-door smile. "Speaking of Superman, you boys really are heroes to all of us. When folks from back home heard I was coming over here, there wasn't a one of them that didn't have a message for me to pass on."

Another cough, and this one seemed to jar the punchline right out of her mind, which was getting foggier by the second. Where did this bit go?

Oh, right. The kiss. That was always the last joke, sure to bring down the house.

Almost done. You can do this, Maggie.

"In fact, a mother from Chicago told me to give a kiss to her boy Jimmy. Anyone here . . . ?"

Before she could finish the joke, the stage pitched up to meet her, and her knees buckled, hitting the ground. Had a bomb hit the stage? No, there was no explosion, only a few men shouting. An earthquake maybe?

But then she saw Douglas rushing over from backstage, and she realized she had collapsed. Voices spoke, and people crowded about, pulling at and speaking to her.

"Maggie." She knew that voice. Gabriel must be trying to help her up, but her limbs felt about as steady as gelatin and the dark patch on her vision grew.

She tried to find the words to say she'd be fine, just needed a little air, but even the word *fine* wouldn't come.

28

April 26, 1943
Constantine, Algeria

The hotel's elevator jerked to a start with an unsettling groan of metal. Catherine tried to turn toward the noise, but with Judith, Howie, and three others pressed inside, she could barely move. Maggie would have made some joke, wondering if the lift was a relic of the Roman occupation from the first century, instead of the more likely date of the early 1920s.

But Maggie wasn't coming back to Hotel Cirta with them, not tonight. After being rushed backstage following her faint, she'd been revived with cool water splashed on her face, but it was clear she was feverish. Gabriel and Mr. Douglas had traveled with her, against her will, to a brand-new army hospital just north of Constantine for treatment.

The elevator lurched to a halt, and the operator pulled open the metal gate for them. Catherine murmured a "thank you" as she passed.

Her worry must have shown on her face because Howie gave her a hearty clap on the back as they straggled down the hallway toward their rooms. "She'll be all right, never fear. She's a tough one, our Maggie."

While Catherine knew it was true, she also felt a weight of guilt. She had heard Maggie coughing all the way to the show, and yet she'd been too focused on her own trouble to do anything more than ask if Maggie was feeling all right. This was, at least in part, her fault.

She sighed. "I just feel we ought to be there."

Judith sniffed. "I'm sure the doctors don't want us getting in the way. They'll have enough trouble getting rid of Gabriel, the poor lovestruck puppy."

Thinking of Gabriel as any sort of puppy was laughable, but it had been sweet to see his concern for Maggie. It seemed that, all their teasing aside, love was blooming in North Africa . . . just not for Catherine.

"See you in the morning, ladies," Howie said, tipping his hat and ambling down the hall, more slowly than usual. Maggie might have been the first one to break, but they were all showing signs of exhaustion.

Catherine's plan to share the news about her departure with the other troupe members after their evening performance had been abandoned. Tomorrow afternoon, she and Arthur would be traveling by bus to the coast while Maggie rested in the hospital.

Will I even get to say good-bye to her? Maybe it was a selfish thing to think of, but leaving without being able to explain herself to the performer she'd known the longest felt oddly incomplete.

Catherine fiddled with the key in her door, trying to focus bleary eyes on the task.

"I *told* her she was running herself ragged," Judith said, shaking her head, "but would she listen? No. I don't know why I even bother saying *anything* around here."

"I'm sure you did your best," Catherine said vaguely, pushing the door open for some welcome peace and quiet.

That, at least, had been her plan, but instead of continuing down the hall, Judith followed her into the room, lounging in the chair by the window and tapping a cigarette out of the narrow pack she kept in her uniform pocket.

"Mind if I smoke?" she asked, already midway through lighting the cigarette.

"No, but . . ." Catherine trailed off, unsure how to finish the sentence, since "What are you doing here?" felt unforgivably rude. "Is there something I can help you with?"

"I thought you might like some company."

Catherine resisted the urge to say that all she wanted right now was sleep. "I'm fine, thank you."

Instead of taking the less-than-subtle hint, Judith stretched out, propping her feet on the metal bed frame, and let up a curl of smoke. "That's what Maggie said, too, and she was about to collapse."

The impolite groan Catherine wanted to deliver escaped as an irritated sigh as she set about the task of packing her things for tomorrow's journey, wrapping up her perfume bottle in her crinoline petticoat for protection. "It's hardly the same thing."

"All right, fine. I'll just come out with it. Want to tell me about your GI beau?"

For one awful moment, Catherine thought Judith was teasing her about Leo, until she added, "The one you met in the lobby the other day."

How did Judith always know these things? Compared to her, the formidable Axis spy network throughout North Africa looked like an amateur tattletale operation. "He's not in the military."

"No, I suppose not. No uniform. A diplomat, then? He's not a bad-looking fellow, though his taste in ties is outrageous."

So she'd actually seen Arthur, then. "You were spying on me," Catherine accused.

"It's not spying to be observant," Judith said archly, without a hint of shame. "I followed you back to the hotel because I was worried you'd step in front of traffic in the state you were in. After that, well, you were out in the lobby for anyone to see."

Try as she might, Catherine couldn't think of a good explanation without getting into all of the embarrassing details. "Arthur brought me some news about a family emergency. I . . . I have to go home. Tomorrow." The half-truth Catherine had settled on for an explanation didn't sound satisfying when she said it out loud.

"With only a month left in the tour?" Judith waited for Catherine to spill all the juicy details, which she declined to do, rolling her socks up tightly instead. There was a luggage weight limit for the steamer home, and she wasn't sure what she'd have to leave behind to make room for souvenirs and tokens from soldiers she hadn't been able to part with.

"You know I'd rather die than meddle in anyone's personal affairs," Judith said, and Catherine couldn't tell if she was being sarcastic or sincere, "but I can't help wondering, you wouldn't be giving up, would you?"

She took a guess. "You heard us talking."

"Observed, darling," Judith corrected, "and not everything. Just enough to wonder. I can't stand the idea of some man talking you out of what you really want to do."

"It isn't like that at all," Catherine retorted, busying herself with arranging her cosmetics in the pocket of the trunk. "Arthur didn't pressure me."

Judith tapped her ashes onto the floor for some poor maid to clean up when they moved on the next day. "I wasn't talking about Mr. Loud Tie, whoever he is. I was talking about that Leo Wallace fellow."

Even hearing his name caused her to wince. "This has nothing to do with him."

"Well, if that's the case and you're leaving just because you want to, the army might call that desertion."

Then the army can step on its own land mines.

Catherine's cheeks burned at the thought that she'd very nearly blurted it out. "Please, I would like to be left *alone*."

"Would you really?" Judith said the words thoughtfully, her expression difficult to read. "Sometimes you think you want to be alone, and then people actually leave you, and . . ." She shrugged. "You wish someone had stayed."

This, Catherine felt sure, was not one of those times. "Why should you care? If I'm gone, your chance at the Pepsodent contract is better."

"Because you're the most talented of any of us, and I'm not going to let you throw all of that away because of some two-timing man."

That made Catherine pause midway through folding her spare performance gown. "You really think I'm talented?"

"Uncomfortably so. Though I'll deny it up and down if you tell anyone I said it." Judith stood and tossed her half-finished cigarette out the window. "Now, tell me all about it, darling. Why are you really going home?"

And somehow the whole story poured out, from joining the Sweethearts to meeting Leo to practically running away to North Africa to escape her parents. All throughout, Judith's face remained unreadable.

"I suppose you're going to tell me I'm a silly, naïve little princess," Catherine said, wiping away a few traitorous tears with her handkerchief.

"Nah, it just proves you're human. Which is a little surprising, actually." Before Catherine could think of how to respond to that, Judith tilted her chin up. "Listen, it's hard getting over a man. I should know. But whatever you decide to do, make sure it's your choice. No one else's. Got that?"

It sounded simple enough, but when Catherine thought

through her life, she was ashamed to realize how many of her choices had been made to keep someone else happy or to avoid an argument.

"All right." Catherine took in a steadying, though somewhat sniffly, breath, feeling oddly comforted. "Thank you, Judith."

"Don't mention it. Really. Don't." Judith stood and stretched. "Better get some beauty sleep, or we'll all end up in a ward next to Maggie. Ta-ta, now." She blew Catherine a kiss as she breezed into the hallway, as if their heart-to-heart had been just another gossip session.

Catherine went through the motions of preparing for bed, but when she was finally surrounded by the clean sheets and the gossamer sweep of mosquito netting, she found herself alone with a question: Which would she regret more, leaving or staying?

29

April 27, 1943
26th General Hospital, Bizot, Algeria

They really ought to be able to keep flies out of a hospital, Maggie decided, batting yet another one away. Even in a tent encampment, it just wasn't sanitary.

Add to that the thin strip of padding they called a mattress, the long hours with nothing to do, and the nurses insisting on accompanying her to the latrine in case she fainted again, and Maggie had had it with the 26th General Hospital, even after just one day. It was ridiculous, really. "Untreated bronchitis developed into pneumonia," the doctor had said. That was the sort of thing you treated with chicken soup and an extra scarf, but she'd duly swallowed the pain medication they'd pawned off on her without complaint. Well, without *much* complaint.

She had been assigned a cot in, of all places, a corrugated metal Nissen hut that would eventually be the dental clinic. For modesty and to protect her from the sights and sounds of the wounded, the doctor had said, but Maggie suspected it was to get her out of the way. They'd officially opened the hospital the day before, and already ambulances from Tunisia were bringing in men by the hundreds. The staff was working furiously to make sure everyone had a chart and a bed and whatever medicine they needed to keep them comfortable.

"Visitor for you, Miss McCleod," one of the white-uniformed nurses called cheerily enough from the hut's doorway, though her smile had flagged somewhat over the hours Maggie had been conscious. Maggie tended to have that effect on people sometimes.

Maggie braced herself for Douglas, come back to scold her about proper hydration and rest, when he was the one setting their breakneck schedule. Instead, she was pleasantly surprised to see Gabriel standing there, hat in hand, looking as worried about her as he had when she woke up after her swoon.

The nurse apparently had more pressing matters to attend to than chaperoning because she disappeared almost instantly.

"Gabriel," she said, sitting up so he'd know that everything was all right. A mistake. She'd moved too quickly, the dizziness that had felled her onstage threatening to return. She closed her eyes briefly until the feeling passed, covering it with a yawn so Gabriel wouldn't get suspicious. "Thank goodness you're here. You can tell them they're making a fuss over nothing."

Instead of looking relieved like she expected, Gabriel only frowned. "Your lungs are infected, Maggie. That's very serious."

Sure, sure, they'd told her all that. When she'd asked for a shot or a pill to deal with it, they'd given her a course of sulfa tablets for the pneumonia but warned her that bronchitis took time and patience to heal. But now that she'd swallowed her pills, drank lots of liquids, and had gotten a good night's sleep, her head wasn't even pounding. Much, anyway.

"I understand you don't want to look weak around Mr. Douglas, but . . ."

"Is that what you think this is?" She laughed, swinging her legs over the side of the cot to stand. Where did they put her shoes? Maybe she should feel self-conscious dressed in nothing but men's pajamas in front of Gabriel, but while they didn't fit perfectly, they covered all the important parts, and they were gloriously comfortable. Maybe they'd let her keep them. "I'm telling you, I'm right as rain now. Don't we have a show this afternoon?"

"Yes, and you won't be in it." Gabriel moved to the other side of the cot to block her path. "The doctor explicitly recommended that even if you travel with us, you rest."

"If? You mean you were going to leave me here?" Douglas would never let that happen. It would ruin his perfect schedule, which was why she was determined to be in the next show, at least for a few songs.

She groaned, spotting the shoes under the bedside table, her green dress folded neatly on top of it. She'd forgotten they were the heels she'd borrowed from Judith. Well, there was no help for it. She sat back on the hospital bed, jamming them on her feet.

"That's not it at all. Mr. Douglas simply wants you to take your medicine and rest the next few days while we perform."

"Without me, you mean?" It was arrogant, maybe, to think that the troupe couldn't go on without her even for a few shows, but Maggie hated the feeling of being passed over. Besides, she knew Douglas wouldn't dream of letting a quitter continue on to *The Pepsodent Show* tour. If she was going to make a comeback, it would have to start now.

"Yes," Gabriel said, leveling her with a stare that felt more than a little condescending, "without you, Maggie. Your act is dispensable. You are not."

She supposed he meant it as a compliment, in his way, but

she was a performer, a fighter. It was impossible to separate who she was from what she did.

"Step outside, please," she said coolly, tottering to her feet in heels. "I have a costume to change into. If we hurry, I'll be gone before the nurses even realize my bed is empty."

Now the look she got was one of plain disbelief. "You're going to sneak out of an army hospital?"

"That was the idea. Don't we have a show to get to?" She snatched up her dress, trying not to let Gabriel see the disorienting tilt of dizziness that came over her as she bent down for it.

"Don't try to tell me you're completely back to normal. I do have eyes, you know."

"Then you can use them to look the other way."

He didn't budge.

Fine. She softened her tone and said what she thought he wanted to hear. "Look, Gabriel, I promise I won't wear myself out. I'll even let someone else load the luggage this time."

He didn't react to this generous concession. "You are a human being just like the rest of us, Maggie, in case you weren't aware. You have limits too."

"I'll go back to having limits at the end of this tour."

He ran a hand through his hair, glancing over his shoulder for rescue from a nurse or doctor, but the hut remained empty. "Listen, it's hard to hear news like that, and I understand how you feel, but . . ."

That was too much. Maggie crossed her arms. "Oh, I seriously doubt that. No one ever treats men like they're helpless."

"Don't they?" Gabriel's voice was low, bordering on angry. "I am in the USO right now because I accepted a polio diagnosis that told me I couldn't fight, might lose the ability to walk, and likely wouldn't live as long as the average man. Not a temporary sickness that would force me to miss a few performances, an illness I'll live with for the rest of my life, and that has shaped all of my choices since then."

The words hit her like a series of blows. Of course. Polio. She should have guessed it was something like that.

Should she say she was sorry? No, that's what people always said at times like this, and it always felt false. From the way Gabriel shifted uncomfortably, looking at the ground, the dentistry equipment, anywhere but her, he probably wished he hadn't said anything at all.

"I didn't mean anything by it" was all she could think to offer, and it sounded hollow.

"No, I'm sure you didn't." With effort, he'd controlled his features until he wore the same blank professionalism as usual, the master of illusion stepping onstage again. "Your choices are your own, Maggie. But I can assure you, it's better to accept your limits than to fight them."

30

April 27, 1943
Constantine, Algeria

It was silly, but Catherine found herself walking slowly from the elevator to the lobby, as if that might delay the inevitable. She'd worried Arthur might be late—he had mentioned visiting an Algerian winery the night before—but when she emerged into the bustle of the main floor, he stood near the main entrance, gesturing frantically at a hotel employee asking him questions in French.

By the time she hurried over, hoping to help, a confused bellhop was pushing the trolley carrying a pyramid of Arthur's red leather luggage set toward the entrance.

He waved when he saw her, despite the fact that she was now only a few feet away. "All's well here, Cathy, not to worry. The fellow thought I was trying to rip him off by tipping him with a souvenir coin instead of a franc." He flipped something small and silver to her, and with the chipped edge and bust of Caesar inscribed on the coin, Catherine couldn't understand how anyone could confuse them. "They make 'em so realistic, you know?"

She handed back the coin, which Arthur returned to the pocket of his double-breasted seersucker suit. "I see. Arthur—"

But he was already looking around, craning his neck like her belongings might be around the corner. "I can tell him to throw on your luggage too, if you like. He's flagging down a taxi for us. Did you know the word for *taxi* is the same in French and English?" He chuckled as Catherine tried to break into the conversation again. "Silly of me. Of course you would."

"I don't need someone to fetch my luggage," she finally managed to get out.

He paused for a moment, taking in the small handbag she carried in one hand, a wrapped parcel in the other. "Already wrangled it to the curb, eh? That's my girl. Are you ready to leave, then?"

Without knowing it, Arthur had just asked the same question that had kept her up late into the night. If she followed through on her promise to return home, she wouldn't wake up to Judith's request for help fastening her dress or Maggie's determination not to get out of bed until the last possible moment. There would be no Howie to give an outlandish "Top o' the morning to you!" or Gabriel to quietly load the women's luggage onto the truck or even Mr. Douglas to remind them, again, that keeping a diary or taking photographs was against army regulations.

She'd known she would miss them, of course, but tossing and turning on her bed, she'd felt it like a physical ache. They would go on without her. The show would be just fine.

But will I be?

"Everything all right, Cathy?" Arthur's voice had the same light tone as ever, but there was something perceptive in the eyes under the brim of his white Panama fedora that had never been there before. Or perhaps it had, and Catherine had simply never noticed.

Either way, the fact that he actually paused to listen gave her a burst of courage. "Arthur, I can't do it. I'm not going to leave."

Instead of the usual torrent of chatter, Arthur simply leaned back on the heels of his spotless two-tone oxfords. "Hmm. Is that so?"

Her words came more confidently now, or at least faster, so he wouldn't have time to interrupt. "I've spent all night thinking about it, and I just can't go through with it. Father always said his business was built on trust, and I've given my word to the USO. I know this can't last forever, but for another few weeks, I really feel I ought to—"

"I'll stop you right there," Arthur said, waving his hands in a poor imitation of a conductor cuing his orchestra. "Listen, if you've made up your mind, I'm not about to try and stop you."

Catherine stared dumbly. "You . . . you're not?"

"I'm a salesman, Cathy," he said, as if she would've forgotten. "I joke about it sometimes, say I could sell dental floss to a granny with false teeth and all that. But the truth is, in my line of work, the goal is to persuade folks to buy what they already want. That's what I thought I was doing with you."

She'd gotten lost somewhere before the false teeth. "I'm afraid I don't understand."

"I can't say as I'm doing the best job explaining," he said, taking off his fedora and fanning himself with it. "It's like this. I figured if your father was paying the bill for me to come all the way out here, I might as well come. And when I pitched going home to you, you looked relieved, like you'd been waiting for someone to give you the excuse. So I figured it was a good deed all around."

"But I've changed my mind," she said, in case he'd talked right over her and missed her announcement.

"That's clear enough," he said, grinning. "So just convince

me you're not gonna change your mind right back again, and I'll say my good-byes."

That was all? Catherine let out a sigh of relief. If Arthur had been angry, if he'd bullied or guilted or tried to persuade her to step on that steamer, she might not have had the resolve to fight back. "I won't," she said. "This is where I'm meant to be."

He pumped her hand up and down like someone had just announced her as the winner of a scholarship or a horse race or whatever was worth celebrating in his world. "Good for you, Cathy, good for you. I'll miss your company, of course."

In the pause, Catherine wondered how to respond. She'd always gotten the idea that Arthur was somewhat thick-headed, oblivious to the matchmaking schemes of his sister and her father, but now she had to wonder.

Thankfully, Arthur never let silence linger. "But long voyages are a good time to make new chums, aren't they?" He snapped his fingers like he'd just gotten a brilliant idea. "I can whip up a story to tell your father when I show up without you. Something about that manager of yours insisting you stay, threatening legal action, whatever you like."

"No." If this was her choice, she was going to face the consequences. "Tell him the truth, please. Tell him—" she paused, searching for the words that might make her father—and her mother, for that matter—understand. "You know, I think I'll tell my parents myself. Both of them. There are some women working very hard at the Central Postal Directory in Algiers to make sure V-mail gets over the Atlantic by air in record time, so letters will likely beat your return trip."

Arthur nodded with enthusiasm. "That's the spirit." The wink he gave her was full of the teasing glint he'd had since he was a boy. "There's some fire in you after all, Cathy, underneath all those Mozart sonatas."

"Yes, I'm a regular red bombshell." The dry retort popped out of her before she could stop it.

Arthur scoffed. "Who called you that? No offense meant, of course," he added quickly. "You're beautiful and all, everyone knows that. And anyone who hears you play knows you have talent. But what matters more is that you're brave, Catherine. Not many people know that. But they're going to." He nodded, almost to himself, and something about it made her blush. "Yessir, I think they're all going to know soon."

To hide her embarrassment, she thrust the small package she held toward him. "Would you give this to Lorraine for me? I found something for the baby at a market in Casablanca."

"Swell. I'll do that." He stuffed the parcel carelessly under his arm, and she was grateful it contained only colorfully embroidered baby slippers and not something more fragile. "And don't you worry about not being around when the little tyke is born. I'll do enough visiting for both of us until you get there."

Impulsively, she stood on tiptoes and kissed his cheek.

"What was that for?" he asked, his face all astonishment.

Though she wasn't entirely sure herself, she said, "Thank you, Arthur. For everything. You could've been a perfect beast about all of this, and I would've deserved it."

"Not at all," he said, ever the gentleman. "It takes most of us time to realize where we fit in this crazy world."

There seemed to be a story there, under Arthur's polished smile, one she'd never asked for. When had she and Arthur last had a real conversation? Only hours before she had been dreading a long voyage with this man, and now she was curious as to how he'd chosen the path he was on.

But his words jostled her back to the present. "Come on, Cathy. No time to dawdle. I've got a steamer to catch, and that variety unit of yours needs you."

And for the first time, Catherine believed Arthur might just be right.

31

April 29, 1943
Bône, Algeria

After a long argument, where Douglas actually took her side for once, the army doctors cleared Maggie to travel to Bône with the rest of the company, though under strict orders to continue resting. Which meant the next day, they'd left her in her own private tent as they prepared for the afternoon show, as if she could sleep in the middle of the day.

Even though her fever was mostly gone and her cough had improved, Maggie knew if she showed up at the performance against orders, she'd get another lecture. She settled for second-best: taking a walk around camp. That was restful, wasn't it?

As she suspected, the east side of the outpost was a ghost town, as each and every entertainment-starved GI crowded around the stage for the USO show.

Well, good. At least she could get some peace and quiet. It didn't take long, though, for the view to get stale. Though Bône was on the coast, the airfield was too far inland to give Maggie a view of the ocean. That meant, unless she wanted to admire the Spitfires ready to take to the skies, there wasn't much to see, the landscape flat and dull like an airfield ought to be.

Except . . . *Is that . . .* ?

From behind, the truck looked like any other military vehicle: boxy frame, drab colors, caked up to the fenders in mud. But the red shield logo visible through a layer of grime on the side made Maggie laugh out loud. "I don't believe it."

She'd skipped church during her tour with the Sweethearts, left her Bible behind with the excuse that they had to travel light, and begged off from chaplain-led services all across North Africa, yet somehow here, in the middle of Algeria, was a Salvation Army Mobile Canteen, parked right in front of her when she had nowhere else to go.

"Fine," she said, throwing out a gesture of surrender to the sky, "you win."

Though she half-hoped no one would be about, Maggie added her tracks to the many that had beaten a path to the mobile canteen. When she didn't see any movement under the service window's metal awning, she thought she'd gotten her wish, until she noticed an older woman in a high-collared blue uniform sitting against the truck's front fender in stocking feet, tapping sand out of sensible black pumps.

She replaced them and stood with a sheepish smile when she noticed Maggie watching. "Well! You've caught me sitting in my stockings."

Maggie blinked. It wasn't that the voice belonged to a woman that surprised her—Salvation Army officers were drawn from both genders—but a strong British accent marked the vowels. Then again, Douglas had said this camp was shared with the RAF, hadn't he?

"No need to stand up on my account," she replied, feeling suddenly foolish. "I'm not here for coffee or doughnuts. I'm only here to . . ."

To what? To appease her conscience? To look for a miracle? To feel a little closer to her father, an ocean away?

"I'm just passing through," she finished.

The woman seemed to take her measure under raised graying eyebrows. "I don't know what made you think we serve *coffee*." The disdain in her voice told Maggie just what she thought of that poor excuse for a beverage. "But if you'd like to come in, we can have a cuppa. Proper black tea, mind. Not that there's anything wrong with the mint sort they serve here, but it won't do when you need something stronger."

Maggie found herself unable to resist the offer, and the woman led her into the canteen with all the decorum of a lady ushering a guest into a parlor rather than an interior crammed with the workings of a functional kitchenette on wheels. She introduced herself as Major Felicity Newton, filling a china teacup out of a tap in a vat of hot water, steam rising to the woman's pinked cheeks.

"No kettle, I'm afraid. I had to fight to let them bring even the most ordinary of cups and saucers."

Sure enough, Maggie saw a collection of several dozen teacups taking up the entirety of counter space next to the sink. "That must make for a lot of cleaning."

"Worth it for the boys to feel a bit more human," Major Newton assured her, handing her the teacup. "Anyway, my husband helps with the washing up. He's out at the moment, went to see some sort of show you Yanks are putting on, with dancers and all that. Have you heard about it?"

The short laugh she gave must have been enough to answer. "Heard about it? I should be performing in it. But not as a dancing girl. I play the trumpet. They hired me for my talent, not my pretty face or long legs."

"I wouldn't have assumed otherwise." Major Newton turned back to filling her own teacup, gesturing to an overturned bucket that seemed to provide the only seating in the confines of the canteen, which Maggie took. "And why aren't you performing? Not that I have any desire to turn you out."

She'd known the question was coming. Still, Maggie resented having to explain her bout of sickness and Douglas's overreaction to it, so she blitzed through it as quickly as possible. "And now, here I am, sitting here drinking tea and being useless while everyone else puts on a show."

"Mmm," Major Newton said mildly, "useless, are you?"

There was something uncomfortably searching in her gaze that made Maggie hesitate. "Well . . . yes. What was the point of coming all the way across the ocean if they won't let me do my bit?"

"I see." The major passed a sugar bowl to her, but Maggie declined, noticing it was nearly empty. Better to save it for the troops. "I can't help but notice you were quite dismissive just now of women who only value their pretty faces."

Maggie blinked, unsure of what that had to do with anything. "Why shouldn't I be?"

"It's just that . . . Oh, how should I put it?" The major clinked a half spoonful of sugar into her own cup, and her face brightened. "When you're allocating your rationed goods and have no eggs left, it's better to use a packet of powdered eggs in your Yorkshire pudding than none at all, but only just."

The second sudden turn in conversation made Maggie blink again in confusion and look around to see if the canteen had any treats stowed away. "We don't ration eggs in America. At least not yet. And why are we talking about baking?"

The older woman gave her a look of mild exasperation. "We aren't. It's a parable, dear."

Maggie was just about to reply that parables went out of style after Jesus's day, on account of their being so obscure, when the major continued, "All I mean is, I suppose it's somewhat better to find your worth in what you accomplish rather than how you look. But it still won't give you what you're looking for."

Maggie began to wonder how she'd ever thought of the major as kindly and matronly. At the moment, her gaze was cutting right through Maggie with the force of an artillery shell. "That all sounds very nice," she finally said, taking another sip of tea, "but I'm not here to find myself or anything like that. I just want to be useful."

"And you're frustrated when you can't be. That says something, that."

Could the major be right? Maggie had to admit it was possible, at least partially. She'd never felt so angry as she had when the doctor barred her from performing, nor so helpless as when she'd been left behind as the others performed.

"Do you know, this is my second war service?" Major Newton nodded to herself, as if Maggie had asked to see a photograph of her in her younger years. "Oh yes, back in the Great War, I volunteered with the Salvation Army in France as a Donut Lassie. We would use artillery shells to roll out the dough to fry up for the boys in trenches only meters away. I was young and wanted so very badly to do something."

Her gaze was distant, as if she could look back three decades and see her younger self, and Maggie felt she was interrupting. "But no matter how many treats I served, no matter how many grateful soldiers I smiled at, it still didn't feel like enough. I began to fear it would never be enough. Still, I kept on. I had to do something great for my family, for my country, even for God."

Her words sounded uncomfortably familiar. "But you're back here again," Maggie pointed out. "For another war, doing nearly the same thing. So it can't be all bad."

"Ah, that's just it. I've learned a bit since then. It wasn't my work that needed to change. It's what I expected my work to do for me." She stared straight at Maggie with eyes the color of long-steeped tea and just as warm. "Your value isn't in what you accomplish, Maggie. If you place your worth there, you'll live just short of satisfied and die tired. But when you give it up"—she held her teacup aloft and smiled—"you learn how to rest."

"I know how to rest," Maggie protested, and when Major Newton raised an eyebrow at her, she modified, "or, at least, they've made me sleep late the past three days."

"There's a difference between sleep and rest. That's the secret behind the Sabbath. It's not about rules of what ought or ought not to be done. It's meant to be one day a week where you contribute nothing at all to the world. Where you're not expected to produce anything, work hard, or prove yourself."

There was something nice in the way she put it. Maggie thought of her childhood, where Sundays were for church and long afternoon naps and inviting friends over for dinner.

"We're often traveling on Sundays," Maggie said, suddenly feeling the need to justify herself since she hadn't been to a worship service in months. "The USO sets our schedules."

"You can't help that. But I've noticed that when we don't take the rest we need, the Lord has a way of giving us a forced Sabbath." She gestured at Maggie's overall person as if she were the prime example. "The question is, How are you going to use it?"

"Drinking another cup of tea, apparently," Maggie said, holding hers out. "Mine's gone cold."

Major Newton chuckled and took the cup. "Certainly. Good for what ails you. And by the way, you should thank the good Lord you haven't gotten on to rationing eggs. That powder is absolutely abominable."

They spent the better part of the next hour talking about Major Newton's adult children, Maggie's early days of learning to play the trumpet in the Salvation Army band, and their shared love of sports—baseball for Maggie, cricket for Major Newton.

By the time she left the dusty canteen with the red shield behind and waved good-bye to Major Newton, Maggie could hear faint cheering rise from the other side of the airfield, where the USO performance was ending. Now, though, it didn't prickle her with resentment.

Gabriel had been right. The show had gone on without her. And maybe, she thought, as she rolled up a blanket to serve as an extra pillow for her nap, that wasn't so terrible after all.

32

May 1, 1943
Tabarka, Tunisia

Catherine looked out on the crowd of men sitting on the ground just past the rickety railroad platform that would serve as a stage. They seemed more subdued than usual, talking amongst one another without the rollicking cheers and demands for the performance to start that they'd experienced at other stops.

Tonight's audience included an American bomber unit, as well as the 753rd Railway Shop Battalion, who patched up bomb-damaged tracks and decrepit boxcars to transport supplies deeper into Tunisia.

Here the men knew that when they loaded into planes, it wasn't for a training run, and if they heard the sound of gunfire, it wasn't merely a distant attack on a strategic location like a harbor. The Germans were coming for them, and their victory or loss could change the course of the war. If they lost this ground, they might well lose the rest of North Africa, the gateway to Italy.

That made the troops all the more willing to laugh at

Howie's antics. As Mr. Douglas had told them many times, the USO members were warriors in the battle for morale, and the stakes had never been higher. Catherine felt the weight of that in a more profound way than usual as she waited to go onstage.

She checked her lipstick for smudges in Judith's compact mirror, wanting to look her best, and caught a glimpse of Maggie and Gabriel in the reflection. They perched on a nearby ammo crate, angling their bodies in separate directions. For the past several days, the two had virtually ignored each other, or as close to it as you could come when in such tight quarters. Judith had hinted that she knew what had gone on between them—no surprise there—but Catherine hadn't asked her to elaborate.

Mr. Douglas pulled out his clipboard, as if taking a routine roll call of all the performers. He'd been just as businesslike when Catherine had informed him of her change of heart after Arthur's departure, asking a few questions and listening to her whole explanation. She'd been terrified he would say they didn't want her anymore, but instead, he'd nodded and said, "In that case, welcome back, Miss Duquette. I don't know how we would have replaced you."

Now the faint trace of a smile she'd seen then was entirely gone, and when he looked up from his notes, his eyes were serious. "They've just lost men, you know."

"What's that, now?" Howie asked, as surprised as they all were by the abruptness of Mr. Douglas's words.

"The bombardment group," Mr. Douglas went on. "A tail gunner and a crew chief on one of the B-25s were killed yesterday on a run."

Silence was not a usual feature of their dressing room banter before shows. Even Mr. Douglas couldn't seem to snap out of the melancholy and go over the order of the program. Thinking about his son, Catherine guessed, remembering how young Theo Douglas had looked. How terrible, as a father, to be this close without being able to protect him.

"Should we do anything differently?" Gabriel asked, and Catherine knew what he meant. With so much fresh grief and the fear that came with it, it seemed the wrong time to be pulling rabbits out of hats.

Mr. Douglas shook his head. "I don't think so. These boys need entertainment and a good laugh more than anyone."

But Catherine wondered if it would be enough. Was anything they were doing more than a distraction?

When it was her turn to step onstage to the usual swell of applause, she did her best to smile, knowing that's what these men needed. All the while, though, the thought rose unbidden: How many of these men would end up in the field hospital back in Bizot, waiting for surgery, moaning for more pain medication, wondering how they'd lived when others had died? And they would be the lucky ones.

She was supposed to lift her bow back to the violin to start the next song, but it suddenly felt far too heavy. "I . . ."

The soldiers' faces in the darkness stared at her, waiting.

The Catherine at the start of the tour would never dream of going off script. But if there was ever a time for it, wasn't it now?

"I hear you fellows have been through a lot today. In my own life, I've found music to be very healing. I don't know what song might help, but if you name it, I'll play it if I can."

It was clear there was something different about this audience. Any hints of audience interaction or participation at other performances garnered a swarm of shouts, but here there was a moment of quiet.

"'Nearer My God to Thee,'" a deep male voice said, and there was a murmur of agreement.

With it, Catherine's newfound confidence was shaken. She'd expected a sentimental radio hit, or perhaps even a common classical piece. She didn't recognize the song, but she knew it was a hymn, one that she'd never heard, much less played.

What should she do now?

While she licked her dry lips, about to apologize and tell the crowd to choose something else, she caught a glimpse of movement from the corner of her eye. It was Maggie, striding onstage, trumpet in hand.

Catherine let out a breath of tension. Rescued by the preacher's daughter. Maggie was still technically on bed-rest and not allowed to perform, so she was in her uniform instead of her costume, but Mr. Douglas had relented enough to allow her backstage.

Before she'd even reached center stage, Maggie raised her trumpet and began to play. The notes soared up in mellow, confident blasts that told Catherine this was no hastily learned-by-ear approximation of a song. She'd played this before, many times, though perhaps never to an audience this enraptured.

"'Though like the wanderer, the sun gone down . . .'"

At first, Catherine thought the soldiers had begun singing, but the direction was wrong. She turned to see Gabriel standing in the shadows at the far edge of the stage. She motioned him closer, stepping away from the microphone to let him take her place.

"'Darkness be over me, my rest a stone; yet in my dreams I'd be nearer, my God, to thee.'"

Gabriel had a fine baritone voice, not professional, certainly, but strong and clear. Seeing him singing the hymn into the microphone seemed to give others permission to join in, and soon several of the soldiers, holding their helmets and caps like they were in church, were singing along. She was sure she could see tears in some of their eyes.

By the second chorus, Catherine could sing along as well,

though she didn't dare attempt even the melody on her violin with no previous practice. Even then, she found herself choking on the words, tears threatening to ruin her makeup.

She would not cry in front of everyone. The USO had told them time and time again that the women of the troupe especially were to be cheerful and optimistic, never reminding the soldiers of the perils of war.

Still, how could she share in their grief without feeling it, at least a little?

When the hymn ended, there was a moment of silence before the applause, and Catherine took the opportunity to hurry offstage as Gabriel and Maggie took their bows.

Howie's voice boomed through the microphone. "That was a fine surprise, wasn't it, boys? Well, as they say in the business, now for something completely different . . ."

As Howie introduced Judith's act, Catherine tried to regain her composure. She didn't have a handkerchief—the slim silhouette of her silver gown had many benefits, but pockets wasn't among them—so there would be no recovering if the tears began to fall.

The tromp of army-issue boots and a burst of coughing told her Maggie was by her side. Catherine tried to wipe her eyes with the back of her hand without smudging her makeup. "You—you shouldn't have done that. Your lungs—"

"Are getting better every day," Maggie insisted. "And, hey, are you sure *you're* all right, Catherine?"

"I'm sorry. It just . . . it hit me all at once." She raised her ducked head and took in a shuddering breath. "No matter how well I play, no matter how much pep and patriotism we pour out on them . . . it can't save them. What is the point of building their morale if so many are going to be injured or killed?"

For once, Maggie didn't have even a hint of a smirk on her face. She rocked on her heels for a few seconds before speaking. "The army might give you a different answer, but here's my two cents. Did you see them out there just now? Did you see their faces?"

"Y-yes." That's what had triggered all of this in the first place.

"Good. Then you know that hymn mattered." Maggie took Catherine's hand, gripping it like she was pulling her out of a muddy trench. "The way I see it, if some of those men are going to die in battle, the best thing we can do is sing them home."

This time, when her eyes welled up, Catherine didn't try to stop it. Maggie was right. Maybe their contribution was only a small one, but they had to give all they could.

"Thank you," she said, giving Maggie a hug that the other woman awkwardly ducked out of a few seconds in. "For that and for the song."

She shrugged away the praise. "Comes from having half a hymnal memorized. Anyway, you ought to thank Gabriel. It was the words they needed."

"Are . . . are the two of you quarreling?"

For a moment, Catherine thought Maggie was going to deny it, but apparently she realized the futility of hiding a tiff in a six-person group. "You could say that." The stiffness in her voice was a clear sign to back away.

But then Catherine thought about how Maggie had warned her away from Leo months ago and how Judith had pried into Catherine's reasons for leaving the troupe and saved her from making a choice she would have regretted.

Because, really, what did people mean when they said another person's choices were none of their business? If you cared about a friend, wasn't it your responsibility to speak up when you could?

"You shouldn't keep things like that between you," she said, as gently as she could. "Whatever happened, wouldn't you at least want to leave this tour as friends?"

"Yes," Maggie admitted, and Catherine caught the brief glance toward Gabriel, who was beginning the meticulous process of packing his props. "But I-I wouldn't know what to say."

Catherine thought of the half-started letters to her parents, attempting an explanation that she'd drafted a half-dozen times. "You could try being honest."

Maggie made a face like she'd eaten something pickled. "That sounds awful."

Wasn't that the truth? "It might be hard. But if this tour reminds us of anything, it's that none of us know how long we'll have to take those risks."

For one rare moment, Maggie said nothing at all. Then she clapped Catherine on the back like she might a baseball teammate after a home run. "I'll think about it. You know, it's a good thing I've got friends like you, Catherine."

Friends. The word lingered in Catherine's mind even after Maggie turned away, and she knew she'd made the right decision to stay, even after finding out the truth about Leo. She may have thought she had found true love before, but she hadn't found a family. Not until now.

33

May 2, 1943
Tabarka, Tunisia

Maggie shuffled with her eyes on the ground, trying to hold the ceramic bowl level so water wouldn't slosh out. She'd searched the market for a container made of glass, but the elaborately designed pottery with swirls of yellow and turquoise was all she could find. At least it had a lid and two handles like a soup tureen, which made it easy to carry.

It had taken a heroic effort to drag Catherine away from the open-air market. Delighted to be asked on a shopping excursion, she'd tried to get Maggie to stop at every stall or blanket with wares carefully displayed, holding up a seashell necklace or bracelet made of beautiful red coral, so bright it didn't look natural. "These would look so lovely with your emerald silk," Catherine had said. "You will wear it again, won't you?"

Maggie had dodged the question, saying it reminded her of fainting onstage, when the real answer was that she wasn't sure if she'd feel like showing off for Gabriel, not with the way things stood between them, awkward and tense.

That's why I've got to find him.

That should be easy enough. He attended the chaplain's Sunday services with the same frequency that Maggie avoided them.

Sure enough, next to the bivouac area, several men sat or knelt near a chaplain's flag with the emblem of the cross. The outdoor service seemed well attended with a few dozen soldiers trying to get right with God before the shooting started.

The chaplain, a tall middle-aged fellow with intense features that made him look like he would charge right up to heaven's gates for an audience, seemed to be done with whatever preaching he'd been up to, and Gabriel stood apart as the soldiers talked amongst one another.

Maggie waved to get his attention, a few drops of water dotting the sand underneath her feet. He jogged over, his right leg dragging slightly in the loose sand, probably to keep her from exerting herself too much, despite the fact that she had followed orders and rested the last several days. Now her fever and cough were almost entirely gone.

"That's quite a souvenir," he said, indicating the bowl. "I only picked up a pair of embroidered slippers back in Fez."

"It's for you, actually." She held it out to him, trying not to read too much into the surprise on his face. Maybe this had been a bad idea.

Come on, Maggie. It's a present for a friend, not a grenade. Or worse, a valentine.

Now that she'd opened her big mouth, she had to go through with it. "I happened to be in the marketplace with Catherine, and I saw this," she said, feeling she ought to give some kind of explanation. "Think of it as a peace offering."

"It's very nice," Gabriel said, hesitantly inspecting it. Clearly, he wasn't sure how he was going to transport a large ceramic vessel all the way back to America but didn't want to be rude.

"Not that," she said impatiently, handing the thing off to him. He lurched slightly under the unexpected weight but thankfully didn't drop the bowl. "Look inside."

With a slightly worried expression, Gabriel lifted the minaret-shaped lid and instantly began to laugh, realizing what she had done.

"It's not exactly a goldfish," she said. "The French call it a rouget, which I think is more like redfish." Inside the bowl, a small mottled scarlet fish with a snub nose and whiskers, about seven inches long, swirled about in the confines of the ceramic walls.

"How did you get it alive?"

"That was a trick," she admitted. "The fishmonger was confused, but Catherine finally explained that we'd pay double to have it fresh, so he sent one of the boys at the stall down to catch one for us."

"He's a fine-looking little fellow," Gabriel said his face breaking into a rare smile. "I'm proud to own him. Although if you were expecting him to earn his keep, I think you'll be disappointed."

She squinted up at him. "And why is that?"

"Since you've gone to all this trouble . . ." Holding the bowl tight against his chest, he picked his way toward their trunks of props, stacked near their truck for tomorrow's departure. Setting the fish down, he pulled the latches of his royal blue one with a quick flick of his long fingers. Maggie leaned forward to watch as he reached inside and unwrapped a scarf protecting the mysterious fishbowl.

Only now, viewing it from the side, Maggie could see it wasn't an ordinary fishbowl at all. It was made of thin clear plastic and couldn't have been more than two inches deep. Even more astonishingly, it was fully flat on the back side.

"How does it do that?" she asked, poking her finger at it. The moment she shifted to see the fishbowl face on, it appeared to be a full globe again.

"Half of a magician's work is clever cheats surrounded by good old-fashioned showmanship." Gabriel set the trick bowl down and looked up at her. "I don't think our rouget friend would be able to manage in a vessel I can easily clip inside my waistcoat with hardly a bulge."

"Then it was all a waste," Maggie said, disappointed. It had taken her over an hour to obtain the fish, not to mention convincing Catherine not to tell Douglas about their outing.

"I wouldn't say that," Gabriel said. "As a gift, it's a great success." He removed the ceramic lid again and studied the little fellow inside. "I'll call him Houdini."

"You know, he seems like a Houdini." Flashy, exotic, and with whiskers that looked like a dignified moustache if you squinted enough. "I bet he'd be able to wriggle out even if you locked him into a straightjacket."

"No doubt." His expression sobered. "As for its value as a peace offering, I hope you know you didn't have to bribe me with a fish."

Now that they'd come down to it, Maggie found it hard to look Gabriel in the eye and settled for a point on his shoulder. "Well, I felt like I had to do *something* after being so horrible to you back at the hospital."

Maggie's siblings had told her she was terrible at apologies often enough that she knew it must be true. It just felt so vulnerable, actually saying the words, then waiting to see how the other person would react. But Gabriel deserved an apology, a real one, so she forced herself on. "I'm sorry I was rude. About your leg and all."

While she'd done her best not to look down at the braced leg, when Gabriel did himself, she couldn't help following suit.

"You couldn't have known. It's not something I speak about often."

Even though she'd told herself a dozen times that she wasn't going to risk driving him away again with more questions, in the moment, curiosity won out. "Why not?"

He countered her question with one of his own. "Why does President Roosevelt hide his paralysis?"

"Roosevelt is paralyzed?" Maggie frowned, trying to picture images she'd seen of the president on magazine covers and such. It was true that she, like most Americans, mainly recognized his voice from his radio addresses, but still, wouldn't she have noticed such a serious disability?

"From the waist down," Gabriel confirmed, "caused by polio contracted as an adult, like me. He never lets photographers capture his wheelchair, and braces himself to stand at a podium when appearing in public to avoid criticism that a crippled man isn't fit to run a country."

That was just plain silly to Maggie's way of thinking. "But he's doing it, isn't he? Running the country during wartime, working hard, and accomplishing things in spite of his physical limits. Which, as you pointed out, we all have."

"I suppose."

The reply was so C-ration bland that Maggie pressed the point. "And you are too, Gabriel. Coming out here, for one. Not everyone would do that, even with two good legs."

He offered a faint smile. "It's the first mildly reckless thing I've ever done. And even with that, I half believe Mr. Douglas only gave me the job out of pity or because of his friendship with my father."

"Douglas gave you the job because you're an excellent magician who puts his whole heart into his act." He had to be joking, didn't he? But no, a second glance convinced Maggie he really meant it. "Good grief, Gabriel, someone must've really made you feel useless, and if he were here right now, I'd punch him in the face for you."

"Her."

That one word and the pain in Gabriel's eyes changed the story in a moment. "Ah." Maggie blew out a breath. "That wouldn't be good form, would it, hitting a lady?"

That got a slight smile. "She doesn't deserve it, in any case. We were young and infatuated with each other, but after my illness . . ." He shrugged, and in that small space, Maggie could see the memory playing out like a movie in his mind: a lovely young woman giving back an engagement ring and turning away. "She had imagined a different future. One that was no longer possible with me. And I realized my future would need to be different as well."

The words were gracious, but Maggie could feel the long-buried hurt in them. "Maybe I'd punch her anyway," she grumbled. "Though I suppose losing you was punishment enough."

Gabriel clutched his chest with his free hand as if she'd just delivered a blow. "Was that . . . a compliment? From Maggie McCleod?"

"Oh, don't sound so surprised. You're not a cripple, Gabriel. You're a good man who happens to need a leg brace. And that's not even the most interesting thing about you."

"No? Then what is?"

Maggie considered how to answer. She could tell him it was the way he helped others without looking for thanks or attention, or his thoughtful insights on the world around him.

She pretended to think about it, unable to fully hide a sly smile. "The fact that you're now the proud owner of a dapper fish named Houdini."

He laughed, and the sound filled Maggie with a kind of pride. As a comedian, she should be used to it by now, but making Gabriel laugh felt different, somehow. More of a challenge for one thing, but also something more.

Don't get your hopes up. You'll likely never see him again after the tour ends.

That date, she realized, was approaching quickly. Like all dreams, the North Africa tour would be over soon enough, and then they'd all have to wake up and face reality.

34

May 4, 1943
On the Nefza-Sedjenane road, Tunisia

So this is what it feels like to ride into a war zone.

Catherine shifted on the truck's troop seats. So far, it was the same standard discomfort but with an elevated sense of danger. All morning, they'd rolled along with a convoy of deuce-and-a-half trucks, their cargo of costumes and props in marked contrast to the fuel, rations, and other vital supplies for the troops in the others.

Out the back of the truck, the darkening sky threatened rain, turning the fields and rolling grass from warm hues of gold and green to a foreboding and monotonous gray.

Despite the gloomy weather, everyone seemed to be in good spirits, in part because of their driver, a cheery fellow from the Transportation Corps, PFC Benjamin Stuart. At all of their stops, he kept up a constant stream of conversation, outrageous tales of childhood pranks and family anecdotes that took Catherine's mind off the danger of German shellings.

This time, though, they were stopping at one of the military posts that served as a checkpoint and refueling station for the supply convoys. There would be no lighthearted banter here, but Catherine hoped that they'd finally get some lunch—breakfast, hours ago, had been meager.

"Have your identification papers at the ready." Mr. Douglas's scripted instruction sounded more tense than usual. Catherine could guess why. In the early weeks of the tour, the checkpoints had been a formality, with the soldiers exchanging jokes and wishing them well.

Here, the stationed guards shielded their eyes from the sun, alert and ready to fire if need be. The difference between an occupying army guarding supply routes and an attacking army closing in on the enemy was obvious.

"Uh-oh," Judith said in a low tone. "Looks like the colonel isn't happy to see us."

Catherine winced, following the other woman's gaze to an officer who could be classified as heavy artillery, and who seemed ready to fire at will. PFC Stuart trailed anxiously behind him, trying to get a word in.

She fumbled for her identification card, but as the colonel stopped stiffly before Mr. Douglas, she had a feeling she might not need it.

"Who authorized the lot of you to be here?" he demanded in a bullhorn tone.

If he expected the bespectacled businessman to crumble in the face of this interrogation, he didn't know Mr. Douglas. "General Eisenhower for the tour in general, and Major General Harmon for our upcoming stop. I assure you, sir, we are quite—"

The colonel's red face indicated he wasn't interested in Mr. Douglas's reassurances. "In case you haven't noticed, these men are busy fighting a war. And let me be clear, Mr. Hollywood—you all are hamming around in uniform by our leave, and if we tell you to move, you'd better ask how fast."

The expression on his face told Catherine just how fast he'd like them to move in this case: very.

Stuart made a faint attempt at an interruption, "B-but sir, I was told to deliver them—"

Before he could finish the thought, the officer had a few choice words for the poor fellow about where exactly he'd be delivered if he didn't jump in that truck and turn around for the Algerian border.

"Colonel, there are ladies present."

For a moment, the officer acknowledged Mr. Douglas's stern objection with a glance at Catherine, Maggie, and Judith. "And they shouldn't be, not this close to a war zone."

In some ways, Catherine had to agree. It was all well and good, keeping soldiers busy and inspired as they awaited battle, but it seemed foolhardy to perform for an armored unit about to pursue a fleeing German army.

"The USO brings their performers as close as is logistically feasible to the front lines," Mr. Douglas said, as if he were the colonel's superior explaining why a retreat would be a tactical disadvantage. "I'm sorry, sir, but unless we hear otherwise, we are under strict orders to—"

That unleashed a whole new torrent of swearing from the major, who didn't bother to look abashedly their way this time. "That's the last time I'll warn you. Pack up and get the devil out of my battlefield. Consider yourselves having 'heard otherwise.'"

With that, the colonel stormed off, shouting orders to the rifle-toting soldiers stationed at the checkpoint, who had been watching the exchange like it was a Saturday matinee filled with A-list Hollywood stars.

Mr. Douglas looked like he might just march after the colonel for a second round. "Of all the self-important, obstructionist—"

"Sir," Stuart said, his voice anxious, "I'd do what he says.

This armored unit is rolling straight to the coast, pushing the Germans back as they go. They'll be ready for a show once the battle's won."

Finally, Mr. Douglas acquiesced, waving for them to get back in the truck. "I suppose we have no choice. Extenuating circumstances and all that. But if there's no way to radio our change of plans, we'll have no reservations, and the home office . . ."

Catherine didn't wait for him to finish muttering the many logistical issues that went into making a hurried plan B and instead climbed back into the truck. It seemed their longed-for lunch wouldn't be coming, at least not here.

"Thank goodness for Colonel What's-His-Name." Judith sat next to her, unlacing her boots and tossing them to the back of the truck bed. "There are lots of things that can damage a singing career, but one of the worst is bullet wounds."

Maggie shook her head, staring dolefully out at the troops who had assembled to greet them, now back at work refueling the convoy. "I can't believe we're giving up."

"We didn't have a choice," Catherine soothed. "And think of the trouble PFC Stuart would have been in if he disobeyed an officer."

If she was honest, part of her was grateful for the change in plans. The closer they'd gotten to actual combat, the more she'd worried.

Still, she understood how Maggie felt. After all, she had made a difficult decision to stay here. If their tour was to be cut short, had it really been worth sending Arthur back alone and offending her father?

After a discussion with PFC Stuart, Mr. Douglas climbed up on the tailgate, still visibly annoyed. A few raindrops spattered a pattern against the dust coating his helmet. "The rest of the convoy's been cleared to go on without us. We're headed back to Nefza, and we'll have to keep a steady pace, as we absolutely must get there by sunset."

"Why is that?" Gabriel asked.

"It's just protocol," Mr. Douglas said, his voice overlapping with Howie's, providing a very different answer.

"Our headlights would make a perfect target for passing Messerschmitt strafing rounds," Howie explained.

Catherine shuddered, sorry anyone had asked. That certainly wasn't a pleasant thought. Surely, though, separated from the large convoy, they wouldn't be visible enough for a strike.

She shivered inside her oversized khaki overcoat and cinched the belt tight, grateful for protection from the rain that was starting to leak into the cracks of the canvas. There was no help for it. The USO had been driven into retreat by their own army.

She could only hope they weren't moving toward more danger than they were leaving behind.

35

May 4, 1943
Toward Nefza, Tunisia

"A fine lot we look." Maggie couldn't help grinning at her fellow performers as they bumped along the road, back the way they'd come earlier that morning. The rain beat a staccato melody on the truck, its canvas sides flapping loosely at the corners, letting in the rain. Even Catherine's usually perfect hair was matted and dirty, and all of them had stains on their uniforms that made it look like they had spent the night in an uncovered slit trench.

Gabriel had joined PFC Stuart in digging out the truck's wheels when they'd slid off the road into a shallow wadi, a dried streambed that formed a shallow ditch, so he was the worst off, patches of mud staining his uniform nearly to his waist. "So much for the glamour of traveling performers."

"I'll say," Judith muttered, her eyes closed. "If I don't get a basin of clean water when we get there, I swear I'll raid a Lyster bag myself."

Maggie wanted to joke that the mud on their faces was good for their complexions, but it didn't look like anyone was in the mood to laugh. Stuart had been increasingly pessimistic about their pace every time they were forced to stop.

As if inspired by Judith's comment, Catherine poured a handful of water from her canteen and splashed it on her face, primly patting it off with what might have been the only dry corner of her overcoat.

"Don't waste that," Howie warned her, his voice uncommonly sharp. "We won't be able to stop to find purified water. Not if we're going to get to Nefza in time." The city had been taken by the Allies in mid-March and held as the fighting moved eastward toward Bizerte and Tunis, so it would be a safe haven—at least, as safe as anywhere in a country at war.

But as the afternoon dragged on, even Maggie, with little sense of distance or navigation, could tell that was a vain hope. It was confirmed when Stuart pulled to a bumpy stop and came around back with Douglas, his expression grim. "We're almost three hours out from Nefza. No way we'll make it in time. We'll have to stop twenty miles down this road. I radioed the commander to let them know we're on our way."

"What's there?" Maggie asked. Surely they weren't bivouacking in a random field by the side of the road.

The driver hesitated a few seconds too long. "An Allied supply point."

"You want us to spend the night at an ammo dump in the middle of a war zone?" Howie demanded. "Why don't we just put a target on our back that says 'German bombers attack here'?"

"Because German bombers don't read English," Maggie volunteered. This helpful comment was met with frosty glares from everyone gathered, and she decided to keep her mouth firmly shut until the delivery of bad news was over. Which might take a while, the way things were going.

"Thank you, PFC Stuart," Douglas said smoothly, cutting Howie off before he could make another protest. "And I assume the goal is still to get there by sundown?"

Mollified, Stuart nodded. "We'll have to keep up the pace. No more stops."

"Tell that to the road," Maggie pointed out, given that it had been responsible for most of their delays.

"Can't we get something to eat?" Judith asked, and Maggie was interested in that particular answer too. They'd forgone lunch, and dinner didn't look promising.

"Where?" Stuart pointed out, gesturing to the grazing lands around them. "We might pass a village soon, but we'd have to invite ourselves over to some local's house for a tagine of lamb, and we just don't have the time."

He did offer them three of his C-ration packs, and they opened the cans of meat and vegetable hash, spooning out small portions into their mess kits as they drove onward.

"No, thank you," Catherine murmured, turning down her share of the entrée that Maggie passed to her, nibbling instead on the rock-hard edge of the biscuit.

"Fine, more for me." Maggie spooned the hash into her mouth quickly to sneak past her gag reflex. It wouldn't be so bad warmed over a fire, probably, but the cold sludge with chunks of vegetable was barely passable as a meal, famished though she was.

After she finished most of her share, Maggie half listened as Judith described the feast she planned to eat when she reached civilization again. All the while, she watched Howie near the back of the truck, looking out at the rain-battered scrub brush. His arms were locked tightly against the chill, flinching whenever a crack of thunder rent the air.

Pretending she needed to stretch, Maggie inched over to him on the troop seats. "Penny for your thoughts, Howie."

He grunted, uncharacteristically serious. "Save your cent.

It's not worth it. Just that whoever called the Great War 'the war to end all wars' must've been some kind of optimist."

He had a point there. It had only taken them a few decades to start an even more devastating conflict. "Still, there's nothing wrong with hoping, is there?"

"Only if hope makes you forget history." His voice, usually cheery, was flat and dull. "The fathers who fought with me now have to watch their sons muddle into this hell. They were right to send us back. A song and dance routine can't make war—real war—any better."

Maggie's father would have a Scripture handy, and even Catherine or Gabriel would come up with something comforting to say, but Maggie found herself at a loss for words.

"Why don't you try to get a little shut-eye?" she suggested. "No telling what kind of place we'll be spending the night, showing up on short notice like this."

"That's the truth." He got out a blanket roll from one of the trunks, and leaning against the side of the bench, was puffing in and out with a light snore within minutes.

Maggie was glad. Being reminded of his war days had to be hard. Back in Chicago, many of the down-and-outers who came to the Salvation Army meetings were former doughboys, some wounded and finding it hard to keep a job, others whose shell shock had proved too much for even their families. "It's a shame," most people said, shaking their head sadly and vowing to contribute to a fund on Armistice Day. Never thinking to do anything about the shame of those troubled men.

Her father had put his beliefs into action, that much could always be said of James McCleod. "There's another battle still going on," he'd always told her, "for these men and for all of us. One on the inside."

As they traveled onward, the twilight landscape, once exciting and exotic, began to blur into a sameness that made

Maggie yawn. Maybe she should follow her own advice and get a little sleep. If you looked at it right, the rocking of the truck and the creaking of the chassis on the road could be a lullaby. For a moment, Maggie closed her eyes to listen as the softer notes of the rain filled in a harmony, joining the rumble of the truck's engine like strings adding into a symphony.

And then a distant sound entered that prickled the skin on the back of her neck. She couldn't name it, but it was out of place. The percussion of war.

"What's—?" she began, before the truck lurched to a stop.

"Everyone out!" Stuart's voice was urgent, panicked, reaching them before he did. "Off the road now!"

Shaking Howie awake as she passed, Maggie obeyed, nearly tripping out of the truck. Stuart was returning to the cab. For his rifle, maybe? What was going on?

"Over there," Douglas shouted, pointing toward the shallow wadi on the side of the road. "Take cover!"

Even though she knew it was a waste of time, Maggie looked up.

On the horizon were three German fighter planes. She didn't have a name for them like the Boy Scout plane spotters she joked about. All she knew was that they were flying low—low enough to have seen their headlights.

The walls of the wadi were steep but shallow, and Maggie threw herself into it, her helmet protecting her head from a hard clunk against the side. She could hear Judith cry out in disgust as they slid into the mud and each other, trying to get as low as possible.

Here, away from the truck, as safe as they could be, Maggie dared to breathe as the planes passed directly overhead. *They won't see us. They'll keep flying past.* If she thought it hard enough, maybe . . .

Then an explosion—mixed with their screams—put an end to the music of the quiet evening.

36

MAY 4, 1943
TOWARD NEFZA, TUNISIA

"We're going to die," Judith whimpered, clutching at Catherine like a drowning woman struggling to stay afloat as the three women huddled together in the ditch. Though Catherine knew it wouldn't do any good to panic, she felt the same fear prickling through her, causing her limbs to shake. Cold drizzle slicked her skin, and the mud had begun to seep through her uniform.

"We are *not*," Maggie said, glaring at both of them. "Even if the planes circle back around, they won't aim here again." At least, that was all they could hope.

Desperate to see what had happened, Catherine struggled to get purchase against the wet earth, propping herself up so she could see over the wadi's waist-high banks to get a view of the road.

Several gouges pocked the ground around the truck, and it looked like one of the shells had hit directly, sending up thick smoke through a crumple of metal. PFC Stuart was on the ground. Killed?

No, he was moving, but flames from the cab reached out and caught his uniform. His anguished cry chilled Catherine more than the light rain that beat against them.

Gabriel was at his side in a moment, pushing him into the mud and extinguishing the blaze. He and Mr. Douglas each took one of his arms, limping toward the wadi in a drunken lockstep, trying to get to cover, to safety.

That only left . . .

"Where is Howie?" Catherine asked.

Not with them, and not safe, unless he had gotten separated in the panic and lurched to the ditch on the other side of the road.

She thought back to the chaos as the planes streaked overhead, remembering him standing stock-still beside the truck, terror on his face.

"He's still out there," Maggie said what they'd both realized. They'd left Howie behind, exposed, open to attack if the planes circled back around to return from their real target.

Mr. Douglas and Gabriel were still hauling PFC Stuart into the wadi, their progress painfully slow. They would have to tend to his injuries as best they could.

Before she could change her mind, Catherine turned to Maggie. "Boost me," she said. "I'm going up to bring Howie back."

For a moment, it looked like Maggie might argue, but then she nodded. She knelt in the wadi with one leg out to form a step, and Catherine scrabbled up, scraping her palms against the muddy ground. Back toward the truck, toward danger.

They couldn't leave him. Not if there was any chance the German bombers might rally for another strike.

The truck listed dangerously to one side, and Catherine's eyes watered from the acrid smoke. As she got closer, she could see Howie curled in the fetal position by the wheel well, the crown of his head tucked down as if refusing to look at the sky would make the planes stay away.

"Howie," she called, trying not to sound as terrified as she felt. "Stand up. We've got to go."

The eyes that met hers in the twilight were not those of the happy-go-lucky vaudeville performer she had come to know. They were almost blank, and Catherine knew she was seeing what the troops called the thousand-yard stare.

"They've got us surrounded," he said, his voice hoarse. "No way out. I've lost my gas mask."

So had she, come to think of it, stashed somewhere with the rest of her gear, but Howie, woken abruptly from sleep, seemed to be trapped in a nightmare of trench warfare from 1918, where mustard gas might be leaking all around him, ready to choke the last of the air from his lungs.

"There is no gas, Howie." Catherine placed a hand on his shoulder, her other hand extended to help him up. If he didn't want to come, she wouldn't be able to drag him away, not even for his own good. "A plane dropped a bomb on our truck. We've got to take shelter."

"It's no use." He raised muddy hands to his face, cupping his temples as if he could block out the scene and the fears it raised within him. "I'm going to die out here. Just like Henry, just like Nelson, just like all of those poor devils."

Catherine felt rising panic as she heard the distant hum increase in volume. The fighter planes were coming back this way. Maybe they'd see the smoked-out ruins of the convoy truck and move along without firing, but she couldn't take that chance.

"Take my hand," Catherine said firmly, keeping it outstretched. "I'm not leaving you, Howie. We're either both getting out of this, or neither of us are."

Whether it was her words or seeing the face of a young woman rather than one of his war buddies, Howie seemed to remember where he was, who he was. Not a doughboy in a muddy trench in France, his unit decimated after going over the top. A performer who had lived decades of life and somehow found his way to a different war—and danger—all the same.

With what looked like great effort, he raised his hand and took Catherine's. She nearly toppled from the sudden weight, but she ground her boots into the mud, not letting go even as they stumbled toward the wadi. Together, they made the short sprint across the open road as the drone of the planes grew to a deafening rumble above them.

Howie climbed in first, then reached up to help her. The planes, now directly overhead, spat a round of machine gun fire at the vehicle, but they didn't linger or drop more shells.

As the whine of their engines faded again, Catherine collapsed against the side of the wadi, fighting dry heaves and tears as the energy that had pounded through her body struggled for release.

"Thank God," Maggie whispered, steadying Howie as he stumbled to press himself lower. Judith, still sobbing, didn't even seem to realize Catherine had gone.

It's all right, she repeated to herself, breathing in the musty smell of wet earth and trying to ignore the creeping scent of smoke that threatened to overpower it. *We're all here. All alive.* Only their driver seemed to have sustained any injuries.

A few feet away, Stuart cried out, his mud-stained face grimacing as Gabriel prodded at his ankle. "Let up, will you? That hurts."

"Probably broken or badly sprained," Gabriel said, in his matter-of-fact way that would make anyone think he actually had medical training. "You're lucky you only have minor burns and no shrapnel injuries." That, Catherine knew, would be far beyond the limited emergency equipment stored in the truck—if that hadn't been destroyed.

She crouched next to Howie, heedless of the mud that soaked through her uniform down to her underthings and hoping that knowing someone was there beside him would keep him from slipping into shock once again.

Next to her, Maggie crossed her arms over her chest to keep warm. "Just in time," she said, her voice barely audible as the drizzle that had followed them around all evening finally broke into a downpour. Catherine couldn't be sure, but she thought there might be a note of admiration in her voice. "I figured you'd be able to talk him down. And you did."

Catherine barely heard, shivering uncontrollably, from nervous tension more than cold. She was filthy, she was terrified, she was . . . proud of herself?

Yes, that was the unfamiliar feeling, different from the satisfaction of a well-executed sonata. She might have saved a man's life, all because when it counted, she'd chosen what was brave instead of what was easy.

Once the rain had died down somewhat and PFC Stuart assured them they were safe—though nowhere in Tunisia seemed to be safe at the moment—they straggled out of the wadi. PFC Stuart needed Mr. Douglas to support him as they hobbled toward what remained of their transportation.

The rain had reduced the fire in the truck's hood to a smolder, but Gabriel followed PFC Stuart's directions to discharge the emergency fire extinguisher to put out what remained. No amount of equipment could piece together the debris scattered in all directions from the direct hit. Even Catherine, with no automotive experience, could tell it was in no condition to take them three yards, much less the three miles Stuart estimated they still had to go.

"Let's see what we can salvage of our equipment and carry

with us," Gabriel said, rapping on the truck's sorry frame. "It looks like we'll be walking into camp tonight."

Thankfully, the cargo was mostly undamaged, and Catherine took out her violin case and tucked it against her under her overcoat—unwilling to leave it behind—along with her canteen, a flashlight, and a change of clothing, still mostly dry.

All the while, she found herself tensing at any unexpected sound, as if a hare trying to find a dry place to spend the night might be the rumble of approaching tanks or bombers. Though she tried not to, she couldn't help tilting her head up to watch the sky, not to evaluate the chance of further rain based on the storm clouds above them but to search for the next danger.

That must be how the men of their audiences had felt all along, and she only now understood the dread of waiting, wondering when the next strike would come, while hope of rescue and safety and a warm fire to huddle around was just out of reach. No wonder they wanted a chance to laugh and enjoy themselves, not only to relieve the monotony but to relieve the tension. Maybe the USO was really here to fill the desert with other sounds than land mine explosions or machine gun fire.

As Catherine turned to rejoin the others consulting PFC Stuart's map, she felt a hand on her shoulder and turned to see Howie, looking abashed. "Thank you," he said, clearing his throat. "You didn't have to come back."

Of course she did. "You'd have done the same for me. We're in the army now, and a soldier never leaves his—or her—comrade behind."

"That's so. Yes, that's so." And whether it was this war or the last that he was thinking of, this time, the place he traveled to in his mind removed the shame from his expression and straightened his bowed shoulders. Whatever came next, they would face it together.

37

MAY 5, 1943
SOUK-EL-ARBA AIRFIELD, TUNISIA

"I still don't understand why we have to *fly* back to Casablanca," Maggie grumbled, trying to get comfortable on the aluminum bench fitted against the cabin wall, a hopeless task. "Especially after what happened last time."

"It would take us nearly a week to drive using army transportation, if we could arrange all of the stops," Gabriel reasoned. He sat beside her, his knee pressed against hers in the close quarters.

Yes, Douglas had explained all that, though how he'd weaseled his way onto a *British* troop-carrying glider going west when they couldn't even scrounge up a decent steak was beyond her.

She'd practically had to be hauled into the narrow cabin by the flight's navigator, all while listening to—and not believing—his long string of reassurances. After their last flight, she was convinced US Army planes were held together with scrap metal and prayers, and their RAF counterparts couldn't be much better.

Maggie watched as the others from the troupe filled their

own seats. Only Catherine looked the slightest bit wary, her hands trembling on the buckle, though her demure smile never wavered. Whether that was bluster or blind confidence, Maggie couldn't say. All she knew was, this time she'd keep the airsickness bag in her grip constantly.

"I just hope the RAF has better flight crews than the Americans." So far, the only difference she'd noticed in the aircraft itself, besides a polite handwritten *Mind Your Head* notice on the low metal girdings above them, was the sheer amount of wood in the interior. If anyone even considered lighting a cigarette, they'd fall out of the sky in a blaze. Not a thought she should dwell on.

"The mechanic checked this plane thoroughly," Gabriel reminded her, which Maggie knew for a fact because she'd peppered the poor fellow with questions before stepping foot in the cabin. "We're flying in the daytime with an experienced pilot."

She raised an eyebrow at him. "Weren't we last time too?"

"Then what are the odds we'll have engine trouble twice?"

It was, in some ways, a good point, but Maggie didn't like trusting in probabilities. "Easy for you to say," she grumbled. "Nothing scares you."

Gabriel frowned briefly. "Before now, I'd have said the same about you, but it turns out we're both wrong."

Well. It made a girl feel a little braver, knowing someone thought she was fearless. "Fine, then. If I stay on this plane, you have to do something terrifying, too, to even things out."

He nodded. "All right. It's a deal."

"I wish we had Houdini with us for good luck." To her dismay, Mr. Douglas had not been impressed with Gabriel's request to transport a live rouget across Tunisia and had kicked Houdini out of the troupe immediately. They'd released him back into the ocean while Maggie played "We'll Meet Again" on her trumpet, to the locals' amusement.

Gabriel shrugged. "I don't think he'd have cared for the altitude anyway."

Neither did she, but no one had given her a choice. Maggie leaned back and closed her eyes, not to fall asleep—the nerves thrumming through her would never let that happen—but to keep anyone else from talking to her.

The moment she felt the plane move, she jerked up, gaze riveted to the opposite window as the shoreline pushed away and it was only the Mediterranean underneath them, jolting forward at a speed that made Maggie's ears ring. Like a bird out of a cage, determined to soar as high as possible before someone could reach up and snatch it back.

Part of her felt exhilarated, while the other part contributed to her doubling over to grip her knees. Every rattle of wind tilted them slightly until they leveled out, the jolts going from terrifying to just uncomfortable.

A sudden warmth covered her hand, still clenched on the canvas strap around her waist. Gabriel had reached over to squeeze her hand, looking reassuringly unconcerned as they hurtled to their doom. He let go again, straightening and not calling attention to her obvious discomfort, but the warmth from his touch seemed to linger.

Maggie shook her head. It was just the sudden change in altitude making her think things like that.

She moaned, closing her eyes. She wouldn't look up again for the rest of the flight. That was the ticket. That way, if they got shot down or crashed, she'd go from the plane to the pearly gates none the wiser.

"The worst of it's over," Gabriel assured her, leaning close to be heard over the engine.

As the plane righted itself, she allowed herself to relax slightly. Maybe he was right.

But then there would be the descent into Casablanca, which, they'd been warned by the pilot, would involve "a good bit of bumping about, owing to the winds off the coast." Given that most military men she'd encountered were prone to understatement in an attempt to sound tough, Maggie was prepared for the worst.

"I'll believe that when I can safely kiss the ground," she fired back, keeping her eyes firmly closed. "Do me a favor—either let me sleep or distract me."

"All right." Gabriel paused, and his next words were spoken more than shouted, so that she could barely hear them. "Maggie, when we get to Casablanca, will you go to dinner with me?"

Her eyes sprang open. That wasn't the distraction she'd had in mind. "To . . . where in the world did that come from?"

"You said if you boarded the plane, I had to do something that frightens me. So . . . ?"

Catherine and Judith would never let her hear the end of this. Their "I told you sos" were practically ringing in her ears already.

That, of course, didn't change her answer. She let the suspense linger for another minute, enjoying the uncomfortable look on Gabriel's face before replying. "That's one way to make sure I survive, giving me plans to look forward to."

"Is that a yes?"

She nodded. "I figure, everyone's teased us about dating often enough that we might as well give it a try."

She liked that she could make him laugh, even if the occasion was a rare one, felt flattered that he wanted to spend time with her, and, yes, had considered the fact that he'd look rather sharp in his tuxedo in some swanky French restaurant in the city center.

That didn't stop her from wincing every time the plane took a turn, but it did give her something else to think about. That, and the fact that when they bumped their way to a landing in Casablanca, Gabriel held her hand again and didn't let go.

Report to the USO Home Office
Floyd Douglas, Foxhole Circuit, Variety Unit 14
May 8, 1943

This may well be my last report before we leave the shores of Africa behind. Despite the setback of canceling the Tunisian part of our circuit, our performers have made the most of our return to Casablanca. Over the past few days, they've held impromptu performances and frequented the many enlisted-men's clubs in the city to provide what cheer they can. Miss McCleod's account of our adventures on the front line grows steadily more outrageous each time she relates it, but the soldiers seem heartened by what we risked, all the same.

On a more formal note, my official recommendation for the Pepsodent contract will be . . . forthcoming. I apologize. I'd fully intended to have arrived at a chosen performer by now, but it became much harder than I'd originally expected.

We're slated for a few performances on the voyage home as well, but since many of the men are wounded and not able to gather on deck, our schedule will be more relaxed than our trip to Casablanca. That will give me plenty of time to contemplate who among my unit is the most worthy—while swallowing seasickness pills I stocked up on back at a Moroccan pharmacy. (Did I mention that sea travel is miserable?)

Once again, my thanks to the entire USO for this opportunity. It's not one I take lightly. Hopefully, this entire ragtag troupe have benefited in some small way from my managerial experience. I have certainly learned a good deal from them.

Sincerely,
Floyd Douglas

38

May 8, 1943
Casablanca, Morocco

"A girls' night on the town to watch a war movie, of all things." Judith tsked as she expertly applied her eyeliner. "Honestly, you two dolls don't know how to have fun."

Secretly, Catherine agreed with her, but Maggie had insisted that they see the premiere of *Desert Victory*, a British documentary that promised "the most thrilling scenes ever taken under fire."

"Come on, Judith," Maggie said, waiting in the hotel room's lone armchair with her feet propped up. She'd put on her green silk gown for the occasion but had shunned Judith's offer of makeup. "The whole city's talking about it."

Catherine twisted the last loose strand of her hair and pinned it just so. "It *will* be nice to get out and see the city one last time."

Mr. Douglas had even given their outing official permission, declaring with a straight face that he considered it "education on the perspective of the troops we serve" rather than sightseeing. Ever since they'd landed in Casablanca, he'd allowed them slightly more leeway on USO rules and regulations.

"However, we are still performing for some new navy arrivals at nine hundred hours tomorrow, with or without you," he'd warned. "Do not be late."

He and the other men had declined to attend, perhaps too tired to stay out for the 9:30 p.m. showing, the earliest Catherine had been able to obtain tickets for, or perhaps out of deference to Howie, who stated that no propaganda film could be anything like being in the heat of battle.

Judith whistled as Catherine turned, letting the skirt of her gown twirl. "Trying to catch a fellow's eye before we ship out?"

"No, I'm not, as a matter of fact."

It had been a long time, Catherine realized, since she'd dressed up for the joy of it, because she loved the color of the lipstick, the feeling of the gown's material against her skin, and the way the curls of her updo framed her face.

All through the tour, before every performance, she'd been careful to fasten her girdle tightly, tuck every bit of hair in place, and apply her makeup to look tasteful yet elegant—all with the hope that maybe this time Leo would be in the audience. Even when wearing her favorite gown, her mind always wandered to what others might think of her—what *he* might think of her.

Maybe that anxiety would return again. But here, so far from anyone she knew, about to enjoy a show instead of performing in one, she felt perfectly at ease for the first time in months, maybe years.

"Don't worry, sister, I'll beat the boys off with a stick for you," Judith said—or at least, that's what Catherine thought she said. A few of the words came out distorted as she applied her lipstick.

Once Judith stepped aside from the mirror, satisfied with

her evening look, Catherine took a cautious step toward it, a slight frown creasing her face as she gave herself a once-over from head to toe.

"What's wrong?" Judith asked. "Stockings got a snag?"

"Nothing." How could she describe the sensation that had come over her? "It's just . . . I feel like an entirely different woman than when we first arrived in Casablanca, but on the outside, nothing has changed."

Judith poked her head into the reflection. "Mmm, I don't know about that. We've all gotten tanner, anyway."

Had she? Catherine looked critically in the mirror, but compared to Judith, she still looked pale, and Maggie seemed mainly to have gained more freckles. Still, there was at least a healthy glow around all of them that she never would have gotten in St. Paul.

The thought forced her to glance over to the hotel's writing desk, where two letters were finally started. She ought to have written to her parents immediately after Arthur's departure. The chances of her letters beating him home now were slim, but every time she'd put pen to paper, exhausted after another performance, she crumpled draft after draft. Difficult truths, long unspoken, took time to craft.

Now, it just remained to be seen if she'd have the courage to post them.

Unexpectedly, Arthur's face came to mind, smiling at her and saying, *"Not many know how brave you are. But they're going to."*

"Come on, ladies." Maggie threw on her drab overcoat, concealing all but ten inches of her lovely gown. "If this show is as packed as you say, we'll have to fight to get good seats."

Despite blackout regulations, Casablanca at night was alive with voices and the press of people. The slightest of chills to the air carried from a seaward breeze, but this time, Catherine didn't feel overwhelmed or content to gape and cling to the others. Instead, she led the way, reading the street signs to find the Cinema Rialto, a stunning building with bold art deco letters proclaiming its name against a white front curved around the street corner. No lit marquees, of course, but the elegant façade still impressed.

She caught snatches of French from the stream of humanity pouring out of the gilded doors from the previous showing: "*Incroyable*," "*Fantastique*," "*Très réaliste*." In them, she heard the audience reviews of the film, as important as any that might be printed in the entertainment page of a newspaper.

Inside, they battled the crowd to find a seat in the plush mezzanine, filing to the middle of a row near the back, taking in the high ceilings hung with gold chandeliers.

"Did you know *the* Josephine Baker performed here for a French Red Cross benefit gala last week?" Judith said, her voice muffled by the heavy carpet and velvet seats. "I was spitting mad when I found out we'd just missed her."

Catherine had a vague image of the performer—an American-born expatriate to Paris, known for her sensational costumes and jazz performances. "Is she the one who has a pet cheetah that wanders into the orchestra pit?"

"Sounds like her," Judith said, with entirely too much pride in her voice.

The temperature of the room rose as spectators packed into the seats—at least a thousand—and Catherine removed her fur wrap just as the lights dimmed and the screen came alive with scenes of war.

How the others reacted to the film, she couldn't say, too transfixed by the details of battle, including footage filmed by German cameramen and captured during their retreat. Gasps from the audience rippled through the theater when the stillness of night crackled with gunfire, shell explosions, and the cries of the wounded. Flares illuminated the rush of soldiers, capturing brief moments of the offensive before plunging back into the darkness.

Though the men fighting at El Alamein were from the British 8th Army, it gave Catherine a new sympathy for what their own troops faced in the heat of combat.

The scene of German planes diving to release bombs in particular made her shudder before it transitioned to a more positive tableau of determined generals making plans, set to an upbeat score.

Now she had more of an idea what Howie had meant. She'd lived this. Her friends and family might go see the film, but they couldn't understand what it felt like to be here, surrounded by desert and air raid sirens and the desperate laughter of men about to risk their lives for their country.

The film ended in November 1942, with British tanks rolling victoriously through Tripoli to the cheers of watching crowds, pushing Axis forces out of Libya.

So much had changed since then. The Americans had invaded North Africa, the Vichy French joined the Allied cause, and they'd gotten word that just yesterday, the British had recaptured Tunis and the Americans Bizerte. Catherine had cheered with the rest of the variety unit on hearing the news. Soon the fighting in Tunisia would be over, with thousands of German POWs captured. Oh, the war wasn't through, not yet. But everyone knew that losing North Africa left Italy exposed and put Hitler on the run.

The moment the applause ended and the buzz of after-show chatter began, Judith turned to Maggie expectantly. "Well, what did you think of your first movie?" She, like Catherine, had been horrified that Maggie wasn't a filmgoer and had checked to make sure she knew what century she was in.

Maggie stood, rubbing her neck like she'd gotten a kink in it from staring at the screen. "It was almost like being there

. . . but I'm glad I wasn't." She laughed, and Catherine knew she should too, but she couldn't shake a lingering feeling of unease.

During all their shows for soldiers, she'd tried her best to separate herself from the actual war, the violence and chaos those boys were headed into, until Tunisia. Now, seeing it play out in black and white in front of her made the combat feel different, more real, even though she knew it was only images flickering on the screen.

While the others put on their coats, preparing to join the throng streaming out the doors, hurried along by the insistent stare of cinema employees eager to clean the seats for the final showing of the night, she couldn't help staring at the names of the army photographers who had captured the film. "Doesn't it . . . make you feel like we shouldn't leave? That there's still more to do?"

Maggie looked back at her and shrugged. "Not really. There are other performers coming through. Bob Hope and his lot, for one, and probably others."

That wasn't really what she'd meant. There was something about knowing that the victory in North Africa could be a turning point in the entire war and realizing how much more work had to be done to bring these soldiers home that gave Catherine pause.

You've done your duty, more than most women have, she told herself. But on the brink of returning to the comforts of home that these soldiers might not have for months or years, she had to ask herself, Was it really enough?

From Catherine to her father and mother

May 9, 1943

Dear Father and Mother,

First, I wanted to say that I'm sorry for not writing or leaving you with my address. It was a cowardly way to avoid conflict, and I hope to make it right by communicating clearly with you now. If you're wondering about the salutation, I am sending an identical copy of this letter to each of you at your separate addresses. This is to make sure you know that I'm not keeping secrets from either of you.

I'd like to begin with what's most important: I love you. Both of you. For a long time now, I've felt like you were forcing me to choose between you, and it's something I simply will not do. Please know that I'll always be your daughter, even as you go your separate ways.

Father, I'm sure Arthur has already arrived in St. Paul without me. He delivered your message. While it was good to see a friendly face, I felt unfairly pressured into a choice I didn't want to make. My love for music may not be something you understand, but it is important to me. Even if it wasn't, it wouldn't be right to break my contract with my troupe and leave early, which is why I did not do so.

Mother, even if you sent in that newspaper article with the best of intentions, it was hurtful to see words in print that I didn't say. And while I appreciate you wanting me to flourish in my musical career, I don't think I'm prepared for an audition with the Philharmonic. Even when I feel like I am ready to perform at that level, I want to be sure I earned my position on my own merit. As a fellow musician, I'm sure you can understand that.

For the moment, however, I've decided to take a different path, one I'm not sure either of you will understand.

Finally, Mother, I may not be your little girl anymore, wearing your pearls at her first public recital, but your guidance and encouragement has been and will continue to be important to me. Father, all my life, you've told me that you hoped I would become a capable woman worthy of the Duquette name. I'm proud to say that I've picked up a good bit of business sense from you, and I'm growing in my confidence to back it up.

Our scheduled arrival in New York is on May 24, and shortly after that, I'll be returning to St. Paul. I plan to visit both of you then to talk about my future plans. Until then, I remain,

Your daughter,
Catherine

From Maggie to her father
May 8, 1943

Dear Dad,

One of my fellow tour members, Gabriel Kaminski, and I stayed up late last night discussing the tour and all. He thought I should share some of my thoughts with you, even though I'm not much for writing. So here goes nothing.

I still swear by the fact that all music is a gift, a little bit of something beautiful left behind in this tired old world. But hymns—I think you called them "those old words that have been passed down from generations of saints who believed they were never alone, not even in their darkest hour"—those are special. You were right about that, for sure. In fact, I've added a few hymns to my repertoire with our manager's blessing. It's not exactly a Salvation Army band show, but I think you'd be proud to hear it.

The men (and some women) we've been playing for need the hope of those songs, but they also need a good laugh. I'm hoping to give them both. There's something about humor that cuts through the awful and ugly and brings some joy back. And I'm starting to wonder if God made me funny for a reason, same as he made me good at music, and if that's worth just as much in the end.

I might get a chance to keep on with the USO, traveling with exactly the kind of Hollywood types you were afraid I'd fall in with. At this point, I'm not sure if I'll take it if it's offered. But what I do know is this has been the best experience of my life. Not because I was away from home, but maybe because it'll make me live differently when I get back home.

Oh, and I miss you, and Paulette, and even that noisy niece and nephew of mine. It'll be good to see you all soon.

Love,
Maggie

39

May 23, 1943
Atlantic Ocean

Champagne spilled onto the front of Maggie's green silk dress, and she found it didn't bother her one bit. Despite the fact that she'd become used to walking on board a troopship, Maggie had chosen the wrong moment to sway with a particularly rough wave.

"Sorry about that, m'dear," Howie said, his chuckle indicating he'd also gotten caught up in the merrymaking. "Don't worry, there's still some left." He gave a steadier pour into her glass this time, then passed the bottle to Gabriel.

With the *George Washington* set to arrive in New York the next day, tonight had been their final performance, given on deck to roaring applause. Catherine had saved her last red flower for this occasion, tossing it to a bandaged navy man missing a leg, and Maggie had used the opportunity to sneak a few new jokes in too, sure Douglas wouldn't mind.

They'd gotten permission to celebrate their final show in the empty officers' mess, enjoying cushioned chairs and real china table settings for their makeshift feast. Though the galley had been closed for hours, they feasted on field-ration chocolate bars that Douglas had begged from the quartermaster and half a decorative tin of small date-filled biscuits Judith passed around in an unexpected show of generosity.

As they all raised their glasses, Douglas stood, and Maggie waited for the toast that would follow, trying to fix a look of interest on her face. He was a great fellow and all, really knew his stuff, but his voice had a droning quality, like a bassoon playing the same three notes over and over, that made it hard to pay attention.

"Thank you all for an excellent show, and an excellent three months," he began, but despite the cheerful words, his face looked as grim as if he were delivering a eulogy. "I felt tonight that I ought to tell you what I've decided about recommending one of you for the Pepsodent contract, led by Bob Hope."

"Sure took him long enough," Maggie muttered to Gabriel. When they'd departed from Casablanca without another mention of it, she'd wondered if maybe Douglas had exaggerated the opportunity, or even forgotten about it.

"The tour departs from New York on a B-17 only a week after our arrival. Since anyone I nominate will need to audition and, hopefully, sign a new USO contract, my decision must be made before we come into port tomorrow."

Maggie exchanged glances with the others. They all knew the reasons each person had wanted to be chosen. Judith, to jumpstart a stalled career and support her son. Howie, to honor his late wife and serve another generation of soldiers. Gabriel, to feel like he was contributing to the war effort despite his disability. Catherine, to prove herself to her controlling family.

And Maggie . . . well, three months had changed a lot for her.

Under the table, Gabriel squeezed her hand.

Should they tell him? Or wait to hear what Douglas had to say first?

Across from her, Judith downed her whole glass of champagne in a few gulps, apparently sensing no toast would be forthcoming.

"It should be noted that I campaigned mightily to be able to recommend all of you. Alas, it seems several managers believe all of their performers are ready for the big leagues, and my proposal was soundly rejected." Douglas gave a heavy sigh. "This was a very difficult decision for me. So difficult that I've decided not to make it."

What? He couldn't mean it.

"I would like the five of you to decide amongst yourselves who will be auditioning." He raised his hand, as if anticipating protests and wanting to silence them before they formed into words. "I don't care if you debate it, gloves off in a verbal boxing ring, or vote by secret ballot, but I feel I owe it to all of you to include you in this decision."

For a moment, they all sat there like the glass-eyed fish in a market stall, gaping at one another, waiting for someone else to speak.

Catherine broke the silence first. "I have something to say." She faltered as all attention turned to her, then thinned her lips in determination and pressed on. "While I loved touring with all of you, these past few weeks have shown me that I have skills beyond my music that I can offer to our country. I've decided to enlist in the new Women's Army Corps once we arrive in the States, with a request to be stationed in Algiers once I've gone through training."

"Ha!" Maggie burst out, reaching across Gabriel to extend her hand to Howie. "You owe me fifty cents."

"You . . . made a bet that I'd join the army?" she sputtered. It was comical to see the surprise on her face, as if she had been the least bit subtle.

"More or less," Maggie said, shrugging. "The way you've been acting all week, we all knew *something* was going on."

She glanced at Gabriel. Now that they knew for sure what Catherine had been planning . . .

"I thought you'd go into nursing, the way you fussed over Maggie when she was sick," Howie grumbled, fishing around in his pocket and pulling out a scrap of dried tangerine peel instead of her two hard-earned quarters. "Are you sure you don't want to give the Red Cross a try?"

"Don't listen to him, darling," Judith said, putting an arm around Catherine's shoulders. "I always did think you were just the type for the military. Following rules and all that."

Maggie wasn't sure whether Judith considered that a compliment, but she seemed to mean it in a friendly way at least.

"So, all that to say, I would like to remove myself from consideration for the Pepsodent contract," Catherine concluded. "And please, don't make me say who should audition. I couldn't possibly choose."

"Very well, and best wishes to you, Miss Duquette," Douglas said, nodding. "What do the rest of you have to say?"

Maggie kicked Gabriel—his good leg, and not nearly hard enough for the exaggerated umph he made. "Actually, some of us have been talking about this already."

"We . . . we have?" Catherine's uncertain glance Maggie's way made her flinch. *Drat*. She hadn't thought about the fact that, as the only one not included in those conversations, it might make Catherine feel left out.

But it would be all right soon enough, once they explained. It had been Gabriel's idea. Once they'd made their daily rounds to help write letters or play cards with the wounded soldiers, when most everyone on board the ship was asleep, they'd had plenty of time to talk. They'd sat on the well-worn sofa of the ship's salon, a remnant of the ocean liner it had once been, and Gabriel said, "You know, Maggie, if we turned down the contract—took ourselves out of the running—maybe the USO could find another tour for us. Together."

Once the thought had entered her mind, it stuck there. What did Maggie want, anyway? To prove herself to her father? To start a career with famous radio stars? To win for the sake of winning?

None of that really mattered. When she thought about it, she'd gotten exactly what she wanted out of the tour through North Africa already—and a few things she hadn't known she wanted besides.

When she'd brought up the idea to Judith, Maggie had been surprised by her response. "It's not a bad idea, come to think of it. We all know Catherine's the one who deserves the contract anyhow." Even Howie had agreed.

The idea of giving the audition to Catherine was ruined now, so Maggie waited to speak. Would they still want to go through with it?

"We thought perhaps," Gabriel continued, while Mr. Douglas waited expectantly, "all other things being equal, if it might be possible—"

"Oh, just come out with it," Judith interrupted, turning her lazy, careless smile on Douglas. "Really, Floyd, can you imagine how stifling North Africa will be in the summer months? I know our boys need entertainment, but I'm sure Bob Hope can manage without us."

From the confusion on both Catherine's and Douglas's faces, this clearly wasn't helping. Maggie sighed. Did no one in this troupe know how to talk plainly?

"What she means is that none of us want to go on *The Pepsodent Show* tour," Maggie said. "Not if we can all join another circuit tour together."

Clearly, from the way Douglas absently stroked his chin, logistics whirring behind his spectacles, he hadn't considered this option. "This is . . . quite irregular."

Howie dazzled him with a crooked-tooth smile. "So are we, Floyd, my friend. So are we."

"Please consider it," Gabriel put in. "It would mean a lot to us if we could stay together."

"As a matter of fact," Douglas said slowly, as if he were performing the needed calculations on the fly, "the home office did telegraph me about another opportunity this summer. I could see if they've already hired a unit or if there might be room to negotiate. . . ."

Maggie grinned, and even Judith deigned to smile. "Huzzah!" Howie all but shouted. "I knew you'd come through for us, Floyd." He sloshed an inch of champagne from Douglas's glass with his exuberant clap on the back.

"You're certain that none of you would like to be recommended for *The Pepsodent Show* tour?" Douglas pressed. "You might be passing up the opportunity of a lifetime."

"You can't fool me. I've been in show business since I was in diapers," Judith said, shaking her head. "Opportunities come and go, but people you truly enjoy performing with? That's what you have to hold on to."

"And, Catherine, let us know your unit number once you're mustered in," Maggie said, popping the last of Judith's cookies into her mouth. A little stale but still tasty. "We'll want to write you, after all."

"Just think," Judith put in, smiling slyly. "Those skirted soldiers in Algiers can go out on a date any night of the week."

Maggie waved her away. After Leo, Catherine was likely to swear off dating servicemen for a while. "Forget *that*. They have comfortable beds and a roof over their heads. You'll never sleep in a tent again."

Catherine couldn't help laughing. "I *will* enjoy that," she admitted.

"This does mean we'll need a fifth troupe member for our unit, then," Gabriel pointed out.

They all became quiet for a moment, and Maggie thought about how awkward it might be for someone new to join, with their established relationships.

Then Judith snapped her fingers. "I know just the person," she said, her eyes alight with more excitement than Maggie had ever seen before. "Douglas, let's have a chat, you and I."

"I'm intrigued," Douglas said, letting Judith tug him toward the door.

Maggie stepped into their path. There was still one last question to be answered. "Before you do, tell us where we're going."

"As you may recall, telling you that would be—"

"Against regulations," they all chorused as one, and Douglas didn't even pretend to be offended.

"Can you at least tell us if it's going to be as miserably hot?" Maggie asked, fanning herself with one of the table's napkins. "I've had just about enough of that."

The smallest hint of a smile appeared on Douglas's face. "It certainly will not."

EPILOGUE

JULY 6, 1943
SITKA, ALASKA

As she stepped out of her metal Quonset hut, Maggie was filled with the same thrill that met her when they first arrived near Anchorage three weeks ago. This was something she'd tell her grandchildren about someday.

She blew a breath through her nose, watching it turn to fog in the cool air, stamping her feet to keep warm. At least they'd had no complaints from Judith out here about a lack of proper silk stockings. The fanciest hosiery they wore underneath their uniforms were flannel long johns, the better to keep out the crisp Alaskan air while sleeping in poorly insulated barracks. And this was summer, when the temperatures usually stayed above freezing, and sunlight stretched late into the evening.

Gabriel wiped his boots on the ground before stepping up to the concrete slab that served as a stoop, cutting a sharp figure in his gray wool coat. "You're early," she said, taking his offered arm to help her pick her way across the mud of the paths worn between the barracks.

"No, *you* are late," he countered, which was probably true. She'd heard reveille come and go, but Douglas had told them to pack up their musette bags and come dressed in costumes, which always took longer than throwing on the same old uniform. Gabriel's appreciative glance made her feel it was worth the effort. "But I suppose a lady can't be rushed."

As they walked, she fiddled with the ropes of pearls around her neck—borrowed from Catherine, who said she wouldn't need jewelry in Algeria. "I always feel like a fraud wearing this. It probably costs more than I make in a year. Some gold-digging GI is going to confuse me with a rich heiress and propose."

"I'll have to keep my eye on you, then." She never got over the thrill of hearing that teasing tone in his voice, the one that only came out for her.

She blew out a snort. "You should talk. I'm the one dating a fellow who literally disappears."

"Don't worry," he said, pulling her closer as a gust of cold wind slammed against them. "I'm not going anywhere."

Technically, he was. He was departing with the troupe tomorrow for the USO club in Skagway, but she'd be with him. Their pace was still breakneck at times. They'd performed for American infantry units in remote outposts, a platoon of specially trained Alaskan scouts, and even a good number of stalwart Canadian infantrymen who weren't above taking in American entertainment. But because of the distance between stops, they had more time to play cards, debate any number of topics, and even nap along the way. Maybe that was why Maggie felt happier and healthier, even as the tour moved toward its second month.

Or maybe she'd finally learned how to rest.

"Any new jokes today?" Gabriel asked.

Ever since Douglas had relaxed the rules on approving all routines in advance, Maggie liked to mix things up every now and then. "What do you think about this one?" She cleared her throat. "I woke up in the middle of the night thinking that one of my bunkmates was composing a letter home on a typewriter. Turns out, it was just her teeth chattering."

Gabriel smiled, always a good sign. "Douglas will like that one." He'd banned her earlier joke about how the Brits weren't cut out for winter defense of the Aleutians because they'd surrender the first morning they woke up to find their tea frozen.

Besides the added jokes and new wool uniform, Maggie's routine was different in one other way: she ended her set with a compilation of the choruses of her childhood hymns. Even though the songs were less boisterous than the jazz tunes that usually made up her set, she never failed to see a few teary faces in the audience by the time she got to "Amazing Grace."

Dad would be proud. He had been happy to have her home for their short leave between tours and had sat at the kitchen table for over an hour while she spilled out stories of what their troupe had done overseas.

She'd paused at the end, waiting for him to say something, to ask questions, to voice his approval for what she'd done . . . or maybe to ask her when she was going to get a real job.

Instead, he stood and walked over to her record player, the one she'd picked up at a discount from a pawn shop. "I received the letter you sent from Casablanca. It seems this USO business was good for you after all."

Relief had filled her. "I meant everything I said, you know."

A smile lifted one corner of his mouth. "You never say anything you don't." He placed a record on the player, and the strains of "A String of Pearls" filled the small sitting room. Not a hymn, not a Salvation Army tune, but her favorite Glenn Miller piece, with a trumpet line that tripped up and down the scale.

"I started listening to the Chicago Symphony Orchestra on the radio while you were gone," he admitted. "It was too quiet without you underfoot." He coughed and drummed his fingers on the radio cabinet, then looked up. "Even before I read your letter, I knew you were right all along. The devil doesn't have any tunes, at least, not any good ones. Everything beautiful is of God."

They listened in silence until the record ended, then her father lit his pipe and opened his Bible to read, and Maggie felt she was truly home again.

She'd have to write him again soon to tell him about meeting a moose for the first time. The city girl in her had been terrified when it had snorted in her direction, to everyone's amusement. Now the only wildlife in sight around the naval operating base were the crows that chattered noisily from their perches on the roofs of the corrugated metal huts. "Pipe down," Maggie hollered, scattering them in a rush of wings.

By the time they reached their agreed-on meeting point, Mess Hall 2, Howie and Judith sat alone in a room full of empty benches, except for a few soldiers on KP duty wiping down tables. Apparently Maggie really had been late.

"Saved you both a cup," Howie said, pushing two mugs of steaming coffee toward them.

Maggie accepted hers gratefully. On this drizzly, windy morning, the hot liquid felt marvelous on the way down. "Where's Kenneth?" she asked Judith.

"Got up early because a pilot promised him a ride in a seaplane," she said, a roll of her eyes telling Maggie exactly what she thought of that. "He promised he'd be back in time." At age fifteen, her son, their newest troupe member, seemed to remind every soldier of his little brother.

That didn't mean he wasn't a worthy performer once the curtain rose, though. He launched himself into spot-on impressions of anyone from Groucho Marx to Mickey Mouse, and his duets with Judith from the new musical *This Is the Army* always received rousing applause. Judith didn't admit to the soldiers that she was his mother—"It would show my age"—but Maggie wasn't sure they could miss the proud way she looked at him as he took his bows.

It wasn't the same as having Catherine with them, and that was better. No one could replace her, but Kenneth made the show his own.

"He'll have one heck of a 'What I Did on My Summer Vacation' essay to write in his composition notebook when he goes back to school," Howie mused.

Judith scoffed, the maternal expression gone. "I only hope he still wants to graduate after all this. It's been all I can do to keep him there between the high pay for welders and recruiters trying to sign them up younger and younger."

"Maybe he'll see this as doing his part."

"I hope so. He's just a boy." Judith's gaze wandered over to the window, where a group of soldiers stood at attention for morning inspection. "Then again, all of them are."

The door burst open, and Kenneth ran in, his cheeks flushed and his sandy hair mussed. "Guess what? They let me be the gunner."

"Charming," Judith said dryly. "I'm not going to ask whether that means you actually fired anything because I don't think I want to know the answer."

The brief pause when Kenneth tried unsuccessfully to hide a guilty look seemed answer enough. "Anyway, I didn't land the plane in the sound," he offered, by means of compromise.

Before Kenneth could tell them everything he'd learned about coastal defense from above, Douglas strode into the mess hall like he knew he was late and had to make up for it.

"There you are, Floyd," Howie called, waving him over. "I was beginning to think we'd have to leave without you."

"I was detained while collecting a special delivery to

Sitka's USO club, forwarded from Juneau." He held a lone letter in the air. "It's addressed to Miss McCleod, but I hope you won't mind sharing with the rest of us."

A glance at the address on the outside told Maggie what he meant: it was from *Private* Catherine Duquette. Maggie still couldn't get used to the title.

"Aha!" Howie exclaimed, leaning over Maggie's shoulder. "What's the news from our violinist?"

Catherine had visited home like the rest of them, then reported to Fort Des Moines for training in the WAAC. Last Maggie had heard, Catherine's parents were still wary about her enlistment, but she'd held her ground and departed with her family's respect, if not their permission. Mail to Alaska was slow, so this was the first news they'd gotten from her since they left the States.

Maggie scanned the first few lines of general greetings, then gave up and just read aloud. "'I've learned to drive, which means many more hours rattling about in a jeep, but this time behind the steering wheel. It wasn't nearly as difficult as I assumed it would be, though I'll admit to shearing off some shrubbery on my first go around the practice course.'"

They all laughed at that, and Howie threw out a "Good for her!"

Maggie read on. "'Once I'm deployed, they'll mostly be using me for translation work for the officers' correspondence, but I have no doubt that I will also spend many leisurely hours in the mail room under the whip-cracking of Master Sergeant Franklin. Whether she'll be glad to see me is another story. In any case, I do plan on bringing a tube of lipstick with me. Uniform or no, a girl must look her best.'"

It was so genuinely Catherine that even Maggie had to smile. "Make us proud," she said to the letter, as if it would form a direct line to her friend as she completed basic training.

"She will," Howie said with a matter-of-fact nod, as if she had already come home decorated with medals, and Maggie had a feeling he was right.

"Time to head out," Douglas said, forcing Maggie to drink the rest of her coffee in a few large gulps. She tucked the letter into her musette bag and shouldered it—no footlockers of props out here with the number of small boats and biplanes they had to take from place to place. They'd performed for the naval air station the night before, and today were headed over to a neighboring island to perform for the army fellows who had guarded the harbor with defense batteries, searchlights, and radar since the start of the war.

Once they'd walked the short distance to the harbor, Douglas glanced at his watch. "The navy patrol boat will be here soon to pick us up. No one wander off, now."

He didn't need to worry about her. Around here, you could do your sightseeing just by looking around, which Maggie did, sitting down on her tightly packed bag. To the west was the harbor, bustling docks, and rocky jetties giving way to calm open sea. To the east, mountains rose from behind the town of Sitka, their bases lush and green, their peaks misty and snow-covered, rising like arrowheads to the sky.

Gabriel sat down next to her, and she tilted her chin to look at him. "Do you wish you were back in that office in Chicago?"

Instead of firing a joke in return, he got that thoughtful look on his face that she loved. "It's not the life I expected. A year ago, I'd have said I had enough uncertainty to worry about without giving up my comfortable apartment and steady job."

"But just think. If you'd never donned your father's top hat and taken a little risk, you'd never have met me."

"I have had that thought once or twice," he said, and the

warmth she felt from the admission worked quicker and stronger than the coffee she'd downed earlier.

It wasn't only meeting Gabriel, though, that made the USO tour worth it. The joy she felt when a wave of chuckles spread over the gathered men was the same whether they were performing in a mess hall in the Aleutian Islands or on a truck bed in the Algerian desert.

No, their little variety unit wasn't famous, and they still missed notes and lost their voices and complained about the weather. They sure didn't have the glamour and star power of the bigger Hollywood tours, or an entourage to help with makeup, hair, and costuming. But they were brave enough to fly into bitter headwinds in biplanes that looked like five-and-dime models, determined enough to give one more encore after a long day of travel, and ordinary enough to remind the soldiers of home. And it turned out that's all the troops needed.

"Hey there!" Howie crossed in front of them, winking. "You two lovebirds better shake a leg. Our boat's here."

Gabriel stood, reaching down to give Maggie a hand. "The touring life never lets up, does it?"

"No," she said, a smile spreading wide on her face, "it never does."

AUTHOR'S NOTE

Readers often ask me where my ideas come from, and this one has an easy answer: *The Foxhole Victory Tour* was born when I first heard about male musicians enlisting in droves after Pearl Harbor—and the women who took their chance to fill the gap and prove their worth. While the Swinging Sweethearts are fictional, they were based on real bands like the Darlings of Rhythm, Hour of Charm Orchestra, the Sharon Rogers All-Girl Orchestra, and the Sweethearts of Rhythm. These determined women recorded stories of grueling schedules, blatant prejudice, and unwanted advances, but also triumphs as their performances convinced even the most skeptical of their talent. You can read more about them in *Swing Shift* by Sherrie Tucker.

As for the USO camp shows, there are many resources available documenting the experience of the stars and Hollywood headliners who entertained the troops during the war (my favorite was *Over Here, Over There* by Maxene Andrews and Bill Gilbert), but far more common were the small obscure variety units featured in this novel. Maggie, Catherine, and their fellow entertainers are products of my imagination, but there were dozens of men and women just like them. They were the unsung heroes who trooped through great hardship to entertain GIs on the USO's Foxhole Circuit, in more dangerous circumstances and with less glamorous accommodations than stars like Marlene Dietrich, Bob Hope, or Carole Lombard.

The rules and regulations for USO performers, especially women, were also taken directly from the USO's Foxhole Circuit handbook. While that final document wasn't in circulation until 1944, it was assembled from memos and other materials presented to earlier groups, so I took the liberty of using it as Maggie and Catherine prepared to go overseas. I also modeled many of my troupe's experiences on those of the performers who toured North Africa during the spring and summer of 1943. Air raids, emergency plane landings, and shellings interrupted many a tour. Some dangerous encounters were so unbelievable that I couldn't use them in the novel, such as the brother-and-sister comedy duo who got close enough to enemy lines to actually be captured by the Germans, accused of being spies.

While I tried to be as accurate as possible with the historical events of the war in North Africa, I made some small timeline changes, such as moving the 703rd Railway Grand Division's overseas crossing up a month so Catherine could encounter someone from home.

Several real figures mentioned in the novel include Bob Hope and his celebrity entourage (who really did tour North Africa in the summer of 1943), as well as the Andrews Sisters, Josephine Baker, and Hélène Benatar, the Jewish French lawyer who worked tirelessly to close the labor camps and find employment and housing for those recently released.

The article by John Steinbeck, quoted at the beginning of the novel, immortalized the sacrificial service of people whose names history has forgotten, and it made me want to learn more about what their journey might've looked like. For more information, be sure to visit my website, amygreenbooks.com, and the "History" page there.

As always, I'm incredibly grateful to my Bethany House publishing team for countless hours of effort to get this story out into the world. Special thanks to my editors, Rochelle Gloege and Kate Deppe, for their helpful insights and detailed corrections, as well as my marketing-team friends for their tireless work to connect readers to this book. I'm always grateful to my writing sister, Ruthie, who gave me helpful feedback as I wrote, with added thanks to her family—Jon, Isaac, and Joel—who compensated for my total lack of knowledge about baseball by helping me edit my lone sports scene.

I'm grateful, too, for the home front team who made this book possible, especially my mother-in-law for watching my baby girl during writing sessions and my husband for bidding his wife good-bye for the majority of deadline month. My family and friends are always my biggest supporters and encouragers, even the ones who don't read my books, and I'm so grateful for the community surrounding me.

The unwitting hero of this book is the aforementioned baby girl for finally figuring out how to sleep through the night a few months before my deadline. It turns out that writing is a lot easier when you've gotten at least five consecutive hours of sleep, and I am grateful.

Finally, thanks to you, the readers of this book. I've met many of you, whether in person, through virtual visits to your book clubs, or through our interactions on social media. Your love of history, books, and the fictional people I've come to know as friends are what keep me going. Feel free to drop me a line anytime at the "Contact" page on my website, amygreenbooks.com. I love hearing from you.

DISCUSSION QUESTIONS

1. During her time with the Swinging Sweethearts, Maggie runs up against the problem of being taken seriously as a female musician. Why do you think that was such a challenge in her day? Do you think the problem has gone away?

2. Though partly motivated by a desire to reconnect with Leo, Catherine also joined the USO as a way of declaring independence from her feuding parents. Do you think she should have handled things differently?

3. Given the risks and the regulations, do you think you would have been willing to join a USO Foxhole Circuit unit? What would have been the most difficult part?

4. The performers visit several cities and rural areas of North Africa. Was there a historical or cultural detail that surprised you? How much did you know about

North Africa during World War II before reading this book?

5. "Pretty girls aren't meant for ugly wars" is a line that comes back to haunt Catherine repeatedly throughout the novel. To what extent, if any, do you think women should be shielded from the hardships and trauma of war?

6. Each of the performers has his or her own reason for wanting to join *The Pepsodent Show* tour. Which did you find most compelling? Did you find yourself cheering for one of them as the story progressed?

7. Early in the story, Catherine displays a fear of conflict, while Maggie is relentlessly self-reliant. Do you feel they have improved in these areas by the end of the book?

8. Do you think it was fair for Senior Leader Franklin of the WAAC to initially distrust the USO women? What factors do you think often lead women to see themselves as competitors instead of friends and allies?

9. While the labor camps of North Africa were much less far-reaching than those in Europe, conditions there were still appalling. Would you have accepted Roosevelt's explanation that relations with Vichy France were too tenuous to close the labor camps right away?

10. Did you have any sympathy for Leo after he explained his actions? Did you have any suspicions be-

fore that he might not be right for Catherine, and if so, why?

11. Maggie's mission-minded father initially sees no purpose in nonreligious music. In what ways did Maggie find meaning in the songs she played, both for herself and for others? What role has music played in your life?

12. Arthur, despite his quirks, staunchly supports Catherine in the end. Do you see them staying friends—or even something more—after the war, or do you think they'll go their separate ways?

13. Major Newton of the Salvation Army tea canteen appears at a critical time in Maggie's journey. What do you think of her statement, "It's somewhat better to find your worth in what you accomplish rather than how you look, but it still won't give you what you're looking for"?

14. Much of the peril faced by Maggie and Catherine's troupe is based in historical fact. Some USO performers even died during their service to the troops, including several who perished in a plane crash. Do you feel it was right to risk civilians, including women, for the sake of entertainment?

For more from
Amy Lynn Green,
read on for an excerpt from

THE *Blackout* BOOK CLUB

In 1942, a promise to her brother before he goes off to war puts Avis Montgomery in the unlikely position of head librarian and book club organizer in small-town Maine. The women of her club band together as the war comes dangerously close, but their friendships are tested by secrets, and they must decide whether depending on each other is worth the cost.

Available now wherever books are sold.

1

Avis Montgomery
January 31, 1942
Derby, Maine

Avis gripped the ladder as her husband climbed, a thick swath of black bunting draped over his shoulder. "Be careful, please, Russ."

He looked down at her from under that dashing swoop of dark hair and grinned. "Careful as I always am." Which did very little to reassure her.

Across from them, her brother Anthony climbed another rung, staring critically at the windows of the library's east wall. "Are you sure the curtain's going to be wide enough?"

Avis nodded to her notebook splayed on the floor, the numbers arranged in neat columns like soldiers at attention. "Of course. I measured it."

"Three times, I bet," Russell chimed in, giving her a teasing wink.

"Four," she admitted.

"See? I told you." Russell bunched a corner of the blackout cloth in his fist. "All right, old man, catch!"

"Don't even think—" Avis began, but it was too late. Russell wound up like a pitcher on the mound and tossed the edge of the fabric, causing Anthony to wobble dangerously as he reached to snatch the hem.

If she dared to take one of her hands off the ladder, she'd be rubbing away a headache. "You're going to fall and break your neck."

Anthony slid the eyelet holes along the curtain rod he'd rigged up, and Russell did the same on his end. "If you'd held my ladder instead of your husband's, you wouldn't have to worry about me."

"I'm fairly certain ladders were covered under my vow to have and to hold." She smiled in satisfaction when both of them laughed, Russell's deep and rumbling, Anthony's breaking off in a snort at the end. Two of her favorite sounds in the world, as different as the men they belonged to. Her husband, stocky and confident, more comfortable on a fishing dock than he was at his job at the bank; her brother, gangly and warmhearted, with a quip on hand for any occasion.

At least there was no one else about to hear their nonsense. This close to closing, the library's patrons had gone home to eat dinner and tune in to radio broadcasts about MacArthur and his boys trying to take back the Pacific.

Her hand trembled slightly as Russell climbed down. *Focus on what you can control.* For now, that meant measurements, regulations, and crisp right angles that matched the edges of the window frame, just as she'd planned. "A perfect fit."

"Well done." Russell kissed her forehead. "Miss Cavendish and the air raid warden won't be able to find even a sliver of light."

The periodical reading tables behind them, arrayed in two rows of three, now looked stiff and subdued in the sudden shadow.

When Anthony returned from stowing the ladders in the

storage closet, a frown clouded his usually cheery face. "Grim as a funeral in here."

"It's wartime chic, pal," Russell said, slapping him on the back. "Better get used to it."

"Home décor magazines across the country will soon be touting these colors," Avis chimed in. Already, *LIFE* magazine had featured Joan Fontaine in a smart cap from a movie where she played a recruit for the British Women's Auxiliary Air Force.

That prompted a snort from her brother. "You and your silly magazines. When will you read a real book?"

"When 'real books' give me tips for altering last season's styles and a recipe for blueberry cobbler," she fired back, a variation of her usual reply. Just because her librarian brother was a snob about books didn't mean she had to be.

"She has a point," Russell interjected. "Last night's cobbler was excellent."

Anthony shot his childhood friend a look of profound betrayal. "There's more to reading than information, you know."

"I've yet to see any proof of that." Why, she probably learned more in a week's worth of her reading than Anthony did in a year of paging through novels. Still, it was no good trying to persuade him. Only twenty-nine years old, but thoroughly set in his ways.

Instead of rising to her taunt, Anthony breathed in deeply. "I'm going to miss this place."

It crept into the quiet after his words: that familiar fear that tingled through her body. For weeks, she'd pushed off the thought of Anthony's leaving, but now, with the trip to Fort Devens only a few days away, there was nothing to be done.

Russell leaned against the shelves, strong arms folded over his chest. "What'll Miss Cavendish do without you around here?"

"Not sure. Though I did give her a suggestion for a replacement."

Something about the way Anthony said it, heavy with implication, made Avis look up. Even in the shadows created by the newly darkened windows, she could see a smirk spreading on her brother's face, and all thoughts of enlistment faded. "Anthony, you don't mean *me*?"

"Come on, sis." He directed his most charming grin at her. "You do half of our cataloguing when I get behind anyway."

"An exaggeration."

"And you have most of the Dewey decimal system memorized."

Not an exaggeration, which unfortunately meant his idea had some legitimacy. "I couldn't possibly. Not as a married woman." She twisted her wedding band, a lovely solitaire, around her finger. Jobs, her mother had impressed on her, were for women who didn't have a husband's suit to iron and dinner to put on the table each night.

"Thousands of women are taking up war work," Russell reasoned, shrugging.

He always took Anthony's side. She gritted her teeth against a prickle of resentment. It was the price she paid for marrying her brother's best friend, she supposed.

She was about to reply that that was quite a different matter when Anthony's grin softened. "Anyway, I thought you'd be glad for something to do when Russ and I ship out."

Despite herself, Avis's jaw tightened, and behind her, Russell coughed. Anthony looked from one to the other, confusion on his face.

At the same time Russell began with "We haven't actually—" she tripped over him with "Russell isn't—"

Russell filled the awkward pause with a vague "We're still discussing it, that's all. Enlistment, I mean."

Even that was only halfway true. It had been weeks since Russell had brought it up after their last argument.

Unlike the enthusiastic flag-waving masses who'd turned out when the United States declared war, Avis looked ahead to the long separations, half-empty beds, and casualty notices printed in the newspapers.

And, try as she might to ignore it, her mother's warning, the night before the wedding and after too much champagne, whispered back into her mind, *"Keep your man nearby as long as you can, or he might be tempted to wander in other ways."*

Anthony blinked behind his narrow eyeglasses, face reddening. "Sorry. I thought . . . anyway, I didn't realize." He cleared his throat, moving the discussion into safer territory. "Still, it would be good for you to get out of the house, Avis."

"But I don't have a college degree," she said, "and, in case you've forgotten in the five minutes since it was brought up, I don't even read books."

"You could learn." Anthony scooped up the library keys from the empty sugar bowl where she'd insisted he keep them after misplacing them one too many times. "Seriously, Avis, we need someone to keep the doors open."

"It's not as if Miss Cavendish will shut the place down."

At that, Anthony hesitated, looking back toward the oil painting of the somber man overlooking the shelves, the only piece of artwork allowed on the walls. "I wouldn't be too sure about that. It was her father's pet project, not hers. Something about this place . . . well, she pays the bills, but she doesn't seem to like it."

"Why's that?" Russell asked.

"Beats me. With Miss C, you learn not to pry." He tossed the keys in the air and headed to the entryway with his usual jaunty step. "I love this place, sis."

As if he needed to tell her. He'd spent at least half his

childhood either here or buried in one of the adventure novels he'd checked out from the shelves.

When he'd left for college, everyone, Mother included, expected he would "make something of himself" and never return. But he'd come back to Derby four years ago, degree in hand, content to spend the rest of his life in the small coastal town working at the association library that had once been his refuge.

"Come on, Avis. Promise me you'll keep it up for me while I'm gone. Please?" He looked down at her with those big, earnest brown eyes that had worn her down since childhood.

"I promise," she found herself saying.

The whoop he let out while tackling her with a hug was probably the loudest noise the staid old building had heard in ages, and Avis couldn't help smiling.

Really, this place might benefit from a woman's touch. Besides, Anthony wouldn't be gone long, and if she could get through the war cataloging books without actually having to read them, why, no one would be the wiser.

Ginny Atkins
January 31, 1942
Long Island, Maine

The way Mack Conway swaggered toward the harbor, Ginny Atkins would have guessed he'd hit the bottle a mite too hard, except it was only afternoon. Besides that, a Sunday suit poked out of his coat, his tousled head topped with a spiffy-looking fedora.

She waved at him with her scrub brush. Now that the busy season for lobstering had passed, it was time for three months of repairing traps and painting buoys for next year. Today, Pa had stayed home—"business to take care of," he had said, and she'd been told to take advantage of the sunny day to work away at the grime and bait that scummed up the *Lady Luck*'s deck.

Instead of sauntering past to the bustle of lobstermen and boys tending their equipment, Mack stopped right in front of her. "Fine day, Ginny," he boomed, his voice deeper than normal, aging him past his nineteen years.

Ginny wiped her cold, wet hands on her trousers, suddenly feeling grimy in her scuffed rubber boots and brother's overcoat. Who'd have thought ol' Mack would outdress her? "Where you been, Mack?"

His grin spread even wider, like he'd been waiting on her to ask. "Took a ferry to the recruiting center."

"Already?" And she tried, really she did, to keep the dismay out of her voice.

It had all happened so fast. One day, Roosevelt was saying they were likely to stay out of the whole mess in Europe; next thing you knew, Japan had sunk those ships in Hawaii and all the young fellows on the island were lining up to stuff themselves in uniforms.

"Can't wait to lick those Japs." Mack rapped his knuckles just under his shoulder. "Once we show 'em who's boss, I'll come back with so many medals pinned to my chest there'll barely be room for buttons."

Ginny watched him for a moment, her breath coming out in white puffs as seagulls filled the silence with unearthly screeches. There was a spark she'd never seen before on Mack's face, a pride in the way he squared his shoulders in the hand-me-down coat.

With the lobster boat, traps, and know-how Pa had gotten from his father, Ginny's family was one of the wealthiest on the island, on account of having steady work. The Depression had knocked other folks, like the Conways, down often enough that they stopped trying to get up. Mr. Conway was snow-in-the-woodbox poor, and she'd heard Mack mumble a dozen shamefaced excuses when her brother invited him to go to the movies or grab a soda.

"I bet you will," Ginny said, rewarding Mack with a smile. If he hadn't been weighed down with spit-shined shoes, he might have floated up to join the planes that were always zooming past from the Godfrey Army Airfield.

Then his smile faltered. "Say, Ginny?"

"Say what?" She jammed her hands deeper into her coat pockets as a sudden breeze rammed against her.

"Want to be my girl?"

She nearly toppled into the ice-cold ocean from sheer surprise, but Mack hadn't noticed, studying the ground like he was. "Aw, Mack, you're like one of my brothers."

"No, I ain't," he insisted, jutting his chin up. "Anyway, nobody but you loves this island like I do."

He had a point there. All that most young fellows on Long Island talked about was how determined they were to get away someday. Ginny hated that, hated it when folks took in the rocky coast with its snow-dusted firs and the scent of the sharp sea air and tossed it all aside like a ball of trash.

Mack was different, always had been. Maybe it was on account of his gran's old tales, somewhere between history and lore, wrapping around his legs like seaweed and making him want to stay. Ginny had to admire that, and he wasn't *exactly* like one of her younger brothers. Hadn't she been thinking about how spiffed-up he looked, golden hair glinting in the sun?

"Fred said before I leave I'd better have a girl to wait for me," Mack went on. "Plus, there's gonna be a dance in town, and I need someone to take."

Ginny's shoulders relaxed. If that's all this was, it was nothing serious. "You know I'd dance with you, Mack. And I'll write you too."

His eyes—she'd never noticed, but they were a nice bold blue, like the sky on a cloudless day—crinkled up with a smile. "This Friday, then?"

"Sure." She was probably one of the only girls on the island with a store-bought dress. Pa had gotten it from a shop in Portland for her twentieth birthday the month before. Nice to have someplace to use it.

"All right, then." Instead of saying something sweet or asking her what time he could pick her up, Mack mumbled a good-bye and charged away like he was getting a leg up on his basic training a few weeks early.

Well. Was she really Mack Conway's girl now? Just like that?

She'd probably have to call him by his real name, Marvin, instead of the childhood nickname after the Atlantic mackerel his family fished.

Nah. No matter what, Mack would always be Mack to her.

Couldn't be any harm in it, from what she could see. Mack was a decent sort, and it would do him good to have someone writing to him. His ma couldn't read much, and his pa—well, it wasn't right to speak ill of a neighbor, but he might not notice his son was gone.

Wasn't very romantic, though. On the walk home, after the *Lady Luck* was scrubbed up proper, she compared Mack's asking to all the declarations of love she'd seen in movies. He hadn't even tried to steal a kiss.

'Course, she would have slapped him if he had.

Maybe that's how it had been with her ma and pa. Just two people who found themselves in the same place wanting to stay there, getting hitched and scrapping out a life. They'd gone through their share of trouble—most of it caused by Ma—but they stuck together.

By now, Ginny had reached the gate of the house. Everything was so . . . quiet. Funny. Right before supper, her younger brothers usually tussled in the yard like gulls after the same fish.

Inside, Pa sat at the kitchen table, head clutched in work-worn hands, and her heart nearly stopped beating. "Pa? What's going on?"

Was something wrong with Ma? Had she been taken to jail again? She'd been better these past few years, once Pa cut her off from the family's money to guard her from herself.

Barely lifting his head, Pa thrust a notice at her. Printed in tall, neat letters that she struggled to read were phrases including *coastal fortifications* and *vacate immediately*.

She scowled at the paper. "What does *eminent domain* mean?"

"It means they can do whatever they want, and folks like us haven't got a chance." Pa's voice was cold as the wind battering the door as he took the paper back, crumpling it. "The government's buying our home, Ginny. Making the whole place into a navy base."

No. They couldn't. Her family could fight this.

But her pa went on, voice as helpless and hopeless as she'd ever heard it. "We've got to leave the island."

Martina Bianchini
January 31, 1942
Boston, Massachusetts

Martina ran her thumb over the worn spines of her books, swiping at the tears that threatened to pock the covers with wet blotches.

"*Affogare in un bicchier d'acqua.*" She scolded herself using one of Mamma's tried-and-true phrases from the old country. "Do not drown in a glass of water." After all she'd gone through, was she going to cry over a few dusty books?

She took a deep breath. Rosa's collection of fairy tales, tattered and threadbare like Cinderella's rags, would need to come. *Swiss Family Robinson* for Gio, with a hope that he wouldn't outgrow that too, as he had with two pairs of shoes this year. *Emma,* of course, her most reread of Jane Austen.

A glance over her shoulder revealed that the faux-snakeskin suitcase she'd allotted herself for personal items was mostly full already.

So *Jane Eyre* would stay behind. It was easier to abandon the biographies and history books she'd used to study for her citizenship test, but *Oliver Twist* was a loss.

Still, it had to be done. The hiring manager at the foundry had given her the dimensions of the one-bedroom trailer home. She'd marked it out with chalk and her sewing tape. So small. With two growing children and all of their possessions, she would have a single shelf at best for her own nonessentials.

"I *will* come back for you," she whispered to the forlorn books. Better not to wonder when.

"No!" Past the thin door, the floorboards of the apartment creaked with hurried footsteps and her son's voice. "I won't give it to you! I *won't.*"

She closed her eyes, longing to kneel by the books a little longer and let the latest trouble run its course. But only for a moment, because deeper than the weariness was the knowledge that she was a mother, so all trouble in the family was her trouble.

When Martina stepped into the hallway, Gio rammed into her, wiry arms wrapped around his prized possession: a portable Motorola radio.

At the end of the hallway, Martina's mother stood with arms folded and dark brows set in a look of *Well? He's your son. Do something.*

What could Mamma want with Gio's radio? She hated the noisy thing.

"Gio! Show respect to your *nonna*." At times like this, Martina couldn't bear to call him George, the name she insisted he use for school.

"It's not *her* I'm disrespecting," Gio shot back, "it's the officer."

Officer? A glance at her mother—who, for all the wrinkles gently scoring her face, looked like a girl caught sneaking cookies before dinner—told Martina there was some truth to Gio's words.

"To your room, Gio." Martina used the tone she heard from matriarchs on every stoop and street corner in Boston's North End, whether the words were in English or Italian. "Finish packing. *Without* the radio."

He reluctantly surrendered it with one last pleading look before she shooed him away and turned her attention to her mother. "What haven't you told me, Mamma?"

"*Calmati*." Mamma bustled down the hall, and Martina followed her into the kitchen, where miracles were produced under Angela Bianchini's wooden spoon. "A nice young man came by yesterday to tell me where to get a registration card. He also said I should not travel far from home, and I must turn in any cameras and radios. That is all."

With each addition, Martina clenched the radio more tightly. "You see? Didn't I tell you? This is what I was afraid of."

"You are afraid of all things, *figlia mia*." Mamma paused to pat Martina's shoulder, as if to soften the criticism. "It is only right they would make sure I am not a spy. I am not an American citizen like you."

"And what's next? Once you've registered, they might put you in prison."

"You—what is the word?" She snapped her fingers, smiling proudly. "*Exaggerate*. This is not the Red Summer."

Martina's shudder was quick enough to cut off the memories from her girlhood that threatened to fill her mind. "Don't tell me it can't happen, Mamma. The newspapers are all shouting for the government to take the Japanese away—even some who are citizens. They might come for us next."

Mamma made a scoffing noise deep in her throat. "There are too many Italians in America. Hundreds of thousands."

"But, Mamma . . ." Martina switched to her mother tongue in case the children were listening. Rosa and Gio could speak some Italian, but school made English drop first from their lips, saints be praised. "I can't leave you now. We'll stay another month or two, to make sure things are all right."

Mamma's hand stilled on the counter, where it had been tapping out an impatient pattern. Then she looked up, eyes steady and sure. "My door will always be open to you, daughter. But you need your own life, away from here. There, you'll have a job with good pay and a home of your own. Somewhere safe, where . . ."

She shrugged, refusing to finish the sentence, but Martina knew what the downward look meant.

Where he *can't find you.* That's why she'd looked for work in Maine instead of one of the many war industries springing up in Boston. A fresh start.

"This is what I want for you, daughter. There will not be trouble."

She had to ask. "But if there is?"

Mamma hesitated only a moment. "If there is, I want you and the children to be far from it."

Martina surrendered to her mamma's fierce embrace, letting it soothe the ache, the fear, the knowledge that, however many books she left behind to travel to Maine, the heroine she would miss most was her mother.

Louise Cavendish
February 1, 1942
Derby, Maine

Fierce barking woke Louise Cavendish in the thin hours of the morning, when the tide ebbed its lowest, leaving behind the smell of rot.

All sleep-induced haze flew from Louise as she sat to attention. Jeeves, her German shepherd, might warn off an errant squirrel during the day, but he hadn't made a fuss at night since his puppy days.

On went her quilted housecoat and slippers, and she hurried down the stairs. Jeeves was a shadow by the front door, his muscled form tense, growling a warning at whoever was beyond the door.

Louise's fingers hesitated before turning on the light switch at the base of the stairs, illuminating the candelabra in the entryway. Father's old hunting rifle was still mounted over the fireplace in the dayroom, and Delphie always kept the kitchen knives razor sharp. Should she . . . ?

No, if there was an intruder, Jeeves had likely scared them off already. And if he hadn't, a woman in her fifties struggling to wield a meat cleaver certainly wouldn't.

He whined and pawed at the door, looking back at her with pleading eyes. "Steady, boy," she soothed, peering out the front window to the grounds of her family's summer home—a flat lawn looming with heavy shadows from shrubbery and the three outbuildings.

And then she heard it: a distant concussive boom, soon drowned out by a renewed burst of barking.

German bombs? Had Hitler's troops really dared attack America's shores so soon after declaring war?

But no, the sound came distinctly from the east, and the only thing east of the cliffs of Windward Hall was the ocean.

"It's only depth charges." She bent down, trying to calm her disconsolate dog. "They've found a German submarine, and planes are shooting it down."

Though there was always a chance they'd gotten there too late, and the U-boat had dived under the surface for another chance at destroying American tankers and freighters.

How Delphie, even with her hearing loss, could sleep through the ruckus of a German shepherd on full alert was beyond Louise, but the older woman didn't venture out to join her. Slowly, with no new explosions to set him off, Jeeves relaxed onto his haunches.

"Good boy," she whispered, running her hands over Jeeves's neck. As usual, he concurred with this assessment, basking in the attention. In the sudden calm, he clearly decided he had single-handedly dealt with and removed the threat.

Maybe the American planes had seen the telltale oil rising to the surface, prompting another boastful newspaper account flashing across the front page with the subtlety of a bad dime novel: *UNCLE SAM SINKS ANOTHER!* and *U-BOAT DISASTER AVERTED.*

But Louise also knew that the U-boats were sinking American ships by the dozens, consigning valuable cargo—and the merchant mariners who crewed them—to the cold depths.

All the more reason average citizens needed to rise up and be useful. The Red Cross motto sprang to her mind: In War, Charity.

It had been years since she'd thought of that, ever since that fateful telegram from Father that kept her from joining the forces of nurses serving in the first world war. And now here she was, too old by a decade to be of use in this one either.

Don't mope, she scolded herself, as she always did at the

first tug of self-pity. *If anything, this should be a reminder that there's work to be done here too.*

Louise had had nearly a quarter century to get used to the unease of being a spinster living alone in a large house—well, alone besides Delphie, her cook. Never before had Louise felt herself in danger at Windward Hall.

That was a consequence of war, she supposed. One couldn't feel safe in one's home, even if the major campaigns were an ocean away. And now war had come to even the shores of peaceful Derby.

Amy Lynn Green has always loved history and reading, and she enjoys speaking with book clubs, writing groups, and libraries all around the country. Her debut novel, *Things We Didn't Say*, was nominated for a 2021 Minnesota Book Award and won two Carol Awards. *Things We Didn't Say* and *The Blackout Book Club* received starred reviews from both *Booklist* and *Library Journal*. Amy and her family make their home in Minneapolis, Minnesota. Visit amygreenbooks.com to learn more.

Sign Up for Amy's Newsletter

Keep up to date with Amy's latest news on book releases and events by signing up for her email list at the link below.

AmyGreenBooks.com

FOLLOW AMY ON SOCIAL MEDIA

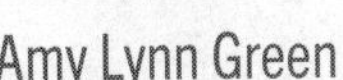

@amygreenbooks

More from Amy Lynn Green

In 1942, a promise to her brother before he goes off to war puts Avis Montgomery in the unlikely position of head librarian and book club organizer in small-town Maine. The women of her club band together as the war comes dangerously close, but their friendships are tested by secrets, and they must decide whether depending on each other is worth the cost.

The Blackout Book Club

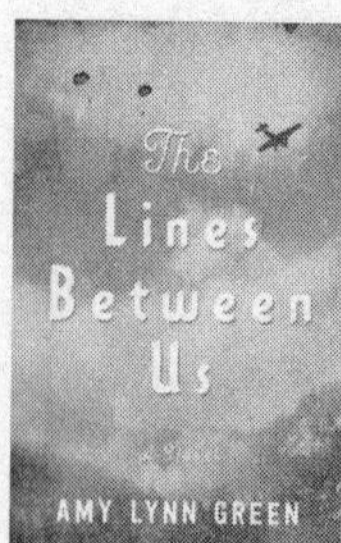

After Pearl Harbor, sweethearts Gordon Hooper and Dorie Armitage were broken up by their convictions. As a conscientious objector, he went west to fight fires as a smokejumper, while she joined the Army Corps. When a tragic accident raises suspicions, they're forced to work together, but the truth they uncover may lead to an impossible—and dangerous—choice.

The Lines Between Us

In this epistolary novel from the WWII home front, Johanna Berglund is forced to return to her small Midwestern town to become a translator at a German prisoner-of-war camp. There, amid old secrets and prejudice, she finds that the POWs have hidden depths. When the lines between compassion and treason are blurred, she must decide where her heart truly lies.

Things We Didn't Say